Issue #3

by Cambria Hebert

Special thanks to Adrienne Ambrose for all the racing talk, time spent reading, and brainstorming!

#Swag
gearshark

"Having swag isn't about what you wear or your hairstyle, but about being confident in yourself."

—Author Unknown

One

Joey

My father always told me I could be whatever I wanted when I grew up.

So I became a woman in a man's world.

Turns out I had bigger balls than a lot of the men. They didn't take too kindly to that. Add on I also happened to be the daughter of the most powerful man in the entire state—well, let's just say I wasn't winning any popularity contests.

I didn't care, though. I wasn't here to win prom queen. I was here for respect, which I thought would be a lot easier to earn than it was.

Thing was, if I had a dick between my legs and a lot less money in my bank account, I'd likely be the most popular asshole on this track.

But I wasn't packing that particular anatomy (even though my name suggested otherwise) and my pockets weren't empty at all.

I was an asshole, though. Experience taught me that trait. Survival gave it practice. Being the only female pro racecar driver on this side of the country required a lot of endurance. Sometimes my endurance came down to a lot of cussing and refusing to take anyone's shit.

So I settled for grudging acceptance from my peers and satisfaction that regardless of what anyone thought I deserved to be here.

I proved it. Time and time again.

It was also another reason I was like a piece of meat stuck between these guys' teeth.

You'd think a bunch of macho, athletic, and driven men would be more secure with themselves that having a "girl" on the track with them wouldn't be such a ball buster.

But it was.

I once suggested perhaps it was the length of what was in their pants that made them so insecure… It got me a couple lewd offers to see for myself (barf) and earned me exactly zero points toward the respect I thought I deserved.

Whatever.

I learned a long time ago you don't always get what you deserve.

You get what you earn.

I earned my spot on the racetrack, and it had nothing to do with Daddy's money.

End of story.

At least I wished it was. The hard truth was there would be no end to this story until I hung up my car keys, which I had no plans to do in the near future.

I would have to fight and claw for every victory, every shred of opportunity, and each drop of success.

Despite what most people thought, I was determined to make my career without my father's influence. Maybe some kids with successful, wealthy parents were happy to take anything that was handed to them. Hell, I'd actually seen reality shows on TV based on the concept.

I wasn't one of those kids.

My father wanted a boy, something he'd never been shy about letting me know. The reason my name Josephine was shortened to Joey from almost the second I was born.

Maybe it was some kind of male successor thing. You know, he wanted a man he could hand over the reins to his empire one day. Maybe he'd been married enough times to know he didn't want to deal with a daughter (God forbid she turn out like any one of his three ex-wives!), because a child wasn't someone he could divorce.

Or maybe, and this was a thought I seldom allowed myself to have, he just thought women were weak.

Regardless of what his reasons were (I'd never asked), he'd gotten a daughter. His only child. I turned out a lot more like him than anyone ever thought. It's likely the reason my mother (ex-wife number three) took off with a hefty divorce settlement, moved into his penthouse in Paris, and never called, visited, or wrote.

Ironic really, my father hadn't wanted a girl because I might turn out like my mother, and my mother ultimately left because I was too much like my father.

A therapist would have a field day with my family.

I would say one thing about Ron Gamble. He didn't leave when the going got tough. In fact, he seemed to thrive on a challenge. And he loved me. I might not have been what he originally planned, but unlike all the other men around me, I'd earned his respect.

I'd like to think, after twenty-two years, if asked, my father would say he was glad he'd gotten me instead of a son.

Maybe it was that which made me so incredibly driven.

Wanting to prove to him I was just as valuable, if not more so, as a son would be.

Or maybe I was just stubborn.

Defeat on any level wasn't something I would ever submit to. My father knew this, yet still, sometimes he tried. Well, not necessarily to defeat me. More like sway me. Change my mind.

It rarely happened… me changing my mind.

It wasn't going to happen now, with this. I could guarantee it.

Still, here I was. Sitting in my father's study after being summoned to what I knew was going to be yet another attempt at swaying my decision.

Balancing a clear, rounded tumbler in my palm, full of top-shelf scotch, I waited for my father to finish his phone call. The leather club chair was soft and supportive against my back. I relaxed into it and sipped at the amber liquid. I liked the warm trail it left as it slid down my throat. It was comforting somehow. Familiar.

Most people would be nervous as hell being beckoned by Ron Gamble. They definitely wouldn't be relaxing in a chair and watching him with open interest bordering on boredom as he finished up some mundane but necessary business call.

I was his daughter, and the chair I was sitting in had been in this room since I was born. The man sitting behind the desk, admittedly intimidating, wasn't just a powerful man to me. He was the man I spent every

Christmas morning with, unwrapping gifts and drinking hot chocolate.

A lot of people didn't know it, but Ron Gamble wasn't just all about business.

He might have always wanted a son, but he never treated me with any kind of disdain or disappointment. I knew he loved me from the time I was born. He never acted like I was a chore or even a bother. *I* was the one who felt the need to prove I was worthy of the love he'd already given me.

Another round of scotch slipped across my tongue as he hung up the phone. Anticipation had me sitting up a little straighter. I wasn't nervous to talk to him, but I knew I was likely in for yet another fight.

He wasn't just my father. He was my sponsor. It was his company, his money, that paid for my racecar and entry fees into the big pro races. I was part of the racing team he built. So technically, he was my boss.

Did I mention I wasn't too great with authority?

It led to some shouting matches over the years.

My newest decision was the conduit for the most recent ones.

I wasn't up for it tonight, the arguing. But I would do it, because letting anyone see I was tired wasn't an option. Instead, I took another gulp of the alcohol and sharpened my gaze.

Dad was still dressed for the office, even though it was almost eight o'clock at night. He'd been home a few hours, but he'd come directly in here to work. I hadn't been home when he first arrived, but I didn't have to be. I was familiar with his routines.

His suit jacket was draped over the back of his chair, the tie around his neck long gone, and the white sleeves of his dress shirt were pushed up. A glass that looked just like the one in my hand was at his elbow, empty.

Papers covered his desk, but not in an unorganized way. I knew without asking he could likely recite every single document in front of him, and he knew exactly where each sheet of paper belonged.

"Need a refill?" I asked, gesturing to his glass. The salt-and-pepper look in his full head of dark hair didn't make him look any older than his fifty-five years; it just made him seem more distinguished.

"Wouldn't say no." He pushed the glass toward me with one finger.

I abandoned my own glass to a nearby table and crossed for the bottle of scotch. "Long day?" I asked when it was full and already at his lips.

"Even dreams take work, kid," he replied.

It wasn't the first time I'd heard that sentiment from his lips; it wouldn't be the last. I never really understood it until I started racing. A dream is just that. A wistful thought, a want. Sure, dreams come true… but in most cases, they did so because it was something that was worked toward.

Gamble wasn't born with a silver spoon in his mouth. He was born to his parents (my grandparents), who struggled their entire lives to make ends meet. His father worked two jobs, sometimes more, to feed his family, and his mother cleaned homes for other people.

Everything he had today was a result of his own effort and belief in himself.

"There's a plate of dinner in the kitchen for you. Want me to go heat it up?" I asked, moving toward the door.

He shook his head and waved me back. "Later. Let's talk."

I crossed back to my chair and dropped down. Dark curls fell into my eyes, and I shoved them back. My hair always got in the way.

"*GearShark Magazine* called," he announced.

I blinked. This wasn't what I was expecting. "Okay…" I hedged, not really sure what this had to do with me.

"Seems those *rumors*"—he began, emphasis on the last word—"are finding their way into the press."

Aaand, there it was.

I sighed. "They aren't rumors, Dad. You know I'm serious about going indie."

He studied me over the rim of his glass. He had a penetrating stare, the kind that could make even the most rock solid a little squeamish. "We talked about this." The glass made a firm thud on the top of the desk when he set it aside.

"No," I said with restrained annoyance. "You told me no, and I told you I wasn't your puppet."

"I pay for that car you race."

I rolled my eyes. "You want to throw that in my face? I already told you I'll get another sponsor. You know I could." It would be hard… Turns out it wasn't just the drivers who didn't like women in racing, but the sponsors as well.

Having a female injured or possibly killed in a racing accident would apparently be more hazardous for business than a male driver. This was one of the reasons my father sponsored me. I hadn't wanted him to at first, but just like with a lot of things, sometimes it was all about who you knew.

The minute my father put up money to sponsor me, several other smaller businesses did, too.

And besides that, I trusted my father and the team of people he employed. I could trust them with my car.

"You're under contract." He reminded me, as if I needed a reminder.

I lifted the scotch to my lips. "I'm well aware, which is why I didn't enter any preliminaries for the NRR. It's why I'm sitting on the sidelines for the first season."

We'd had this conversation more than once. It was always the same. I said I wanted to go indie, and he told me no. I didn't know why, but me switching from pro to indie wasn't something my father wanted me to do.

I sighed when he just watched me. "You know all my contracts are up for renewal this winter. All of them but yours. You could easily transfer it to the indie side. Hell, you own the division."

"Not all of it," he corrected.

I waved off his words. "You know what I mean."

My father started the NRR (New Revolution Racing), but it quickly grew so large it needed more than just him heading it up. Now there were three big owners of the corporation, with a lot of sponsors and employees under them. My father was one of the three, but since he was the man who started it all, he had the most pull.

"I already have a driver in the NRR."

My back teeth clenched, and I forced them to relax. "And Drew's the best. If he keeps going the way he is, he'll bring you the championship trophy at the end of the season. But you can have more than one driver, just like you do on the pro side."

He moved like he wanted to say something, but I cut him off.

"Plus, I'm part of the reason Drew's so good. I did help train him."

"I wonder what Drew would say to that?" He pondered.

"He'd probably tell me to shove it," I said, amusement making me forget some of the irritation this conversation caused.

Drew was just another reason I wanted to switch to the indie side. Having a real friend on the track was something I'd never had before. Trent, too. He might not be driving, but he was in the pit, and I knew he was an ally.

"Most people in your position would be grateful. They wouldn't be trying to get out."

His words made me hot and cold at the same time. He didn't understand my reasons. He likely thought I was just being fickle and wanting in on the new *in* thing.

I could try and explain, but I didn't want to. I wasn't sure he'd get it anyway. Or maybe he would.

I wasn't sure which was worse.

"Most people probably bet against you when you started your first business at nineteen," I quipped.

His eyes sparked with amusement. It was a look I was familiar with. It meant he was proud of me but also didn't necessarily want to show it. Kind of like when a child does something inappropriate and has to be scolded, but the parent really just wants to laugh.

Slowly, he sat back, picked up the scotch, and took another drink. I didn't squirm in my seat or fidget. I knew what I wanted. I wasn't going to change my mind. I drank my whiskey and stared back.

"You're in the middle of the season. Races you're already registered for."

Was that a crack in his staunch position of no?

I forced my face to remain as it was. I wasn't about to get all excited over the possibility I was wearing him down. I knew better.

"I honor my commitments. I'm still all in for this season with the pros. I've been training and working with Hopper and the rest of the staff at the speedway almost around the clock."

"I know." He nodded.

"The season will be over this winter; my contracts will be up for renewal. I can make the change and be ready for spring preliminaries and the summer race season."

The pro racing season was long, nearly ten months. The NRR season was shorter, spanning only the summer months for the actual season races. Preliminaries were held in the spring, and while they technically weren't part of the season, most would argue they were. At least, that was the way of the NRR for now. In a few years, that could change. If it continued to grow in popularity, more races would be added.

It was pretty much luck a lot of my sponsorship contracts were up for renewal this winter. It was the perfect time for me to make the switch.

"*GearShark* wants an interview," he stated, not responding directly to my words.

Shock had me gawking at him like he'd just announced baby aliens landed on the roof and would be moving into my bedroom.

"With me?" I asked, dubious.

"Why not you?" he asked.

I rolled my eyes. "You know why," I replied. "You know I never get as much mention as the men."

"Like I said, they're interested in the rumors you want to leave the pros and cross over into indie territory."

It kinda pissed me off they were calling now. Like the only reason I was suddenly worth interviewing was because I was doing something they probably thought was foolish. I could imagine the headlines now:

Female racer can't hack it with the pros, goes indie!

or

Ron Gamble's daughter making a big mistake.

"Tell them to call someone else for the empty corner in the back of their rag," I told him. I didn't even care I sounded bitter. It was hard not to have a chip on my shoulder when it felt like everything worked against me.

"It's a feature interview."

I glanced up. He'd shocked me again. Why in the hell would the fact I wanted to go indie make me a featured headline?

It didn't matter anyway.

"You told them they were barking up the wrong tree, right?" I said, settling back into the chair, disgruntled.

"Actually, no."

I glanced down at the scotch in my hand. What the fuck was in this? I was hearing things. "I'm sorry, what?"

Dad chuckled; it was a warm sound. His looks had changed over the years. His hair had become peppered with grey, his face more creased with lines.

But his rich laugh never changed.

"A feature interview is a good opportunity for you. Look what it did for Drew and the NRR."

"What are you saying, Dad?" I sat forward. I was ready for the bottom line.

"Finish the pro season strong, get the media good and interested in you…"

"And…?" I pressed.

"And then I will transfer your sponsorship contract over to the NRR."

I jumped up out of the chair, a wide smile splitting my face. "Really?"

He chuckled again and nodded. Then, like any parent, he had to go and ruin it with a bunch of conditions and yapping. "But Hopper is going to manage you."

"But what about the pros?" I asked, perplexed. Hopper worked with me and the rest of the pros my dad sponsored now.

"I'll find someone else to help take his responsibilities."

I frowned. I liked Hopper. Working with him was definitely not a hardship. He was a friend, but I didn't want him to feel like he was being pushed out of a job he loved just to babysit me.

"He wants to do it," Dad said, reading my face.

"He does?"

"Apparently, no-rules racing appeals to him as well," Dad quipped.

I grinned.

"You'll also be attending more events with Drew. He's the face of the NRR, poised as the first champion. His press will be good for you."

I nodded, readily agreeing. But then I scowled. "People are going to say I'm only sponsored by you because you're my dad."

I hated it. But at the same time… my father opened doors for me.

"Prove them wrong." He challenged. "Just like in the pros."

A wave of fatigue washed over me. How many times did a person have to prove themselves? I wanted a fresh start… not a new beginning of the same thing.

As I grappled with my own thoughts, he continued. "When you aren't at pro races, you need to be at indie ones."

I just nodded. I already planned on that anyway.

"It's basically double the work."

He listed all these conditions like they were somehow death sentences and things I wouldn't be thrilled to take on. He seemed almost regretful he was agreeing to transfer my contract.

"I'm not afraid of hard work." *Even if it does make me exhausted.* It was a point I felt I shouldn't have to make. I worked harder than any other driver he sponsored. I didn't say it out of arrogance; it was merely a fact. A fact my father well knew.

He rubbed a hand over his face, suddenly looking tired. "The indie world is different than the pros. The drivers are of a different…" He searched for a word. "Caliber."

It was like a megawatt lightbulb flickered to life inside the darkened areas of my brain.

That's why he doesn't want me in the NRR.

I forgot about proving myself. I forgot about the work I was taking on. I was transported backward. To a different time. "I'm not that girl anymore," I said, tight. "I haven't been for a long time."

"A division with no rules might be tempting, though." He cautioned.

"Who's talking right now?" I asked, my voice low. "My sponsor or my father?"

"Both."

I wanted to laugh. If he only knew half the crap I dealt with being the only girl in my world, he wouldn't even be bringing this up.

"I can assure my sponsor I'm not a bad investment. You've seen my driving, and you know my work ethic. I won't do anything to jeopardize all the time and effort I've put into getting myself where I am today."

He nodded. "I know. It's the reason I'm agreeing to this."

So it was really just the father in him talking, then.

"You don't need to worry about me, Dad." I vowed. "It wasn't the pros that straightened me out or the rules of the division. I grew up."

His voice was gruff. "I know I don't say it often, but I'm proud of you, kid."

That meant something to me.

No. Not something.

Everything.

"Thank you," I whispered.

"The interview with *GearShark* is next week. All the details are being sent over."

A giddy feeling rose up inside me, like I was suddenly filled with all the bubbles a soda came alive with when it was first poured into a glass. "I'll be there."

I started for the door, assuming the meeting was over. I would heat up his dinner and then head across the house to where my rooms were and maybe take a hot bath.

"Joey." His voice stopped me.

I turned back.

"There's something about the interview I haven't told you yet."

Of course. Hadn't I known I couldn't possibly escape with only the third degree? "What's the catch?" I asked.

"It's not a solo interview. There is another driver being interviewed as well."

I laughed, a harsh sound. I'd known it was too good to be true. For whatever reason, I alone wasn't a good enough story. "Who?" I asked, already pissed at the unknown person.

"He's an indie driver. I think they want to do a dual point of view about the potential crossover."

Of course they did.

"Who is it?" I asked again. Knowing it wasn't, but hoping it was going to be Drew.

"Lorhaven."

The bottom fell out of my stomach. "You've got to be kidding me." I fumed, swinging fully around to face my father. "That guy is a class-A asshole. And he hates pro drivers."

"Which is probably why they want his perspective." My father pointed out, the business tycoon in him recognizing the spin the magazine could put on this.

I made a rude sound.

"It's not too late to change your mind." He reminded me.

I made a face. "I'll do the interview."

I wasn't about to back down. It was exactly what men like Lorhaven wanted.

Everyone, including *GearShark*, thought they had the upper hand. They thought I was just some piece on a chessboard, a rook instead of a queen.

They were wrong.

I'd prove it.

All of them could kiss my ass, including the man who thought he was so epic he only needed one name.

TWO

Lorhaven

It never gets old. The feeling behind the wheel of a car breaking barriers, of carrying a man faster on land than he ever thought he'd go.

Adrenaline spikes through my blood like fuel through a fuel injection line. The juice hammers beneath my skin, making my hands jitter, but my foot is steady and sure as it tamps down on the gas.

Even though I'm sitting, the physical aspect of driving is intense. My heart rate spikes like I'm sprinting on a treadmill, sweat slicks beneath my clothes, and I'm so immersed in what I'm doing, the concentration almost hurts.

But it's a good kind of hurt. The kind a man like me craves.

It doesn't matter what kind of track I'm on, who I'm up against. The second my tires squeal off the starting line, it becomes a little less about who's on the road with me and a little more about pushing myself to the max.

I love the control of driving. The absolute power thumping beneath my palms and purring through the engine of a jacked-up car. I'm at the helm here, in complete command of the machine rumbling beneath my body. My only limits are my own.

The back end of the Corvette turned out, drifting forward to lead as smoke from the burning rubber of my very expensive tires saturated the space around the white body. Even though I was inside the car, I knew what it looked like to all the people lining the streets.

It looked fucking badass. So fucking bad it was good. Almost ethereal, with the white fog lifting and the sleek, shiny white body cutting through it with perfect precision.

Just when it seemed I might drift too far, I cut the wheel and put the end back where it belonged and hammered the nose forward to shoot ahead on the last straightaway.

Behind me, a Dodge Charger came in fast, nosing close to the back of my Vette and putting pressure on me to move or get taken out.

I laughed.

Beneath my grip, the steering wheel obeyed my every command. The car swerved in small, decisive jerks. Right—left then right—left again.

The Charger behind me jerked, thinking they were going to power around me, but they should have known better by now. I came back solidly in front, cutting him off and stomping on his hope.

I guess I was the kind of lion who liked to play with his food before taking the fatal bite.

Aggression and frustration of the driver in my rearview crackled in the air, and I pressed down on the gas, milking my car for even more performance. The engine responded, and I glided forward, creating more of a gap between us.

His emotions were starting to cloud his driving. I could sense it almost immediately. It left a foul taste in my mouth. Those emotions were going to be his downfall.

Not the fact that he had any. Hell, we all did.

But they didn't belong in a street race.

Turns out I was right. In his haste, he pressed down on the NOS injector installed in his car. I heard the groan of his engine even over the purring, smooth hum of mine.

The Charger shot forward, making mincemeat of the distance I'd put between us, and came in hot on the fender of my Vette. I swerved over, but it didn't matter.

The kid behind the wheel couldn't hack the power. He didn't have enough knowledge to use the muscle he'd just summoned.

Time slowed down. My own breathing echoed in my lungs as he lost a split second of control. A split second was sometimes all it took.

The front corner of his car slammed into my fender, sending my ride in a wide circle. I drove into it, not fighting against it, knowing I could use the momentum of the hit to spin myself back out, straight over the finish line.

He wasn't so lucky.

The Charger flipped and began to roll.

I had a prime view through my windshield as my car swung around.

Coming up behind the AWOL Charger was a car I knew very well. The black Camaro my brother always drove came dangerously close, and every muscle in my body locked up.

"No!" I yelled and started fighting my car, intent on putting it into submission.

The Charger rolled and flipped over the pavement as if it weren't a huge, heavy piece of metal, but an acrobat performing some fabulous routine.

My attention zeroed in.

The Vette shot forward, fishtailing a bit as I forced it out of the spin and surged forward, now driving in the complete opposite direction I'd been going.

A bleached-blond head was my focus. Through the windshield of my brother's car, I saw his eyes round, his shoulders tense, and his hands white-knuckle on the wheel.

When a man was driving as fast as we all were, everything happened so fast, often way too fast for there to be enough time to anticipate or even react.

By the time my brother saw the wreck in motion, he was already so close even slamming on his brakes wouldn't stop him from becoming a casualty.

The fucking Charger headed right for him. They were going to collide, my little brother landing underneath.

Remember how I said you couldn't let emotion get in the way of driving?

There was an exception.

Family.

My little brother.

I forced my eyes off him. I couldn't let it paralyze me.

My foot punched the gas all the way to the floor. I rarely did that; there was never a reason to. Pushing my car to its absolute max was never a necessity.

Until now.

The sound of my tires on the pavement was so loud it echoed through the night. The end of the Charger bounced off the pavement and catapulted into one more rotation, the rotation that would land it on top of my bro.

It was a split-second decision. One I would have made even if I had five minutes to consider it.

As the car peaked in the air, my Vette slid beneath it, and I hit the emergency brake hard and swerved the wheel with more violence than I usually treated my ride with.

The car jolted around. My body slammed against the door and bounced off, and the car continued the sharp U-turn.

My back end smacked into the Camaro, shoving it sideways, as my car took up the spot my brother was supposed to be.

I threw the car into reverse and hit the gas again. I didn't even bother looking where I was going. I just went.

The Charger dropped out of the sky like a plane in full engine failure.

Crunching metal, shattering glass, and loud groans filled my ears. The impact of the Challenger on the Corvette felt like my body hit a wall of water from a twenty-foot drop. The harness strapping me in tightened painfully as my body jostled once more. The airbag deployed, punching my body and robbing me of air. My head snapped back, the taste of blood slicked my tongue, and then everything fell silent.

* * *

The kind of silence that follows destruction is always sort of eerie. Kind of like the calm after the storm… you know, where everything around is taking stock of what the fuck just happened and how much damage there was to recover from.

I blinked, my movements sort of sluggish as I pushed at the airbag filling my vision. The weight of my arm moved it enough that I got a close-up view of how close I came to being a pancake on this dark back road.

The Charger lay upside down across my hood. It teetered there like a seesaw in the wind. Shattered glass lay everywhere like rubble, and the headlights cast a glare off to the side of the road. The body of the Charger was mangled and dented, the paint partially scraped off from the tumbling, and windows all blown out.

My own windshield was filled with a thousand cracks, making it look like a giant spider web. All it would take was the slightest nudge and the entire thing would crumble.

The sound of metal scratching against metal caused chills to brush over the back of my neck.

All at once, everything seemed to burst into motion again, and the sounds of people yelling filled the air, and the body of my car jolted like someone was jumping on the hood again.

"Lor!" a familiar voice screamed. I heard the alarm, the scared-shitless tone, and my body stiffened.

I grappled for the handle to get out, but the goddamn airbag wouldn't get the fuck out of the way.

"Lor!" he screamed again, and my door was ripped open. Night air came whooshing inside the stifling cab.

The airbag was shoved away, and my brother's bleach-blond head appeared. Worry lines creased his face, his eyes frantic.

"I'm fine." I assured him and reached for the buckles on my harness.

"What the fuck were you thinking?" he yelled, ripping away the ends of the harness after I unhooked them.

I didn't take offense because the underlying fear in his tone cut me.

I didn't want you to die. That's what I'd been thinking.

"You okay?" I asked, pushing out of the driver's seat to stand. I was a little unsteady, but I pushed that back, refusing to show any kind of weakness, even after I was almost fish food.

I spared a glance at my once perfect icy-white Corvette. The entire front end was crumpled in, the hood bent up around the Charger at odd angles. Smoke from my tires and the scent of burning rubber and brake fluid tinged the air.

My car was likely totaled. I wasn't going to be able to fix the damage done. It totally fucking sucked because this was my favorite car.

"Me!" Arrow scoffed, reminding me I was supposed to be making sure he wasn't hurt. I focused back on him as he shoved at the long strands falling over the side of his head. "You just drove head on into a wreck."

I gave him a smirk. "But did I die?"

"Your mouth is bloody," he said, not finding humor in my joke.

I dabbed at my teeth; my fingers came away red. I shrugged. "Bit my tongue when the airbag deployed."

"Don't do that again," Arrow said, his voice a little hollow and low.

I glanced up sharply. His face was ghostly pale, his eyes like wide, white saucers in his face.

"He was headed right for you." I dabbed at my mouth some more, not taking my eyes off him.

His body shifted, his voice harsh. "I had it handled."

Maybe. But he was my brother.

"Where would I be if you died, Lor?" He shoved at my shoulder. "I'd rather go than be left here without you."

The bold statement squeezed my heart. I pulled him roughly against my chest and wrapped him in a tight hug.

"Don't talk like that," I whispered and slapped him on the shoulder.

He gripped my back like he was afraid I might disappear. I wasn't one for showing any kind of emotion, especially not at a race on my own turf.

But the kid was clearly shaken. He'd been through enough already; he didn't need me pushing him away like I was too macho to hug him.

Movement coming toward us had me looking up. Anger cut through all the family fuzzies, and I shoved back from my brother.

"You goddamn son of a bitch!" I roared and burst forward.

My fist drove right into the side of his face. I felt the bone give way as his body recoiled back from the force of the hit.

When he was sprawled out over the pavement, I stood over him, chest heaving.

"Your green, cocky ass almost killed my brother," I snarled. His eyes were slightly unfocused as he looked at me, but I knew his ears worked just fine.

He seemed rather unhurt considering his car just slammed down over mine.

My hands shook with the need to rectify it.

"It was an accident," he mumbled. "I lost control."

"You never had control!" I spat. "Don't ever come back on my turf again. You're out." The way I saw it, any man could drive, but he had to be real about it. Thinking you could handle too much power too fast was a way to get people killed.

Driving the way we did wasn't a safe sport by any means. But some people were just fucking idiots.

This idiot was a poser with a nice car who thought he could best me and make me look like a fool on my own territory.

"But…" He tried to push himself up but fell back down.

I felt my upper lip curl in disgust.

People crowded in around us, watching warily. I felt the judgmental stare of someone close by, incredulous that I would deck a man who just almost died.

He must be new here. Everyone else knew I didn't give a shit.

If he had died, it would have been his own fault.

"Get him the fuck outta my sight!" I growled. I didn't have time for this.

A couple guys moved in and picked him up.

"Jones!" I barked and turned my back. A guy in a set of coveralls and a backward hat appeared. "Gonna need your tow trucks tonight, man."

He nodded. "Have 'em here in five."

I held out my fist, and we pounded it out. "Thanks, man."

Here on my turf, we didn't call the cops. They'd just throw us in the slammer anyway. I wasn't too fond of the metal cages they liked to lock racers in. Accidents happened, and we cleaned them up ourselves.

Besides, I was pretty sure if this got around, my sponsor would read me the fucking riot act.

I was lucky it hadn't been worse. I had a race coming up.

Might be time for a little break from the streets. At least until my next race was over.

"You sure you're okay?" Arrow asked, coming up beside me as I studied the mess that was my Corvette.

"I'm fine," I replied.

"I had it under control. I was going to move," he said, regret and agitation in his tone.

He was pissed I jumped in front of him. Pissed I protected him.

My brother lived too long without protection from assholes. He could be pissed all he wanted, but it wouldn't stop me from being the brother I should have been before.

"Losing control of the streets," someone said from behind.

I turned away from the mangled cars and stared, unflinching, at the approaching man.

Kurt Bodean was a regular on my streets. He raced here, lived here, and generally annoyed me here.

It wasn't always that way, at least the last part anyway. We actually used to be pretty tight. We'd grown up together, worked in some car shops together, but over the years, we'd grown apart.

We'd always sort of balanced on the line of friends and rivals. The older we got, the more it felt like we were just keeping each other close to keep an eye on the other. The fact I had money had always been a sticking point with him.

But when I started out-driving him and took control of the turf, all the "advantages" I had become too hard to ignore.

Jealousy was an ugly monster.

"I think I controlled the street just fine tonight," I drawled lazily.

"Letting juniors in your races doesn't speak of control to me."

I rolled my head toward Kurt and levelled my eyes on him. "You know damn well that junior has been around for a while. He'd have been fine if he hadn't installed a bunch of shit in his car he wasn't ready for."

Kurt glanced toward the cars, then back. "I'm thinking your attention must be pretty divided lately, with the NRR and trying to maintain control here."

He had a buzz cut that suggested he didn't have time to bother with his hair, but on his chin was a goatee he clearly kept trimmed. So my thoughts on his style and maybe some of his problem was premature balding.

"You got your eye on my place?" I asked, my own eyes narrowing on his face.

What was it with everyone tonight?

Couldn't a man get one night off from someone trying to take something from him?

"Maybe," Kurt replied.

Well, at least he was honest. And unlike the junior who wrecked my car, he actually had some shit to back it up.

I stepped up to him. We measured each other as if we'd never met before. "My spot here isn't vacant," I said evenly.

"Maybe it should be."

I didn't like the glint in his eye.

"You should watch yourself," I warned.

He didn't back down, but I didn't expect him to. I wouldn't have if I were angling for the top spot. I wasn't dumb. I knew this was coming. The way some people saw it around here, now that I was driving for the NRR, I didn't need to be on the streets.

I begged to differ.

Never forget where you come from.

It's exactly there that made a man who he was.

I came from these streets.

I wasn't some pampered pro driver who had everything handed to them. As far as I was concerned, these streets were the path that led me to the NRR.

Jones pulled up in a tow truck, followed by another one that looked just like it. People around us burst into action, preparing to pry the Charger off my car and tow them both away.

I'd seen what happened when men forgot. One victory, one step into a level higher than where they'd been made them arrogant. It made them think they were better than those they left behind.

In truth, we were all the same. Me, Kurt… hell, even Junior who ruined my car.

What set us apart was sheer determination. Sheer will… And a heavy dose of hard work.

Even though the most bitter <insert Kurt> liked to say it was money and luck.

Money and luck didn't hurt. But it wasn't defining.

Sometimes not even all of the above was enough. Sometimes we got smacked back down to where we started, and we had to begin again.

That's why knowing where you come from wasn't something you could leave behind.

If I had to begin again, I would, here, on *my* turf.

Until that point, my feet were going to be firmly planted in both racing worlds. This one and the NRR. And no one was going to get in my way.

Three

Joey

There were boys in my kitchen.

Not just any boys.

Trent and Drew.

"How did you get in here?" I scowled. I was happy to see them, but it was morning and I hadn't had any coffee yet.

Plus, today was the day.

"The housekeeper loves us," Trent said around a bite of an oversized homemade muffin.

Drew was busy nursing a cup of steaming coffee, but he did smirk when Trent replied.

The housekeeper did love them. Everyone did. They were practically the most lovable pair of guys on the entire planet.

And the fact that they loved each other only made them more endearing.

"My father summoned you here," I stated as I poured the dark, richly scented brew into a white mug sitting beside the pot.

Drew appeared soundlessly beside me and shoved his identical half-empty cup under my nose. I fought a smile as I refilled it for him. He looked as disgruntled as

I felt about the early morning hour. His hair was either artfully arranged to look unkempt or…

Knowing Drew, it was just uncombed.

The scruff on his jawline was a permanent fixture. It seemed a little more pronounced this morning, and for once, he wasn't wearing a leather jacket and black jeans. Instead, he was dressed in a pair of battered, loose blue jeans, a white T-shirt, and an open, cotton plaid button-up. It was bright yellow and cobalt blue. The colors seemed to make his already blue eyes even bluer.

"Finally got him to cave about you coming over to the dark side," he mused, approval written all over his coffee-guzzling face.

When I first met him, I'd been interested in being more than friends. If I hadn't seen the way he looked at his best friend, I probably would have pursued him.

But his heart was already spoken for, and now I couldn't imagine him as anything other than a friend.

"Ron Gamble doesn't cave." I poked him in the chest. "And his agreement came with a list of conditions."

I turned to lean back against the counter and let the first sip of coffee slide down my throat and touch my soul.

It was some good shit.

"One of those conditions being a dual interview with Lorhaven," Trent unnecessarily pointed out while shoving the rest of his muffin between his lips.

I gave him a sour look, and he grinned, blueberries stuck in his teeth.

Besides the food crammed in his mouth, Trent was a lot more pulled together than Drew, in appearance anyway.

He had the whole "effortlessly preppy but still managing to look cool" vibe going on. His dark-blond hair was styled in a disheveled way, a pair of navy board shorts hung low on his hips, and a white cotton polo with the top two buttons undone hugged his wide upper body and seemed to stretch around the muscles in his biceps.

Perched on the top of his head were a pair of Oakleys, and on his feet were flip-flops. I honestly never thought men looked good in flip-flops… but he did.

"One of the conditions being to get some media time." I corrected. Then muttered, "Lorhaven comes with the damn interview."

Now that he had a full mug of coffee, Drew retreated to where Trent was and leaned up against the counter beside him. Automatically, Trent shifted so their sides were pressed together.

Drew held out his mug, and Trent palmed it to take a sip. When he was done, he placed it back in Drew's hand, allowing his fingers to linger on Drew's for a few seconds before pulling away.

The room practically crackled whenever they were in it. I'd honestly never seen anything like it. Certainly not with my father and my mother, not with my father and any woman that had come and gone from his life since I'd been born.

I'd never experienced it either.

I would have argued attraction like that didn't exist, but I couldn't deny what was right in front of me.

Made me wonder if something like that would ever touch my life, or if it was reserved for only a select few.

"The tables are turned," Drew mused, the dimple in his cheek making an appearance. Clearly, the coffee was starting to hit his bloodstream.

"What?" I asked. Clearly, it wasn't hitting mine yet.

"Seems like just yesterday you were sent to help groom me to drive for the NRR. And now it's me being sent to help you cross over."

I scowled. "You didn't need help. I don't either."

Drew just smiled. He never seemed to take my independent nature to heart. "Nah, but it will give us an excuse to hang out."

"Yeah, you gonna let us into the pit for your next race?" Trent asked, wagging his eyebrows.

Drew chuckled.

I laughed. I missed them. Sometimes we went weeks without seeing each other, especially when Drew was racing in all the preliminaries for the first indie season. Even though we were expected to see each other more now, I knew it would still be hard to come by.

The NRR season was starting, and my season was already in swing. I told my father I'd honor my commitments, and I would. I never backed out on my word.

But I kind of wished I could.

I'd never say it out loud to anyone, but the pros were wearing me down. It was hard to fight (and fight alone) when there was no end to the struggle in sight.

I loved cars. I loved racing and the feel of the road beneath my tires. I even loved being strapped into a racecar without much room to move.

But I was ready for a change.

I was ready to embrace the indie world, and I hoped they would embrace me as well.

"I got a pit pass with your names on it," I told him and snatched up a muffin. The idea of Trent and Drew in the pit with my crew made me look forward to my races a little bit more.

"I got you a T-shirt."

"A shirt?" I asked, wrinkling my nose.

Trent smiled quick and motioned toward the lump of fabric on the island. I hadn't even noticed it.

Abandoning my breakfast, I snatched the cotton off the counter and held it up. The shirt was yellow, a color that seemed to become Drew's signature, and on the back it read:

Drew Forrester
PIT CREW

I smiled and pulled it back against my chest, holding it up for them to see. A quick glance down, and I saw the outline of a racecar on the front.

"I love it," I told them and folded it carefully to place it down. "Thank you."

"We'll coordinate schedules later. Dinner?" Drew asked.

I nodded. "You guys in town for a while?"

"'Til after next week's race," Trent answered.

That was right. The first indie race of the official season was at Gamble Speedway.

"You can't stay at a hotel all week," I told them. "Stay here."

"I don't know," Trent deadpanned. "This place is kinda small."

Drew laughed.

I rolled my eyes. "I think we can fit you in. You can have the suite near my wing."

"I was kinda hoping you'd say that," Trent admitted. Beside him, Drew's face grew dark.

What was that about?

Before I could ask, Drew pushed off the counter. "You ready? Can't be late for your big interview."

"I'm sure Lorhaven wouldn't mind," I muttered. "He'd probably prefer it. Attention hog."

Trent barked a laugh and flung his arm across my shoulders. "Give him hell."

We went through the house, but at the front door, Drew paused with his palm on the handle. "You mind driving?" he asked over his shoulder.

That look was back in his eye.

"Of course not. The Skyline is right outside."

Trent nodded. "We saw it on the way in."

I pulled the keys out of my pocket, and we headed out into the summer sunshine. It was early, so it wasn't too hot, but I could tell by the balminess in the air it was going to be a warm day.

I got in the driver's seat, Drew climbed in the back, and Trent took shotgun. No one said anything on the way down the long driveway, but as we approached the gates, the tension in the car seemed to increase.

I glanced at Trent and then back at Drew.

"What?" I said finally.

Trent hitched his chin toward something on the other side of the gate.

One black SUV and one unfamiliar car was parked out on the street. As I watched, the SUV's passenger window rolled down and a camera with a huge lens appeared.

"The press is following you around?" I asked, irritation in my tone.

"Fucking bloodsuckers were waiting in the lobby of the hotel when we came down this morning," he spat.

And that explained why Trent seemed relieved when I offered him a room here. Behind the gates where press couldn't get.

Anger warmed my cheeks. "They hound you guys a lot?"

"Just when we're on the road," Drew said. "We have gates at home now."

"Thank fuck," Trent muttered.

They were on the road a lot. I couldn't imagine having a camera up my ass every time I stepped outside. I dared a glance at Trent. He was staring down the black SUV with something close to rage simmering beneath his stare.

"Hey," I said and touched his arm.

His hazel eyes collided with mine. I saw the hard edge there, the absolute steel and determination to protect Drew from as much of the intrusion as possible.

It made me sad for them.

They weren't a circus act.

They were two really awesome men in love. They were friends, brothers, businessmen. They deserved privacy and a chance to live their lives without Trent being on the defensive every time they left the house.

"You can stay at my place anytime you come to town," I told him softly, patting him with my hand.

The relaxed, almost playful guy I saw this morning in the kitchen came back to the surface. He grabbed my hand and kissed the back of it. "Thanks."

"You two are looking awfully cozy up there," Drew drawled from the backseat.

Trent winked at me. "Don't get your boxers in a bunch, Forrester. You know you're my favorite."

Drew grunted like he was satisfied, and I pulled the car out onto the street, noting that almost immediately, the paparazzi pulled out to follow.

Guess it didn't matter we left the Fastback behind; the assholes knew Drew and Trent were with me.

"So tell me," I said, turning away from the rearview and hoping to distract the guys from the vultures behind us. "How much of an asshole is Lorhaven going to be today at the interview?"

Drew snorted. "On a scale of one to ten?" he asked. "Twenty."

Oh, good. Something to look forward to.

Not.

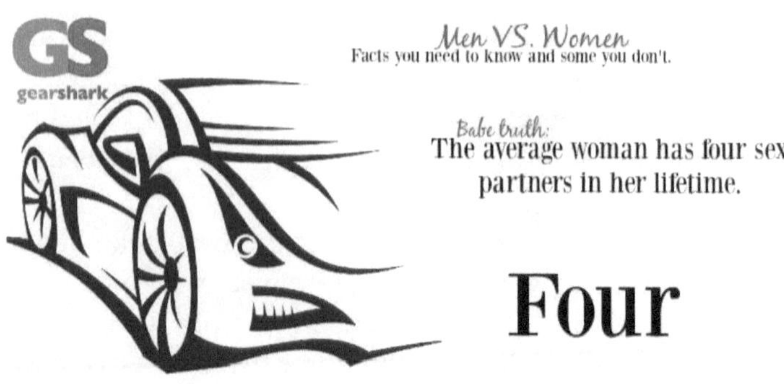

Four

Lorhaven

Scrap metal.

Not fixable.

Totally fucked.

All of these things describe the condition of my beautiful white Corvette.

Once we got it back to the hangar, it looked even more hopeless beneath the bright, harsh beams of the floodlights.

Refusing to admit defeat, I went over that car like I was searching for gold. Arrow helped, even though I knew he thought it was hopeless.

After several hours and a long moment of silence, I pulled a cover over her and called it.

Dead on arrival.

Arrow offered me the Camaro. I wasn't going to take my brother's car. He loved it the way I did the Corvette. We had a few other cars in our hangars. They were all nice cars. A Nissan, a Dodge, even an older model Corvette.

I drove around in a Mustang for a week.

It wasn't a Fastback, but I felt like a Forrester wannabe.

So I sold it.

It didn't take more than a day. All I had to do was put out word I was selling one of my cars. One of the drivers I was accustomed to seeing around my races bought it. Paid all cash. I didn't ask him where he got all that cash, because I didn't really care. It was green, and it increased my bottom line.

Personally, I thought it was pretty fucking stupid for the guy to buy my car, because I knew he'd show up at my races with it. He'd never beat me driving a car I practically built. I knew all the nuances of the Mustang. Unless he did a lot of work under the hood, I'd beat him without even trying.

But he would pick up some wins on my turf when I wasn't racing. Maybe he didn't care to be the best like Kurt. Maybe he just wanted to be better than he was now.

I could respect that.

I looked through listings for another Vette. Even test drove a couple. It didn't feel right. It was sort of like trying to replace a favorite pair of jeans. It didn't matter if they were exactly the same, because the original was always better.

In short, I was in a goddamned pissy mood.

And I'd never say it to anyone, but my neck fucking hurt. Guess having my head snapped back in the wreck pulled a muscle or some shit.

The morning of my *GearShark* interview, Arrow got up and left the hotel room early. I figured he was going to get some coffee and breakfast. I took a hot shower and put on a pair of jeans and a black T-shirt with my sponsor logo on it.

It hadn't taken long for a few offers to come my way. I held out, though, until the best one came along.

Ted Bayer was one of the three men who owned the New Revolution Racing corporation. He was rich and connected. His main business was a huge tire company that had chain stores in every state in the country. He had his hands in other businesses as well, but it was Brickstone Tire's logo that was prominently displayed on most of my shit.

When Arrow walked in the room without any coffee or food in his hands, I gave him a WTF look.

"You didn't bring me any coffee, asshole?"

Arrow grinned beneath the baseball hat he wore. "Brought you something better."

On the way to the elevator, I shoved my wallet and phone into my jeans and gave him the death glare until we stepped outside on the brick sidewalk of the hotel.

I stopped in my tracks at the sight.

I glanced between Arrow and the object parked there. "You did this?"

He grinned like he thought he was fucking brilliant. "Dude, you've been like an old man with a bad case of the gout and some extra-large hemorrhoids lately."

"Fuck you," I told him, still staring.

It was a fucking Lotus.

A pristine Lotus Elise.

This car was basically mystery and sensuality wrapped up in a two-door package. There was a lot of racing history and some mighty impressive wins around the Lotus Elise. It was the kind of car people would drop their voices an octave when they spoke about it.

It just had that kind of majestic pull.

Lotus was actually a well-known brand in my circles, the manufacturer having basically pulled off a Hail Mary.

A few years back, a lot of car manufacturer's in Britain were going under, and it appeared they would be going down with them. But the company threw every last resource they had into the Elise.

And it paid off.

It literally saved the entire brand.

That's the kind of magic I was talking about here.

And sitting not twenty feet away was a damn fine specimen.

Plus, it was white.

I approached the car slowly, studying every line and curve on its flawlessly designed body. The wheels were black satin in a lightweight Y-shaped cast. The front tires were sixteen inches, while the back were seventeen.

The rounded vents behind the two doors were fierce. Round taillights anchored the word

L O T U S spelled out between them. The roof was a removable hard top and installed auxiliary lights on the front. It was a small sports car, only enough room for two, but my God, it had a presence.

Frankly, it was giving me a hard on.

"Where the fuck did you find this?" I asked Arrow, glancing over the hood to where he was standing on the sidewalk.

You can find anything on the internet.

He searched for a car for me.

And he found this.

I was in awe.

My momentary come to Jesus moment was interrupted when someone flung over the driver's door and got out.

I stiffened and rushed around the hood to the man.

"Who the fuck are you!" I demanded. Did he think he could just steal this car?

My car?

He cleared his throat and looked at me. I snarled. He was wearing a pair of dress pants that were too short and gave a nice view of his dress socks and shoes. His shirt was tucked in like it was shoved so far into the back of his pants his ass probably could taste it.

What the fuck was a douche like this doing even touching my car?

Arrow glanced at me. "He owns it, Lor."

I laughed.

The man with the keys and bad pants frowned.

"You own this car?" I scoffed.

"I'm a car collector," he replied, his voice tight.

I shook my head. A fucking shame.

He probably never even drove this beauty. It probably sat in his temperature-controlled garage and wept every night when the lights went out.

I glanced at the car. *I'll save you.*

"Sorry about that, man," I said, approaching him and offering my hand. "I thought you were trying to take off with it."

He cleared his throat and shook my offered hand. "Your brother says you've been looking for a new car."

I nodded. "This one for sale?"

"For the right price."

Fucking businessmen. Always thinking they could get one over on someone like me because I looked like some rich boy who only wanted to impress his friends with a shiny new toy.

"One point eight-liter engine. Toyota, right?"

The man's gaze sharpened a little. "Yes."

"Five or six speed?" I asked.

"Five."

I pursed my lips. "Zero to sixty in four point two seconds, zero to one hundred in four point six," I said as I walked around and admired the body some more. "Two hundred seventeen horse power, and a max power at one forty-five?"

He nodded. "Yes."

I scoffed. "I could make it to one sixty."

"It's a good design," he said. "Speed wasn't sacrificed for safety. This model has both."

I nodded. It would have even more speed when I was done modifying it.

I motioned for Arrow. "How about a test drive?"

"Well, I'll need to ride with you," the man said, glancing at Arrow.

I plucked the keys out of his hand. "Not necessary. I'll handle her with kid gloves."

"You can't just take my car," he protested, his voice hard.

I pulled my driver's license out of my back pocket and handed it to him. Then I handed him the keys to Arrow's Camaro.

"Here's some collateral. You can't expect me to pay for a car I'm not even able to drive."

"You can't expect me to let you drive off with it," the man retorted.

"I have an interview with *GearShark Magazine*." I shrugged. "Can't be late."

"*GearShark Magazine*." He scoffed.

"I'm a driver in the NRR."

His eyes turned speculative. I shut that shit down instantly.

"Here's the deal. I'll drive her. We'll meet back here in, say, three hours? If I like the car, I'll give you sixty grand on the spot. Cash."

"This car is worth seventy!" He fumed.

I crossed my arms over my chest. "No. It *will* be worth seventy when I'm done with it."

"You can't just give me a number and expect me to take it," the man argued. "And you aren't leaving here with my car."

"Fine." I held the keys out between us.

Over the hood, Arrow watched with apt interest.

Hope you're learning something, little bro.

"Excuse me?" the man asked, staring at the keys.

"You don't like my number or my terms? I'm sure you have another buyer willing to give you seventy grand on the spot."

The man's mouth drew down.

He knew as well as I did he wasn't going to get seventy grand for this car. Maybe if it were brand new and had some upgrades, but as is?

He could go fuck himself.

"I'm gonna need the keys to my brother's Camaro back." I held out my hand. "And my license."

He glanced down at the stuff he was holding. His eyes seemed to sharpen on my ID.

"You're the Lorhaven who drives for Brickstone?"

"One in the same," I drawled, impatiently motioning for my shit.

"Well, I guess it would be okay if you took the car for a bit." His hand curled around my ID like he intended to keep it.

I think my price just went down to fifty-five thousand. Asshole.

Without another word, I turned and slid into the driver's seat. There was less room in here than in my Vette, but I liked the way the car seemed to hug my body.

The engine purred when I hit the button to start it up, and the man on the sidewalk stood there like he was in shock. I rolled down the window.

"See you in a few hours," I said, then drove off.

Arrow looked over from the passenger seat. "Nice choice for your next car." He grinned.

I held my fist out to him above the leather console.

The interior was all black leather, trimmed with Alcantara in red.

"Good looking out, bro," I told him as we pounded it out.

Out on the main road, I opened her up. She responded beneath my hands better than any lover ever had.

Damn, this was a sweet car.

"So?" Arrow said when I downshifted as I approached Gamble Speedway where the *GearShark* team would be waiting. "You gonna buy her?"

"Thinking about it," I replied, wondering why I said that and not an immediate hell yes.

We turned into the Speedway lot and coasted across the pavement.

I wanted the car. This was the closest I'd come to driving nirvana since the Vette was totaled. Yet for some reason, something held me back from saying so.

There was a slight hesitation to my usually quick willingness to pull the trigger.

And it wasn't the price tag.

As I steered through the smaller gates into the stadium, I caught the distinct sight of a bright-yellow Skyline.

Nah, it wasn't the money. It was something else.

Five

Joey

My hair.

There was so much of it, it got its own sentence.

My mother was Latin. Yes, the irony of a Latin woman living it up in Paris was not lost on me. She was all curves, dark hair, and olive-toned skin. She was a gorgeous woman, actually; it was the reason she'd caught my father's eye and managed to become his third and final ex-wife.

I'd inherited a lot of features from her, like my endless curves and the thick mass of dark, curly hair, which frankly, I found unruly and sometimes bothersome. My skin tone wasn't pale, but it wasn't quite as olive and golden as some Latin women. That was courtesy of my father, along with my height, for which I was grateful. I had so many curves I couldn't imagine trying to pack them all into a shorter frame.

At least being five seven, the length of my body attempted to slim out my hips and chest.

Not that it worked much.

So many days, I'd cursed my womanly body. Working in a male-dominated field—correction—a field where men thought they were God's gift to women, I'd wished more than once my chest was flat and my booty was, too.

Even so, I didn't often cover up my curves with baggy, oversized clothes. I tried that; it only made me feel like I was wearing a sack, and I still got lewd comments and propositions anyway.

Always out of earshot of my father or any of his loyal employees of course.

And I never said a word. I wasn't about to run back to my father and tattle. I was a big girl and I could handle a bunch of dicks.

Not literally. Figuratively.

Physically, I preferred my dicks one at a time.

:-)

I didn't dress suggestively either. Frankly, I didn't have to. My body had the ability to turn any outfit into something I worked.

Usually, on the track, I wore leggings and tank tops covered up by jumpsuits I had made with all my sponsor logos and brands on them.

I wasn't in a business where I necessarily had to dress for the part. Although, I had a feeling that might be changing in the next couple months.

Or, um, right now.

That's where my hair came into the equation.

We were the first to arrive on the set of the interview. Once again, *GearShark* had a whole team of people on standby to make the interview and shoot happen.

I'd never done a photoshoot before. Sure, I'd had headshots done, but it was from the shoulders up. Photographers my father hired would never dare take a full-body shot of his only daughter.

<insert eye roll here>

On occasion, at races, the press would capture shots of me, usually when I was half dressed in the jumpsuit and it hung around my waist like I had a giant sweatshirt tied there.

I'd been in magazines before. Never a feature article, though.

At first, I'd come into the pro racing circuit thinking being a female might actually help me. It might set me apart and grasp some attention.

It set me apart all right. From everyone.

Sure, some magazines ran articles about me, never more than half a page, and they were always accompanied by the kind of shot a photographer accidentally snapped when he was taking shots of some of the other drivers.

I knew for a fact some of those paps had shots of me on the winners' podiums, but none of those pics ever made it public.

Conspiracy? I tried to think not.

Some days it was hard.

The second Drew, Trent, and I got out of the car, we were surrounded. It seemed the team today was the same team from both Drew's and Trent's feature interviews. Both of them had graced the cover of *GearShark*, and both those issues had sold a lot of copies.

Especially Trent's because he was sans his shirt.

I was whisked almost instantly into hair and makeup. The stylist took one look at my very long, very curly strands and asked me if I would allow them to blow it out.

I laughed.

But she was serious.

I told her it would take hours.

She patted my head as if to say, "I'm a professional. Watch this."

Game on. I liked my hair straight; it was something to be able to run my fingers through it. I also liked the way it reflected light when it was sleek.

But getting it straight?

Nearly impossible.

I was a wash-n-wear kind of girl. You know, I'd shampoo, condition, and then use some products to attempt to make it controllable.

Then it would air-dry into ringlets that took on a mind of their own.

A lot of women envied it.

It wasn't that I thought it was ugly; it was just a pain in the ass. I couldn't even cut it. I did that once, in a fit of rebellion.

I looked like a pyramid for an entire year.

I was invited into a small trailer where my hair was washed, conditioned, and some other stuff. Honestly, I stopped paying attention because one of the girls handed me a mimosa.

When the blow-dryer and styling tools came out, so did my earbuds and my playlist.

I actually kind of liked sitting here being pampered like this. I hardly ever got my hair done. I hardly ever got to just sit and relax. I was too busy of a person, always on the move.

Being forced to sit while my hair and makeup were being done was a welcome respite.

They even waxed my eyebrows.

I might have been offended it was taking so much effort just to get me photo ready if I cared enough what they all thought.

I wasn't a model. I was a racecar driver.

Trent and Drew were in and out of the trailer. So was Emily, the woman doing the interview. She said she wanted to interview both of us at the same time.

I tried to talk her out of it.

That only seemed to make her want to do it more.

Finally, I was done. The stylist turned me around in the swivel chair and pointed me at the mirror surrounded by lights.

I did a double take.

Slowly, I reached up and pulled the earbuds out of my ears and leaned forward.

My hair looking amazing. So good it almost made me jealous. I glanced through the mirror at the two girls standing there. "How did you do this to my hair?"

"Blow it out?" she asked.

"Make it *behave*," I replied, glancing back at the mirror.

It seemed darker this way. Almost black. Maybe because it was so shiny, almost like glass. And smooth… I didn't even know my hair would go this smooth. My fingers combed through the strands falling down my chest. It was even longer now; it fell past my breasts.

"It's soft," I murmured.

"Totally gorgeous," the girl behind me said.

"I need a list of everything you used on it," I told her.

She laughed and nodded.

I wouldn't do this on a daily basis, but it would be nice to sometimes have it look this way.

"The blowout should last three or four days. You can use some dry shampoo at the roots, if needed, to give it a boost."

"Makeup went on like a dream, too," the other girl spoke up.

I hadn't even noticed the makeup. I was too busy admiring my hair. But it looked nice, too. They went for a natural look, which I was grateful for. I didn't want to look like someone I wasn't.

"We're going casual for the shoot." The girl went on. "Here you go." She handed me a stack of clothes.

"When you're done, meet us outside."

Once I was alone, I glanced down at the ripped up jeans and white "wife-beater" tank top.

Wasn't exactly what I was expecting, but I liked it.

I changed out of the shorts and T-shirt I was dressed in and then took a few more minutes to look at my hair. I wasn't vain. Far from it.

But it was almost shocking to see it so contained.

After slipping into the high-heeled black sandals, I left all my stuff and stepped out of the trailer into the morning sun. It was warmer out here already.

The second my eyes adjusted, I actually forgot all about my hair and the shoot.

There was a Lotus Elise Sport 220 sitting nearby. It was gorgeous and so like a siren beckoning me forward.

I wouldn't go so far as to say an Elise was rare, but I don't think I'd ever seen one here in Maryland.

I stepped up to it and let my fingertips trail along the hood, noting the engine was still warm and hoped *GearShark* had brought it as a prop for the shoot.

Maybe they'd let me drive it.

I loved my Skyline, it was the best, but this car was… captivating.

"You like?" a voice behind me drawled.

I was still spellbound by the way the sun sparkled off the white. "It's freaking sex on wheels." I sighed.

"That good?"

I perked up, jerked my fingers back and spun. The stupid heels I was wearing almost tossed me on my ass but I threw out a hand and steadied myself on the car I just equated to sex on wheels. "You." I intoned.

"I got a name, sweetheart," he drawled, in a smartass kind of way that he probably thought was sexy.

"Call me sweetheart again and your balls will become intimately acquainted with my foot."

He grinned a slow, self-satisfied kind of smile, like my promise to dent in his boys was somehow a turn on.

My stomach dipped a little.

"Just can't keep your hands off her, can you?" he motioned toward the car I was still leaning on for support.

I pulled my hand back and straightened.

"Can't help but admire it," I said, trying not to antagonize him right before our interview. A breeze picked up, bringing with it a warm stirring of air. The glossy strands of my hair slid back over my shoulder and brushed across my shoulder blades. I reached up and tugged a hand through the sleek style just because I could. "Have you ever driven one?" I asked.

He was silent a moment, his dark gaze caught by something just over my shoulder. I cleared my throat, and he blinked. "What?"

I pointed at the car. "Have you driven a Lotus?"

"Once or twice." He smiled.

God, the way he smiled. It was like I'd just asked for some fancy prime rib dinner and he agreed to give it to me, even though he knew he'd just eaten it.

"I hope they let me drive it," I mused, bending to look in the driver's side window. It had red accents on the black leather.

It was a sex machine.

"They?"

I nodded absentmindedly. "*GearShark.*"

"It's not the magazine's car." His voice was low but loud, closer than before. I jerked up.

A wide, warm hand settled over my hip, steadying me.

I jolted backward, effectively bringing my entire back up against his chest.

How the hell did he get over here so fast?

I swallowed thickly and spun. I couldn't go anywhere, though, because I was pinned between him and the car.

Like a sex sandwich.

Oh my God! Why did I keep thinking about sex? *Stop it!* I commanded my brain.

There was nothing about Lorhaven that was sexy. Nothing. He was a total douche-nozzle.

"What'd you say?" I pressed back into the car, trying to get away from him.

His eyes swept over my face. There wasn't an inch his eyes didn't touch, and I swear I felt every sweeping gaze.

His eyes were very dark. Almost black. Like endless dark wells.

When I was a girl, my mother would take me to Argentina. In the center of one town square, there was a wishing well. I used to stand above it and stare down. I'd toss coins in and wait for the sound of them hitting the bottom.

It never once came.

It was as if it ran so deep there was no bottom.

I used to tell my mother I wanted to leap in and see just how far it went. I wanted to see what awaited when I finally hit the floor.

She'd laugh and tell me I was silly.

But oh, the mystery of that well.

The possibilities I used to be sure it contained.

Those were his eyes.

It was disconcerting.

It was intriguing.

I wanted to leap in and find out just how deep Lorhaven could go.

The breeze blew again, brushing against my suddenly hot skin. It felt cold even though it wasn't. I shivered.

"Did you hear me?" he asked. The depth of his voice was also something I found myself wanting to explore.

"What?" I muttered.

He shifted, the movement mostly in his hips. It brought his body that much closer to mine.

I plastered myself even more against the Lotus.

His fingers dug into my hip. Gripping me, holding me there.

"I said that's not *GearShark's* car. It's mine. You can drive it anytime you want."

My mouth went dry. Like I'd suddenly been walking through the Sahara and was in dire need of a cool drink.

"Hey," a familiar voice growled. "Back off."

I blinked.

Drew was standing several yards away, scowling, his arms folded tight over his chest. The way he glared at Lorhaven reminded me I didn't like him either.

I brought my hands up between us and shoved him back hard. He stumbled, a look of surprise crossing his face.

I tossed my hair back and drew myself up. With these heels on, I was almost as tall as him. He didn't intimidate me. No man did.

"I didn't think it was actually possible," I said.

"What's that?" he countered. Ugh, the arrogance in his face and body was so disgusting.

He needed someone to bring him down a peg or two.

"That a car could instantly be dropped to the bottom of my must-drive list." I shrugged. "But it's happened. Turns out I want nothing to do with anything you've touched."

His eyes narrowed. A dangerous air floated about him.

I pushed off the car and walked—*no*—I sauntered away. Right to Drew's side.

His eyes bounced between mine. "You okay?"

I smiled. "Of course."

He smiled back and caught up a handful of my hair. "Looking pretty good, J."

Behind us, Lorhaven made a rude noise and then walked off.

"You get under his skin," Drew said, pride in his voice. His arm dropped over my shoulder, and he guided me toward a group of people where Trent was. "Makes me fucking giddy."

I laughed.

"Let's get this over with so we can go have some fun."

"Amen," I prayed.

The faster I got away from Lorhaven and his *gift from heaven* persona, the better.

Six

Lorhaven

You know what was more gut punching than the sight of my *maybe* white Lotus for the first time?

The sight of a midnight-haired, long-legged goddess standing next to it.

She thought it was sex on wheels.

My *maybe* car just became certain.

Seven

Joey

We had an audience.

Not that there was a we.

More like me and Lorhaven had an exchange of words, and people watched.

One particular person seemed to be intrigued by the way we argued with each other.

Too bad she was the one in charge of the shoot.

I was standing in a small group with Drew, Trent, and Hopper (he came as my manager but also for moral support) when Emily approached. I remembered her from when she interviewed Drew for his article. She looked the same. Blond hair, slim figure, and a tight skirt.

"Joey." She began, and we all stopped our conversation so I could turn toward her. "We'd like to get the photography done first. Would that be okay with you?"

"Sure." I nodded and fell into step beside her as she led me to wherever they planned to take the photos.

My steps staggered a bit when I looked ahead at where Lorhaven was standing. The stylists must have just finished with him because his clothes and hair were different than just a short while ago.

"Uh," I said, noting he seemed to be waiting for Emily.

"We were thinking…" Emily began, measuring me out of the corner of her eye as she kept walking.

No, no, no.

"It would be really fun to get some photos of you two together. You know, a symbolism of both racing divisions. And since it's a dual interview…"

"You want us to model together?" My voice was clipped.

"I couldn't help but notice the way you two looked standing there together," she said. My shoulder's stiffened. "You're both gorgeous. You make a stunning combination. Plus," she hurried to add, "it would lend a new dynamic to a *GearShark* cover. Usually, we just have single models or cars. A couple… a racing couple would really be a seller."

Did she say cover?

"We aren't a couple." I pointed out.

"Of course not." Emily allowed. "You know what I mean."

My reply was blunt. "Actually, I don't."

The reporter seemed taken aback I didn't just readily agree to what she wanted. She began to stutter, like she didn't know what to say. As if telling me what she really meant would only piss me off more.

My mood darkened.

This interview was a bad idea. We'd barely just started, and I was already irritated and insulted.

Lorhaven chose that moment to inject himself into the conversation. His arm fell across my shoulders, and

I jerked upright. The movement and weight of his arm pulled my hair and sent tingles of pain over my scalp.

I glanced over, giving him a scathing look.

He acted like he didn't even notice. It pissed me off. I thought longingly of stomping my heel down on his booted foot. Let Emily put that in her article.

My father would have a cow.

And then I'd be stuck in the pro circuit.

"She's just nervous I'll look better than her."

God, he was incredibly cocky. I made a sound and shoved his arm away from me.

Emily lifted a brow. "Is this tension because you're on opposite sides of the track, or is it a different kind of tension?"

Lorhaven opened his mouth. I gave him a warning look. "It's because he's an asshole," I said.

"My feelings are hurt," he declared, turning sad, dark eyes on Emily.

The only thing sad was the fact I had to pose for pictures with him.

"So…" Emily glanced between us. "Is that a no to the shoot?"

"No. We got this," Lorhaven replied. His hand met the small of my back and pushed lightly to propel me forward. "We're professionals."

"Good." Emily smiled and motioned for the photographer.

He leaned down in my ear as we walked. Even though I was moving right beside him, he kept his hand on the small of my back. "They want some shots with my car. Shouldn't be hard for you since you were already drooling all over it."

"This is ridiculous," I muttered.

Abruptly, his hand left my back, and his body rotated around directly in front of mine. I stopped walking. His eyes bore directly into mine.

"This is the cover we're talking about." He spoke low, not a hint of the ass-like sarcasm typically in his tone. "It's good publicity. We could both use it. I'll be on my best behavior."

He was right. This was an opportunity I'd never been presented in the three years I'd been racing. Even if I was bitter they didn't think I could carry a cover on my own, even if they did want this jackass beside me for it… I could use it to my advantage.

I could use this to propel myself further and get the press my father wanted so I could cross over.

"Fine." I relented. "But keep your hands where I can see them."

His face dropped a little closer to mine. He had full, wide lips… "Now what fun would that be?"

I lifted my chin a little in a challenge. The ends of my hair brushed my back. "Best behavior." I reminded him.

He lifted his hands, palms out as if he were surrendering.

I knew better.

The photographer started barking orders, and we moved over to the hood of the Lotus.

"I'm gonna have you sit there," he said to Lorhaven, pointing to the hood, between the headlights. "Open your legs," he instructed.

Lorhaven had long, lean legs, and when he sat on the white hood, his ripped-up jeans seemed to stretch on forever. The fabric was so worn and tattered one of his knees was completely exposed.

I watched as he followed the directions of the photographer and propped one black-booted foot on the front so his knee was bent and even more of his skin showed.

"Good," the photographer said, backing up and checking the shot in his camera. "Unbutton the shirt."

Lorhaven was wearing a thin, gauzy-type white shirt that buttoned up the front. I watched his long fingers skillfully work the front open and pull the sides to reveal his muscled, sinewy torso.

He had genuine olive-toned skin. The kind that stayed tan all year round. It was the kind of skin tone most people in Argentina had, where my mother grew up. Robust she would call him—a prime specimen of a virile man.

As the breeze blew, a stand of dark hair fell out of place and over his forehead. He smoothed it back by running his hands through the longer strands at the top, which gave him a done but not too done appearance.

"Joey…" The photographer motioned. "If I could get you between his legs."

I reminded myself this was for work and did as I was told. I expected to see some kind of humor or sick satisfaction on his face, because I was literally instructed to get between his legs, so when I looked up, it was with defiance.

He needed to know I was doing this because I had to. Not because I wanted to.

Lorhaven's eyes were already on mine when I met his stare.

There was no look of satisfaction on his face. Instead, there was a predatory glint, like I was a rabbit stepping right into his clutches.

But he wasn't going to eat me. He was going to play.

And I was going to like it.

Invisible electricity of some kind flared between us. Like a rope, it towed me forward. If my hips swayed a little more provocatively, it was because of the camera, because I was doing my job.

His stare dropped away first, slipping down to my chest, where it lingered. The girls were pretty much on display because of the tank they'd put me in, and it wasn't as if I'd never had men leer at me before.

But he wasn't leering right now.

Lorhaven was… making me hungry.

I snapped my eyes away and spun, making sure my hair hit him in the face.

The sound of his sputtering made me smirk.

"Okay, good," the photographer called. I could hear the clicking of the camera. "Lean back," he told me. I did. "Closer," he urged.

My body was tight. I was uncomfortable. Modeling was clearly not for me. And neither was sitting in a dickhead's lap.

"Relax," Lorhaven murmured, snaking an arm around my waist to pull me back fully against him.

My ass fit right against his crotch; my back pressed against his chest.

I went stiff for a few seconds, but then, without any kind of force, I relaxed into him. He felt like a blanket just out of the dryer or a shirt I'd let hang in the sun while I was in the pool. He radiated the kind of heat that could only be generated naturally.

His bare chest brushed against the backs of my bare arms, and without any warning, the arm wrapped around my waist found the hem of my tank top and lifted so his hand could splay out over the curved part of my exposed waist.

I sucked in a breath and went taut once more.

"What are you doing?" I ground out.

"Giving them what they want," He whispered against my hair.

I glanced over, and indeed, the photographer looked enthused. "Yes," he said, clicking a few more times.

"Just go with it." His fingertips caressed my side, and my skin broke out in goosebumps.

His free hand lifted, pulled all my hair to one side, and let it fall over my shoulder. My arms loosened and one hand fell down to rest on top of his thigh. Just beneath my fingertips was a rip, and I brushed, accidentally, against his skin.

Against my lower back, his stomach muscles tightened.

Inside, I smirked, and I did it again, this time letting my fingers stop atop the rip, pressing fully against his skin.

A scruffy chin hit my bare shoulder, and his arm tightened around my waist.

"Wrap your legs…" The photographer started, but Lorhaven was already moving.

I was tugged farther onto the hood of the Lotus, kept tightly between his legs. How he moved and kept hold of me, I wasn't sure… but it was making me a little breathless.

Once we were in the center of the hood, those long, lean legs I'd just been staring at wrapped around me from behind. My stomach muscles quivered and jumped. I sucked in a breath.

"Now both arms," called someone.

Lorhaven's one arm was replaced with both, and suddenly, I was totally surrounded by him. My eyes closed. I let my hair fall down to shield some of my face because… because… *Oh God.*

He affected me.

He was strong and hard. Not shy at all about putting his hands on me, and even though I knew this was just a photoshoot… I felt owned. Claimed.

I started to jerk away. I didn't like this.

"Hey." His hand caught my face and tugged, gently, so I was looking over my shoulder at him while his body nearly wrapped around mine.

I wasn't a small woman… but I fit inside his circle. There was enough of his body to cover all of me.

Our eyes met. The breeze picked up again. My hair blew backward, trailing out behind me as I sat there on the hood of his damn sexy car, wrapped up in a pair of achingly steady arms.

My lower lip quivered.

He didn't break eye contact, but he smiled. A knowing look came into his eyes.

I pulled away, so quickly I would have slid right off the car if he hadn't had such a strong hold.

"Let go," I growled.

He released me instantly. I got up and strode a few feet away.

The photographer came rushing over, beaming. "That was great. Now if we could move inside?"

"Inside?" I said, alarmed.

He nodded. "I have a portable studio set up. It's small, but it gets the job done. The lighting today isn't ideal, so some indoor shots with my equipment would be a good option to have."

"You want some pictures of just me?" I asked.

He frowned. "I was actually hoping you'd be up for some more duo shots."

"I'm game," Lorhaven sang, dragging a thumb across his lower lip. It was like he was trying to remind me my own lip had been quivering. And he was the reason.

It was like a challenge. He thought I couldn't handle it.

Well, buddy… Wasn't he in for a surprise?

I looked back at the photographer and smiled wide. "Let's do it."

Eight

Lorhaven

I got under her skin.

I preferred to be under her clothes.

It seemed so wrong she had the name of a dude, because that body of hers? It was all woman.

I wasn't a stranger to females, good-looking ones like her. They were practically a dime a dozen on the streets. They showed up at every race, every party. Their clothes were tiny and their morals tinier.

This isn't the part where I tell you how boring it was.

I liked ass. I liked sex. And I had both. Often.

I didn't have a problem with an easy lay. I didn't need the thrill of chasing a girl who played hard to get.

I got my thrills behind the wheel of a car.

Joey didn't want me. But her body damn sure did. It pissed her off, too. That turned me on. The fact that I could sway her own body against her mind.

The way that had just been proven to her. I saw the defiance in her eyes, felt the fight in the corded muscles of her neck. But her body melted like butter. It slid right up against mine and surrendered to my touch.

If only we'd not been surrounded by people.

If only it had been just her, me, and the hood of my car.

I'd have taken her right there, and it would have been satisfying to hear her scream my name.

I honestly thought she'd refuse more photos. So I made it into a challenge. Truth was I wasn't done yet. I wasn't done feeling her conform to the shape of my palms.

I saw the flare in her eyes when I spoke, the way my words incited a burning need to prove me wrong.

Bring it on, baby.

The photographer (~~I forgot his name.~~ I didn't care enough to listen when he told me what it was.) led us to a makeshift-looking building. How they erected it I didn't know. I didn't really care about that either.

I got to the door first and pulled it open, stepped back so everyone else could go in first.

The guy with the camera hanging off him stopped abruptly and turned, Emily (the journalist) almost ran right into him. She shrieked and pulled up short, just shy of barreling into his back.

"It's a tight space," he said. "Just me and the models, please."

Forrester and Trent were on either side of Joey, like they planned to go in with her to protect her honor. It irritated me.

"I don't know," Drew intoned and stepped forward, he glanced at me with a hard, untrusting look in his eye.

I smiled, letting all my pearly whites show.

"Hey, bro." I called out to Arrow. He spun around, pink blooming over his cheeks. I glanced around, wondering what the fuck he'd been staring at, but I didn't see anything.

With a grunt, I pulled my keys out and tossed them through the air. "Watch my car. I might be a while."

Drew growled.

Trent stepped up, hands at his sides like he was ready to throw down.

Joey rolled her eyes and glanced at them. "I can handle this."

Trent nodded, but then both men stared at me. Was I supposed to be intimidated?

The photographer was already inside, and Joey breezed past, not even giving me the time of day. Her scent lingered even after she'd moved past. It wasn't a girly, flowery smell.

Instead, it was sweet and deep… like sugar and spice.

Naughty and nice.

I waved at Drew and Trent before allowing the door to swing shut behind me.

Assholes.

Inside was bright, like so bright my eyes needed to adjust. Goddamn. He must have had a million lights turned on. All of them pointed at a white backdrop, lighting it up like the Fourth of July.

"It's going to get hot in here because of all the bulbs," he cautioned, moving around to flip on a few oscillating fans. "We'll try and get this done quickly so you can get to the interview."

Joey was standing at the edge of the backdrop, sort of in the shadows of all the lights. I moved up beside her. I thought she would step away, but she didn't.

Instead, her green eyes caught mine, and she smiled like a cat. "Ready for this?"

"Bring it on."

"Okay, let's start out with some basic shots," the photographer instructed, taking up position on the white-draped floor.

We moved in front of him and followed his instructions as he took what felt like five hundred pictures.

They were boring and basic. They made my hands itch and a very large part of me pissy. And, true to his word, the small square space felt like it was a million degrees.

Enough was enough. I reached out, palmed Joey's hips, and pulled her into me. Instantly, Joey arched, like a cat. Her narrow waist bowed out, but her neck and shoulders thrust against my upper body.

One of her hands came up and wrapped around the back of my head; her fingers brushed over the nearly buzzed hair at my hairline.

"Oh, that's good," the photographer murmured, taking pics.

I delved my hand into the front pocket of her jeans, and she rocked her hip into my hand.

"We need music." The photographer said and looked away to switch on a portable music source.

Sound filled the space. It was heavy with bass and made my hand pull her arched-out ass to me. I got two seconds of the luscious junk against me before she spun away.

Her eyes beguiled me, eager hands grabbing the open edges of my shirt and yanking. The fabric slid free of my shoulders and bunched low around my elbows, baring my entire upper body.

I arched an eyebrow at her, and her heart-shaped mouth curled upward. The fans blew her hair out around her face and tugged at the tank she wore. I dug my fingers into her waist, enjoying the way it curved in. Her hourglass figure was basically built for my hands.

"Sex sells," the photographer mumbled, but I barely heard him.

I was too focused on her.

We took a few more photos facing each other, my bare chest against her clothed one, and then the camera stopped clicking.

I glanced around, irritated. Were we done?

I wasn't done.

Joey still clutched at the front of my shirt, but she released the fabric and smoothed her palms out over my pecs.

"Your skin is smooth," she murmured, peeking up from beneath a thick, dark lash line.

I lifted a hand, wrapped it around her shoulder, and let the pad of my thumb brush back and forth over her skin.

"I have an idea." The photographer cut in.

A displeased rumble vibrated my chest. Why was he still here?

Joey pulled her hands and body away, turning toward the man.

"I don't want to come off as forward. I know you two aren't a couple…"

"Just say it," I snapped out.

He swallowed.

Joey gave me a reproachful look. "Don't mind him. He's just a dick."

Amusement as well as full-on horniness filled me as I watched that round ass sashay away. I liked hearing dirty words out of her pretty mouth.

The photographer nodded and focused on her. I saw the desire in his eyes. He thought she was sexy, too.

I glanced down at his jeans. If he had a boner, I'd fuck him up right here.

"I want to do something really broken down, simple but at the same time really sexy. I think it would be a big hit with not only the magazine's demographic, but the audience the NRR is trying to pull in."

Non-race fans. People who didn't feel like they belonged anywhere. The NRR wanted to be a home for everyone—especially those who felt like outcasts and underdogs.

"Sounds good," Joey replied encouragingly. "What did you have in mind?"

"Uh…" He rubbed the back of his neck. "Would you mind taking off your shirt?"

Oh, hell yeah! my dick shouted.

I watched her shoulder blades come together. She wasn't expecting that.

She glanced back at me, almost peeking around the curtain of her fuck-me hair. Seriously. It was all satin and silk. It begged for my hands.

I shrugged.

"Sure," she said instantly.

Ballsy.

I liked it.

Joey turned, glanced at me, then stripped that white, not see-through-enough tank right over her head. I watched the fabric fall from her fingertips and onto the floor.

After that, I saw nothing else but the way her big, round tits bounced beneath the lace of her bra as she strode back over to where I was.

Most tits that big were fake. Hers were all natural.

I felt my tongue run across my lower lip. Suddenly, I was really thirsty.

She smirked, and I had a moment of clarity where I thought, *Is she playing me right now?*

But it was here and gone, because her hand reached for mine.

I stepped up. We stood staring at each other, chest to chest.

"The bra?" the photographer called out.

Joey's teeth sank into her lower lip. I saw a flash of something in her eyes, but then she tossed back her hair and reached behind her.

Before I could even comprehend what the fuck was happening, she was standing there completely naked from the waist up.

Her skin looked like silk, called to me like velvet… And her nipples… they were the deepest shade of pink I'd ever seen, and they were erect.

"What the fuck!" I roared, taking everyone off guard.

Joey jumped in alarm when I yelled.

Quickly, I ripped off my open shirt and shook it out behind her, tucking the front closed, hiding the most perfect pair of tits I'd ever seen.

"Lorhaven?" My name was a question.

It irritated me. Something about my name on her tongue didn't seem right.

"Hold this," I said, harsh, gripping the shirt closed.

She grabbed it. I stalked over to where the cameraman was standing. I grabbed him by the front of his shirt and yanked him right off his feet.

"What game are you playing?" I growled.

"N-no game," he stuttered, shock and fear in his irises.

"You tell women to take off their clothes in front of your camera all the time?" I spat. My chest rose and fell rapidly.

It was one thing to admire Joey's body, to think about burying deep… to making her squirm a little beneath my touch.

But it was entirely something else for some guy (who was *not* me) to ask her to take her clothes off for photos he could jack off to later.

Hell. No.

"It's for the cover!" he insisted.

I felt my upper lip curl.

"I didn't want the straps of her tank top to disrupt the fluid motion of the image."

"Blah, blah, you were trying to look at that girl naked."

"No!"

"Lorhaven," Joey said from behind me. Her voice held a note of surprise.

"Stop calling me that," I snarled.

"Your name?" she wondered.

I made a sound. What the fuck was happening?

I put the cameraman down and stepped back.

A slender hand slid over my lower back, almost dipping into the waistband of my low-slung jeans. "I'll put my shirt back on."

I stiffened and turned. Two of the buttons on the shirt were haphazardly done up, hiding her chest. "Whatever," I said. "I don't care."

She blinked.

"I truly meant no disrespect," the photographer told her, stepping forward.

I gave him a withering stare, and he stopped.

"I just saw a shot in my head and wanted to recreate it."

Joey smiled. She fecking smiled at him. "Creative minds," she said, like that made up for it.

He was a goddamn perv.

"We can be done," he said, staring at me warily.

"I don't mind taking a few more. Maybe I'll leave the shirt on." I felt her sidelong glance.

"I don't know…" The photographer hedged.

"Oh, for shit's sake," I declared. "Let's do it."

I grabbed Joey's hand and pulled her in front of me, pushing her along. I was being ridiculous, but I couldn't help but put my body between hers and the perv's.

"Maybe a couple with his shirt on?" the man suggested when she bent to pick up her bra.

Joey glanced at me. "Can I borrow your shirt a little longer?"

"Whatever," I said, playing it cool.

'Course, I'd already ruined the cool guy card with my outburst.

"Lorhaven, turn around," the photographer instructed, slipping back into work mode.

I did, and he instructed Joey to press her front along my back, her arm came around my hip, and her thumb hooked into my front jeans pocket.

I felt her sigh when her cheek hit the top of my shoulder.

"I like the way you smell," she murmured, almost like she spoke to herself.

But I heard.

I definitely heard.

"Hair back," she was told, and I felt her brushing at the locks.

He snapped a few pics and then glanced at Joey and motioned for her to drop the shirt off one shoulder.

My entire body tensed.

Did he think I was fucking stupid and blind?

"He can't see anything," she whispered, soft enough only I could hear over the fans and music.

Her palm brushed down the center of my back, a motion meant to reassure me.

It worked.

I relaxed, not all the way, but enough.

I heard the soft rustle of my shirt, and then her arm was back around me, and the feel of her round, perfect, bare breasts was pressed into my back.

Her nipples were hard. I felt the stiff buds in the center of the warm softness.

My eyes closed briefly.

"This okay?" she asked, her cheek pillowing back on my shoulder. It was the first hint of insecurity I'd ever heard from her.

Emotion swelled in the center of my chest. I swallowed it down. "Yeah, baby, it's good." I murmured over my shoulder.

She pressed a little tighter.

"Oh, that's good." The photographer cut in.

I tensed again. Automatically, my arm went out a little, in front of her arm, instinctively shielding her.

I thought this would be fun.

I thought I could tease her, rile her up, make her want me.

That's not at all what was happening.

Instead, *I* was the one riled up. *I* was the one standing here with an ache beneath my jeans.

I didn't like her.

She was a pro driver. A pro driver with a rich daddy who thought she could waltz into my world like she owned it.

But here I was, standing here with my arm out as if it dared that man to even look at her wrong. Here I was standing here with watchful eyes lest he get too close.

She'd turned the tables on me.

I was played.

By my own damn game.

Abruptly, I pulled away. Without my body there to support hers, Joey stumbled forward. With a low swear, I reached for her.

As I steadied her, I caught a flash of boob.

My dick throbbed.

"We're done," I barked. My hands were still on her, so I pulled the shirt up, taking a moment to flip the collar up around her neck and button several of the buttons.

"Lor—"

I snarled. Her voice fell away.

My body spun. I watched the man bustle around, turning off most of the lights and the fans. The music cut off.

The three of us were left in a shadowy, partially lit square box.

"I'll send the proof of the cover over for final approval before I submit it," he said, looking at me.

I was pretty sure the contract I signed said all images were the magazine's and I had no say.

"You do that," I replied. I wanted to make sure he wasn't trying to pull a fast one by putting her half naked on a magazine just to make money.

I'd never cared about this shit before. Hell, I looked at nudie magazines and watched porn just like every other guy.

But not her.

She was off-limits.

The man nodded sagely.

"She needs to change," I said, a hint of steel in my implication.

He scurried out of the box faster than I thought he was capable. I shut the door behind him and leaned against it.

Joey was standing there with her hands on her hips, glaring at me. "What the fuck is your problem?"

"I like when you cuss," I said, staring at her mouth.

She rolled her eyes. "I know you're an ass, but what the hell possessed you to go off like that?"

"Say one more filthy word," I warned, taking a menacing step toward her.

My blood was pounding in my veins. Sweat clung to my shoulder blades, and my palms itched. Her nipples were still tight little buds, and when she breathed, they pressed against the thin fabric of my shirt.

"Or what?" She challenged, lifting her chin.

"I'll show you," I intoned.

"You are such a *dick*."

I shot away from the door and snatched her wrist, yanking her so she fell against my chest. Her eyes blazed up at me, and I growled.

Within seconds, I lifted her off her feet, her legs wrapped around my waist, and I slammed her back up against the door.

I wasn't gentle.

She didn't care.

Just like I'd longed to do since I saw her standing there by my Lotus, I shoved my hands in all her midnight hair.

A groan ripped from between my lips, and then I attacked her.

The back of her head hit against the door as my lips locked over hers. Her fingernails dug into my neck, pulling me close as our mouths went at each other like the first round in an MMA fight.

She kissed like she spoke.

Dirty, hard, and sassy.

She wasn't easy like all the other girls. It was like she gave me a fight, our lip-lock was exciting, intoxicating, and it thrilled me all the way to my core.

We went rounds with each other. I would have eaten her lips if I could. She was a craving I never knew I had, the most expensive bottle of champagne a five-star restaurant could offer.

And her tongue.

She wielded it like a sword. It fucking slayed me. The way it wrapped around mine and delved deep into my mouth…

Fucking right.

I reached around, filled my hands with her ass, and squeezed as I screwed her mouth with mine.

I was so stiff I thought I might rip my jeans. I wanted to pound myself so deep in her I might never come out. I wanted to feel those shapely hips rotate over my cock, and I wanted her inner walls to squeeze me until I shot a load deep in her depths.

I ripped my mouth free and pressed my forehead against the door just over her shoulder.

Joey took in deep, gulping breaths. Every rise and fall of her chest made me hungry for more. Against her body, my hand flexed.

She was a pro driver.

A pain in my ass.

As bad as I wanted to dip inside her, it wasn't going to happen.

Fucking wrong.

I stepped back, and she slid down my front like Jell-O.

"What should I call you?" she asked, her voice still breathless.

I glanced down. The intense, clover green of her eyes pierced me. Her lips were swollen and slick with my kiss.

I wanted to kiss her again.

I couldn't.

"Jace," I bit out. My voice was made of gravel. "Call me Jace."

I picked her up and moved her away from the door, then nearly ripped it off the wall as I rushed outside into the summer sun.

People looked up, surprise on their faces.

I gave them all a look like they were imagining things and went casually toward my car to get the T-shirt I'd showed up in.

I'd told her to call me by my first name.

No one called me by my first name.

That's the way I'd always wanted it.

Until now.

Nine

Joey

Why did all the dickheads have to kiss so good?

He issued a challenge.

I replied in turn.

I wanted to rile him up. Give him a taste of his own medicine. Serve him up a slice of tasty humble pie.

Yet I was the one standing here with aching, heavy breasts. My lips still tingled from the way he devoured me. My ears still echoed from when he called me baby.

I wasn't a girly girl. I didn't get all dressed up or spend hours on my hair and makeup. I didn't bat my eyes or bite my lip to get a man's attention.

Men were pigs. I didn't want their attention anyway. I wanted their respect.

But he called me baby.

For a moment there, I'd forgotten about the photographer. For a moment, it had been just him and me. My body and his. God, the way it felt to curl up at his back and press against him.

I'd never felt like that before.

Small. Protected. Desired.

Yes, desired. I'm not talking about the desire every woman saw when a man looked at her rack, whistled as she walked past, or even propositioned her with or without a dinner date.

That wasn't desire, not really. It was lust. Want.

Desire was wholly different; at least just then it was. Desire became tangible. It transcended the physical; though, the physical pull was definitely there. For it wasn't just his body that was present in that moment; it was part of him I'd never seen or felt before. A part I felt him wanting to share, as if while, yes, he might lust for my body, part of him whispered for a piece of my heart.

He told me his name. The one I'd never heard before. It was like that piece of him, the one whispering to my heart, wanted to be recognized. By me and only me.

A girl could get high on thoughts like that.

It was dangerous, and it shook me.

This was Lorhaven, the guy who, when we first met, literally tried to run the car I was in off the road. He and Drew were always at each other's throats, and Trent seemed to hate him for some unidentified reason.

He was a snob. A racing snob. He hated the pros because he was an indie.

Call me Jace.

Quickly, I stripped off his shirt and left it right there on the floor. It carried his scent. I liked it, so I left it behind.

The second I stepped out of the makeshift studio, I was surrounded. Trent, Drew and Hopper all stood there with worried looks on their faces.

"What?" I snapped.

"I was about to come in there," Drew intoned.

"And?" I motioned with my hand. *So what?*

Drew's blue eyes narrowed. "Did something happen between you and Lorhaven?"

"Besides him being his usual mule's ass? No."

I felt Drew's stare, like he was trying to decide if I was lying. I looked him right in the eye.

He relented after a minute.

"It was hot in there. I was just freshening up." It was a lie veiled in truth.

I felt Trent's watchful gaze and glanced up. He didn't say a word, but I saw. He knew I lied. He somehow sensed a storm churning inside me.

"Emily's ready for you," Hopper told me, drawing my attention away from Trent.

His light-blue eyes were piercing. It was like he, too, was trying to read me. But he wasn't as good at it as Trent.

I felt myself exhale.

I followed along behind Hopper, noting the deep-blue color of his jeans and the tension in his back muscles. The wrist at his side was wrapped in the dark-brown leather bracelet he always wore. There were dull-gold studs all around it with something else of the same metal in the center. I'd never actually looked at it close enough to see what it was even though he wore it every single time I saw him.

He led me to a small area where Emily and Lorhaven were already seated. Before stepping out of the way, he turned to face me, placing a steady hand on my upper arm. "You okay, Joey?" he murmured low. "If you're done, we'll go."

"No," I put my hand over his. "I'm good, but thank you."

He studied me for one second longer, then nodded and stepped aside. Jace and Emily came into full view.

The only vacant chair was beside him. He didn't even glance at me when I sat down.

I felt my hackles rise.

"One forty-five you say?" Emily purred. Her voice grated on my nerves.

He nodded and sat back as if he owned the chair. "I can push her faster."

"I've never gone that fast before." She pouted.

Oh, good Lord. If she had a dick, she'd probably pull it out and ask him to suck it for her.

"Maybe I'll take you for a ride sometime," he replied. The smooth tone of his suggestion made vomit bubble up the back of my throat.

"Could we begin?" I asked, blunt. "I have somewhere I need to be."

Lorhaven's stance in the chair didn't change; if anything he lounged back farther. I didn't look at him. If I did, I'd probably punch him.

I didn't like being played with.

"Of course." Her eyes cut to me, and a look I recognized well shone in their depths.

So this was how it was going to go, eh?

My hands gripped the armrests.

For whatever reason, she saw me as a threat. I knew jealousy when I saw it. I knew when a cat had out its claws. I could eat this little reporter for breakfast.

But I was full.

Lorhaven saw to that.

"I'll just ask you a few questions, and then I can do the rest of the interview with Lorhaven."

I couldn't help it. I glanced at Lorhaven. His eyes flashed up at mine, then away.

There was a brooding quality to his eyes, perhaps because they were so dark?

Because there's a lot more beneath Lorhaven's surface. Like a Jace.

My back teeth snapped together, and I pinned little Miss Pencil Skirt with a hard look. "Oh, just a few questions? So you can relegate me to the back page with just a couple lines of text."

Her eyes widened. "Of course not."

"Wouldn't be the first time." I went on. "*GearShark* seems to have a reputation for being a good ol' boys club, one that has a *No Women Allowed* sign front and center."

"I'm not sure I know what you mean?"

"Of course you wouldn't," I spat. "Because you flirt and do as you're told."

Her eyes lit with anger.

I held up my hand. "I apologize. That was rude." I wasn't really sorry. But I pictured my dad bursting a vein in his head if what I said to the "press" got out. "I'm just a little… bitter," I admitted. "The last time I was mentioned in the magazine, I got one line of stats. All the other racers got bios with headshots."

"So you think you're discriminated against because of your gender?" The reporter brushed her hair back and looked at me with interest.

Well, maybe a couple of the crayons in her box still had some sharpness after all.

"I know so."

"Most people would laugh or scoff at that. This is the twenty-first century. Women's rights were in place a long time ago."

"So were rights for gays, people of different races…" I replied without heat. "But my best friends are hated on for loving each other. The news reeks of injustice against all races."

"Touché."

"The truth is," I said, blunt, "men don't want women in racing. They just don't. It ruffles their feathers."

Lorhaven made a sound. I glared at him over my shoulder. "Something to add, *Lorhaven*?"

His eyes narrowed and between the slits, they glittered like black diamonds.

Jace is still in there, somewhere, or he wouldn't care I called him something else.

He spread out his hand for me to continue. "I find this fascinating."

I just bet he does.

I turned away from him. Screw him and the car he drove in on.

Even if it was a sexy white Lotus.

"Out there on the track, a lot of testosterone is pumping. Men are in a primal form. Be the best. Be the strongest. They're intimidated by a female coming along and trying to beat them."

"You said trying. Have you ever won?" Emily questioned.

I sat back. "Of course. If I had more print time in these racing magazines and sports channels, you'd already know that."

"And what was it like for you after you won?"

I felt one shoulder shrug. "It doesn't matter if I win or lose, it's always the same." I had to work to keep the exhaustion from my tone. "I'm not wanted; they make it clear. I'm often isolated, left to work on my own. They don't want to talk to me, but at me. When I try to interject into a conversation, say about engine parts or torque ratio, they suddenly start acting like I'm dumb or a child."

"Have you ever been hazed?"

I felt the weight of a thousand eyes, even though it was just one set belonging to the man beside me.

I shifted uncomfortably. "The pro racing circuit prohibits hazing of any members."

"Spoken like the daughter of a business tycoon."

"Another strike against me," I replied.

"The boss' daughter."

"I couldn't possibly have talent or ambition, you know," I said, bitter. "My daddy buys me *everything*."

"He is your sponsor, isn't he?" Lorhaven interrupted.

"My main sponsor, yes," I replied. "But I have others."

"Do you think he sponsors you because you're his only child?"

I turned steady eyes on Emily. "My father is a businessman, and I think his accomplishments attest to that. Do you really think a businessman would sink as much money into a racing sponsorship for someone if he wasn't going to get a return on investment?"

"For his only child?" Lorhaven mused. "Absolutely."

"Don't you have a wealthy father?" I asked.

His eyes narrowed. "He doesn't sponsor me in the NRR. Brickstone Tires sponsors me."

"But I guess he's never helped you in your career. Or bought you a car or car parts," I said.

Emily looked at him expectantly.

Lorhaven shrugged.

God! What an asshole. Why was it okay for him to take from his father, but not me?

"What happened to your Corvette anyway?" I asked. "Did you finally wreck it trying to run someone off the road?"

"Something like that," he said, looking away.

"This is all very interesting." Emily cut in. "I'd like to talk further with both of you. But first, I just really want to know…" She turned to me. "Is it true you'll be leaving the pro racing circuit for a sponsorship in the NRR?"

"Yes," I said, not holding back. This is what I was here for. "I'm finishing out my pro season, and then I will be crossing over."

Lorhaven's boots hit the floor when he sat up all the way.

"You don't like pro drivers. You've never hidden that fact," Emily said to him.

"Nope."

"What's up with that?" she asked.

I turned to him, waiting.

"Because they're a bunch of stuck-up assholes."

"Let me guess. You tried out and they didn't want you," I said.

"I wouldn't let my daddy buy my way in," he snapped.

Touchy.

"We'll come back to that," Emily said. "So what are your thoughts on this crossover and a female driver in the NRR?"

I was dumb.

Played. With one kiss, one shared name, I'd somehow become forgetful of just who it was sitting beside me.

And why that one kiss was all we'd ever have.

"I think she can't hack it in the pros. She thinks it's going to be easier in the NRR." He sat forward. I was so mad my entire body had gone rigid. Our eyes warred with one another, and not the kind of war that felt good. "Guess what, sweetheart?" he murmured. "The NRR is harder than the pros. No rules racing ain't for girls."

Slowly, I pushed up out of my chair.

Emily watched me warily as I moved stiffly. "Thank you for having me. I do appreciate the opportunity to speak, however briefly, on women in sports. More specifically, women in racing."

"We aren't done," she said, alarmed.

"Oh, I am," I said, no room in my voice for argument. "Besides," I added, "I think you wanted to finish the majority of your interview in private." I leaned forward toward her to whisper loudly, "You know, so you can offer to blow him inside that fast car of his."

Her mouth formed a little O.

I rolled my eyes and straightened.

Lorhaven was sitting there still sprawled out like he was some kind of racing king. The smirk on his face pissed me off even more.

Without another word, I brought my leg up and slammed the heel of my shoe down on his toe.

He howled, his relaxed posture going rigid.

"What the fuck!" he yelled.

Everyone on set stopped and glanced our way. Somewhere close by, I heard Hopper sigh insufferably.

He started it.

"That's for calling me sweetheart," I intoned. Then I slapped him across the face.

The sharp, high-pitched sound was like music to my ears.

His nostrils flared as he worked his jaw where I'd just hammered him. My hand stung, so I hoped like hell it hurt.

"And that," I said, "was for saying I can't hack it."

I turned and strode away.

I heard him leap up and his footsteps pound behind me. I kept going. I didn't even glance back.

"Joey," he growled.

I kept walking.

Drew and Trent appeared. I didn't let myself look at them too close. I was afraid I'd cry.

You know when you get so filled with anger and humiliation all that's left are tears?

I was there right then.

There was no way in hell I'd let any of these people see me cry.

"Move," Lorhaven demanded.

Drew's voice rumbled a low reply.

"Joey?" Hopper called. "What did he say?"

"The truth," Lorhaven spat from behind. "All I said was the truth!"

"Just let me go." I urged Hopper, my voice very low so only he could hear. I got maybe a few more steps before I was stopped again.

"Hey…" A familiar hand wrapped around my wrist. I looked up. Trent gazed down at me. The restraint I had on my tears began to stretch thin. "Talk to me," he implored.

"I can't right now," I said, clinging to my composure.

"Want me to beat his ass?" he offered, but it was said without humor. Trent would totally kick Lorhaven's ass.

But I fought my own battles. I shook my head. "I have to go. I have to drive."

He released my arm and stepped back. "Go. We'll catch a ride with Arrow. See you at home."

"Thank you," I whispered. *Damn my watery voice.*

The Skyline's engine fired right up. I tore out of the lot without looking back.

I had a momentary lapse in judgement that hurt more than I cared to admit. There was no Jace inside Lorhaven. He'd probably used that line one hundred times. Hell, everyone on his turf, all the women, probably called him Jace.

He was just like all the others in this sport.

To him, I was nothing but a game.

Ten

Lorhaven

Third place.

Know what that is in racing?

Loser.

I was pretty fucking livid with myself. I knew I'd have a time behind Drew's ass, but I planned to give him a wedgie the whole go around the track.

Instead, I gave him a wedgie about eighty percent of the race. Then the other twenty, I was busy getting my ass beat.

My first fucking official race with the NRR, and I came in third.

I was embarrassed.

Off my game.

It was all her fault.

During the day, my cheek still echoed with the force of her slap, and at night, my lips tingled with the memory of her kiss.

I'd acted like an asshole during the interview. She just dug so deep beneath my skin it made me crazy. Hearing her talk about the way men treated her in this sport made me angry, but then I'd gone and done the exact same thing.

It did what I intended. To push her away. To get that distance back between us, that line of separation drawn in the sand.

I hated to admit it.

In fact, it was just one more thing to be embarrassed about.

Figured I should just get it all out here and now. 'Cause I didn't plan on being embarrassed ever again.

Kissing her scared me.

It was like a piece of her reached down deep and grabbed a piece of me. I wasn't one of those guys who scoffed at love. I didn't *not* believe in it.

I knew it existed.

I also knew it could twist you up and hurt you.

I didn't have time for any of that. My focus was my career. And my brother.

I didn't have room for anyone else.

But I came in third.

Fuuuck.

No one else seemed to think my placing sucked as big ass as me. My pit crew cheered and congratulated me. I smiled and accepted it, and I thanked them for the shit they did to keep me on the track.

Ted Bayer called. I'd expected a scathing review of my performance. He, too, was positive. Third place was still at the top. It was good advertisement and promo for Brickstone.

I promised him I'd step it up.

He didn't seem worried.

I was.

Arrow knew, though. With him, I could be real. I let him see the frustration in my eyes for a few seconds before banking it and stepping back into my big brother shoes.

The pit crew was packed up and just pulled out. My car (a cherry-red modified Chevy) was packed up and driven out. It would meet me at the next race, which was next week in Colorado.

The stands were empty, and the grounds were a lot quieter than they'd been just an hour before. I was still wearing my coveralls, covered in logos, most of them the Brickstone Tire image. Underneath, I was sweating and tired. I wanted a shower and a beer. Not necessarily in that order.

I want to see her.

I wanted to apologize, but apologies weren't really something I was very good at. I didn't have much practice. I usually never cared when I pissed someone off.

Thing was I didn't think she *should* be racing with us. It wasn't because I was sexist either. It's because this was a dangerous, risky sport. And truthfully, she'd been right. The men didn't want a woman on the track. What kind of life did that give her?

I'd seen her reaction when asked about the hazing.

She gave the politically correct response.

A lie.

I bet her daddy didn't know what those peckerheads probably did to her on a daily basis.

In my lap, my hand clenched. She wasn't my problem. Her father was Ron Gamble, for Chrissakes. And she packed a hell of a hit, even with an open palm.

Joey made it more than clear she could take care of herself.

And she was a good driver. I'd looked at her stats, even watched a race (or two) she'd been in. I shouldn't have told her she couldn't hack it. She could. I just wanted to get under her skin the way she was under mine.

The sound of a familiar engine revved behind me, and I turned. Forrester's cobalt-blue Fastback pulled to a stop, and the doors popped open.

"Wanted to congratulate you on your win," Drew said, coming toward me.

I gave him the finger.

He guffawed. "Seriously, that was some nice driving out there. Mahone seriously wanted around you, but you held him off."

"Mahone," I spat.

Drew laughed.

I glanced at him and then at Trent, who was standing close by. He was wearing a bright-yellow shirt with Drew's car number (forty-five) on the front.

"Congrats, man," Trent said.

They were serious.

"Must be easy to hand out congratulations when you're number one," I said, looking out over the track.

"Home track advantage," Drew said. "I won't be number one in every race."

"I wanted at least number two," I muttered.

"You almost had it." Drew slapped me on the back. "We all have off days."

Not on the first race of my career.

"Look, your ego is showing," Drew said, blunt. "You know damn well third place is fucking awesome. It puts you on the watch map for the next few races."

"My ego?" I echoed.

"It needs a leash, man," Trent deadpanned.

"Don't get pissed at yourself because you're one spot behind where you wanted. It's solid, and I've seen you drive. You'll be in the number two spot soon."

"Then I'm coming for number one," I said.

"Don't get ahead of yourself," Trent warned.

Drew snickered. "Sorry, man. I got my eye on the championship."

So did I.

"So what's fucking with you?" Trent asked.

I rotated. "Huh?"

"Something going on that's messing with your head today?"

Drew frowned. "It's not Arrow, is it? He seemed fine last time I talked to him."

"My brother's fine."

"He told me about the Corvette," Drew told me.

I screwed up my face. "What is this, *90210*? *Soap Opera Weekly*? Do you and my brother sit around and gossip every time you see him?"

Arrow had been spending a lot of time with Drew and Trent the past few weeks. I approved of it. Even if I did think Trent was sometimes a douche and Drew was my rival.

They were good friends to my brother, and he needed that. They were a solid example of how two men in a relationship could make it work. Fuck, they were paving the way in the NRR for acceptance of all kinds of people.

With a brother who was gay and who (yes, I admit) looked just like Justin Bieber, I was grateful to these guys.

So yeah, maybe I sort of like them, too.

"Joey really laid into ya at the interview." Trent pointed out.

I stiffened. "She's just pissed I said I didn't think she should cross over."

"What do you care?" Drew scoffed.

I shrugged.

"Right," Trent drawled. "We're out. Picking up some fries and going home for a few days. See you in Colorado next week."

Fries? Those dudes were weird.

I waved, and they left.

Home sounded good, though. The streets. Maybe going back to where I came from would help me remember where I belonged.

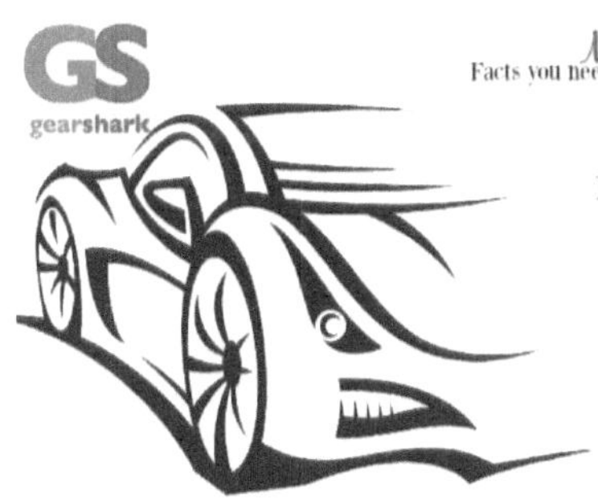

Eleven

Joey

I was still fuming.

I'd been fuming about what happened with him for so long I was nearly out of fuel.

My race had been a total bitch. The guys were worse than usual. Guess they didn't like I was drawing attention away from the pros and toward the NRR.

'Cause you know, my *one* disastrous meeting with the press went *so* well.

Well-meaning people told me not to take it to heart. You know, the usual *haters gonna hate* and *they're only jealous*. Screw that.

The men in the pro circuit were just assholes. And I wasn't wanted here.

Screw *them*.

I wasn't running to the NRR because of it. But I was tired. I just wanted to do what I loved without so much damn drama. And people said women were the dramatic ones.

Yeah right. Men were just as bad. Big bunch of babies.

But I could handle it. I could and *would* handle anything they threw at me. Not just because I was strong, but because I was too stubborn to let them get the best of me.

My next race wasn't for two weeks. I wasn't racing in the one a week from now, something I wasn't disappointed about. So I came home for a few days. My Skyline needed some work, and it was a good opportunity to take a day or two of downtime, because I wasn't going to get much from here on out.

Just because my race wasn't for a couple weeks didn't mean my schedule was empty. I was going to Drew's next race and doing some press.

I was closed off in my wing of the house (my wing = a private living room, a small kitchen, a huge bedroom, and a private en-suite bathroom). Drew and Trent had gone home, and it seemed a little quieter than usual. I'd gotten used to having them around for the past week.

I missed them already.

They had no boundaries as far as space was concerned. They'd barge right into my rooms without even knocking (well, except the bathroom). We'd had a movie night and eaten pizza. We drove and talked cars.

There was never one ounce of any kind of competition or sourness because I was a female driver or because my father was influential.

After a warm shower, I pulled on an oversized T-shirt and nothing else (I don't have to wear pants in my own room) and pulled up my email. I'd ignored it for a few days and couldn't go any further. There were invites and scheduling that needed confirmation. If I didn't get it done, Hopper would be over here kicking me in my pant-less ass.

I sat down with a cold bottle of beer (I liked Miller Light) and tucked my bare, lotion saturated legs beneath me.

One of the first emails was from Emily Metcalf at *GearShark*. The subject line read: These Drivers Got #Swag. Draft of your feature article.

I snorted. It wasn't going to be much of a feature because I'd basically walked out of it. A little prickle of embarrassment creeped up the back of my neck. I kind of acted like a brat that day. I shouldn't have let him get the best of me, or Emily for that matter.

Some days were just hard to not feel so… suppressed and judged because I was a woman.

Not to mention the photoshoot, the kiss… him. It had all been an overload to my circuits.

I took a pull off my longneck and stared at the subject line.

Fuck it. I clicked on it and opened up the article. I wouldn't allow myself to be embarrassed. I was strong. Capable. And I felt the way I did and acted the way I did for a reason. I didn't have to apologize to anyone.

Except my father.

I drank some more beer. If Emily outlined my… uh, behavior in this article, my father was going to shit a brick.

Forget the NRR! he'd say. *You're sliding backward, Joey. You better get control before you end up where you were.*

My long curls were still damp from the shower and the ends saturated my shirt with moisture. I snatched up the towel off my desk to squeeze out the excess water (never rub curly hair with a towel; the frizz is real) as I began to read the article.

Lorhaven & Joey G.
These drivers got #SWAG

written by Emily Metcalf
© GearShark Magazine

(Side note: I noticed Lorhaven was the only name used. He hadn't given his first name. Made me wonder how many people even knew it. *Jace*.)

(Side side note: I went by Joey G. with the press. I tried to downplay my relationship with my father. I wanted my own identity. I didn't want to be known only as "daughter of Ron Gamble.")

The pages of GearShark *magazine have been filled with many firsts for the past year. First time features, breaking news of the then unnamed new indie racing circuit now known as New Revolution Racing (NRR), and a diversity in drivers that hasn't been seen in the past.*

We've even seen and heard from people behind the scenes on the track, like Trent Mask, who unknowingly started a lot of discussion in sports about athletes and acceptance.

Perhaps that's what brought me to this interview today. Well, that and a good dose of *buzz* surrounding the new NRR and the pro racing circuit.

To be blunt, the pro division isn't too happy. They've been having to share the spotlight, the pages of racing magazines, and their vast fan base with men most of them consider to not be professional drivers.

The world of racing is changing at a speed that rivals that of a Formula One car. Most of it has been met with excitement and anticipation. But for the drivers on the pro circuit, it's been a time of closing ranks. Here at GearShark, we've learned many pro drivers find the birth of the NRR a slap in the face to all the hard work they've put in to get to where they are.

Personally, I think it's all about supply and demand. Race fans want to see more driving. They want the thrill of watching underdogs duke it out with their gas pedals. And as Drew Forrester and other NRR drivers, like my featured guest today, Lorhaven, have proven, having a pro contract doesn't make you a more skilled driver.

They've also given something a voice it seems pro racing has not: diversity.

That's where my other featured guest comes in today. Yes, I have not one, but two drivers here for a unique perspective on the racing world. You might be familiar with Lorhaven and the previous mentions of him in GearShark.

He's an NRR driver with a lot of promise, so much so he scored a coveted sponsorship by one of the owners of a new giant corporation. Brickstone Tires has put a lot of backing into the driver with only one name.

What's more interesting is this guy has a man-sized chip on his shoulder regarding the pros. I saw it the day he drove into my interview with Drew Forrester and accepted his rival's challenge. Lorhaven doesn't like the pro circuit. He doesn't like pro drivers.

I wanted to know why.

This prompted me to call Joey G. Not only is she a pro driver, but she's a woman. Right now in the world of racing, there are two female drivers. Joey is the only one on this side of the country. She has huge sponsorship deals with Gamble Enterprises, Friars Fueling, and Rimmel London (the first cosmetics company to ever sponsor a driver).

Oh, and she's also the daughter of business tycoon Ron Gamble.

I admit I first set up this interview because I wanted to see sparks fly when I put Lorhaven (the guy from the wrong side of the tracks?) and Joey G. (pros racing royalty?) in the same room.

The tension certainly runs high between these two. Add in the fact that I've been hearing a lot of rumors about a potential crossover for Joey G. from the pros to the NRR… Well, let's just say this interview was so hot I was nearly burned.

Due to the tumultuous nature of the interview and some noticeable bitterness on Joey G.'s part, the dual portion of the interview was not as long as I would have liked.

But not to worry, this journalist doesn't give up that easily, and I did get some information, some food for thought, and an answer to the burning crossover question. Also, I got some one-on-one time with Lorhaven that is sure to please.

Before I cut to the interview portion of this feature I'd like to just point out if my description of the fire between these two drivers wasn't clear, perhaps you should close the magazine (but save your spot!) and check out this cover again.

Pictures speak a thousand words, you know.

The number one word this cover is speaking? Intensity.

Another fun fact: this is the FIRST issue in GearShark history featuring two models instead of only one. Way to embrace diversity GS!

And now, readers, start your engines. Buckle up. We're about to take you for a sizzling ride.

GS: I'll just ask you a few questions, and then I can do the rest of the interview with Lorhaven.

JG: Oh just a few questions? So you can relegate me to the back page with just a couple lines of text.

GS: Of course not.

JG: Wouldn't be the first time. *GearShark* seems to have a reputation for being a good ol' boys club, one that has a *No Women Allowed* sign front and center.

<I was taken aback by this response and pretty much said so.>

JG: I'm just a little… bitter. The last time I was mentioned in the magazine, I got one line of stats. All the other racers got bios with headshots.

<For the record, I did not write the article she seems to be referencing. However, I cannot imagine a time GS would treat any driver differently because of their sex.>

GS: So you think you're discriminated against because of your gender?

JG: I know so.

GS: Most people would laugh or scoff at that. This is the twenty-first century. Women's rights were in place a long time ago.

JG: So were rights for gays, people of different races… But my best friends are hated on for loving each other. The news reeks of injustice against all races.

GS: Touché.

JG: The truth is men don't want women in racing. They just don't. It ruffles their feathers.

<Up until now, Lorhaven had been lounging back in his chair, his long legs, accentuated in a pair of destructed, low-riding jeans, kicked out in a relaxed way. He'd been listening, watching… Something I got the impression this driver did often. Joey G.'s words had him making a sound.>

JG: Something to add, *Lorhaven?*

L: I find this fascinating.

<She ignored Lorhaven a lot in this interview. Something I found interesting. Lorhaven is a very good-looking man, with olive skin and an intense stare. I found it hard to not look at him.>

JG: Out there on the track a lot of testosterone is pumping. Men are in a primal form. Be the best. Be the strongest. They're intimidated by a female coming along and trying to beat them.

GS: You said trying. Have you ever won?

JG: Of course. If I had more print time in these racing magazines and sports channels, you'd already know that.

GS: And what was it like for you after you won?

JG: It doesn't matter if I win or lose, it's always the same. I'm not wanted. They make it clear. I'm often isolated, left to work on my own. They don't want to talk to me, but at me. When I try to interject into a conversation, say about engine parts or torque ratio, they suddenly start acting like I'm dumb or a child.

GS: Have you ever been hazed?

JG: The pro racing circuit prohibits hazing of any members.

<I found that answer to be very interesting, and it also made the journalist in me want to dig around to learn more about hazing in sports. It also became increasingly clear that Joey G. also felt stifled by the fact that Ron Gamble is her father. This journalist now knows why she only uses the first letter of her last name. It's clear this is a strong woman who wants to drive her own path in the world.>

GS: Do you think he [Ron Gamble] sponsors you because you're his only child?

JG: My father is a businessman, and I think his accomplishments attest to that. Do you really think a businessman would sink as much money into a racing sponsorship for someone if he wasn't going to get a return on investment?

GS: This is all very interesting. I'd like to talk further with both of you. But first, I just really want to know… Is it true you will be leaving the pro racing circuit for a sponsorship in the NRR?

JG: *<without hesitation>* Yes. I'm finishing out my pro season, and then I'll be crossing over.

<Lorhaven's reaction to this admission was very interesting. He was almost angry.>

GS: You don't like pro drivers. You've never hidden that fact. What's up with that?

L: Because they're a bunch of stuck-up assholes.

JG: Let me guess. You tried out, and they didn't want you.

<Clearly, this woman has no problem saying what's on her mind.>

GS: So what are your thoughts on this crossover and a female driver in the NRR?

L: I think she can't hack it in the pros. She thinks it's going to be easier in the NRR.

<Joey stiffened at his words, and the two commence with a stare-down that made me uncomfortable.>

L: *<to JG>* Guess what, sweetheart? The NRR is harder than the pros. No rules racing ain't for girls.

<At this point in the interview, Joey G. decided she was done. Frustration and determination shone on her face as she thanked me for my time and drove away in a spotless yellow-and-black Nissan Skyline. I turned back to Lorhaven after a few moments of digesting what just happened.>

GS: Don't you think no rules racing is a good place for a female driver? Because there are no rules?

L: No.

GS: Fair enough. Could you maybe elaborate on your experience with the pro driving division?

L: I've been driving all my life. My cars are top of the line; so are the parts. It took me years to get an audition, and I admit, my father had to use some connections of his.

<Lorhaven's father is a successful businessman here in Maryland. He owns many companies, including two airports.>

GS: I take it the audition didn't go well?

L: *<laughs>* I didn't have an agent or any interested sponsors, and for some reason, the guy I drove for had a stick up his ass about Corvettes.

GS: You auditioned with a Corvette.

L: Yep. And as he well knew, the sponsors would come if the interest came, but he wasn't willing to show any interest.

GS: Why do you think that is?

L: *<His expression is that of someone who just ate some bad cheese.>* Because I wasn't in the "in crowd" with the division. My father didn't know the right people. Neither did I. And because *<he says grudgingly>* I have a record.

GS: A criminal record?

L: Yes.

GS: For what?

L: Illegal betting.

GS: Well, I could see how that might raise some trust issues.

L: *<shrugs>*

GS: You don't seem very apologetic about it.

L: *<His black boots hit the ground as he sits forward. I have to say when eyes as dark as his settle on me, I feel partially swallowed up, and I catch myself leaning toward him.>* Why should I be? I might have a wealthy father, and I didn't grow up without or in what some people call the ghetto, but I was raised on the streets. That's where I come from. That's the disconnect between the pros and the rest of the world. Not everyone is groomed from birth to be drafted by an exclusive club. Some of us have to work for it. Some of us have to build our reputations from the ground up. Racing isn't like playing *My Little Pony*. Cars are on the streets, where real drivers are born. That's the kind of driving that earned me a spot in the NRR.

GS: What does your father think of your racing?

L: It doesn't matter what he thinks. I drive for me. Not him.

GS: Does that mean he doesn't approve?

L: My father supports me.

<Something tells me there's a lot more to the dynamics of that father-son relationship, but that particular topic seems to be off-limits.>

GS: You mentioned a Corvette and so did Joey G. I'm assuming you have one, yet you drove a Lotus Elise here today. What happened to the Corvette?

L: Casualty of a street race.

GS: You wrecked it?

<His jaw worked like the question made him angry.>

L: Yeah.

GS: I would think someone as skilled at driving wouldn't wreck his cars.

L: Shit happens.

<Instantly, someone stepped off the sidelines. I did a double take because, quite frankly, the guy looked a lot like Justin Bieber.>

Bieber: That's not exactly true.

L: *<Turns to look.>* Shut it, Arrow.

GS: Who is this?

L: My brother, Arrow. He's also a driver.

GS: Arrow Lorhaven?

Arrow: *<Glances away, uncomfortable.>* No. My last name is Ambrose.

GS: You two are half-brothers, then.

L: We're brothers.

AA: Lor didn't wreck his car because of his driving. He actually wrecked it on purpose.

GS: I can't imagine why he would do that.

AA: *<Glances at Lorhaven, who sighs and shrugs. This seems to be some sort of approval because Arrow continues.>* Another driver was being erratic and flipped his car. Lor was in the lead, turned his car around, drove under the flipping car, and pushed my car out of the way.

GS: What happened next?

L: The other car fell on the Vette and totaled it. So I bought a Lotus.

GS: You have a reputation of…

L: *<Laughs>* Being an asshole?

GS: Frankly, yes.

L: I am an asshole. But that's my brother.

GS: Where do you see yourself at the end of the first season for the NRR?

L: At the top.

GS: The man to beat is your rival, Drew Forrester. Think you can do it?

L: Yes.

GS: Do you and Drew really hate each other as much as the media purports?

L: *<shrugs>*

GS: One more question before we wrap up. You told Joey G. you think women don't belong in racing and you don't think she'll be able to hack it. I've seen her stats. She's a good driver. Do you really believe that?

L: I think being a woman in a male-dominated sport takes guts. She clearly has that. I'm down with the whole women equality and diversity. You gotta let people be who they want to be.

GS: But do you think she belongs in the NRR?

L: No.

As you can see, both of these drivers got #swag. And no, I'm not talking about the kind of swag that propels young men to wear their pants below their butts and allow their behinds to hang out (seriously, what's up with that?). I'm not talking about some kind of rap term used in a popular song.

The kind of #swag I'm referencing is the confidence in which a person carries themselves. In order to have #swag, you have to be loaded with it. Something, I think, both of these drivers have in spades.

Furthermore, this interview has raised a lot of good discussion points that I don't think have been addressed at length by the racing world.

What do you think about women in racing?

Do you think females are just as skilled and capable as men to drive and drive fast?

What are your thoughts on Joey G.? Do you think she's right to think she's been treated unfairly by the racing world?

Do you have a stance on the Pro vs NRR regarding which is a more "legitimate" racing division?

Does diversity belong in sports?

Let's start a discussion! Hit up our online forums at GearShark.com/RacingDiversity to share your thoughts and opinions. As this continues to be a topic at the front and center of the racing world, we here at GearShark promise to bring you continued coverage and updates about all things racing, whether it be on the pro side or the NRR.

I sat back away from the computer screen and raised the beer to my lips in thought. None of the smooth liquid hit my tongue. I tipped the bottle back farther, and when I still wasn't rewarded with the cool taste of comfort, I yanked it away with an aggravated grunt.

Empty.

Apparently, this article made me chug it down.

I pushed out of the desk chair, tossed the bottle in a nearby waste bin, and grabbed another longneck out of my fridge. Once the top was open and the first taste of a freshly opened brewsky slid down my throat, I was able to ponder what I just read.

Leaning a hip against the counter, I gazed across the room at the lit-up laptop screen. It could have been worse. I honestly thought Emily was going to rip me to shreds in her piece, considering I basically alleged she'd be giving Jace a blowjob when I left.

Uh-oh.

He'd become Jace in my thoughts. Not Lorhaven. That was dangerous with a capital D.

Emily skipped over my worst parts of the day and even erred on the side of giving me the benefit of the doubt. I would almost venture to say she could see my point in all of this. But it still wasn't great.

I felt like it had been too telling… I'd been a little too honest.

Not that I was against honesty. I wasn't. I hated liars.

But I couldn't help but wonder what kind of effect this article was going to have when it came out and what the dudes I raced with on the pro side would think when they read what I said about them.

And then there was the NRR side. Lorhaven literally came out against me. He said he didn't want me there. Would the other drivers follow his lead? Would I be an outcast among my peers before I even had a chance to prove them otherwise?

No. You have Drew and Trent this time. You already have support. That made me feel marginally better, because having them behind me was more than I had when I started in the pros.

But still… why did he have to be so blunt and unsupportive in the article?

At the end of the article, he did sort of backtrack a little. He said I had guts. He stated he was all for diversity.

And then there was the Corvette.

He'd put himself in danger to knock his brother out of the way. He showed loyalty and even love toward his family in that one act.

Actions speak louder than words.

And the way he acted when he kissed me… I shivered.

So once again, I got a glimpse of Jace.

"He literally said you couldn't hack it, J," I told myself and pushed off the counter to go change out of the damp shirt so I could finish checking my emails.

In my walk-in closet (that was partially empty because I wasn't one of those girls that loves to shop and buy a bunch of clothes I'd probably only wear once), I pulled on a pair of black jeans and a grey T-shirt.

My mind kept wandering to the article, to Jace and to the mention Emily made of the cover. I wanted to see it.

Taking my half-empty beer along with me, I padded back to my desk. X-ing out of the article, I went back to Emily's email to read it, since I hadn't bothered in the first place.

Joey,

Here is the finalized proof of the feature for GearShark. *If you have any changes, please send them in immediately, as our production staff has decided this article is going to run in next month's issue (instead of the following month's), which means it's going into production in just a few days. The article is a big hit at the office, and the editor is anxious to get it onto stands.*

I have also attached the cover so you can get a peek at it. No changes will be allowed to it.

Also, I'd like to just apologize because I feel like you and I didn't get off to the greatest start. As a female who works at a magazine with predominately male readers, I want you to know I can see the kind of... challenges you must face in your chosen career. I wasn't as sympathetic as I should have been. I'll blame it on the fact Lorhaven was sitting there with us, and his presence was very distracting ;-).

Emily Metcalf

GearShark Magazine

Emily and I would never be friends. She irritated me the way synthetic fabric irritated my crotch.

And I called bullshit on the fact she was "distracted" by Jace. She was turned on, horny, and jealous because she saw me as competition.

However, I appreciated the parts of my interview she omitted.

I clicked on the attachment to pull up the cover. The image appeared on the screen.

My stomach clenched. My breasts tightened, and heat pooled between my legs. They chose the image of me against his back, in his shirt, with it slipping down my arms.

I still remembered the way his body felt against mine, the way my cheek fit against his shoulder.

It was all right there in my eyes, the attraction and heat I felt for him. It was almost electric.

And Jace… that photo was all Jace, no trace of Lorhaven.

The way he held his arm sort of in front of me and the look in his eyes… I hadn't seen his face during the shoot because I, too, had been focused on the camera.

God help me, he was sexy.

And dangerous.

It was as if he dared anyone to come near either of us.

The image was black and white, done in shades of grey. I couldn't help but draw a parallel with that. It was like me and him.

Joey and Jace existed in the grey of the racing world. Like we were on separate sides, apart but together… Together we were somewhere else altogether.

I minimized the pic and got up to pace away.

Suddenly, I felt full of energy and tension. My need for a restful, relaxing day was blown to hell.

I felt the need to shed it all. The feelings he incited in me. The image of our photo burned a hole in the back of my brain. Most of all, I wanted him out of my system. I didn't want to be in such a tightly tied knot.

I snatched up my cell and hit a button. He answered on the first ring.

"I need a race. NRR style," I said, still pacing.

"Our door is always open," Drew replied.

"See you in a few hours," I said and cut off the connection.

I went back into my closet to throw a few things in a duffle bag. Jace was going to eat his words.

He didn't think I could hack it in his world?

I would prove him wrong.

Twelve

Lorhaven

I owned this part of town.

Not in the monetary, sign here on the dotted line sense, but in the unspoken yet acknowledged sense.

I'd been running the streets in this part of Maryland for a long time. Since I was old enough to drive. I never really fit in my father's world.

No. Scratch that. I fit in. I just didn't want to. I didn't like it.

His world of numbers, suits, and boring, stodgy dinner parties made me feel like I was suffocating. Like I had one foot in my grave.

I enjoyed comfort. I enjoyed having a nice home to grow up in and a father who took care of his family. But in the back of my head, there was always this voice. This urgency inside me.

There's something more out there.

When I hit my teen years, I was just like every other boy, no matter how he was raised. Curious, wanting to test my limits and explore. I ended up on the other side of town one night, at a party for someone I didn't even know.

The music was loud, the girls were fast, and the cars were even faster.

I'd been to lots of parties. I'd been drunk, experimented with drugs, and most definitely wasn't a virgin. But this was a whole new world to me. A whole different vibe. That voice always whispering in my head suddenly shut up.

I loved the stripped-down nature of the streets. The way everything was black or white. There was no room for BS here, and while money talked (it didn't matter where you were, money always talked) it wasn't number one. Respect was.

Everyone here lived by a code. And the cars, hot damn, the cars were off the chain. To a kid who was used to nice stuff, this was a whole new ballgame.

Nothing compared to a shiny body, brand new tires, and an engine that made your insides vibrate when revved up.

This world was a stark contrast to the smooth lifestyle I grew up in. It was gritty here.

I loved it.

After that, there was no going back.

I met Kurt, whose father owned a garage, and I started spending time there after school and on the weekends. Kurt and I worked on cars, chased women, and went to every street race we could.

I used to be the guy on the sidelines. I used to be the one who sat amid the exhaust, loud music, and planned when I would get to be the one on the start line.

We ran from cops when they showed up, and we partied with the drivers.

It was home, more so than the place I grew up in. I felt more accepted here, more like myself than any other time or place.

But I wanted more.

I wanted to be the one to own it. I wanted the loyalty and respect. I was my father's son after all. I guess some things just came with genetics. I wanted to be the best.

My first car was a Toyota. I tricked it out, souped it up, and started racing. I lost a lot, but every loss was a lesson. I started up at the Chesapeake Speedway and picked up a lot of skill.

My father wasn't too thrilled with my new hobby. He thought my time would be better spent being dull and stodgy like him. He stopped paying for my car parts and my gas.

I started taking bets and raking in a lot of cash at the speedway.

Until, of course, someone ratted me out. That was my mistake. If I'd been on the streets and not the speedway, no one would have said shit. You don't rat out one of your own. Period.

But I wasn't boss yet, and the powers that be didn't take too kindly to me raking in a shit ton of cash to make my car better than theirs on their own turf.

My father paid a lot of money to get me out of trouble. I didn't even spend one night in jail. But I did get banned from the tracks.

But to me, that was just details.

Some people called me a cheater.

Fuck them.

I didn't cheat. I had honor. I drove honestly. Like I said, I wanted respect, and cheaters were like gum on the bottom of a real racer's shoe.

After that, my allowance started showing up in my account again. I guess my father figured he'd rather let me spend the money on what I was doing than using it to bail me out of trouble.

I took the money. For a while.

I started racing more on the streets, and I started winning. People started clapping when my car pulled into a lot. Kurt was always there, either in my rearview or riding shotgun.

My father didn't approve of my lifestyle choices, and I made it clear I didn't give a flying fuck. He accepted it, never turning me out, and I knew he'd always be there if I got into any trouble.

I always wondered why, until, of course, I found out.

I became obsessed with winning, with being the best. I entered a couple races across town, on someone else's turf. It was hostile and tumultuous, but I did it anyway. They just saw me as a kid they could take a car from.

It was me who walked away with the slips.

I won some nice cars with expensive upgrades.

I sold them all and bought myself the Corvette. It took a while to make it unbeatable, but using all the skills I'd learned at Kurt's dad's garage, plus some patience, I did it.

When word got out the number one driver in town was picking up and taking off, there was suddenly an open spot at the top.

I wasn't technically in the running.

I'd spent a lot of time in other circles, winning and taking cars. I made some enemies and earned a reputation. I challenged the exiting driver sort of the way a beta challenges an alpha.

There was a big race; all the best drivers were there. They laughed because I'd thrown down the challenge.

I rolled up in the Vette and smoked them all.

No one ever laughed again.

I became number one, and this became my town.

Kurt and I had been drifting apart, and this was the nail in our coffin. Some friends grow up together, and some grow apart.

Now he looked at me with some sort of derision. With anger that I took the spot that was rightfully his. I didn't technically grow up on the streets, but he had.

Thing was he never beat me.

I'd never let him.

So we became strangers instead of friends.

I didn't hate him. In fact, there was a time I thought about trying to mend the fracture between us. I pulled him closer, but that's as far as it got.

I went to the hangars one night after racing and found my brother…

After that, everything changed. In my obsession with racing, I'd missed a lot of shit, and he'd dealt with it all on his own.

It became crystal clear that night why my father never cut me off and why I knew he put up with my racing.

In his eyes, there were worse things I could do.

And in my eyes, he'd never been worse.

My obsession shifted to include my brother, and he took up residence by my side. I cut off everyone else. I was at the top, and I isolated myself in order to protect Arrow.

My isolation, in many ways, worked in favor of solidifying my leadership because it made people wary. My reputation among the other circles of racing, my illegal betting arrest, the fact I had access to more money than anyone else on the streets—it all made taking me over almost impossible.

Oh, and the fact I beat the shit out of a few people who deserved it made a lot of people think twice before they even challenged me. And I'm not talking I won a couple fights.

I mean I literally beat some people within an inch of their lives.

My father paid to get me out of that, too. Not many people knew the details on that. He buried it, and I wasn't opening my mouth.

But there are always whispers. The streets have a way about them. Word spreads.

Basically, I got everything I'd wanted since that first night I went to that street party.

I was at the top. Nothing happened here that I didn't know about. And it paved the way for my sponsorship with the NRR. Plus, I had my brother at my side.

Funny thing when you get everything you work for only to realize you need more.

But what was lacking, I didn't know.

I did know one thing, though. Coming home felt good.

When I first pulled up in the Lotus, people stopped, turned, and the crowds in the street parted naturally like a sea to let the elite-looking ride pass. That's the thing with the Lotus. It might be small, but it carried presence.

There was also the fact it was in my signature color (I had a thing for white cars), and everyone knew my Corvette was trashed.

The windows were tinted so dark I knew when people peered inside, they couldn't make out who was driving.

But then my brother and his black Camaro appeared. The looks of speculation turned to knowing.

I stopped in the center of the parted crowd, a familiar rush of energy and a sense of belonging washing over me. Before I even climbed out, the Lotus was surrounded, with only enough room for me to get out.

Just ahead, there was already a line, and several cars were parked there, ready for a race.

I wasn't sure if I would race tonight. I might just sit back and soak it all in.

"Lorhaven!" My name rippled through the crowd, and I grinned and slapped hands with everyone in reach.

"No place like home," I drawled.

"Third place is pretty fucking epic for your first race," one of the guys closest to me said.

These people were all my friends.

But none of them knew me.

"Appreciate it," I said without letting on I was disappointed as hell with third place.

Talk turned to my new ride, the first NRR race, and a bunch of people talking smack to each other. A few of my closest "friends" filled me in on anything I might have missed, and Beneto, the guy who usually oversaw the races, ran around setting up tonight's stakes.

I kept an eye on my brother (without him realizing it), but he was all good. He had friends here just like me. People he hung with. But as far as I knew, he kept them at arm's length as well. It was just as well. Arrow had enough disappointment to last a lifetime. He didn't need any more.

No one had yet to try and get any closer to him. Probably because they knew I was a mean bastard.

The closest friends he'd made since I brought him into the fold was Drew and then, shortly after, Trent. He spent time at their family compound, too, and I knew the rest of Drew's family treated him good.

I'd seen a change in my brother because of those relationships. A change I was grateful for.

A short time after I arrived, the girls made their way through the crowds and sidled up to me and my car. They were street rats—not a derogatory term around here; it just meant they were at every race.

What could I say? I had my own groupies.

Richelle had long, straight hair that was dyed red, and she favored shorts that left nothing to the imagination and tight tops that bared everything but her rack. Lots of her skin was showing, so I looked at it more than her brown, heavily made-up eyes and pink, glossy lips.

Her friend, Veronica, had shorter hair, but it still hung over her shoulders and was a more natural shade of brown. Half of it was pulled up, and she had a pair of big glittery earrings in her ears. She also was scantily dressed in a white, short skirt that showed the bottom of her ass cheeks when she walked. The shirt she wore was low cut and backless, so she wasn't wearing a bra. She was clearly going for the whole "naughty schoolgirl" look because the socks she wore stretched up to her knees and had bows on the sides.

I wasn't into the naughty schoolgirl look. I liked women.

Like Joey.

"Ladies," I said, leaning back against my car.

Richelle came close, dragged a finger down my chest, and then boosted herself up to sit on the edge of the hood.

She crossed her legs and swiveled toward me and slid her tongue across her teeth. "I like the new car."

She was basically a walking sex invite for me.

I grinned lazily down and slid a little closer to put an arm around her waist.

It doesn't dip in at the side like hers. It isn't made for my hands.

"See anything else you like?" I asked, my voice dropping.

She laid a hand on my chest and tipped her head back. "I hear you're going to be on the cover of a magazine."

Surprise that word spread *that* fast filtered through me, but I didn't show it. "Think I make a good cover model?"

"Oh yeah," she purred, her palm rubbing over my pec.

I'd gotten the email yesterday, with the article draft and the cover proof. I'd actually received the cover twice, once from Emily and once from the perv photographer.

Seeing that photo for the first time had been like a punch in my stomach. I still felt slightly hollow in the spot, even though I tried to ignore it.

God, she was insanely gorgeous.

And to see her practically curled up against me that way…

I almost told that perv to change the photo. I didn't want anyone to see her like that. It was too intimate. Too sexy… And it reminded me of the way her breasts felt against my bare back.

But then I deleted the email.

I wanted people to see.

In a sick way, it was like staking my claim on something that wasn't even remotely mine.

"Wanna go for a ride?" I asked, shoving the image, the article, and the woman out of my brain.

"Not racing tonight?" she asked.

"I'd rather be ridden instead."

A sexy glint came into her eyes. "A ride it is."

The sound of purring engines cut through the sound of the crowd. My head snapped up. I found Beneto in the crowd. "You invite some racers?"

"Nah, man. Wasn't me."

I knew by the sound of the engines, the cars were top of the line. Made me even more curious and suspicious.

I started to pull away from the girl in my arm, but she wasn't about to let me go. "Where do you think you're going?"

The crowd started to part the way it had for me. Richelle, plastered herself against my side, like she was marking her territory, but I barely noticed her.

A bright-yellow and black Skyline maneuvered into view. The last time I'd seen it, the tires were carrying it out of sight.

I felt in that moment the way I did right now.

Like a wad of something was stuck in my throat. Like it was slightly hard to breathe in deep. My chest felt kinda empty, matching that hollow feeling I'd had since I saw the cover.

It made me oddly suspicious that the space beneath my ribs was vacant because my heart had just relocated to my throat.

Behind the Skyline was Drew's cobalt Fastback. Of course he'd be trailing along. He and Trent acted like they were Joey's bodyguards.

Both cars stopped almost simultaneously. Drew's name rippled through the crowd; everyone knew him here. His presence at my races was annoyingly common.

But no one knew the yellow Skyline.

I did.

Joey's here.

I thought when she'd driven away over a week ago, I wouldn't see her again for a long time.

The driver's door opened, two long, shapely legs unfolded, and a pair of black heels hit the pavement. She straightened, tossing back a heavy curtain of long curls, and shut her door.

The catcalls and whistles started almost instantly.

They set my back teeth on edge, and my fists clenched.

"You know her?" Richelle asked, rubbing against my chest.

God, was she still there?

Joey had on a pair of black jeans with rips up the thighs. The contrast of her skin against the dark fabric was like a damn neon light, and it pissed me off. The waistband rode her hips, and the shirt beneath the black leather jacket was cropped so her belly button was exposed.

Unlike all the street rats, she wasn't wearing a shit ton of makeup; in fact, I couldn't tell if she wore any at all.

She didn't need it anyway.

I heard Drew and Trent exit the Fastback and greet some of the people surrounding the area, but my eyes never left Joey.

As if she could feel my stare, she looked my way. The urge to grab her and fuck her mouth with my tongue like I had before almost robbed me of my sight. Black spots swam before my eyes, and when they cleared, she was still looking at me.

As I stared, her chin lifted, and her eyes narrowed.

She was still pissed.

Oh, that excited me.

"Aren't we leaving?" Richelle purred and arched against me.

Joey's eyes slipped off mine to the girl wrapped around me. The angry look she wore intensified, and the corners of her lips pulled up in distaste.

I glanced down at Richelle. "Leaving now would be rude," I said, making it look like the quiet words I spoke were a lot more exciting. "Guests just showed up."

Richelle stuck out her lip in a pout. "I thought you wanted a ride."

Oh, I do. I wanted Joey to straddle my lap and grind herself so hard against me my lower half went numb.

I smiled at the thought. Richelle thought I was smiling at her.

I felt Joey still watching. I hoped she was jealous.

"You must be lost, little girl," Kurt's voice boomed. "Because pro racers aren't welcome in this part of town."

I whipped my head around as Kurt stepped up toward Joey.

She turned away from me completely, planted her hands on her hips, and stared at my friend-turned-stranger.

"The only thing little around here is the dick in your pants," she retorted.

There was a moment of shocked silence that she would dare say such a thing. My laugh murdered that silence.

It burst out of my chest full throttle.

Kurt's eyes fired toward me, and he scowled. Everyone within earshot roared. Laughter, catcalls, and more erupted through the night.

His face flared with embarrassment but also anger. The girls around here weren't like Joey; he hadn't been expecting such a sharp comeback.

He wanted to make her pay for that.

I watched him step close and lean forward. His lips moved. It was too loud for me to hear what he was saying.

I watched Joey's face because that would be a clear indicator of what he said.

She rolled her eyes.

My lips twitched, but then a not-so-humorous feeling stomped out the amusement.

Joey didn't seem so upset by whatever Kurt said, but it pissed off Drew and Trent. Both men stepped forward defensively. Trent went so far as to shove Kurt back.

I abandoned Richelle where she was, ignored her call, and strode forward. People moved as I walked.

"Pro racers aren't welcome on this turf. So unless you want to take me up on my offer to find out just how small my dick *isn't*, I suggest you leave before—"

Trent lunged at him, but Kurt was ready and sprang back out of reach. But he collided with me.

He twisted around, surprise on his face.

I crossed my arms over my chest. "Sounds like you're over here delivering orders when it ain't your place."

"They're your orders, not mine," he snapped and pointed at Joey. "You know who that is?"

"I'm well aware who Joey Gamble is," I replied, hard.

It pissed me off he didn't know. He didn't know who she was to *me*.

She isn't anyone to you.

Liar.

"Gamble?" Kurt echoed. The ferocity in his eyes slipped, and he glanced back at her.

The back of my neck tingled.

My jaw clenched. "Don't play fucking games, Kurt. You know who she is."

"The G is for Gamble. You're Ron Gamble's daughter," he said, like he was only just working it out.

He was either really good at acting or really fucking stupid.

He wouldn't be winning any Academy Awards in this lifetime, so I guess that made him a moron.

Joey lifted her chin. "You got a problem with that?"

She was nothing less than defiant, but I couldn't help but feel like I'd just done something wrong.

I thought everyone around here knew who she was. The first and only other time she'd been on my turf was when Drew showed up with her. The second she got out of the car, people knew her. They called her out right away.

You hadn't known she was Gamble's daughter…

I glanced at Kurt. I watched the realization click, watched his eyes fill with an emotion I did not like.

"Pros aren't welcome here," I told her, hard. I glanced at Drew. "You know you ain't, either."

Nearby, Arrow stiffened.

Great. Later I'd have to listen to him bitch about me treating his BFF bad.

So much for hanging back and chilling tonight, enjoying my home.

"I'll go when she does," Drew said. He understood. He knew I couldn't just open my arms and act like he was my long-lost brother.

It kind of irritated me I had to put on a front.

I never had to before.

"I'm not going anywhere. Not yet anyway," Joey replied, dismissing Kurt and looking at me. "You invited me."

I felt my brows shoot halfway up my forehead. "*I* invited you?"

"Yeah, when you told *GearShark* I couldn't hack it in the racing world."

A bunch of ooohs and ahhhs accompanied by a few hollered, "Burn!" remarks made me smile. "I said that?" I scoffed.

She made a face. "What's the matter, *Lorhaven*?" she drawled. "Afraid I've come to prove you wrong?"

Pro or not pro, when a racer—a female one at that—came onto my own turf and threw down a challenge such as this, a man had no other choice but to accept.

"All right, *sweetheart*," I drawled in return. I figured if she was gonna call me the L-word, I'd call her the S-word. "Show us all what ya got."

People started cheering and making bets.

"Beneto," I called over my shoulder. "What's the pot up to tonight?"

Joey made a sound. "Uh-uh. I don't want your money."

"No?" I smirked and sauntered a little closer. She still smelled naughty and nice.

I loved naughty and nice.

She peeled the cropped leather jacket off her arms and tossed it on the hood of her car. It afforded me a better view of all those curves.

And everyone else.

My eyes narrowed.

"If I beat you, I want to drive your car." Her arms folded over her chest, and her shirt rode up even higher.

More oohs and ahhhs echoed. I never let anyone drive my cars.

Over the melee, she added, "And you'll admit I can drive."

I scoffed. "And if I win?"

"If you win, I won't kick your ass."

More laughter.

I shook my head. "If I win, you'll let me look under your hood."

What was under a driver's hood was sacred. It was private. It was a culmination of their hard work, money, and dreams. And for a winner, it was a secret to a portion of their success.

She pursed her lips, then nodded once. "Deal."

"Sure you don't want the cash?" Beneto cut in. "Pot is ten grand tonight."

I shook my head. What was between me and Joey wasn't about money. 'Course, no one else knew that.

"Nah. We'll leave that for the other racers."

"This is an open race?" Kurt spoke up.

I looked at Joey. She shrugged.

There were already cars on the starting line. More cars might make it more interesting. "Yeah, previous race stands. First one behind me wins the cash."

"Or me." Joey cut in confidently.

I flashed a smile. "First one behind me *or* Joey takes the money."

Excitement crackled through the air. Everyone dispersed toward the sidelines, and the drivers planning to race (there were four) went to their cars.

Kurt was one of them.

"You in?" I called out to Drew.

He gave me a barely-there nod, acknowledging the fact I threw out the invite. "Nah," he drawled. "Think I'm gonna watch this one."

Joey was already in her Skyline, nudging it toward the start line.

I headed for the Lotus.

Tonight just got a whole helluva lot more interesting.

Thirteen

Joey

When the crowd parted and my car slid through, I had a hard time braking.

You know why?

Because there was some five-dollar hooker with a bad dye job draping herself all over Jace.

My foot hovered between the gas and the brake. The urge to run her down was strong.

Her tombstone would read:

Here lies a bitch who touched what she shouldn't.

The second I felt the intensity of his stare, which amazingly had become familiar to me after just one photoshoot, truth socked me in the eye like a cheap shot from a lucky boxer.

I was here for him.

Not just to prove him wrong about my driving, either.

I wanted to see him.

Saw him I had, and now I was sitting at the starting line of a street race.

My first street race. Yeah, technically, I'd been in one with Drew, but I hadn't been driving.

As I sat and waited, nervous energy made me jittery. It was the same before every race. It was like my body knew what was coming and was already fiending for a taste of the first surge of adrenaline. I was an addict.

My addiction was speed.

A sharp rap on my driver's side window brought me around. A GPS loaded with the race coordinates was slipped toward me, and I had a moment of panic I wouldn't be able to work it.

Then I told myself to stop being a wiener and do it. It was a GPS for crap's sake, not a word problem in geometry.

Seriously, I had nightmares about geometry.

Everything was already pulled up and ready to go. All I had to do was stick it to my windshield and listen.

Around me, cars started up and people cheered. Lorhaven was parked right beside me. I glanced over, through the passenger window, at his Lotus. The windows were too tinted to see him, but I didn't have to.

I sensed his stare.

"Ready in one," the GPS announced.

I ripped my eyes away from the Lotus and wrapped my hands around the steering wheel, blowing out a deep breath. The moments just before I laid on the gas were always the hardest.

My body was already there, already on full throttle, but I was still sitting motionless.

Basically every cell inside me urged me forward, screamed at me to go, but my mind fought against that impulse and forced me to remain immobile.

Thoughts of Lorhaven, the pros, NRR, and everything else ceased. I was about to know a freedom only a select few ever experienced.

"Get ready in three, two… one." The robotic female voice counted down, and then we were all peeling off the start line and racing down the empty street.

I didn't know how long this race would last. I didn't even know how many miles or where we were going. All I had was a red line on the GPS, a moving dot that represented me, and the electronic voice telling me where to go.

The race was going on some back roads, roads less traveled so traffic wasn't an issue. Six cars were in the running, but in my mind, the only one I was racing was Jace.

I so badly wanted to make him eat his words.

When I first fired off the starting line, I hung back a little, resisting the urge to force my way to the front. I preferred to hold back, just a little. I might only be concerned with beating Jace, but there were other cars on the road with us. I watched them, getting a feel for the way they drove.

The guy who offered in a rather crude way to show me just how small his dick wasn't was behind the wheel of a cherry-red Nissan. Currently, he was ahead of me, something I was certain he was eating up.

I would use it to my advantage. I always liked playing a little bit of a game with some of the biggest idiots I raced with. I wanted him to think he had me, that I'd been all talk. Just when his head got nice and big, I'd blow right by and destroy his ego.

Boom.

No, it wasn't nice to manipulate drivers, especially while we were traveling at such high speeds, but I didn't care.

Every driver behind the wheel knew the risk they took. Including me.

I overtook two cars, positioning myself behind the red Nissan and a Toyota right beside him. Jace was ahead of them both, having shot to the front, not instantly, but fairly quickly. I liked how he didn't just swoop around and take the lead right away. Then again, I already knew he was one for games.

The Toyota beside the red car started to fall back a little and then was overcome completely. The GPS flashed a curve in the road up ahead, so I took it, easing around, then punched the fuel and overtook them.

I rode up hard on the Nissan's tail end, putting pressure on him to speed the hell up. It shot forward, but not enough. I swerved out while the road was wide enough for us side by side and slid right up alongside him.

Anger radiated from the driver's seat, and his focus was torn between the road and the rage he felt because I was gaining on him.

I smirked.

A fraction of a second later, I caught the way his hands squeezed on the wheel, and I reacted. The Nissan cut over toward me, trying to slam into my side to push me off the road.

I swung wide; his car missed mine by centimeters.

Suddenly, the tires on my side of the car vaulted off the road and into loose gravel and dirt. The sound of the rocks pinging my undercarriage and kicked up by my tires assaulted my ears.

The car fishtailed slightly because of the uneven pavement, straddling the shoulder and the road at the same time. The Nissan kept the pressure on, hogging up the road, and swerved toward me every few seconds.

Did he think I'd be surprised by his behavior? Did he think I'd be scandalized at his no-rules approach and disregard for respect?

That's what these men didn't understand.

I might be coming from the pros, but I was never treated like one. I knew the tricks. And I wasn't thrown off by this.

More gravel flung up; one chunk hit the side of my windshield, and I winced a little.

I swerved a bit when the inside of my tires hit the lip of the road, and a horrible sound filled the night. The millisecond flash of brake lights ahead tore my attention.

Jace had hit his brake, just for a fraction of a second. Enough for the brake lights to flicker. Did he see what was happening? Had he thought about intervening?

Screw that shit. I didn't need him to intervene. I didn't need anyone to fight my battles for me. I was strong enough to do it myself.

I glanced out the window at the guy in the Nissan. He smirked and blew me a kiss.

I yanked the wheel of my car and slammed against his side fender.

Because he wasn't expecting it ('cause you know, only men act like tools; ladies would never… Guess now he knows I'm not a fucking lady), his car spun.

I blasted ahead and veered all four tires back onto the road. Through my rearview mirror, I watched the red Nissan skid in a full three-sixty before coming to a complete stop in the center of the road.

In only a matter of seconds, he'd be back on my tail, but that was okay. Now he knew when he fucked with me, I fucked back.

All my attention focused ahead, noting the Lotus now had more distance between us.

It's almost as if now he sees I'm okay and pulled ahead.

"Roadwork ahead," the GPS warned.

I glanced at the road map. It indicated everything was being condensed down into one narrow lane that was technically the shoulder of the road.

I was so gonna need new tires after tonight.

I grinned. This was fun as hell.

The gas punched down, and my car responded like I knew she would. Landscape blurred around me as I came up on the Lotus.

I swerved out to see how much room I had left and if overtaking him now was possible.

It wasn't.

He downshifted, maneuvered the car, and shot between two rows of orange cones.

I did the same, not backing down from his rear. The road twisted and turned a bit. The dust and dirt from the shoulder rose up around the cars like black clouds in the already night sky.

A car came up behind and flipped on their high beams. I squinted, turning away from the blinding light.

What messed-up kind of shit was this!

I'd been through a lot of crap with drivers, but trying to blind one when they were driving through narrow, unfamiliar roads?

Dirty.

I flipped my rearview up to deflect a portion of the beam and slapped on a pair of sunglasses.

Up ahead, the Lotus swerved out, the road having widened again. Anxious to be done, I burst ahead to do the same.

I drove up alongside Jace, but didn't allow myself to glance his way.

I wasn't playing wave to my neighbor.

He gunned his engine, sliding ahead. I did the same.

For about a mile, the pair of us did this sort of dance together. I'd swerve one way; he'd go the other. I'd go forward, and he would, too. It was almost like we could anticipate the other without even trying.

"One mile to your destination," the GPS informed.

I glanced at the screen. There was an S-shaped curve up ahead, then a straightaway where the finish line was blinking.

I figured everyone was already there, waiting to see who would cross first.

It was going to be me.

I shifted, gave my Skyline more juice than usual, and burst around the Lotus. With a loud, *"Whoop!"*

I didn't let off the gas, choosing instead to keep on flying forward.

I spared one glance back, noting Jace wasn't far behind, and just behind him was the red Nissan. He didn't have his high beams on anymore. Guess that had been a little bonus just for me.

The S-turn was just ahead. My stomach dipped a little as I anticipated the maneuvers I would have to make. I wasn't familiar with this road, this kind of turn. And because it was dark, I only saw as far as my headlights would allow.

I decided not to plan, just to allow my pure driver instincts to lead me on this one.

As I was leaning into the first curve in the road, the sound of an engine nearby had me glancing up. The compact Lotus literally slid/drifted around the curve on the inside, like I wasn't even there.

From there, it moved into the next curve like he'd done it a thousand times.

My focus shifted back to my own driving as I straightened from the first curve and prepared to go into the next one.

Behind me, the Nissan tried to swing inward, to also overtake me. I moved over, forcing him back. His tires squealed when we took the second curve, and I punched the gas before I was even completely out of the move.

My front end was practically touching the Lotus now, and my blood pounded, my fingers burning.

I had to do it now or I'd lose. He was going so fast, probably almost at the max that car would allow.

I glanced down at the button for the NOS I had installed but didn't often utilize. I could use it out here on the streets; all was fair in competition. I pulled out, nudged my car ahead, now almost even with the driver's side door.

My finger stroked over the button, and I smiled.

Suddenly, I was jolted from the side. I bounced around in the driver's seat and smacked my head on the window.

THUMP THUMP THUMP…

My body stiffened as the sound erupted. At the same time, my back end fishtailed off the road, and I caught a flash of red.

That son of a bitch hit me! Somehow, he'd rubbed against my back passenger tire and nudged me out.

I turned into the way my car swerved and hit the brake because his car came forward, so we were parallel. If I didn't love my car so much, I'd have hit the gas instead and ran into his side head on.

My car stopped, the scent of burning rubber scorching my nose.

The driver in the Nissan flipped me off and then shot forward. I followed suit, and even with my now wonky tire, I buzzed around him and over the finish line where Jace was already parked.

Son of a bitch.

I lost.

I was never going to hear the end of this.

And now I would always wonder if my loss was because I got bumped from the side or if it was because Jace was a better driver.

His eyes were on my car as he got out, came around, and leaned against the hood of his Lotus. People swarmed around him, but it was like they weren't even there. All I saw was him.

I expected more of a smirk. Instead, the dark power in his eyes seemed focused on something besides his win.

On me.

The Nissan stopped near my car, and just looking at it was like a red flag, and I was the bull. My door shot open, and I lurched out. I didn't even bother slamming it closed. My heels clapped against the ground as I rushed across the pavement, around the car to where the guy with the tiny junk unfolded from his ride.

He glanced at me with a smirk, and I pulled back my fist and decked him.

The bones in my hand jolted with the force of my hit, but I didn't regret it. I'd never thrown so much force into a swing before. This guy deserved it. He deserved a lot stronger of a punch than I was able to deliver.

His head snapped back and his footing shook. He didn't fall, instead righting himself quicker than I wished he could. Shock and fury crowded his eyes, and fresh, red blood smeared the corner of his lip.

"Must really sting to know you can't beat me fair," I spat. I had to fight the urge to shake out my hand and pull it into my chest. "Hell, you can't even beat me when you *cheat*."

He dabbed at his bloody mouth. Once. Twice.

Swiftly, he flew across the pavement, closing the small distance between us, and grabbed my arms, jerking me forward.

I brought my knee up and made contact with his balls.

His eyes widened, and I wrenched my body away from his and stumbled back.

"You bitch," he growled and came at me again.

The look in his eyes was real and it was mean. I'd gone too far, I knew, but sometimes I just couldn't help myself. Sometimes people deserved it.

"Whoa!" someone shouted, and instantly, bodies larger than mine converged.

I was pushed back. Drew and Trent planted themselves in front of me, and in front of them, sounds of a scuffle made me crane my neck to see.

Tiny dick went flying back, smacking into his car and falling sideways. Jace stood in front of Drew and Trent, his body completely rigid and his hands at his sides.

There was an air of menace about him, the kind that made me draw up short.

"Real men don't hit women," he declared.

Tiny dick scrambled back up and shoved his body toward Jace. "I helped you! She almost smoked you."

Jace cracked his neck from one side to the other and made a rude sound. "You helped me?" He scoffed, glancing around at the intent audience.

People smirked and cackled.

"When have I ever needed help winning a race? Real drivers win on their own merit, not because someone *helped* them."

"You're seriously gonna stand here in front of your entire territory and side with that bitch pro over your own brother who is loyal to you!" he yelled.

"Kurt. You didn't do that back there out of loyalty to *me*. You did that because you're pissed you were losing to a woman."

Kurt rushed Jace, like a bull in a china shop. His head dropped down, his shoulders jutted out, and he charged.

Jace barely even moved. In seconds, he swept Kurt's feet out from beneath him and had him on his back. I pushed to stand between Drew and Trent to get a better view at what was going down. Drew's hand cupped my elbow like he thought he might have to restrain me.

Jace leaned down, grabbed fistfuls of Kurt's shirt, and yanked his upper body off the asphalt. "I ever see you raise a hand to a woman again, I'll blacklist you."

He sputtered and floundered, trying to get out of Jace's hold. "She swung first! That ain't right. A man should be able to defend himself."

Jace's upper lip curled. "If you need to defend yourself against a woman, you need to ask yourself why."

With that, he tossed Kurt back down and crossed his arms. "Get the fuck out of here."

"I won the pot," he said, scrambling up. "That money is rightfully mine."

Jace measured him for a long moment. Everyone waited to see what he would say. I swear the tension in the air was so thick it was hard to breathe.

"Give him the money," Jace said, gruff, to a guy at the edge of the crowd. I think he'd called him Beneto earlier.

After that, everyone seemed to sense the drama was over. It was as if Jace told them it was finished without saying a word. People started talking again, moving off in groups like nothing even happened.

Jace stayed in place, his body still rigid, as Kurt pocketed the money and got in his Nissan.

Drew and Trent turned their eyes to me.

"That was some fucked-up shit," Drew drawled.

"You got a nice right hook," Trent added.

I laughed beneath my breath and exhaled. "That guy had it coming. He tried to run me off the road more than once tonight, and when that didn't work, he tried to blind me with his high beams."

Drew's mouth thinned. "No rules racing," he murmured. "Some guys think no rules also means no honor."

"You totally would have won if he hadn't pulled that punk-ass move," Trent announced.

"No way in hell."

The guys turned toward Jace, who was fast approaching. I glanced over at Kurt's disappearing taillights.

All three guys measured each other, and everyone else seemed to have switched into party mode, so I took the split second of reprieve and shook out my hand.

Ouch.

I didn't go around punching guys very often, and my poor fingers were feeling it.

"Admit it, Lorhaven," Drew ribbed. "She's a damn good driver."

He shrugged. "She still lost."

I shook my head. I actually thought he was better than that. "Didn't peg you for a driver who took a win based on a technicality."

"There are no technicalities in racing," he retorted. "You're either first over the finish line or you're not."

Drew didn't say anything, but deep in his eyes, I saw he agreed.

"All right." I relented. I wasn't a sore loser. "You win. Nice driving out there tonight."

Surprise flickered in his eyes, like he didn't expect I would accept the code of the street. A slow smile pulled his full mouth upward and reminded me of what it was like to feel it slanting over mine.

"Thank you." he said. The words sounded rusty coming out of his lips, like using manners wasn't something he was accustomed to.

Big surprise there.

"So per our bet, I believe there's something you owe me."

I rolled my eyes. "I suppose you plan to collect right now?"

Please say yes.

^^^^^*I think I might be having a psychotic break.*

"No time like the present." His onyx eyes locked on mine. A light shiver worked its way down my spine. "Show me what you got underneath that hood."

Fourteen

Lorhaven

Drew and Trent appointed themselves Joey's protectors.

I'd just seen her literally coldcock some guy after racing a car through dark backroads she'd likely never been on before.

I was pretty sure she could take care of herself.

Didn't stop you from jumping in when Kurt went after her.

I was an asshole. I'd broken a lot of laws, and no one actually liked me. They just liked my status.

However…

Men didn't hit women. Period.

And they especially didn't do it on my territory.

Besides, Kurt fucking deserved what he got. I saw the way he rode her the entire race. It was almost like he wasn't racing for the cash, but just as an excuse to try and hurt her.

She managed it well, better than a lot of the guys I knew. Joey could handle a car; that much was crystal clear. It was also clear tonight wasn't the first time she'd had to deal with someone like Kurt.

It was like I said, though. There were no technicalities in racing, just wins and losses. I won tonight. A bet was a bet.

I had no idea when I'd see her again, so I was collecting before I let her out of my sight.

Looking at her definitely wasn't a hardship, and tonight, she'd taught me a lesson. Women who drove like badasses, threw punches without hesitation, and filled out a pair of jeans while they did it were my ultimate type.

Sexy. As. Hell.

I'd started the race with a damn stiffy. It only went down when I saw her car take a nudge from Kurt and spin off to the side.

But no worries. It recovered. My dick was a champ like that. Couldn't much keep him down for long. The second she'd marched out of her car and literally drew blood from Kurt's face, I was back to rocking some wood.

The old airport always had a certain stillness about it after the sun went down. The slightly too long grass around the strips of asphalt, the old abandoned planes sitting like giant relics no one cared about anymore, and weeds poking up between cracks on the roads.

We had four hangars with cars in them.

All of them were metal buildings with wide doors on the front that opened to allow small plane storage. We used them to drive our cars in and out.

One of the four hangars was set up like a garage, and at the back was where Arrow stayed.

I didn't like that he lived here.

I'd asked, ordered, and demanded he come live with me. I had a townhouse not too far from here, and there was more than enough room for him.

He refused to budge, refused to move in. I knew he liked his space and he liked being here with the objects of his passion.

But there was more to it than that.

He'd never said it out loud, and I never called him out, but I knew there was a part of Arrow that thought living in a garage was what he deserved.

I tried not to think of that often, because, frankly, it cut me like nothing else did.

The guilt I felt when I thought of my brother and the shit I missed was unmatched. Which was probably why when push came to shove, I never forced him out of here.

Besides him thinking he didn't deserve better than a hangar, this place was his solace. It was a retreat. The fences surrounding the property, the locked gate…

It afforded a sense of safety.

Violently, I shoved away those thoughts. I was already in a tenuous enough state without adding all my demons to the mix.

The Lotus was first through the gate of the airport. Behind me was the yellow Skyline, then the Fastback, and finally Arrow and his Camaro.

When Joey refused to pop the hood right there on the street in front of everyone partying, I suggested we go somewhere a little more private.

She agreed, but so did her bodyguards.

I told them they weren't invited, yet here they were.

Whatever. My brother liked them.

And I guess they weren't that bad. I had to respect the fact they were looking out for her.

I stopped in front of Arrow's hangar, and everyone else pulled up alongside me.

Arrow hit the remote he carried in his car, and the large door drifted open. The front center was empty, and once the door was open far enough, he pulled the black Camaro inside where he parked it every night.

Probably kissed it before he went to bed, too.

I snorted. *Loser.*

Even though it was dark, there were tall streetlights lining the perimeter of the property. It wasn't a huge airport, but there was a lot of land.

The lights cast a yellowish tone about. One of the lamps closest to us flickered and made a buzzing sound. The air was balmy and warm; a breeze moved around us. It always seemed a little windier here, and I wondered if it was because of the lack of trees.

Joey was all business once she was out of the car. I heard her pull the latch for the hood, and she moved around like she was going to prop it open right there.

I liked a person who paid their debts.

"Whoa." I stalled her. "It's too dark out here. You can pull it in there," I said, pointing to another hangar. It was a short distance away, on the other side of the one next to Arrow's.

"What's wrong with that one?" she asked, motioning toward the closer one.

"It's already got cars in it. No room."

"That one over there has some garage space so it would be better," Arrow said, backing me up.

"Whatever," Joey said.

"Be right behind you," Drew called from near his Mustang.

Joey waved and returned to her seat behind the wheel and coasted over to where I'd instructed. Arrow jogged into the open hangar and hit a button so the door would open up.

"There a reason you're so up her ass, Forrester?" I challenged before he could scurry to follow.

Drew swung around to look at me. Trent pushed his partway opened door back closed. "There a reason you're trying to get rid of us?"

"Besides the fact I don't like you?" I drawled.

Arrow cut in. "I thought you guys were friends now."

Little brothers. Making everything harder since the day they were born.

"I'm thinking this don't have to do so much with friendship," Trent said. Damn him and his knowing tone.

"Fuck you, Mask," I shot out. "Y'all wanna stay and hang out with my brother, go for it. But that hangar over there ain't big enough for the five of us."

Trent smirked. Sometimes I really just wanted to punch the guy.

Drew shoved away from his car and strode forward. If it weren't for his light hair, he would totally blend in with the night. His black jeans, jacket, and T-shirt gave him a cloak of partial invisibility.

"You look like a floating head." I scoffed, watching him approach.

"Good. Then you won't see my fists coming when I start throwing them."

My eyes narrowed. We stepped up to each other, measuring for weaknesses. Behind us, I felt Trent and Arrow watching as if they thought a fight were imminent.

"What's your deal with Joey?" He spoke low.

"Deal is I get to look under her hood."

"Which hood you talking about right now?"

My tongue slipped over my front teeth, and I half snarled. "I'm pretty sure she can take care of herself."

"I'm positive if you fuck with her, you'll see a side of me you've never seen." Forrester vowed, speaking forcefully and only at a volume I would hear.

"You really think I'm gonna hurt her?" I asked. I wished instantly I could take back the words. Not because of what I said, but the way in which I said it. It was like I practically admitted to wanting more with her than just to fulfill the terms of a race.

So? Maybe I did.

Maybe I wanted to fuck her brains out.

That wasn't Forrester's business. Neither was the fact I was appalled at the thought of hurting her.

"Before tonight, I would have said absolutely." Drew shifted, relaxing a fraction.

"And now?" I prompted.

"After having seen you bolt into action the exact same moment T and I did when that fuckwad Kurt went at her, now I'm more inclined to say maybe not."

"Was that a ringing endorsement, Forrester?" I grinned.

He snorted. "Yeah, and I'm the tooth fairy."

"Good talk." I slapped him on the shoulder. "Beer's in the fridge. Help yourself."

He grabbed my arm as I was pulling it back. "I'm serious, Lorhaven. She's not one of your so-called street rats.

I yanked my arm out of his grip. "Yeah, well, she ain't a wilting violet. She don't need you trailing her everywhere she goes."

He glanced away, then back.

I folded my arms over my chest. "Say it."

"Gamble asked me to keep an eye on her." He admitted.

"You mean spy," I spat, actually feeling pissed on her behalf. "I thought you were friends."

"We are," he said, tight. "Which is why I agreed." He paused, then sighed. "Look, when Ron Gamble asks you to keep an eye on someone and help with the crossover, he has his reasons. This is his daughter, man. He wasn't asking me as a businessman. He came to me as a father."

"Why is he so concerned?" I asked.

He shook his head. "I don't know. Maybe he's just being a dad."

But Drew didn't think that. He thought Gamble had reasons, so he agreed, because truthfully, I knew Drew and Trent cared about Joey.

Have you been hazed? The question Emily asked Joey the day of the interview floated through the back of my head. Right after it came Joey's PC reply.

Was that it? Did Ron Gamble find out Joey was being hassled?

Seemed like a man like him would just squash that problem then and there. There had to be more to it.

"I'm not going to hurt her," I stated.

He cut right to the chase. "But you might fuck her."

I felt my grin slowly spread. "Oh, I'm definitely gonna do that."

Drew's eyes narrowed.

"Don't you worry, Forrester. She's gonna like it."

Fifteen

Joey

Drew and Jace were having words.

Funny how he was no longer Lorhaven to me, not at all. He'd slowly, over the course of the past week and a half, become Jace.

The article was a big push in that direction, and it wasn't because he was so sensitive and sweet in it. Those two words could probably never be used in the same sentence with him anyway.

Sensitive and sweet would never be my thing. I was too jaded for that. Too independent. I wanted strong. I wanted capable. I craved a man who would be confident and resilient enough to handle me, even at my worst.

It was cumbersome to be a "rough and tumble" woman. I still searched for balance. Balance between the woman I was and the one deep inside that wanted something… maybe just a little softer to give all the hard edges in me a break.

Strength was the only thing that could achieve that softness, though. Most would assume the opposite, that in order to give me something soft, they would have to *be* soft.

Not true.

Authority was the key in allowing someone like me to be vulnerable. So was trust. I could never trust someone with that side of me if they weren't made of steel. Not many men were made that solid. It wasn't something that was learned. It was a trait one was born with and honed with life.

I wasn't sure if Jace was that man.

But I found myself more and more drawn to him, more and more interested to find out.

Watching him even yards away as he and Drew seemed to size one another up, I felt it. He still looked like Lorhaven. Tension and danger emanated off him; so did his asshole persona. Danger permeated the energy always surrounding him, and he was still as smug and sexy as he'd ever been.

But there was more.

I thought I might be the only one to see it. To feel it.

No. He wasn't Lorhaven to me anymore.

He could only be Jace.

And I wanted more.

The two men broke apart, Drew remained planted where he was, but Jace started toward me and the hangar.

I felt his eyes, Drew's, and Trent's.

First, I glanced at Jace. He was shrouded in the darkness, but the familiar way he walked and the way his hips swiveled was entirely visible.

Excitement tingled my nerves, causing my belly to jump.

In an effort to calm myself, I looked to Drew, who still stood in the same position, only now Trent was right beside him. Both men looked at me like they waited for a sign, some kind of gesture to let them know I didn't want to be alone with Jace.

But I *did* want to be alone with him.

I waved, a sort of see you later kind of wave, then dropped my hand.

They stared for one more long moment before Arrow called out to them. My stare followed his call; he was inside the hangar beside the black Camaro, with a few bottles of beer in his hands.

Drew and Trent relented and went toward their friend.

More excitement unfurled inside me.

Jace was much closer now. His hands were in the front pockets of his jeans, and his footsteps were heavy against the ground. He was tall, he had a good, strong build, but he wasn't huge like Trent. He didn't need it, though, because everything about him screamed strength.

His dark hair looked a lot like it had the last time I saw him (at the shoot), cut very close on the sides, but the top was long and brushed back off his face. The angular planes to his face might have been too much, but the light dusting of scruff over his jaws served to dull the edges.

And make him look even sexier.

He arrived close enough all his features were visible from the light inside the hangar. It didn't matter how much light there was, though—whether it be the dim lighting from an overhead behind us or the brightest light from a bright sun—his eyes remained the same.

Dark as secrets but as all-knowing as truth.

Slowly, the black leather jacket tugged over his shoulders and slid down his arms behind him. He wore a white T-shirt, plain, thin, and surely soft to the touch.

It was the same kind of T-shirt you saw on the underwear commercials or in those hot as hell Calvin Klein ads. It made me think of sex, like he was dressed for the bedroom and not the car garage.

The right sleeve had somehow rolled up a little beneath his jacket, exposing more of the well-defined muscles in his arm.

Because the shirt was really what I suspected was made to wear beneath another shirt, it was shorter in length, and the hem caught on the front of his jeans, almost like it tucked itself into the front behind the fly because he was just that desirable.

It drew attention he already didn't lack down to the bulge between his legs.

I worked with men on a daily basis. A lot of them were good-looking, but I never had a problem focusing on my job or what I was doing until now.

He reeked of sex. Like he'd just had it, like he wanted it right then... And the way he moved promised he'd want it again in just an hour.

Hunger gnawed at me, low in my belly, at the tips of my fingers. My lips tingled remembering what he felt like, and my brain whispered, *More.*

"Pop the hood," he said, barely pausing beside me, continuing to toss his jacket on the workbench nearby. Turning on my heel, I went around my car to where the hood was still unlatched.

Jace flipped on some more lights, making it brighter as I propped up the hood to let him have his coveted *look* inside my engine.

Before he came to see, a switch was thrown, and the sound of the hangar door sliding closed filled the space.

I leaned back against the front of my car, bracing my hand on the metal body. Jace appeared, his body close, his eyes touching on mine before sweeping over my body.

It was hot in here, too hot for the jacket I'd put back on before driving to the airport. I wanted to take it off, but I didn't want him to think I was taking it off because I wanted to make him look at me.

Wait. Fuck that.

I didn't do anything in the name of someone else. If I was hot, I would take off my jacket, and he could get over himself.

I tugged it off and tossed it on the roof of the car. When I came back, he already had his hands down in my engine, looking at all my shit.

"Whoa," I called. "I said you could look. I didn't say anything about touching."

He finished what he was doing before pulling back. "You had a cap loose." He gestured to it, but I was too busy studying the way dark grease smeared his fingers.

"This is some nice shit," he said, putting his hands back where I told him not to and tinkering with more.

A strand of hair fell over his forehead, but he ignored it and kept looking. Some of the parts were special ordered from places only pros could order from.

He gave me the third degree about some of them: performance, cost, maintenance, etc.

I answered, relaxing into the conversation and forgetting all about how riled up he made my insides.

I liked talking cars with him. He didn't talk down to me or assume I didn't understand exactly what all the shit beneath my hood did. That's what usually happened. Even after I proved I knew what I was talking about, they still had shit to say. It never ceased to amaze me how big of dicks some guys could be.

After a little while of car talk, he shifted, pulled his body up, and glanced at me. "You break your hand?"

"What?" I asked, startled by the turn of conversation.

Without any thought, he wiped his greasy hands on the front of his once pristine white shirt. Instantly, it became smudged with dark streaks and shadows.

"When you punched Kurt." He gestured at me, noted more grime, and lifted the hem to wipe his hand further.

The action exposed his flat abs and hips.

"Uh…"

The shirt fell back into place, now wrinkled and even dirtier.

I cleared my throat and glanced down. I'd been favoring it without realizing. "No," I hurried to say. "It's just kinda sore." There was no point in lying; he'd already seen the way I'd been acting.

"Let me see." He reached for my hand, lifting it between us. "It's red," he murmured, brushing the back of his thumb over the knuckles.

A streak of oil got on my skin.

"Flex your fingers," he instructed.

I did without thinking. Did I mention yet that his dirty appearance only added to the rogue reputation he exuded?

"Not broken," he announced.

"That's what I said." I reminded him.

"Looks like it hurts, though." He glanced up. His endless night-colored eyes teased me. "That's what happens when you slam it into someone's face."

"That asshole deserved it," I snapped, moving to pull back my hand.

Jace nodded. "He did."

He agreed with me? I thought it might be a first.

"I got what you need for this," he said. The words stroked down my spine like an hour-long massage.

Instead of releasing my hand, he tucked it under his arm and towed me toward the back of the hangar.

I barely made out anything beyond the silver metal walls because I was too focused on him.

The seam on the corner of his back pocket was loose. It caused the material to pull away from the pants a little. Every time he swung his leg forward, I'd get a tiny glimpse of the boxers he wore beneath.

"Here," he said, stopping in front of a full-size fridge and freezer. He produced an ice pack, which he deftly wrapped in a towel and applied to the back of my hand.

"I got grease on you," he murmured, noticing the smudge.

I shrugged. "Hazard of the job."

"It's sexy."

I tugged the ice over it, hiding it. As if in retaliation, he swiped two fingers across my cheek. It must have left behind a streak, because his eyes became smug. "I'd like to see you covered in streaks, every last one of them made by my hands."

Sex was something I enjoyed, but the way he stared at me made me feel like I'd never experienced it before. At least not in any way, shape, or form the way it would be with him.

"They look good on you, too," I said, gesturing to his shirt.

Just because my insides felt like a bubbling volcano didn't mean I had to show it.

His body shifted just a bit closer. "What's your real name?"

I lifted a brow. "How do you know it isn't Joey?"

"There's no way in hell someone who looks like you only has a boy name."

"It's Josephine," I answered, taking some pleasure in the fact he liked the way I looked. "Everyone calls me Joey."

"I'm not calling you that." It wasn't a question, a suggestion, or a statement.

It was what would be.

"No?" God, just the way he looked at me. I actually tore my eyes off him to make sure the ice on my hand wasn't completely melted.

With a low sound, he moved past me, going back over to my engine.

I followed along, once again staring at the rip in his jeans.

Once there, he turned, grabbed a fistful of the stained white shirt, and pulled it over his head.

This wasn't the first time I'd seen him sans shirt. Hell, I'd felt his skin against mine in an intimate way.

But the setting had been anything but.

Now we were alone.

I didn't have to pretend, and I didn't have to play a game.

He knew I was attracted to him, just as I knew he was to me. The energy was undeniable. The tremor in my hands dared me to deny it, and the slow thud of my heart was impossible to ignore.

I stopped in front of him, facing each other in front of my car in the shadows cast by the open hood.

Jace took the ice I was holding and threw it over his shoulder. I barely heard the smacking sound it made against the concrete floor. Beneath the hem of my crop top, his still filthy hands wrapped around my waist, his thumbs pressing into the flesh and swiping.

I looked down. Two black marks marred my waist.

I reached over. Without looking, my hands found the dirtiest parts of the engine and worked around. Seconds later, I pulled back, fingers coated in the stuff, and dragged it down his chest, over his pec and toward his abs.

Three long lines were left behind, and I discovered something.

"You were right," I said. "It is sexy."

The sound he emitted was nothing short of a growl. He snatched my hand and put it on him again, covering it with his, pressing it hard against his shoulder and rubbing. When my fingers started moving, pulling toward his collarbone, he allowed it, and I traced more lines across his skin.

He smelled like a cross between unidentifiable soap and motor oil.

His skin was smooth; my fingers were slick.

Abruptly, my playing became too much. One long arm wrapped around and pulled me against his body. The palm of his hand flattened and rubbed upward, snaking beneath my shirt and all the way up past my bra straps, beneath my hair, grabbing the back of my neck.

I looked up.

He kissed me.

No. He devastated my mouth, my body, and every coherent thought I could have had. There was nothing but the feel of him against me, the pressure of his lips upon mine. I didn't know how he did it. How he kissed with so much intensity but never seemed to need air. My lungs were close to exploding, so close I squirmed against him.

Jace ripped away his mouth, but I didn't automatically breathe. It was like my body was no longer my own…

It was his.

"Take a breath, Josie."

I gasped. The burning in my chest was alleviated, but the pounding of my heart increased.

My stomach jumped so much, so fast it almost hurt. It almost scared me.

Before I could make sense of the way he made me feel, his lips were on mine once more. The feel of his thick tongue made my knees wobble, and the pain in my hand was forgotten.

He wasn't wearing a shirt, and the hair low on the back of his neck was too short to anchor myself with. Instead, I reached up and grabbed his ears, tugging his head down even closer. I was tall, but he was taller, so he came, hunching down around me.

A moan vibrated my throat and echoed through my mouth into his. There was nowhere else for the sound to travel because Jace wouldn't let me free.

His kiss was a prison. His tongue my warden and his body my cell.

In one fast movement, he ripped his hand from underneath my shirt, and both hands found the hem.

I lifted my arms, and he laughed.

We broke apart so he could remove the fabric and make short work of my bra.

My rack spilled out. The fullness of my breasts was heavy and felt even heavier right now. Need pooled in them; they tingled and ached.

I didn't have to ask or even wait. His hands covered them, kneading into the flesh, and I moaned. My head fell back, and I arched into his ministrations.

His lips found the hollow of neck and began sucking. I grabbed his hips. My fingers dug in as he sucked down my neck and across my collarbone.

So good.

So. Fucking. Good.

When he started to pull back, I flattened my hands on his back and dug my nails in, forcing him close once more.

Two warm, willing lips latched onto a rock-hard nipple, and I cried out. Tingles of pleasure shot through my body, all the way down to my toes. I stroked his back and finally shoved my hands in his hair, making sure to rough up the combed strands so he looked as out of control as I felt.

It didn't take long for my mouth to get jealous of my tits. Not being gentle, I pulled his hair, forcing his head back.

Dark, glittering eyes met mine. His lips were plump and red, and I dove at them.

Our tongues battled it out, trying to prove who wanted the other more. Desire pumped through me, erasing everything else. My panties weren't just damp; they were soaked.

Between my thighs, I ached; actual shooting pain vibrated up into my lower abs. When Jace's hand found the button on my jeans, my body screamed in relief.

The button gave way and my fly slid down. His large, warm hand shoved down the front of my pants to cup my sex.

My lips faltered on his. My face fell, my forehead hitting his shoulder.

He didn't stroke me. He didn't dive beneath the fabric of my panties. Instead, he took one thick middle finger and pressed it fully against my slit. It rested there with heavy pressure, and I literally throbbed against him.

I squirmed, wanting more.

"Jace," I demanded.

He pulled back totally. His hand left my crotch, and his body left mine.

I watched the muscles ripple in his back and the way his abs contracted when he unlatched the hood and slammed it back into place.

He swung back around, a look of pure dominance on his face.

"Are you on the pill, Josie?"

I nodded.

He grabbed me around the waist. Without being rough, he pulled me so I was standing in front of my car, back to the windshield but facing him.

"Let me make one thing very clear," he intoned. The husky quality in his voice made me shiver.

"I'm the one in control right now. You can demand all you want, baby, but you won't get a thing until I'm ready to give it to you."

I felt my eyes narrow.

"Go ahead and try to boss me," Jace growled. "It turns me on more. Out there"—he motioned with his chin toward the doors— "is something else, but when you're naked beneath my hands, it's me who calls the shots."

Here it was. The chance to surrender some kind of control, the chance to be handled.

"Let *me* make one thing very clear," I purred, unfastening the button on his jeans with one simple flip of my hands. "You can be in control, but I'm still participating. I give as good as I get."

"Honey, I'm counting on it."

His mouth crashed over mine. There was aggression in his kiss, ownership. It burned me from the inside out. Strong hands latched around my waist, lifted, and sat me on the hood of my car.

I kicked off my heels, and he tugged my jeans down my legs and whipped them off my ankles.

Wearing nothing but a pair of black satin boyshorts, I spread my legs, and he stepped forward. I loved the size of his hands. Big, strong, not to be missed.

They wrapped around my thighs and pulled. My satin-covered bottom slid over the sleek hood of the car, and my crotch collided with his body.

Jace eased me back so I lay across the hood, my body stretched out over the curves of the car, and my legs wrapped around his ass. I arched up, shoving my chest close as he bent over me and his hot mouth licked over the center.

His hips moved, grinding into my center, and the feel of his rigid jean-covered rod was delicious.

My hands explored him, learned the curves of his body, the length of his back. Traces of grease marred our bodies and only added to the grittiness with which I wanted him.

Impatient, I pushed at his shoulder so I could sit up and reach for his jeans. He made a sound and pushed away my hand.

Dark hair spilled over my shoulders as my chest heaved, and he stripped the pants and his boxers off his body.

He had the biggest dick I'd ever seen. It was thick and swollen, the head round and full. His balls were large despite the fact he was already so far gone; they were drawn up tight against his pelvis.

And he was completely shaved. Not a trace of hair around his cock, on his balls, or above it all.

I licked my lips, knowing he would fill my mouth totally.

When he bent to kick the pants off his feet, I bent my knees, resting my feet on the front fender.

When he straightened, my eyes went right back to the glorious specimen right in front of me.

"Touch it," he demanded.

I grabbed him, stroked up and down the shaft, and then licked the head. A satisfied sound rolled out of his mouth, and I became even bolder to suck it deep into my mouth and rub his balls as I worked with my mouth.

Just as I was beginning to really revel in the way he felt against my tongue and dragging against the roof of my mouth, he grabbed my head and guided me away.

Once more, he laid me out over the hood and pushed me back a little farther so I was totally on display.

The satin boyshorts were gone in seconds, and one finger dragged up my crease. He made a sound of appreciation, and I peeked at him through partially closed eyes. He was staring at my center, watching his finger swirl in my silky heat.

I was also shaved bare, so he had a complete view of exactly what I looked like.

The tip of his finger nudged my aching clit. Just the briefest touch made me shudder, and my legs automatically fell closed. I was already losing the ability to hold my limbs up.

He seemed to know and held my thighs wide, pressing against them, and lowered his face to my crotch.

I glanced up once. All I saw was the top of his dark head, and then everything fell away.

His tongue speared me. I gasped. And he did it again. One thorough lick across my clit fired ripples of pleasure throughout my body. While I was still tingling, two fingers eased inside my opening and began to fuck me slowly.

"Jace," I whispered, my head falling to the side. My eyes were open, but I saw nothing at all.

"Josie," he answered, then said nothing else.

Seconds later, his fingers abandoned their position, but there was no time to recover.

He pulled my ass down and straightened between my legs.

"Say my name when I enter you, Josie," he told me. The command in his voice was replaced with sheer desire.

The tip of his large head nudged at my entrance. I gasped. Hands grabbed my hips and pulled.

His entire long length thrust inside me. My heat eagerly sheathed him, stretching and making room to take him all.

I moaned his name, the sound echoing through the metal room.

"That's it, baby," he growled and began moving.

He fucked me hard and fast, exactly the way I wanted it. Every single time he surged deep into me, I moaned.

I wasn't quiet; there was no way in hell I could be.

I said his name until it was the only word I knew, and then he told me to say it again.

"Jace," I whimpered, having teetered on the peak of blinding release for so long I was actually starting to feel emotional. It made panic creep beneath the edge of bliss.

Three things happened at once:
1.) His fingers reached between us, found the quivering, needy bud, and stroked.
2.) His chest came over mine, pressing down over me, and his tongue slipped softly between my lips.
3.) Bliss rolled over my body in the form of the most intense orgasm I'd ever known.

I was still high with pleasure when his body turned rigid, his lips fell from mine, and his face buried deep into my neck. He shouted, followed by soft moans as he jerked and jolted into me with release. He was so hard and so big I felt every inch of his orgasm.

I felt the tightness in his dick, I felt the way he exploded, and I felt the little tremors that wracked him when my body squeezed his cock for more.

We were both saturated with sweat, breathing hard, and I could already tell I was going to be sore.

Sore in all the right places.

I thought he would pull away. Quickly he'd leave my body and perhaps turn back into the cold bastard he normally was.

But this was Jace. The man I couldn't seem to resist. The man I saw more and more often whenever I looked into his bottomless eyes.

Both his arms slid beneath me, cradling my back against the car. With a full push, he kept his length inside me, and I wrapped my legs around him to help keep it there.

He straightened, taking me with him like I weighed nothing at all. His arms tightened, pulling me close as he walked across the room.

I didn't know where we were going. I didn't even look. I laid my head on his shoulder, willing to go anywhere he took me.

Seconds later, he sat down, still completely naked, in a nearby chair, keeping me in his lap.

I wiggled down over him, and he stroked my back, played with my hair.

The intensity with which I wanted him just moments ago was still there; it just shifted into something else.

Feelings.

I sat back in a feeble attempt to get away.

It was easy for a girl to think she was feeling things she really wasn't when someone fucked her brains out the way he just had.

His hands wouldn't release my waist; he kept me in his lap, lifted his head, and looked me directly in the eyes.

I liked him. I liked his directness. I liked the way he just took me without all the pretty talk or empty promises. And even more… I liked the way he didn't shove me off when it was over. I liked the way he stayed inside me and had no hesitation to look me in the eye.

After what we'd just done, one would think shyness would be impossible, but it seemed after something as intense as that, shyness was the perfect response.

Still, he made me feel like this wasn't just us combusting in a fit of attraction. He made me feel like he didn't regret it. Even after the high of release began to fade, he was still here, still inside me.

Jace didn't do what was expected. He didn't do perfect, and he definitely didn't do what every other guy I'd ever dated did.

Not that I was dating him. You know what I mean.

"Leave your car here. I'll fix what Kurt did to it," he said, brushing my hair back over my shoulders so my chest was accessible to his eyes.

"I fix my own car," I informed him.

"You can't drive all the way across the state on that temp tire."

Before we'd left the race location, I'd put on the spare, because the one Kurt nudged was ruined. I was pretty sure I was going to need a new rim, too, because I drove on it anyway just to beat him to the finish line.

It was worth it.

There were also some scratches and minor bodywork needed as well, nothing the shop back at Gamble Speedway couldn't knock out in one afternoon.

"I know. Drew will take me to get a new tire, maybe another rim, tomorrow."

His jaw tightened, but he didn't say anything. I wasn't about to start depending on any man for maintenance on my car. Good drivers did their own work, or at least knew well enough to stand around and watch while someone else did it.

When a driver was out there on the street, on the track, or anywhere at a race, the quality of his car sometimes meant life and death. The work done on the car was equally important. Shoddy service got more than one man killed.

It was the reason the pro's racecars were thoroughly inspected the night before every race. Once they passed a series of checks, they were signed off on and moved under lock and key. No changes. Not so much as even a steering wheel cover could be added without accusations of cheating, hefty fines and penalties that could include being disqualified.

It wasn't that I didn't trust Jace (though, I admit he was still earning that from me. I didn't give trust easily); it was a code of the sport. Just like letting other drivers look under hood was something sacred.

I fixed my own car. I didn't need or depend on anyone else to do it.

"I'd get a new rim." He agreed. "If it was my car."

I nodded. "Yeah, it's a good call."

"Drew have everything you need to put it on?" he asked.

I shrugged. "I'm not sure. I think him and Trent are still putting together a working garage on the compound they share with their family."

"Text me if you need a place. You can come here, use the garage."

See? You can support someone and still make them feel looked after without swooping in and fixing everything.

"I don't have your number, Jace." I used his name, not because I needed to, but because I loved saying it. It was my favorite word. My favorite sound, and I loved the way he looked at me when it rolled off my tongue.

"No one else calls me that." He confided.

His tone coupled with the statement chipped away at a piece of my heart.

"No?" I tilted my head, considering his words.

Warmth from his palm seeped into my cheek when he cupped it. "No one."

"No one has ever called me Josie." I admitted, wanting to give him a little of what he'd just given me.

"It suits you," he murmured, stroking my cheek and then running his fingers over my long curls. "You're so very beautiful."

Total girl moment. Emotion welled up in my throat. It surprised me, and I could tell by the wary look that crept into his eyes he saw. I couldn't help it.

"No one ever calls me beautiful," I whispered.

He made a scoffing sound and rolled his eyes.

I grabbed his face and forced him to look at me. "I'm serious."

Disbelief clouded his eyes. Mirroring my position, he cupped my face with his hands. "That's impossible. You are without a doubt the most beautiful woman I've ever seen."

"I don't need pretty words, Jace," I told him.

"Good, 'cause I don't have any. I tell it like it is, and your beauty just is."

A million things bubbled up and spilled onto my tongue.

No one's ever looked at me the way you do.

I love the darkness in your eyes. I like the way your hair is way too short on the sides but too long on the top.

You have a really big cock.

I didn't say any of it out loud. I kept it all in. I let it swirl around inside me and hoped it soon found a place to land. One night of really good sex didn't mean I had to tell him how awesome he was.

"They're even harder on you than you let on, aren't they, Josie?" he asked softly.

My heart stopped beating for one beat, but it felt like much longer. Tightness in my throat abounded. "Who?"

"The other drivers."

I shrugged a shoulder. "It's not so bad."

He looked at me like he knew better, like he saw deeper.

I kissed him, wrapped my arms around the back of his neck, and pressed in. It was a slow, lazy kiss, very unlike the ones we shared before.

I got lost in sensations, in the way his breath mingled with mine, how he breathed in without parting from me completely. I enjoyed the way his fingertips rubbed along my spine as we made out and the way his cock started to grow within my body.

My eyes opened, surprised he was filling me up again. He couldn't be getting hard already... It hadn't been that long. Hell, he hadn't even left me yet.

I felt him smile as we continued to kiss. His eyes opened and stared into mine. His hips thrust up.

He was definitely getting hard again.

His desire was enough to incite my own. New moisture pooled, mixing with the old I'd yet to clean away.

I ripped my mouth free to kiss down his neck, across his shoulder, and then onto his pec.

He sprawled back like he was lounging, the same way he'd sat the day of our interview. Except this time his long legs were bare. I felt the corded muscles in his thighs intimately as he moved beneath me.

I started to move as well, using the rhythm he began. Hands reached behind me, filled with my ass cheeks, and kneaded as I rode him.

I worked him the way I drove, full throttle, but always knowing when to back off. That was the key to good driving—knowing the road.

I might have only just been with Jace, but my body instinctively seemed to know him. I let go and did what I felt.

He moved along with me, and soon we were straining against each other and my teeth were sinking into his shoulder as bright light exploded behind my eyes.

I collapsed, completely spent, on top of him, knowing he wasn't quite there, feeling his twitching cock inside me. I tried to push up, but I was so damn languid. He was just so incredibly good.

Jace took over, even from beneath me.

I don't know how, but he lifted me up and down, literally sliding my core over his cock. It made me moan all over again.

I saw the edge in his eyes when he was about to come, and I bore down on him and rocked so his head rubbed against my inner walls.

He shouted my name.

The one only he called me.

Another little piece of my heart chipped away.

Jace was dangerous.

But I was too far gone to care.

Sixteen

Lorhaven

I offered to fix her car.

She told me no.

I liked her even more for it.

The fact she was naked and cradling my dick inside her body when she said it? Made it the sexiest no I'd ever heard.

I knew it would be hot with her because I saw the passion that ran under her skin. Everything I'd seen Josie do was not without passion. The way she raced, the way she spoke, the way she took pictures… hell, even the way she slapped me in the face.

Josie wasn't exactly who I thought she was.

Okay, she wasn't what I assumed she'd be at all.

My initial opinion was she was a spoiled daddy's girl who got everything she wanted, and right now, she wanted a pretty racecar and a fancy racing gig.

Usually, I was a good judge of people, but this time, I was so far off base it was like I'd been in outer space.

What was worse was most people thought the same as me. Did any of the other drivers ever try to get to know her? Did they ever look past the fight she put up every day?

She must be exhausted.

I knew she could take care of herself; I saw it. Oddly, her independence made me want to do it more.

Josie asked for nothing. It made me want to give her everything.

Not only that, but she was fucking fantastic at sex.

A lioness to my lion. A twenty-four-inch hoagie to my raging appetite.

Fuck. Yes.

Currently, my naked ass was sticking to a chair. It wasn't the best position to be in, but I wasn't ready to move yet. Josie was draped across me, her hair pretty much everywhere. I didn't know how long she was in town, why she was even here, or if I'd see her anytime soon after she walked out tonight.

I did want to see her again; that much I knew.

Her warm body stirred. Her hand pushed against my shoulder, using my body as leverage to sit up in my lap.

Unabashedly, I stared. Her curves were rocking. The hourglass shape all her strength was packed into was pleasing to the eye. And to the touch.

Her waist was narrow, her bust and hips flared out, and her long, slender legs the perfect fit around my waist.

"They're probably wondering where we are," she said.

I shrugged. "They aren't stupid."

"Is that what you and Drew were arguing about earlier?"

"We weren't arguing," I rebutted. "But yeah, he's protective over you."

"He's my friend. Trent, too."

I made a sound. "You staying at their place?"

She nodded.

I wanted to tell her to come stay at mine. The image of her in the center of my California king was very enticing.

The things I could do to her body when I had hours and a bed…

But I said nothing.

My cock slipped out of her when she moved. After everything we'd done and two orgasms, we both were a little messy. I lifted her out of my lap and grabbed a couple towels out of a nearby locker.

"Here," I said, taking it across the room and handing it to her.

She looked down.

"It's clean." I assured her.

Our fingers brushed together when she reached for it. My stomach felt like I'd just sped over a dip in the road at full speed.

We were quiet as we cleaned up, but it wasn't awkward.

When we were done, we untangled our clothes and found the rest. I watched her as she dressed, the way the black boyshorts slid up her legs and molded to her round, perky ass. Her underwear wasn't tiny like most women's.

They hugged her hips and ass, looking like tiny shorts. I liked them better than the ass-floss shit. They were sexy.

When she bent to pick up her bra, I didn't like the distance between us. I moved right up behind her and pressed my hips against her ass.

She stood, her back brushing my chest. I wrapped an arm around her.

We stood there for a few minutes, not saying a word, while I held her one last time tonight.

There wasn't anything sexual about this contact, and for that reason, it shook me more.

After a minute, I pulled back, and we finished dressing. When she was done, I used the clean end of a towel to wipe a smear of grease off her cheek.

"Where's your phone?" I asked.

She grabbed it out of her car.

I took it and entered my number. "Text me tomorrow. I'll open the garage for you."

"Okay."

I grabbed her wrist. "Text me anytime you want. For anything."

"Even sex?" She wagged her eyebrows.

I laughed. "I'm down with a booty call." I paused, then added, "But for anything else, too."

"Where's your phone?" she asked.

I produced it, handing it over.

She added herself to my contacts, then handed it back. "In case *you* need anything."

"Cheeky," I drawled.

"You really wrecked your Corvette to protect your brother?" she asked after abandoning her phone back inside her car.

I groaned. "I told her that was off the record."

"Well, something tells me Emily doesn't listen very well."

"She talks too much," I muttered.

"Aww, you didn't take her for a ride?"

A slow smiled pulled my lips. "Someone's jealous."

She shrugged one shoulder. "I like your car."

"Is that all you like?"

"Someone's fishing for a compliment." She poked me in the ribs.

I caught her hand, folding it inside one of mine. "You gonna give me one?"

She debated. Like, I saw her thinking in her stare.

I was offended. Clearly, I was very compliment-able.

"You're not as bad as I thought."

I scoffed.

She giggled.

I'd never heard her giggle before. I liked it. "That's all you got, Josie?" I cajoled.

She mumbled something I couldn't hear. I squeezed her hand.

"I want to come back tomorrow." she said again. This time I heard every word. "So I can see you again."

It felt like I just rushed over the finish line first in a big race.

I tugged her close and kissed her slow. I liked the way she melted against me when I took my time against her mouth.

When I lifted my head, she ducked hers. Her forehead hit my chest for only one second before she pulled away.

"Jace?"

"Yeah?"

"I would appreciate it if we could keep what happened here between us. I'd rather not give anyone anything to talk about."

Now that pissed me off. I crossed my arms. "You really think I'd do that?"

"I know how guys can be in the pit."

I tamped down my temper. Even though I wanted to be an asshole, I decided not to be, because she was right. "No one's going to hear shit from me."

"Thank you."

The fact she said it all without derision or accusation was what drained the rest of my annoyance. She was relieved… almost grateful.

It was just one more thing causing me to wonder what her life was like in this sport.

Was her father right to ask Drew to keep an eye on her?

Was this the reason she wanted to crossover?

What exactly was Josie not saying?

Seventeen

Joey

The latest issue of *GearShark* hit stands a week later.

Emily hadn't been playing when she said they put in on the fast track and would be going into production immediately.

After spending just a short time with Drew and Trent at their house (and spending that one bone-melting night with Jace), I came back home to take care of all the business I put off yet again to drive across state.

Hopper was breathing down my neck, and I'd even gotten a call from my father, making sure I was okay.

Making sure I was okay = father speak for get your ass home and deal with your responsibilities.

It took several days to catch up, a full day at the pro shop getting the Skyline back in perfect condition, and by the time I was caught up on all the "business" stuff I had to deal with, I only had one day before I was to fly to Colorado to attend the NRR race.

I fixed my tire before driving back home, but I didn't use Jace's garage like he told me I could. Once I was out of his arms, I missed him.

It wasn't a bad thing to miss someone. Unless of course that someone wasn't really part of your life. Then it hurt. It ached.

It made me feel like I was somehow losing a piece of me.

A big piece… a piece I might not ever get back.

So I stayed away. Drew and Trent helped me with the tire. We hung out with their family (who were all really cool), and then I drove home.

Jace didn't text me, and it took effort not to wonder why.

He didn't owe me anything, just as I owed him nothing.

Yet here I was, almost a full week later, with need pooling in my limbs. I looked at my phone more than I cared to admit, wondering if he would text or call. I was preoccupied a lot, thinking, remembering… reliving the way I felt beneath his touch.

Sex with him had been the best I'd ever known. Anyone or anything that wasn't him would be a step down.

I realized I could text him; phones worked both ways. His name and number were in my phone, but I didn't reach out.

Know how I found out the magazine was out?

I was standing in line at Target, behind a woman with more kids in her cart than actual items, with my arms full of things I needed before I boarded a plane the next day, when I saw it.

Right there on the top shelf, with all the other magazines, was ours.

The black and white image of Jace and me pressed together, both staring off the page, took my breath. It was an instantaneous feeling of being punched right in the stomach.

I'd never seen *GearShark* so prominently displayed, but even I had to admit it fit there alongside the fashion magazines, the celebrity rag mags, and the entertainment-themed ones.

I stepped closer to the rack, my eyes unable to move from the image we made. Looking at this photo now, it struck me as foreplay. As a definite prelude to the fireworks that went off when he laid me across the hood of my car.

At the time, I'd been slightly annoyed, put off, and not really feeling like a model. Then the photographer directed us behind closed doors. He seemed to sense what I hadn't. Was that why he asked me to get half naked?

Did he know?

The second my bare skin pressed against Jace's, the shoot itself shifted. It became much more real. This photograph captured what I'd been feeling perfectly.

It captured the intensity Jace and I seemed to generate between us.

That look in his eyes. So fierce. So dangerous.

I picked up the issue, the glossy cover smooth against my fingers. I didn't think it was possible to feel his absence more.

I did now.

I drove home and threw a bunch of stuff in my suitcase. The magazine lay out on my bed, the cover on full display.

The phone beeped with a text, and my heart jumped.

Then fell when I saw Hopper's name on the screen.

I rolled my eyes at my own behavior. I was acting like I was in eighth grade. "Get over yourself, Joey."

Be there early to pick you up for airport. Flight leaves at the ungodly hour of 7 a.m., Hopper texted.

See you then. I confirmed as I snickered.

Hopper was traveling with me to Colorado. Since he was managing me through my crossover and once I was firmly in the NRR, it only made sense he come to this NRR race. The more we could pick up, the better. Most people probably thought racing was racing, but they were wrong.

The dynamic between drivers, racers, and even sponsors was different everywhere. The NRR was in a league of its own; it wasn't like the pros. It wasn't supposed to be.

Once I finished packing, I glanced at the clock and realized it was dinnertime. Tonight I was eating with my father; he wanted to have a "family" meal with me before I left.

I was twenty-two and still lived at home. But sometimes it felt like I had my own place. This was a big house, and my father worked a lot. Sometimes we would go days without seeing each other at all.

I still lived here because, well, why wouldn't I?

This was a gorgeous home. I grew up here. I had my own wing, didn't pay rent, and there was a small staff that helped out with things like cleaning and keeping food in the fridge. And honestly, I liked not having to do my own laundry.

Plus, there was the added bonus of having gates around the property. It served as added security and privacy. My father was a high-profile man, so things like that were very important.

I didn't bother changing for dinner, but left on my leggings, white T-shirt, and oversized buttoned flannel. I'd been reaching for the white T-shirts in my drawer a lot lately.

It wasn't because it reminded me of Jace.

Well, maybe it was.

With the magazine under my arm, I made my way into the dining room, expecting to be the first one there.

I was last.

And more people sat there than just my father.

Trent and Drew sat on the same side of the table, facing away from the entry. But the second I stepped in, they both turned and grinned.

I smiled immediately. I liked their faces.

"There you go, just sneaking in on me again," I said fondly.

I was glad to see them. Truthfully, the loneliness I'd been feeling lately was something I wasn't accustomed to, and it kinda freaked me out.

I went forward, set the magazine on the table, and threw one arm each around their necks.

"Group hug," Trent declared, and I laughed.

"Bringing reading material to dinner?" Drew asked, picking up the magazine before I could snatch it. "We aren't that boring."

As he spoke, he flipped it over in his hands so it was cover up, revealing Jace and me.

"Damn," Drew said, getting an eyeful.

I reached for it, slightly embarrassed, but he pulled it away.

"That's a pretty sexy shot," he said, still gawking at it.

My eyes skittered to my father seated at the head of the table and watching the three of us.

Sexy and my father did not belong in the same room.

I never blushed, but I felt my cheeks heating.

"I just did what the photographer asked. He had an artistic vision, you know," I muttered.

The reality that thousands of people would be seeing this magazine suddenly crashed over me. Nerves flared in my tummy and made me nauseous.

Suddenly, all the moxie and determination I felt to turn the tables on Jace the day of the shoot and call his bluff seemed like a really bad idea.

"That photographer is good at getting people to take off their shirts," Trent said, leaning over and taking in the full cover. "He did the same thing to me."

Drew made a rude sound. "Then he tried to get T to model underwear for him. Freaking underwear."

Trent gave me an amused look and winked. I couldn't help but smile because it was so obvious Drew's jealousy entertained him.

My father cleared his throat, and I practically jumped and reached for the magazine again. Drew tried the keep-away game again, and I gave him a pointed stare. "Dad hasn't seen it yet."

I gave him the stink eye, hoping they would all shut up about my state of undress on the national magazine.

Drew grimaced and handed it over.

"Sorry," he said to my father.

I walked around the table opposite Drew and Trent and beside my father to sit down. The table was already set with plates and glasses, and there was bread in the center.

I wasn't about to be all timid about the shot. Obviously, Dad was going to see it. I wasn't going to act ashamed because I didn't do anything wrong. I leaned over, setting the magazine (cover up) beside his plate.

He didn't even look down.

"I've seen it," he announced.

"You have?" I demanded.

He gave me a look that said, *You underestimate me.*

"Ten copies were delivered to my office yesterday morning."

I gasped. "You didn't say anything."

"You were busy."

"I didn't even know it was out until I saw it at Target earlier."

"They didn't send you a proof of the article?" Drew asked.

I nodded. "Yeah, but I didn't think they were going to push it out this fast."

Dad made a sound. "It's called good business. No point in sitting on a product that will clearly drive sales."

"So you like it?" I asked.

I was a grown woman, my own person. But every daughter cared about her father's opinion.

Even if she never wanted to admit it.

"I'm assuming there was an entire staff present for the shoot?" he questioned.

I nodded. "When we went inside, the staff was pared down because of space limitations, but yes."

Lorhaven counted as staff… right?

Drew glanced at me and smiled. I thought about throwing a piece of bread at his face.

"As long as you weren't pressured." Dad went on.

"I wasn't. They said it was the first issue they've ever done with a couple, and they wanted something a little edgy." I glanced over at Drew. "Apparently, Trent's shirtless cover sold *very* well."

Drew scowled, and Trent choked on the iced tea he was drinking.

My father nodded. "Well, it definitely does have… appeal. And the other model, he was respectful?"

Trent laughed like it was the funniest thing he'd ever heard.

My father frowned.

"Lorhaven—" Trent began, and I gave him a look that shut him up instantly.

"Jace was perfectly respectful, Dad. In fact, he yelled at the photographer for asking me to take off my shirt and then made me put on his."

"Jace?" Drew observed.

Trent lifted his eyebrow.

OMG! They were like two annoying brothers who just wanted me to get in trouble!

"That's his name," I snapped.

"Interesting," Trent murmured, like he was speaking only to Drew.

They shared a look between them.

"Where's Ellen? I'm starving." Actually, I wasn't, but I wanted to give big mouth and never-shut-up-mouth something to do besides talk.

As if on cue, she appeared. A few covered platters were placed down, and I jumped up to help her retrieve the rest. Once all the food was out, we began passing it around.

Tonight, we were having Maryland Crab Cakes, cornbread, roasted vegetables, and some kind of pasta dish with a butter and cream sauce.

Yet another reason I chose to take a wing here rather than get my own place. I couldn't cook. At all. In fact, if it weren't for room service, I'd starve when I was on the road.

Once everyone had full plates, Dad glanced at me. "I read the article."

"What did you think?"

"They gave Lorhaven more press time."

I wanted to wince. *If I hadn't walked out, I could have made sure he didn't.*

"Are you surprised?" I asked. "The fact I'm on the cover shocks the hell out of me."

"The interviewer said you had to leave early." He gave me a look. "You didn't tell me that."

"I don't get the same respect the other drivers get," I said, setting aside my fork. "You know that. Sometimes I get sick of it."

"Lorhaven didn't seem to think your reception with the NRR would be any better." My father pointed out.

I reached for my water, wishing it was beer.

"Lorhaven has a reputation for being an asshole," Trent put in.

Drew nodded. "I'm pretty sure he doesn't think that now."

"Why is that?" Dad turned to the guys.

"Because she nearly creamed him on his own turf last week." Trent showed his teeth. "It was sweet."

"Almost?"

"Blew a tire," I hurried to say.

Both guys looked at me, knowing there was more to it than that. My eyes told them to shut the hell up.

They listened.

"Overall," Dad said, taking a bite of food, "I think the article will be good for your career and will help put the spotlight on you."

"Have many people at headquarters seen it yet?" I asked, thinking of all the pro racers that drove with me over at Gamble Speedway on a regular basis. My stomach twisted when I imagined them reading the article, looking at the cover…

"I had several copies sent there, so I imagine some have seen it by now."

I digested that information, suddenly feeling too full to eat my food.

After a while of everyone eating, I glanced up at Drew, realizing I hadn't even asked, "What are you doing here?"

"Figured we could all fly to Colorado together," Drew answered.

"I have my plane at the airport ready for you all."

After that, I let the guys guide the conversation, only chiming in when asked a question. Otherwise, I pushed food around my plate (except the crab cake; I ate that. It was totally good) and spared lingering glances at the copy of my magazine still lying on the table.

Once all the plates were cleared and coffee was served, my father announced he had some paperwork for Drew.

"Would you mind looking over it now?" he asked.

Drew shook his head.

"You mind, Joey?" my father asked.

I waved him away. "Of course not. Thanks for dinner, Dad."

"Come see me in my office before you go upstairs so I can say good-bye."

I nodded.

When they were gone, I focused on my coffee, but my attention was on Trent, who stared at me with this knowing expression in his eyes.

Finally, I glanced up. "What?" I asked, irritable.

"I know a little about wanting someone you aren't supposed to."

My stomach bottomed out. "What?" I croaked. The word sounded a lot different than just seconds ago.

He smiled, not the *I've got you all figured out* smile, but the *I understand and I don't judge you* smile.

Abandoning his chair, palming his coffee, he walked around to where I sat, pulled out the wooden seat beside me, and dropped into it.

My heart fluttered, nerves coiling in me. I didn't know I was being obvious. I didn't want to be. I prided myself on being a closed book.

"Relax," he said, leaning back in his chair. "You aren't that obvious."

My mouth fell open. "How did you know?"

He made a sound. "I've been there."

I nodded. I guess he had. He and Drew didn't have the easiest of starts. But look at them now, so happy, stable, and seemingly impervious to what other people thought.

I glanced back at the magazine.

If Drew's reaction to first seeing it was it was sexy, if my first reaction to finding it on the shelves was how we looked together, then what would everyone else think?

Trent nudged my leg with his foot. "Wanna talk about it?"

He had this calmness about him no one else I knew had. This way of relaxing someone even when they felt judged. It was like with Trent, he understood and he listened… Most of all, I felt like no matter what I said, he wouldn't hold it against me.

All those knowing looks I'd caught from him, the quiet way he watched every situation.

I put my chin in my hand and tried to ignore the wild hair trying to steal my vision. "I don't think I need to say anything. You already know, don't you?"

The side of his mouth curved up. "Probably."

"I'm not sure what happened," I whispered, dropping my hand on the table.

"Your heart chose."

I glanced up. "What?"

"People think…" He paused as if searching for what to say. "They think they have a say. That when the "perfect" person walks into their life and checks all the boxes, they will instantly fall in love. It doesn't work that way. We get no say whatsoever. In fact, I'd be pretty much willing to bet the universe laughs when we create those check boxes of the perfect mate. Then it sends us the complete opposite to show us who's really boss."

I felt hot and cold at the same time. I felt understood and confused all at once. Yet his words settled inside me, like deep in the very bottom of my gut as if that were exactly where they belonged.

Still, I scoffed. "You think I'm in love with Jace?"

"Are you?"

"Of course not," I refused, picking up my coffee to cradle it in my hands, lifting it to my lips. Suddenly, my throat felt very dry.

"Is that your head or your heart talking?"

Well, damn him and his knowing ways.

"We don't have a relationship, not even a friendship," I argued. He'd at least had a friendship with Drew that was at the core of them falling in love.

He squinted. "You sure about that?"

"It was just sex. One time." *Two times*. My mind reminded me. As if my body could ever forget.

And no, I didn't feel awkward telling Trent I had sex with Jace. I already said Trent had some kind of exclusive ability to make me feel I could say anything.

And to be honest? It felt kind of nice to talk to someone.

I didn't have girlfriends. Not the kind I could call up and chat with. Not the kind who met for coffee and no one I could talk about my sex life and relationships with.

My mom moved out when I was fourteen, right around the time a girl might start thinking about dating and boys. I wouldn't dare talk to my father about it, even though I knew I could.

It was probably the reason I didn't have many relationships. Other than a boyfriend in high school and a couple hookups since then, I didn't date.

My job was my life. People probably assumed I had the pick of all the men. So not true.

If anything, it only made it worse. No one wanted to date someone who was just as good at driving as them, or even better.

Plus, even if I managed to find someone who actually wanted to date me and could look past my job, just hearing the shit said to me on a daily basis would be enough to make him think twice. That didn't even include what they said when I wasn't around.

Once in high school, Ellen found me crying in the kitchen over ice cream, and I talked to her about my boy troubles, but that was just one time. Frankly, it only got worse the older I grew.

"Sometimes it is just sex, but sometimes it isn't," Trent replied, going right along with the topic without missing a beat.

"Who says it isn't now?" I challenged.

"How many people call him by his first name? I didn't even know it 'til you said it. Seemed awful familiar on your tongue."

Every word out of his mouth was like a wisdom bomb.

I decided not to tell him Jace called me Josie. That would just prove him right more.

"He's an asshole." I sighed.

Trent laughed. "Totally." But then he shifted. "Even assholes are capable of love."

"Why don't you like him?" I asked boldly.

Trent pondered the question, sipped his coffee, then set it aside. "Well, there is the obvious asshole factor."

I smiled.

"But maybe it's because he's a lot less asshole than everyone gives him credit for."

My eyes widened. I hadn't expected that.

"There's a difference between being an asshole and being a mean bastard. I think Lorhaven acts the way he does because he has to. Because there's a lot of weight on his shoulders."

"That doesn't really explain why you don't like him." I pointed out.

"Damn, it doesn't?"

I laughed. "Tell me."

"He's a lot of stuff I'm not. Really confident. Really outspoken. His driving is close to Drew's level…" He cleared his throat.

"You can't be jealous of him," I deadpanned.

Trent shook his head. "Not really jealous. Just, I guess part of me thought he had the ability to take over my role in Drew's life." He smiled lopsided. "You know, before we became more than friends."

I nodded. I guessed I could understand that. It was sort of the same reason he didn't like me when I first showed up in town.

Trent stretched out his arm and slid the magazine over between us. "Lorhaven got pissy when you took off your shirt, huh?"

I rolled my eyes. "Told the photographer we were done."

Trent smiled. "A man who's only interested in sex doesn't do that. He also doesn't challenge one of his own when they go after an outsider."

He meant the night of the street race, with Kurt.

"I don't know," I whispered. It seemed like getting my hopes up would be a mistake. "He doesn't like pro drivers. It feels like we're from two different worlds."

"Nah, you're just on different sides of the street. But you're crossing over."

"He doesn't want me to." I tapped on the magazine, referencing the article inside. "He's made that very clear."

"Yeah, and I said I was straight for a long time."

"You think he lied?"

"Maybe not lied. I think when someone protests as much as Lorhaven has, it's because they're scared. *Doth protest too much* and all that shit." He waved his hand around when he said the last part.

"Maybe," I murmured.

Trent patted my knee as we heard Drew making his way back to the dining room.

"That dude sounds like a horse," Trent said fondly.

"Thanks for talking to me," I whispered.

"Anytime, Joey. Give it some time, okay? See what happens in Colorado."

Drew bounded into the room, totally stealing Trent's attention.

It was just as well. I sat back in my chair with an *oomph*.

As much as my thoughts had wandered to Jace this past week, I never thought about the fact I'd be seeing him at the NRR race.

I'd only been thinking backward, about the night in the hangar.

Now all my thoughts shifted to the present, to the future.

Eighteen

Lorhaven

I'd been summoned.

The only times that happened was when I was doing something he didn't approve of.

He = my father.

Our relationship was tumultuous at best. It hadn't always been like that. Well, yeah, maybe it had. But the past few years, it became more so.

For a long time, I told myself it was because a boy couldn't be his own man if he was still standing in the shadow of his father.

However, the fact I was answering his summons and stepping into an elevator at his office kinda proved, in a way, I would always be in his shadow. I guess it never mattered how grown a son became; he was still in some ways vulnerable to his father.

A point that actually made me bitter.

Not on my behalf, though, but on my brother's.

It seemed to me a powerful man such as Sullivan Lorhaven raised two kinds of kids:

1.) Powerful, strong-willed ones who could withstand anything and had a hungry drive

or

2.) Insecure, shy ones who were afraid they would never meet their father's expectations.

I was the first kind. Unfortunately, Arrow was the second. I didn't blame him. I blamed my father for making him that way, and that was just one more reason the chasm between us had grown.

I also blamed myself.

I actually thought after so many years, my father would grow to approve what I'd chosen to do with my life, but it was as it had been since he bailed me out of the betting trouble.

Reluctant acceptance.

There was a time a couple years ago when I thought that changed, back when I'd caught the eye of the pro division only long enough for me to notice them looking. After that, I spent all my energy trying to get a tryout.

I failed at every turn. Rejection sucked.

I learned my father kept tabs on me, on my career. He got me an interview and a tryout. He even came to the hangar to see my car, and I showed him how I was preparing it for the tryout.

That tryout was a big fucking waste of my time. I felt so stupid that sometimes I still tasted the bitter flavor of it on the back of my tongue.

Here's the thing about the pro division: they're a bunch of stuck-up pricks.

A bunch of snobby, rich old men in suits who've never driven a car in their life (that's what limo drivers were for, you know) called all the shots. And they liked exclusive. It made them feel superior, because without their money and ties, they'd have nothing at all.

I didn't pass quality control.

Yeah, I had a rich father, good breeding, and a healthy bank account. Not even money could buy my way past the fact I'd spent all my time leading up to my tryout on the streets with people who didn't have the right names and reputations.

Fucking burned me up inside. Still did when I thought about.

It didn't matter I drove like a champ, had a father who would back me if necessary (my first choice was my own sponsor, but my father would have sponsored me in some way), and met all and I mean *all* of the qualifications necessary to be drafted into the pros.

All they saw was a *street racer.*

Third place wasn't good enough in my first NRR race. You know why?

Because it wasn't a big enough fuck you.

Sometimes when people refused to notice you, you had to make them notice.

Oh, and the pro division would notice me. They'd fucking regret the day they told me I wasn't good enough.

Unfortunately, I wasn't the only one who took that rejection personally. My father did, too. Instead of taking it out on the men who made the decision, he looked at me like I'd somehow been lacking something, causing the refusal.

In his eyes, if I couldn't be the best in the pro division and hopefully make it to a NASCAR race, then there was no reason to drive at all. To him, my efforts were a waste.

It didn't matter that while doing all this and running my own turf, I held down a job. At one of his companies.

It paid well, so between my salary, all the races I won, and cars I sold, I didn't need his money anymore. My trust fund literally sat untouched.

The day I signed my sponsorship deal with Brickstone, I quit my day job.

It was my way of giving the old man the finger.

I'd seen him only once since then. Made me wonder why I got a call this evening, why my presence at his swanky office was practically demanded.

I didn't have time for this.

We were leaving in the morning for Colorado. I should be focusing on the race. Yet here I was, stepping off the wide-paneled elevator with its sleek, polished stainless doors. The floors were made of large marble tiles the color of sand. They stretched out across the wide, rectangular room with a giant mahogany desk sitting in the center, toward the wall.

On that wall was a large custom-created fountain. The sound it made reminded me of a rushing stream and added to the atmosphere of basically my father's "reception" area.

There was a large inlaid L on the front of the reception desk, polished so completely I could see the reflection of my jean-clad legs.

Hell no, I didn't dress up.

I was here. That was all he was getting.

Bethany, my father's assistant, was sitting at her post with a Bluetooth device hooked over one ear. When she looked up, I gave her a lazy, charming smile.

Bethany was probably my age, maybe even younger. Her long, blond hair probably wasn't real; neither were her huge tits. Her eyes were blue, and her lips had injections. She stood as I approached, revealing her very professional outfit of a red, skintight pencil skirt and a blouse with a bunch of ruffles around the neck and a plunging neckline.

She was an attractive woman, which was why she worked here. I wouldn't be surprised at all to find out she was sleeping with my father. Hell, she probably climbed under his desk when he had an hour's worth of conference calls and sucked him off.

That's how she paid for half her beauty.

Yep, I was an asshole. But it was the truth.

"Hey, Bethany," I said.

"Lorhaven," she said, breathless. I wondered if she talked like that because she thought it made her sound sexy. Personally, I liked women who didn't have to try to be sexy.

Like Josie.

"I didn't know you were coming this evening."

That's because you weren't blowing my dad when he called and told me to come over.

"Last-minute call," I explained, and she nodded. "I'll see myself in."

"Well, I should call him." She worried.

"He's expecting me," I called over my shoulder as I headed toward his office. It was located at the end of the hall behind two mahogany doors. His name was on both doors.

You know, in case Barbie, I mean Bethany, forgot his name on her way in to bring him his coffee.

So maybe I was angry. I had every right to be.

I shoved open the door and let myself in. Sullivan Lorhaven was standing in front of the wall of windows stretching across the entire back wall of the office. He was dressed in a three-piece designer suit and designer shoes.

His hair was dark like mine, almost black, without a hint of grey. I was thinking he had it colored, but I didn't care enough to ask.

"It's rude to just barge in," he said without turning.

"It's rude to call the son you haven't spoken to in months and expect him to drop everything and just come over."

He turned to finally look at me. His tie was blood red, eyes as dark as mine, and I'd never seen him with anything less than a clean shave. "Were you busy?"

"You know the season for the NRR started."

I might speak to him barely ever, but Sully knew exactly what I was up to. There was no way in hell he didn't know everything about my career. He was too controlling to *not* know.

"Going to Colorado soon, right?"

See?

"I'm leaving tomorrow, so if this can wait…" I spread my hands as if to say I had no issue leaving.

He went over to a bar on the opposite side of the room to pick up a crystal glass; it was hand carved and completely stocked. "Drink?" He lifted the glass decanter filled with dark-colored liquor.

"I prefer beer," I said. Honestly, I liked it all. I just liked to get under his skin.

On another note, I wasn't going to drink in front of him. That implied I needed a drink to be in the room with him. I didn't. I was stronger than that.

He shrugged and poured a few fingertips of the stuff into his glass and carried it over to sit down behind his desk.

There was a couch near the bar and a couple club chairs. He could have sat there. But then he wouldn't be able to "intimidate" me with his power.

I sat in a chair opposite his desk, kicking back in a relaxing manner. The ends of my leather jacket fell open and away from my body.

All I had on beneath it was a white T-shirt. I'd been wearing a lot of them lately.

"I read the article on you in this month's *GearShark* issue."

It was out? How the fuck did I miss that? "Rushed right out to the stands to get it, did you?"

"Actually, the publisher sent me several copies. They know you're my son."

Was he trying to imply he was the reason I was on the cover? That I got into the NRR?

He could kiss my ass.

I made sure my voice sounded good and bored. "That's right. I forgot. You don't do mundane things such as buy magazines."

He sighed and sat forward. "Actually, when Bethany came in this morning, she was waving it around. I thought the copies I received were advanced. I didn't realize they were out. But she'd gotten it at the coffee shop around the corner. I sent her back to buy the rest."

I didn't say anything. Just waited for him to get to the point.

He sighed again. "I do care about you, Jace."

"Don't call me that," I bit out.

He frowned. He couldn't understand why in the past several years, I pretty much chewed off everyone's head who dared use my first name. He and Mother might have chosen that name, but that didn't give him the right to use it.

Not anymore.

It denoted a certain familiarity to me. A closeness he and I did not have. My father didn't know me. Not many people did. My first name was reserved.

Reserved for those I deemed fit enough to use it.

Right now, that was only two people: Arrow and Josie.

Arrow barely used it, choosing instead to mostly call me Lor. That left Josie… the girl who maybe didn't know me that well, but maybe would. I should have called her. Texted. Something. My pride got in the way. My need to never chase after a person.

Maybe some people were worth chasing.

"I know we don't talk much, but I'm always here if you need me." My father spoke, reminding me I was in his office.

"What about your other son?" I challenged.

He sat back, voice becoming tight. "I didn't call you here to argue."

"Why did you call me here?"

"To tell you I'm proud of you."

There were a few seconds of dead silence while I processed what he said. "You're proud of me," I echoed.

"Yes, that article was well done. It's clear you've made a name for yourself and your career is really taking off."

"Are you surprised?"

"No, I always knew you'd succeed in everything you wanted to."

I made a scoffing sound. "That's a load of horse shit."

He took a sip of his drink and studied me as I swallowed. "Why?"

"You really need to ask me that?" I challenged. What was the point of this?

"Have I not always supported you? Gotten you out of trouble, making sure the details stayed buried so you could continue to do what you do?"

"Writing some checks isn't what I call support; it's making sure your name doesn't go up in flames."

"Protecting one's image isn't something to be ashamed of. I would think you know all about that. You have quite an image and reputation of your own."

He had me there.

"I haven't shunned one of my sons, though, for the sake of my good name," I retorted with some anger.

"I have my plane at my airstrip. It's fueled up and on standby. You just need to call in your flight plan so it can be filed. The pilot has instructions to wait in Colorado until you're ready to return home."

"I already have plane tickets." I hadn't expected him to reply to my previous accusation. He couldn't.

"Yes, well, this will be more comfortable. No lines, airport headache, and no layovers."

"Why would you do this?"

"I told you. I'm proud of you, son. I want to support you. I want to see you succeed."

"I took third place in my first race," I said. It wasn't a win. Not to me and, therefore, definitely wouldn't be to him. He was the only person to which I would essentially slam myself to get the better of.

"Third place is commendable. You'll only come up from there."

I blinked. I wasn't expecting that. So I tried again. "Arrow is coming with me to Colorado."

"I assumed as much."

Was this the *Twilight Zone?*

"I'm trying here, Lorhaven." He spoke. "I've been thinking a lot lately. When a man gets as old as me, he starts to do some reflecting, and I've come to regret the way our relationship has been."

"You? Regret?" I raised my eyebrows.

"When your mother died, I should have been a better father, more present. I just… Losing Jackie was very hard. I loved your mother very much. You remind me of her, you know." His face softened, which gave way for his age (his late sixties). A wistful tone I didn't think I'd ever heard filled his usually crisp voice.

My stomach knotted, and I swallowed past the lump in my throat. My mother died when I was five. I didn't have a lot of memories of her because I was so young, but the ones I did have I carried close to my heart. She was a good person, kind, generous, but also strong.

I always heard she was the kind of woman who never put up with my father's bullshit and would storm right into his office to put him in his place whenever she thought it necessary.

I had a picture of her in my head I knew was from my own experiences, not just the photograph that still sat framed on Dad's desk.

Her hair was long, the color of glittering black diamonds. In my memory, it was so straight it reflected light, and when she smiled down at me, it fell like a curtain around her slim face.

She'd been a model in Paris before she married my father. She spoke French, and her English had an accent that used to lull me to sleep. She was tall, nearly six feet, very thin, and had brown eyes with a hint of honey inside.

She loved me, enough that even now I felt it. Sometimes I thought of her at night when I lay in bed, and I wondered what my father would be like if she hadn't died so suddenly.

"Funny, most people say I'm like you," I replied, trying to get a little distance from the memories flooding through my emotions.

"You are." He laughed. "But she's the reason you've gone your own way and you have no problem giving me a hard time."

I saw the love he had for her in his face just then… It made some of the anger I always felt toward him slip away.

"You remarried." It was meant to be a statement but came out like an accusation.

"I thought you liked Donna. She was good to you. Still is."

Donna was my father's second wife. He married her about two years after my mom died of a freak heart attack at an age no one thought women died of heart attacks.

Donna was Arrow's mother and really the woman who raised me. The second she came into my father's mansion, she looked at me like her own, never once implying I wasn't. That was one thing about my father… He had good taste in wives.

But the women he cheated on them with were another story.

"I do like her. Still see her a lot."

He nodded. "I figured."

They'd gotten divorced several years ago. Another product of his treatment of Arrow (and probably his affairs). Donna wasn't about to stand by and accept it. Arrow was her son, and it didn't matter to her if he was gay or looked like Justin Bieber. She loved him.

I just wished she'd been a little stronger, a little faster, because maybe if she had, my brother wouldn't have suffered so much.

"She's doing all right, then?"

"She's fine," I said. He knew that. He's the one who bought her the million-dollar estate she moved to.

"It's one of the main reasons I married her, you know. Because I knew she'd be wonderful to you. Since I couldn't seem to pull myself together, I wanted you to have at least one parent who was present."

"Do you want me to be grateful?" I asked. "Thankful you got me a replacement mother and not mad you were never around except to tell us when we weren't good enough? Your money can't buy that."

"I realize that. I'd like an opportunity to not make up for the past, but perhaps have a better relationship in the future."

"Why?" I asked, blunt.

"Because I don't want to die with regrets."

Clearly, he was better at being blunt than me.

"What about Arrow?" I challenged.

His eyes clouded over. "I'd like to try with him as well. I thought maybe you could speak to him."

I barked a laugh and stood. "Is that why I'm here? Because you want me to convince my brother to forgive you for all the shit you've done? Fuck that and fuck you. My loyalty is to him."

"Don't you take that tone with me." He also stood. "I'm well aware of how fucked up my relationship with my son is. I don't need you to tell me, and I sure as hell don't need you to fix it."

I got the asshole side of my personality from him.

"I thought maybe you could just see if he'd be willing to talk to me."

"He isn't," I said, stubborn.

"Ask."

"Don't hold your breath," I replied and started for the door.

"Lorhaven." His commanding voice stopped me. What a stark contrast it was when he talked about my mother.

He never sounded like that when he talked about Donna.

Had losing my mom been something that altered him forever? Was she the only one he'd ever really loved?

"I really did just want to tell you I read the article, I'm proud of you, and I've been watching your career. You've earned where you are today."

I swung back around. "Thank you."

I wished I could say his words didn't mean anything. But they still did.

"Your mother would be proud, too. She'd be in the stands at every race."

Again, my stomach clenched. It felt heavy, like it was going to sink down inside me and, on its way, take out all my other organs in the process.

"I have to go," I said.

"So the girl," he said, ignoring my words. "The one on the cover with you."

"What about her?" I challenged. That sinking feeling I had in my stomach rapidly left, and familiar tension coiled inside me.

He'd better watch himself bringing up Josie.

"You don't think women belong in racing," he stated.

"I don't think you can say shit to me about discrimination."

He smiled. "That's the thing, son. I know all about discrimination, and that look on your face…" He lifted a copy of *GearShark* off his desk.

I hadn't even noticed it lying there. My eyes went right to Josie, to the way she curled into my back.

It made me hungry.

So goddamn hungry.

My father went on. "The look on your face in this photo, that's not it."

"What are you saying?" I crossed my arms over my chest.

"Don't be stupid like me, son. Don't push people away. I had the look you have in your eyes once, a long time ago. I lost it. I spent the rest of my life buried in work and pissing everybody off. Here I am at sixty-seven, with piles of money, but I have to practically threaten my own son to come see me."

"I don't know what you're talking about." I lied.

"You're on the cusp right now. A career, a woman, a life you want. Don't fuck it up."

His words made me uncomfortable. He was an asshole, but he wasn't dumb.

Once again, I started to leave.

Stopped.

I didn't look at him. Instead, I kept my back turned. It was easier to ask what I wanted without looking him in the eye.

"When the pros shot me down a couple years ago, why'd you drop me? Why'd you forget I existed again?"

"You've always existed to me, Jace," he said, and I stiffened. "But you had to do the work to get to where you are right now. I couldn't do it for you, because you're the type of man who has to make it on his own for it to count. I backed off. I see now I backed off too far, but it was only because I knew you would make your way. I've always been here, watching, silently cheering you on."

I cleared my throat and pulled the door open. Out in the hallway, his voice followed.

"Don't forget about the plane. It's waiting."

I pulled the wood shut and went to the elevator. If Bethany said anything to me, I didn't hear. This conversation was the last thing I expected. I was used to heated exchanges and criticism. I was angry with my father for so many things.

Right now, it was hard to be one hundred percent angry.

Some of me was too tired for that. I felt in a lot of ways shell-shocked.

Was my father not exactly who I thought all these years? Was there a little more buried beneath his cold, distant, and judgmental persona?

Did it really even matter? A lot of damage had been done in the past several years, some of it irreversible. One conversation wouldn't make it better.

Sure made me feel like I'd been kicked in a kidney, though.

If I'd been missing Josie before, I did even more now.

I wasn't sure when I'd see her again, but suddenly, whenever that was just wasn't soon enough.

I pulled out my phone and shot off a text.

It was only one word, but to me, it was more. Maybe in some ways, it was a test. A way for me to see if the look my father said was in my eyes was reciprocated.

Would she understand what I didn't say?

Or maybe…

Maybe that text was just my way of reaching out to someone who didn't want anything from me. Someone who made me feel a little like the man I was (though flawed and fucked up) was all I needed to be.

Nineteen

Joey

Trying *not* to think about him was hard enough, but now I knew he was thinking of me, too.

I reread that text more than once. I never knew a simple exchange of two names could ever say so much.

Twenty

Lorhaven

She understood.

I didn't know because she called me back or even in the response she texted (though that was pretty telling).

How did I know?

I saw it in her eyes.

She was here. In Colorado. I looked up from the pit as people scattered all around, and there she was.

I didn't know she was going to be here, but she was impossible to miss even from a distance while she, too, stood in the center of chaos in Forrester's pit.

Our eyes locked, like they'd known exactly where to look. I saw the understanding in the green depths. She knew.

Just as I knew.

I didn't know a look, such a simple thing, could alter my mood so unequivocally. A mood that had been precarious, quiet, and more brooding than usual.

I felt energized suddenly, more in control. It was easier to shut out the shit storm in my head my father had churned up and just be in the moment.

It was like a heavy curtain lifted and everything around me came back into focus.

I needed that, more than I think I ever had before.

Her hair was down, not in the wild mass of curls from the last time I'd seen her. Instead, it was sleek and smooth, just like on the cover of *GearShark*. It fell over her shoulders, down over her chest, and framed her face. She was fucking beautiful, the most beautiful sight I'd ever laid my scrutinizing eyes on.

She wore a white tank-top and a pair of jeans that weren't painted on. They were worn, slightly loose, and had a couple rips in the knees and what looked like oil stains in various places. All her curves were on display, but it didn't make me jealous; it made me proud. It made me horny.

It made me want her.

I liked her strength, the unapologetic way she was who she was. *No fucks.* That was her vibe. Like she didn't care at all.

This one didn't need saving. She didn't even need protecting.

She could stand at a man's side. She could go toe to toe with him.

Maybe it was the span of a few seconds, or maybe it was a few minutes. I'm not sure how long we stared, but eventually, the chaos around us reached out and enveloped us back into its many folds.

A camera crew led by a man with a mic approached and called out to her.

Arrow appeared at my side and called out to me.

The moment was broken, but it had been enough.

I kicked up the side of my mouth, feeling more like myself than the past twenty-four hours. She also smiled something similar, then turned to the people vying for her attention.

"Car's ready," Arrow said.

I slapped him on the back. "Good man."

"You okay, Lor?" he asked, giving me a suspicious look.

"Do I look okay?" I held out my arms.

"Actually, yeah, you seem great all of a sudden, which is a total one-eighty from how you've been since we stepped on the plane."

Our father's plane.

Something Arrow hadn't been too thrilled about. But like me, he saw the benefit. Flying private was definitely the way to go.

Maybe I should have been a no-show for Dad's plane, but it seemed like a seamless, quiet flight would be a lot better than a commercial one. Especially since my head was already on overload.

Arrow asked me about three hundred times what was wrong. I didn't tell him. I wasn't ready to get into it. Obviously, he knew it was something to do with daddy dearest, because our asses were sitting in his plane.

He didn't push, though, out of respect for me but also because he probably was afraid to ask.

"Just getting in the zone to race," I drawled, looking over at my modified car. It was red, with the Brickstone logo prominently displayed on the hood. Several other logos covered the car as well.

I was dressed in a red jumpsuit. I made it look good. On my feet were black boots, and there was a pair of Oakleys on my head.

About four members of my pit crew swarmed around the car, making sure it was one hundred percent ready to race.

"Joey's here," he said, giving me a look.

"Is she?"

"Like you weren't just making eyes at her." Arrow scoffed.

I slung my arm around his neck and pulled him into my body. "I don't make eyes at people," I declared, messing up his too-blond hair.

He shoved me back with a fierce look in his eye and smoothed out his wild mane. "I'd deck you if you weren't due in the damn car."

I flashed my teeth. "Ahh, little bro, don't hate."

"Fuck you."

"That's some mouth you got," I remarked, dry.

"I'm sick of everyone treating me like a kid," he announced with a stubborn glint to his jaw. "I'm not. People need to start treating me like it."

"Whoa." My eyes narrowed. All my attention swung to him. Clearly, I'd hit a nerve, and clearly, I wasn't the only one stewing. "What's going on, A?"

"I know you saw him." His voice was low and tight.

Well, shit. My refusal to talk about what went down with Dad and me was only intended to give me some time to think, but I was still as convoluted as ever. My silence only served to make Arrow feel the same way I was, only he didn't understand why.

"Yeah, I did," I replied. "And it mind fucked me, okay? I'm not keeping it from you on purpose. I was just trying to protect you and keep my head on the race."

He nodded once. "I get keeping your head in the race. But you can't protect me from this. It's not your job."

My stare fired directly into his. "Yes. It is."

He drew himself up. He wasn't quite as tall or wide as me, but he wasn't completely lacking in size. "I know you think that. Hell, I even understand it. I used to be pretty messed up. But I'm stronger now… better. I can handle this. I have to. It's my life. I won't hide in your shadow, Lor. I respect you, I'm loyal to you first, always… but I gotta be my own man."

I don't know when it happened… but somewhere along the way, he became more than my little brother. He became my best friend. But beyond that… it was almost like he became mine.

Weird. I know.

And I didn't mean it in some romantic sense.

God, all that shit where guys are like, *She's mine.* Fuck that.

I didn't want to own a woman. Owning something was just that, claiming it. Like going to an auto parts store and paying a set price for an item.

A woman wasn't for sale.

People in general weren't for sale.

To me, owning a woman was a fancy way of retaining her. I didn't want to retain anyone. I wanted to be chosen. Day after day. Night after night. That was real love, freedom to choose and for her to make the choice for me every single day.

Shit. Maybe my brain was still more convoluted than I thought.

Get it together, Lor. This is about Arrow right now.

I guess what I meant was in a sense, I became his protector, pulled him under my wing, almost like a father to a son.

It was almost impossible to stop feeling like that, to hear he wanted to be his own man. I didn't mean to hold him back or suffocate him with my protection.

It's just the image of him a couple years ago in the back of the hangar… I would never forget it.

But I couldn't allow him to suffer from it either. It was something he was pushing back at me. Something he wanted to be on more equal footing. I had to let it happen, even if it felt impossible.

I could still protect him. Hell, I always would. I'd just have to find a quieter way of going about it.

Or maybe less quiet.

Since, you know, my silence about what went down with Dad was what got me here in the first place.

Shit. I needed a beer. Or four.

After you win this race.

"I get that," I told him. "You got a right to know. I wasn't keeping secrets, just wasn't ready to talk about it."

"Yeah." He pushed back the blond hair falling over the side of his head. "I know. Sorry."

I grinned. "Don't be. We'll talk after the race."

"I didn't fuck with your headspace, did I?" He worried.

"Nah." I glanced over my shoulder to where Josie was still standing, talking to the reporter. She looked confident and cool. "I'm tight."

"Give 'em hell out there, bro." Arrow grinned and steered me toward my waiting wheels.

Oh, I planned on it.

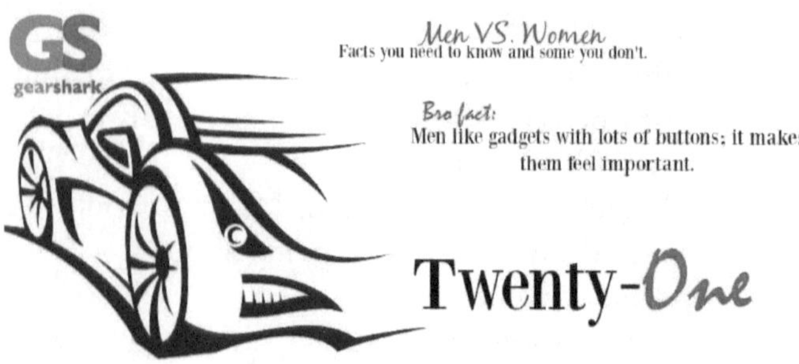

Twenty-One

Joey

I felt like a real girl.

I mean, I *am* a girl, but I've never been one to get that fluttery, anticipatory feeling when a guy was around and I was just waiting to catch sight of him.

Then I did.

My blood pressure spiked. I actually felt it rise like it shot out of a cannon. My pulse began to hammer, and an almost giddy feeling erupted deep in my stomach.

I was totally embarrassed.

I'd never ever felt like this before. Not even in high school with my first crush, my first boyfriend, or even the first time I had sex.

I was usually more cool, more even tempered. Sure, I would get excited to see a guy in the past or someone I really liked. We laughed and had fun together. Sex was always good.

Jace was different.

He made me feel like a woman in ways I'd never felt before, in ways I thought I never would.

I honestly believed growing up under my father's roof, where it once had been hoped I were a son and not a daughter, influenced me. Sure, my mom would dress me up when I was little and she'd try to teach me to be a lady and take me to where she'd come from and try to mold me in her image.

I never took to it. To her.

Most would describe me as a tomboy. I don't know what the hell that even meant. I was just me, and that me wasn't a girly girl. I liked fast cars, ripped-up jeans, action movies, and I didn't depend on a man for anything.

Yet when I arrived in Colorado (a day before the race), we all went downtown and walked around the shops and had dinner at a restaurant with the *best* homemade fish and chips. Across the street was a place that caught my eye. A place I'd never seen or been to before.

A blow-dry bar.

If you're anything like me, then you're sitting there saying, "A what now?"

A blow-dry bar is a place women go to get their hair shampooed and blown out. It's not a salon. They don't do cuts; they don't do color. They simply shampoo, condition, and then blow your hair out into a sleek and gorgeous style that supposedly will hold for several days because, apparently, the blow-dryers are filled with fairy dust.

Okay, they aren't.

But the way they advertise it, they might as well be.

Naturally, I scoffed at the sight as I sat in the window of the restaurant across the street and chewed my steak. I'd walk in and those women would probably be horrified. They wouldn't know what to do with a head of hair like mine. Hell, I didn't even know what to do with it.

The thought amused the hell out of me. Naturally, I then wanted to go there.

I told myself it was because I wanted to show these blow-dryer wielding fairies nothing they did could tame this beast on my head… but really, the lure of perfectly straight, glossy hair, the way it was on the cover of *GearShark,* totally called to me.

Jace had liked it. I saw the way his eyes followed it, and I recalled exactly how it felt to have his hands running through it. Granted, I liked my curls just fine, but this was a chance to sit in a chair and have it tamed without having to get a shoulder cramp trying to do it myself.

FYI: When I "blow-out" my hair, I end up wearing a hat. 'Cause, you know, I do a shitty job.

So after dinner, I went there (they stayed open 'til 9:00 p.m. at night! Clearly, the ladies around here were serious about their hair) and walked in, waiting for the shrieks.

"Girl, have a seat. We'll fix ya," one of the girls said. She wore an apron that made her look official.

About an hour and half later, I paid a price I never thought I would pay for someone to shampoo and dry my hair while gazing in the huge mirror behind the checkout desk.

They did it. They actually tamed the beast.

It looked even better than it had for the magazine shoot.

I was thinking maybe there *was* some fairy dust in all the products she used… It was long, sleek, but not flat, and it reflected the overhead lights like glass. I couldn't help but notice how my eyes looked even greener when it was like this. It was almost darker, richer.

So here I stood, in the center of the second NRR race, realizing I had a lot more girl in me than I imagined. My hair. The butterflies courtesy of being somewhere near Jace.

And for once? For once, it didn't seem like a bad thing. So what if I liked having my hair done, and so what if I totally looked for Jace in the crowd? I felt like I spent my whole life trying to make up for the fact that I was born a girl. I fought against stereotypes and tried to prove my worth.

All this time, I thought I was breaking down barriers. I thought I was strong and kickass. What if I wasn't? What if all I'd been doing was trying to make other people happy by being who they wanted me to be? By letting them push me down when I was trying to rise.

Why couldn't I be a driver with really good hair? Why couldn't I want to date and be treated like a woman even if I worked with a bunch of men?

I could be tough and soft.

I could, but then I'd make it harder on myself. Showing any kind of softness is sometimes like opening a door enough for someone to wedge their foot in to blow it open wide.

I spent all this time giving everyone the theoretical finger, but in some respects, I suppressed some of who I was to please them.

Wow. I felt fucked up.

All because I got my hair blow-dried and locked eyes with Jace.

Strange how sometimes the littlest things brought on the biggest change.

Was I changing? I wasn't sure.

We were standing there staring at each other when the reporter showed up. Hopper was with them, like he'd been leading the way. I focused on him, trying to dislodge Jace from the forefront of my mind. He was dressed in his standard dark-colored jeans that didn't look faded or worn like the kind Jace wore. His shirt was black, tight, and long-sleeved. The elbows had patches of leather, and there matching patches at his shoulders.

Hopper was lean, not a huge guy, but he had broad shoulders from which the rest of his body tapered in. The tight material of the shirt molded around those powerful shoulders, shaped biceps, and narrow, tight waist.

He was wearing a hat, a red one (it matched my sponsor logo), pulled low over the piercing lightness of his eyes. The dark-brown mop of hair on his head was covered, but the too-long ends curled up around the base of the hat at his neck, sticking out like he hadn't even bothered combing it.

His chin was pointed, but not overly so, and it seemed with the hat pulled over his eyes, all the emphasis went to his chin and the full lips currently pulled into concentration as he led the camera crew toward me.

Usually, reporters weren't allowed down in the pit, especially before the start of a race. But this was the NRR, and lots of things went here that didn't go in the pros.

"Joey G.?" the man said, a press pass clipped to the breast of his suit jacket. He gripped a mic in his hand and was trailed by a cameraman. The camera was fairly large. You'd think as advanced as we were with technology these days, he wouldn't be saddled with such a huge piece of equipment.

"Yes," I said, wondering what the heck he wanted with me.

"I'm John Lennox from KW3. I was wondering if you had a few minutes before the race starts to give us a short interview."

I glanced down at his badge again. It bore the logo of the national TV station that covered a lot of races. It was the first time any national station had approached me, including after some of the races I'd won that I thought were pretty big deals.

My eyes slid to Hopper, who was standing close by. He nodded encouragingly.

"Sure." I smiled at the reporter.

"Great!"

I had no idea what to expect. What he would ask, what would come out of my mouth. But this was what I was here for. This was what my father wanted.

And me, too. Didn't I want more attention? More equality on the track?

Now's your chance.

"Ready in three…" John said to the cameraman.

"Isn't it too loud right here?" I worried, glancing behind me where the pit crew was working and yelling to each other. Drew and Trent were beside his bright-yellow racecar as he prepared to strap in and drive onto the track.

"The background noise is authentic," he explained. "We can tone down the sound in the editing room."

"Sounds great." I agreed. "Can you give me a second?"

Hopper peered up from beneath the brim of his hat like I'd lost my damn mind. I grinned at him.

"Sure," John said, a little surprised.

I jogged over to the bright-yellow car, noting the small French fry decal on the corner of the dash. It had to be something Trent put there.

"Wanted to tell you to rip it up out there," I called over the noise. The breeze blew through my hair and whipped it around behind me.

"Thanks!" Drew called back, his white teeth flashing. The blond strands of his hair were wild, and there was a spark of excitement in his eyes.

He is totally high.

High on adrenaline, the crowd, and the race.

God, I loved that feeling.

I jumped forward and flung my arms around his neck for a quick hug. "Burn rubber," I whispered in his year. Okay, more like yelled over the roar.

He laughed. "Will do!"

I left him with Trent and jogged back to the reporter. It wasn't lost on me the camera was following my movements.

"The news broke in the new issue of *GearShark Magazine* recently that you have confirmed your crossover to the NRR from the pro racing division."

I nodded and practically heard Hopper shouting at me through his mind. Clearly, nodding was not acceptable for a TV interview. "Yes, that's right," I said. "I'll be finishing my season with the pro circuit this year, and next year, I'll be entering the NRR."

"You seem to be pretty close with NRR star Drew Forrester. Is that because you like him or because your father sponsors him?"

"It's because he's a damn good driver, which he's about to prove yet again today."

John nodded. He seemed a little disappointed he wasn't able to goad me with that question. I glanced at Hopper and noted the way he was looking at John.

I settled a little more firmly onto the ground and smiled for the camera.

"Will your father, Ron Gamble, also be sponsoring you in the crossover?"

"Yes, along with several other large sponsors." I had no idea who those were yet… I just prayed I got some.

"Will you still feel as warmly of Drew Forrester when he's your competition?"

"I don't think of him as my competition. I don't think of any other driver that way. They're my peers, and we all do the same job. I just hope to do it a little better." I smiled and ran my hand through my hair.

John blinked.

I smiled wider.

"Some people are speculating the reason you're crossing over is because of a brewing romance with another NRR driver."

I laughed even as my stomach tightened. "I'm pretty sure you know Drew is off the market."

"I'm not talking about Drew Forrester. I'm talking about Lorhaven, the man who appeared on the cover with you."

"I think if anyone read that article, they would know he's not fond of my crossover," I replied, short.

Figures everyone was jumping to that conclusion. Why hadn't I thought about this when we were doing the shoot? Because my hormones had taken over. Ugh.

"According to some of our sources and online reports, some of the pro drivers aren't too happy with it either."

That was news to me. I'd been so busy I didn't even pay attention to people's reaction to the feature story… Apparently, that hadn't been too smart.

"Well, considering they weren't too fond of having me in the division in the first place, I'm surprised they care I'm leaving."

"Do you think their reluctance to your pro career is because of your father?"

I thought about it for a second, glancing at Hopper. His icy-blue eyes held a warning.

Fuck that.

"Honestly? No. I don't think it would have mattered if I was a man. I think the fact that I'm a woman is what everyone in the pros hates so much."

Hopper sighed loudly.

I ignored him.

"Is that why you're crossing over? Your interview with the magazine seemed to be cut short before you could answer that," John said, glancing at the camera as if he were telling the viewers.

"It's definitely part of it."

"So what I'm hearing is you feel you're discriminated against as a woman in the sport of racing?"

"I know I am."

"Care to give us and the viewers at home an example?"

"Well, take this interview for instance." I pointed out. "The first couple things you asked were about my father and relationship status."

"I fail to see how that's discrimination."

I shrugged one shoulder. "Not technically, but I've watched you with countless interviews. My fellow male drivers are never asked about who their fathers are or what their relationship status is. You were effectively turning all the attention to the males in my life instead of asking me about being a female driver."

Hopper was staring daggers at me. *Behave yourself!* his expression said. The cameraman looked amused, and John seemed a little shell-shocked.

He cleared his throat. "So what's life like as a female racecar driver?"

I smiled brilliantly. "It's been pretty interesting lately."

He seemed afraid to ask me to elaborate. Admittedly, I think I was, too. "What do you hope to gain out of your crossover with the NRR?"

Here's your chance…

"More drive time, more fun, and less rules." He started to pull the mic away, so I quickly added, "And to spend more time with Drew Forrester, who is likely going to be the first NRR champion."

"So I guess we know who you're rooting for today?"

I laughed. "Of course."

"So one last time…" He paused. "Would you care to comment on your relationship with Lorhaven?"

Unbelievable.

"I don't really have a comment," I said. Then with a smile, I added, "Maybe if he ever asks me out, I will."

John Lennox turned in front of the camera and smiled into it. "There you have it, folks. An exclusive talk with Joey G., the first driver to give up the pros in favor of an unestablished division of racing."

I bristled. He made me sound so… fickle. Rage boiled up inside me. Made me sorry about all the things I hadn't said.

"And…" He continued, his voice cheeky.

Cheeky = something stupid was about to come out of his mouth.

"Sounds like it's a direct challenge for NRR driver Lorhaven to ask out this little firecracker."

Little firecracker?

The red light on the camera went off, and I dropped my smile. John turned back around. "Hey, thanks—"

My finger jabbed into his chest, and his words cut off. "Why were you trying to bait me?"

"I don't know what you mean?" he asked, like he was an idiot.

I rolled my eyes. "Right. Well, thank you for taking the time to interview me."

John and his gigantic camera-toting friend rushed off. Hopper scowled and started forward. I turned away, toward the race, which was already in progress.

The pit crew was standing at the ready with everything Drew might need front and center. I glanced up, squinting against the blinding summer sun at Trent, who was standing on top of the long tractor-trailer with Drew's name scrawled across the side, along with my father's business logo and the logo for the NRR. His shirt was bright yellow, Drew's name scrawled across his wide back, and there was a black baseball hat pulled over his face. Sunglasses wrapped around his eyes, and a headset rested over his ears with a mic at his lips.

His eyes never once left the track, more specifically, Drew's position. I watched as Trent's lips moved, and he smiled fast. Then he turned serious again and went back to the job he took very seriously.

Trent served as Drew's spotter, his eyes for the entire track, to warn him of blind spots, potential issues, and he also would be able to make sure the crew could burst into action with exactly what Drew needed when he pulled in.

I'd never been to this track before. It wasn't a pro raceway. It wouldn't pass all the codes and requirements to make it pro quality. It wasn't a perfect oval-shaped speedway like I was used to. The pro racing circuit was more about science and precision. We measured how much fuel we put in so as not to weigh the car down to heavily. The tire pressure was always exact, and we planned each pit stop to perfection, because one misstep could cost a lap, a lag, or basically a total loss. The variables in pro racing were more standard in a lot of ways… more controlled. Essentially, the drivers were all on equal footing.

This was not the case with the NRR.

This track was bigger, longer, and had a lot more curves, like a country backroad. No track was exactly the same. While the first race of the season was more standard because it was at my father's speedway, this one was much more exciting and showed the fans what the NRR was all about.

More variables. More unknowns. That was the NRR.

There was a section of gravel instead of asphalt the drivers had to transition on as they drove, and there was a dirt road that cut right through the center of the course that they had to drive across. The dust from the commotion filled the air and floated down the entire pit row.

In this division, it all came down to who was a better driver. It was more like off-road racing. It came down to which driver could maneuver the best, control his vehicle the best through the curves, the transitions of the road types… It was about more than speed.

I liked it. It added a lot more elements to the race. It added more drama and grit. And to me, it added more heart. It let a driver really show what they were made of. By the sound coming from the stands, it was a huge hit.

I loved the feel of race day. It was like being contaminated with a virus, except it wasn't a gross sickness; it was more of an epidemic you enjoyed sweeping through your body. The vibrations of the car, the tone of the roaring crowd. The cheers, the announcers, people yelling at every turn.

I didn't always get a side seat to a race. Most of the time, I was in the driver's seat where a lot of the sound was muffled by my own car.

But man, I loved both equally the same.

"Discrimination, Joey?" Hopper said, nudging me in the side. Guess I couldn't pretend he wasn't there forever.

I glanced at him out of the side of my eye. "Like you don't agree one hundred percent."

"Look, I know it hasn't been easy, but that interview could have gone a lot better."

I made a sound, still watching the race. Drew was in the lead, Jace was in fourth, but I knew just by looking, he'd have third after the next turn.

"Trust me; it could have been a lot worse," I murmured.

All the things I wanted to say, the words and emotions I sometimes felt were choking me, were all right there. Stuck.

Because I was afraid.

Afraid what would happen if I opened my mouth.

"And what's this about Lorhaven? That cover, J, it's been a PR nightmare. Everyone thinks you're crossing over because of some guy." He was clearly exasperated trying to manage me and keep my father happy as well.

I laughed.

It isn't just one guy. It's a whole lot of them.

"Look." I ripped my eyes off the track and laid them on Hopper. The bite in my attitude fell to the wayside when I saw the expression in his blue eyes. He wasn't trying to be a jerk. He was my friend. He was concerned, and he was also my manager. I knew Hopper cared about my career. He was the only one in the pro circles that treated me like I belonged there.

I sighed and looked back out, craning my neck in time to see Jace take third place. A feeling of pride filled me. They sped out of sight, and I started toward a big monitor where I could see the section of the track I couldn't view from here.

Hopper grabbed my wrist, not roughly, just enough to get my attention. I didn't pull away.

"I'm sorry, Jay," I said, using his first name, hoping to show him I really meant it, and shifted closer. "I just… He pissed me off in the beginning, trying to goad me. It's like they all want me to snap or something. So they can say I don't belong. And then the stuff with Jace…"

"Jace?"

"Lorhaven." I corrected.

"Was that a joke for the media about him asking you out, or were you serious?"

I rolled my eyes.

He made a sound. "You like him?"

I shrugged. "He's not as bad as I originally thought."

Hopper nodded and glanced over toward Jace's pit crew. His attention seemed to focus on something there and off of me. I started to turn to see if something was wrong, but he looked back. "Is that his brother?"

I glanced around at Arrow, who had a headset already over his blond head. "That's Justin Bieber." I joked.

Hopper grinned, but not the kind of smile that usually graced his face. This one was a little… fonder? Charmed? I stared at him, but he didn't notice; he looked back in Arrow's direction.

"Yeah, that's his brother. Arrow."

"He's a driver, right?" There was definite curiosity in his tone.

I nodded.

Hopper crossed his arms in front of him, a thoughtful look coming over him. "Is he any good?"

"I haven't seen him drive, but if he's anything like Jace, then yeah, probably."

"He looks young," he said, almost to himself.

I tilted my head. Was Hopper checking out Jace's brother? *Like checking him out?* Interesting.

He must have noticed my scrutiny, because he focused on me and cleared his throat. "Next time you're in front of a reporter, maybe be a little less…"

"Myself?" I finished for him.

He laughed. "More yourself. That wasn't you back there, Joey. That was the woman you want everyone to think you are."

Ouch. That hit its mark.

I mumbled a reply, then went off to watch the race.

Maybe I'd been lying to myself all along.

Maybe I wasn't fighting stereotypes… Maybe I was hiding behind them.

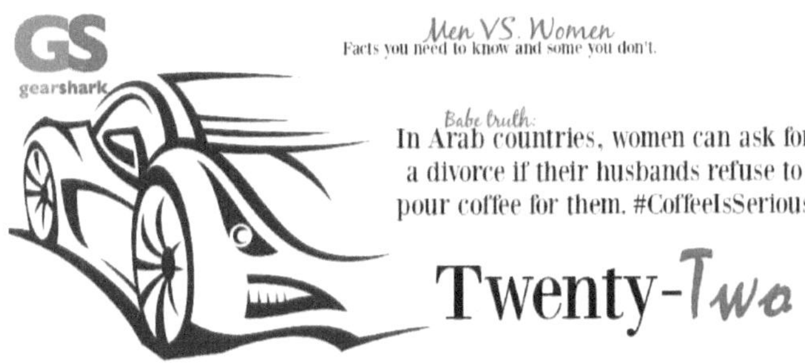

Twenty-Two

Lorhaven

My second, as I liked to call him, was Arrow.

You know the guy whose voice filled my ear when I was racing. The spotter. When I first started learning more about driving racecars (like besides on the street) the idea of anyone in my ear while I drove ticked me off.

I didn't need some prick standing on the sidelines with a shitty view, telling me how to drive. I was in control of my car, my race. Not him.

I learned it was necessary. Guess even the stubbornest of dogs could be taught new tricks.

Or maybe I just really wanted to win.

My manager and head of my pit crew on race days technically would fill this role. He was a good guy, we got along, and he was invested in my career, so I liked him.

But he wasn't my brother.

Trust and loyalty wasn't something I handed out on a silver platter to anyone who smiled. It would take a lot more than working with him for several months and even traveling to tracks, interviews, and work shit to get me to want him as my eyes.

I only trusted Arrow with that.

He might not be the most experienced spotter, but that kid knew how to keep his eyes open for trouble. He learned that the hard way.

He also knew a lot about driving. I'd taught him everything I knew.

For months and months after he first moved into the hangar, that's all we did. Drove, worked on cars, and drove some more. It was his sanctuary, his savior, and in a lot of ways, his revenge.

Because of that, he learned a lot fast, and he was a natural.

There was no one else I'd rather have on the top of my trailer today.

Currently, I was in third place.

I fucking hated third place. It was the worst place to me, and I wasn't going to end up placing here again. Third place was lame. It denoted I wasn't lousy enough to come in at a lower position, but not good enough to come in higher.

Second wasn't my choice (obviously), but it was a hell of a lot better than third. At least second spoke to talent, to the potential to overtake the top at any given moment.

Basically, third place meant I, as a driver, was mediocre.

Fuck mediocre.

We were driving down the clock, there was only one lap left, and I was riding number two's bumper like a heat rash in summer. He was gonna have to powder himself for a month after this shit was done because I was not backing down.

Not too far up was the gravel section. I could use it to my advantage. I spent one entire summer a couple years back driving on a gravel section of my turf near a lake no one ever really went to.

I was confident I could take it at an even faster speed than I had even just the lap before. Some of the guys were backing off the gas when we hit the section. I understood why; even I didn't want to rip up my tires.

It was risky this close to the finish line. If I blew a tire (and they were already getting worn from this race), I wouldn't be in second. I wouldn't even be in third.

I glanced up ahead, my foot twitchy on the gas. Sometimes even when I debated a move, when I knew it was dangerous or could even backfire, my gut already knew.

I felt the decision long before I made it. It made my foot happy on the gas.

Clearly, I already knew what I was going to do today. Sometimes you just had to go balls to the wall and do it.

Forrester was holding steady in the top spot. I hated looking at that guy's taillights. I hated even more knowing he was a damn good driver.

Maybe that's why coming in second wasn't as fucking embarrassing as it should be.

I'd never admit it out loud, but I wouldn't be opposed to seeing Forrester win the first NRR championship. That didn't mean I was going to hand it to him, though. Hell no. If I got the chance to beat him, I would take it.

"I'm gonna take the gravel at full speed, try and lap this tool on the inside and take up number two," I said into the piece to Arrow. "How's my blind spots looking?"

"That's a pretty ballsy move," came his reply.

Only it wasn't my brother's voice.

It was Josie.

My fingers tightened around the steering wheel, learning the curve of it even more precisely than ever before. I kept my eyes trained on the road even though they sorely wanted to seek her out.

Just the sound of her voice was like premium octane injected right into my heart. Even though I was starting to run a little low on adrenaline and energy stores, she was like a shot of epinephrine right to my chest.

"You got this, though. He's getting antsy with you so far up his ass." She went on like she had no idea what she did to me.

"Josie," I said, putting the pressure on the guy in front of me. "I like the sound of your voice in my ear when I drive this fast."

"Had to pry the headset off the Bieb's head," she quipped.

I laughed.

"All right, settle in." Her voice changed, became a little more clipped, more serious. "I've been watching him a while. Like I said, he's antsy. I don't like the looks of his back passenger tire. He's gonna have to slow so it doesn't blow. But you need to be on guard in case it does. He'll take you out, too, with you so tight against him."

"Roger," I said, focusing back in.

She wasn't a distraction, maybe because I couldn't see her in spite of knowing she was watching me. Her instructions were clear, concise, and put me in a steady state.

I trusted her.

With my life.

Not dramatic. That's what this was sometimes, life and death. Right now, if I took a hit at this speed, my time could be over.

"Coming in hot on your blind spot, on the outside," she warned. "Glide over, smooth, just a couple inches."

I moved.

"That's it." I could hear the grin in her voice. "Way to put him in his place."

"Gravel coming."

"He's gonna swing out a little. He's gonna have to because of that tire. He can't drift through gravel, and he can't take that turn on the inside so sharp."

I nodded, understanding her thought process.

"Guy behind you is a non-issue," she said. "Get ready to punch it. I'll tell you when the tool starts to edge over."

I grinned even as I sat up a little straighter. If my heart pumped any faster, I'd need meds to bring it back into normal range. Doing this with her, taking this gravel, and trusting her to tell me when to punch it was like foreplay to me.

Hot fucking foreplay.

Her breathing increased. I felt her focus. My front tires met gravel.

"Go, now!" she yelled.

I pushed the gas in so much my back tires made a squealing sound on the pavement just before they transitioned into gravel. The rock spun up, and the sounds of it hitting my car were like the sound of rain on a window at night.

Chaotic but soothing at the same time.

"Inside," she demanded just as my hands starting pulling the car inward.

"Shit!" she cursed. "He's not moving over fast enough."

"I got this," I said.

"Move over, motherfucker!" she yelled.

I liked her sinful mouth. Especially when she yelled at my competition.

I glided into the inside, farther in than I wanted. My car was going almost at top speed as the gravel curved with the road slightly.

I took a page out of Forrester's book.

I didn't curve with it.

My two side tires stayed in the gravel, practically spraying the guy in second place as I pulled up beside him. The two tires on my side hit dirt.

It actually kinda helped with traction.

I manhandled the wheel and forced my car in the place I wanted. The driver beside me backed off just an inch, but an inch was all I needed.

"Pull it up!" Josie yelled. "Take him over."

My back end fished a little. My stomach jerked.

"You got this, Jace," Josie whispered in my ear.

I hit the gas.

Fired ahead.

Lapped up my competition and swerved into position behind Forrester's bright-yellow bumper.

Josie whooped with glee, and I could hear Arrow shouting nearby.

"Fuck yeah!" I roared but tried not to think about it too much. I couldn't celebrate yet. I still had to maintain for the rest of this lap.

"All right, his tire's toast. The guy who tried to pass you is coming up on your inside." Josie warned.

I swerved in a little, holding him back.

I wasn't giving this shit up. He'd have to shove me off the road.

Which, frankly, wasn't out of the realm of possibilities.

Josie's thoughts seemed to be in line with mine. "Put some distance between you."

"On it." I did. I could practically hear my tires groan.

"These tires are done," I bitched.

"Just focus," she said, calm. "I can see them. They'll hold."

She was right. They held. They carried me all the way over the finish line, right behind Forrester.

Second place.

Fucking right.

In my ear, Josie and Arrow were yelling and cheering. She laughed at something he said, but I couldn't make it out.

I grinned, elation making me almost dizzy.

"I'm handing it back over to your commander," she said, a smile in her voice.

"Hey, Josie," I said as I slowed.

"Jace?"

"Don't go too far when this is over. I'm coming for you."

"I'll make sure I'm easy to find."

Slow enough now I was able to glance over toward my pit, dust rose up in the air, creating a veil in the sky. But there she was. Standing on top of my trailer, my brother right beside her.

Dark strands of long hair flowed out behind her like a flag waving in the wind.

Now that was a woman. One who could drive as well as she could ride… (my cock, that is).

Yeah, I would definitely be coming for her tonight.

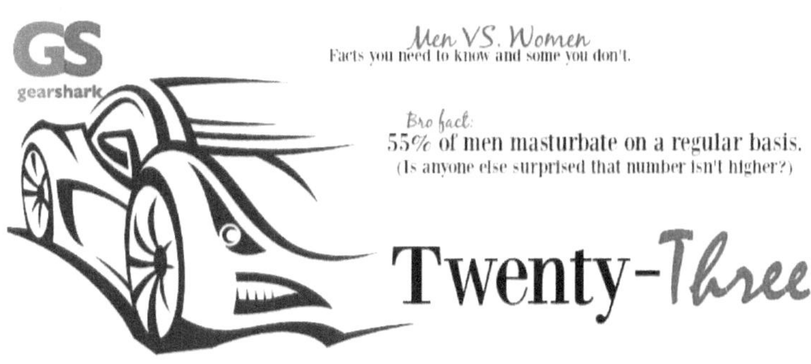

Joey

I'm coming for you.

So ominous. So delicious.

The promise Jace whispered into my ear thumped just beneath my skin like a second pulse. I felt it there hammering away beneath my outer layer, but it wasn't annoying. I reveled in it.

By the time he made good on his promise and found me, I'd be so worked up I wouldn't need foreplay. God, I wanted him. I wanted the overwhelming size of his unbending cock pounding inside me.

I wanted his hands in my hair, his lips on mine, and more than anything, I wanted to hear him say my name about a thousand times before the night was done.

By the time the race was wrapped, the equipment and trucks were packed, all the fans had left the stands. I knew some would be loitering out in the parking lot; some with special pit passes still milled around. But this place was about eighty percent emptier than it had been before.

The scent of burning fuel, hot rubber, and exhaust still lingered. Dust still drifted across the wide-open spaces to occasionally hit me in the face, and the sound of laughter still echoed.

Drew was celebrating his second victory. He was now two for two. My father was going to be happier than a pig with organic feed and fresh mud to roll in. Everybody in the pit was sky high, and most of us were hoarse from cheering so loud when they handed Drew his shining trophy.

Right up on the podium, Jace stood beside him, his grin less smirky and his eyes less broody than I was used to, but he still made my heart race.

The longer hair on top of his head was all mussed and crazy, his face was streaked with sweat and dust, but his smile was genuine. The way he and Drew shook hands and posed for pictures was honest.

After a while, we made it back to the hotel, this great place that had a lodge feel. Even though it was summer, the huge stone fireplace crackled with a fire at the main entrance. I was pretty sure they were running the AC and the fireplace at once, but I understood why. The ambience of the glowing fire was a wonderfully welcome sight.

All the floors in this hotel were hardwood, something I didn't see much. Usually, it was carpet or tile, but the distressed wood floors were perfect for this place. Everything was neutral, done in warm tones with pops of red.

My suite was on the same floor as Drew and Trent's. We rode up the elevator together and parted ways down the hall.

"We're gonna stay in," Drew told me when I stopped at my door. "Order some room service, chill."

I nodded. "Of course. You're probably both exhausted. I'm probably going to do the same."

They both looked a little guilty standing there, feeling like jerks for leaving me on my own. I thought they were cute and obviously still so wrapped up in each other they still needed alone time. "Go." I shooed them off. "Have some guy time." I winked. "We'll have breakfast in the morning."

"Not too early," Drew grumped.

Trent laughed.

I nodded sagely. "Just knock on your way down, and I'll meet you in the dining room."

I was mildly surprised when Trent stepped forward, kissed me on the top of the head, and whispered, "Good luck."

I glanced up at him, and he winked.

He couldn't possibly know what Jace said. He couldn't conceivably know I was waiting for him.

Could he?

I watched the guys walk to their room. Drew opened the door, let out a long sigh, and went in. Trent stopped in their doorway, glanced back, and chuckled.

He totally knew.

Perceptive or psychic?

I made a face. He laughed again, then disappeared inside the room.

Inside my own room, I glanced around, noting the large king-size bed in the center. It was done all in white with a red throw at the foot of the bed. The room was pretty much standard for any hotel, just with a lodge feel.

I glanced over at the room service menu, my stomach growling. But my skin felt gritty with a fine layer of dust. Shower first, food after.

With my shower shoes in hand I went into the bathroom, kicked off my race day clothes, and slid on the shoes. Once the water for the shower was on, I brushed out my hair, surprised it was still straight and sleek. I wasn't about to wash away the style. Instead, I wrapped my hair in a small towel and secured it with a clip from my bag.

The water felt good, the soap even better. I loved the track, but it was dirty, and I didn't love feeling grimy. It didn't take long to clean up, especially since I didn't have to complete the task of my hair. Soon as I was toweled off, I smoothed some freshly scented body lotion into my skin and completed the rest of my routine.

After brushing out my hair a second time, I dug for some clothes. After putting on a white bra with a sheer lace band beneath the cups (that I thought accentuated the way my waist curved in) and a matching pair of panties, I chose a pair of dark cut-off jean shorts and a silky dark-green top with cap sleeves.

Just as I finished, his text came through.

The second I typed out my room number and hit send, I tossed the phone down like a teenager and rushed into the bathroom. It only took a few seconds to get some BB cream on my fingertips and rub it into my face.

BB cream = a fancy tinted moisturizer.

I wasn't big on makeup, but I liked to look nice and put together. The BB cream gave me a natural glow and just evened out my skin tone. When that was done, I quickly dusted on a bit of bronzer and some lip balm that tinted my lips pink because it was cherry flavored.

When the knock echoed through the room, the stuff fell out of my hand, landing in front of me. Quickly, I capped it, glanced up to make sure everything was on right (hey, I barely looked when I put it on!), and then fled the small bathroom.

Jace was leaning in the doorjamb when I pulled it open. The movement seemed to bring a burst of his scent right at me. My fingers tightened on the handle, holding me steady as the rest of me took in all of him.

Loose jeans that didn't seem very committed to staying high up on his hips, a black T-shirt pulled taut across his chest, flirting with the waistband of those teasing jeans, as if it, too, were in on the game of maybe concealing his skin from my sight.

The jacket he wore wasn't black, but white with black seaming and two black bands around his left sleeve. The cuffs were rolled up enough that his forearms were showing, and black Converse covered his feet.

Clearly, he was also fresh from the shower. Not only did he smell good, but his hair was still damp, as if he'd rubbed a towel over the wet strands at the top and brushed them back, away from his face.

I noticed then the way we were just now. Standing in a doorway, eyes roaming the other like we were completely new to each other.

It felt that way… like I hadn't already been thoroughly sexed up by him. Like I was waiting for that first touch.

"Josie," he finally said, his voice deep like the smoothest liquor, his eyes hungry like a wolf.

"Jace," I replied.

We had a thing with each other's names. Probably because with them came exclusivity. Names weren't supposed to be exclusive; they were attached to us at our first breath as identifiers. A name was a person's calling card, a signature that went beyond scrawling a line of letters on a page.

It was different with Josie and Jace. It wasn't just the names that were exclusive; it was the people we were when we used them. Like letting someone into a place no one was ever granted access. It was the possibility that the person standing right here in front of me saw me better than anyone else.

Whenever my name slid off his tongue, I felt as if chains were being unshackled from my wrists. I felt the things no one knew I hid became transparent, leaving the only thing for him to see was all of it.

All of me.

He pushed off the doorjamb, his movements almost lazy. One hand curled around my side. Through the silky fabric of my shirt, his fingers pressed as he stepped forward, bringing me in.

All at once, his body brushed close, his mouth teasing mine. Thoroughly, his lips rubbed over me, the flavor of my cherry gloss exploding between us, adding yet another layer to the already satisfying kiss. I sighed into him, and he smiled but didn't stop kissing, instead increasing the pressure times two. My hand grabbed his hip, my finger sliding through the belt loop on the side. The jeans stopped teasing and slid down so my thumb could caress the newly exposed skin at his hip.

Jace cupped my face, shifting even closer, the pads of his thumbs pressed beneath my cheek bones, right in the hollow space, and coaxed my jaw to open.

Fluidly, his tongue invaded, massaged against mine, and everything went fuzzy.

My free hand fisted in the front of his worn T-shirt while we stood halfway in my room and halfway in the hall and made out like two teenagers who were victims of their hormones.

But, *oh*, I wasn't Jace's victim. I was an instigator. And judging by the way he kissed me just now, I would also call myself a victor.

My skin felt flushed when he lifted his head. I couldn't even be upset when he shifted back an inch because I loved just watching his body move. My hand loosened against his shirt and slid down to fall away. He caught it, linked our fingers together, and gave my arm a tug.

"C'mon," he said, motioning to the hallway. "Let's go."

I felt my nose wrinkle. "Go where?"

"You'll see."

I started forward, only to stop and turn back. "Wait."

"You don't need any of that shit girls carry around. I got cash."

My stomach flipped a little. Such a stupid, silly thing to stumble over. I mean, really. It was hardly the first time anyone had offered to pay for a date.

Wait. Is this a date? Oh, man, I should have made more effort with my face.

This didn't feel like that. It didn't feel like impatience for him to get me moving either. It was like he was taking on responsibility for me tonight. Like he would make sure we had everything we needed wherever we went as long as I stayed at his side.

The feeling weighed a lot. But not in a too heavy to move kind of way. In a grounding kind of way, like maybe I'd found a place I belonged.

Funny, I never knew I was searching.

I didn't let go of his hand. Instead, I tugged back, trying to bring him with me.

"I need shoes."

He glanced down. I wiggled my toes at him, and he chuckled.

"Those look like shoes." He pointed out, still looking at the black flip-flops I wore in the shower.

"Yeah, for in the shower."

"You have shoes for the shower?" He wondered, allowing me to pull him back inside the room just a foot.

"I've seen pictures of toe fungus." I shuddered, kicking them off only to slip my feet into another pair of flip-flops. These were a little more stylish, though, with brown leather soles and straps. In the center was a dark-green gem I thought looked pretty when the light caught it.

I reached for my phone, still on the bed where I threw it.

He made a sound. "Shoes, yes. Phone, no."

"No phone?" I gasped like I was outraged.

His white teeth flashed. They were perfectly straight, like mine. His father probably insisted on braces, something we had in common.

"No phone," he echoed.

I left it there and stepped to his side, I noticed the way his fingers enclosed mine just a little tighter as I snatched the room key off the dresser and shoved it in my back pocket.

Behind us, the door closed with an audible latch, and together we walked down the hall. Such a simple thing, but it seemed just having him next to me inspired all sorts of excitement.

Balmy was the best word I could use to describe the air when we stepped out of the simultaneously AC and fire-crackling lobby. The sky was dark, stars lit up the sky, and a calmness that only darkness could bring shrouded the evening.

We walked without saying a word into the lot where it didn't take long for me to find his Lotus.

"You brought your car?" Mild surprise tinged in my voice.

"They drove it out here for me on the trailer with my racecar."

"Didn't they already pack up and go?" I questioned.

"My driver leaves tomorrow. I have some press to do, and they wanted the racecar for the shoot."

I tried not to feel a little jealous he had yet another big press opportunity. It wasn't his fault, if given the opportunity I would take it as well. Besides, he had to do this. It was his job. Brickstone sank a lot of money into him, I knew. Not only with the car, the travel, entry fees, etc., but with whatever he was getting paid. I was certain the powers that be behind his deal were insistent they get their money's worth.

"I'm sure everyone in your camp was beyond thrilled with your race today." I poked him in the ribs.

He grinned and opened up the passenger door. I angled so I was between him and the seat, the door in front of us so I was boxed in on almost every side.

"It was a good call to get," he allowed but ruined his humble speak with a huge grin.

"You drove really great today," I said. It didn't bother me to compliment other drivers, especially when they deserved it. I guess I'd always hoped they would do the same for me.

The only one who ever had so far was Drew.

"We make a pretty good team," he murmured, stroking his palm against the side of my head. "I like your hair like this."

"Yeah?" I murmured, pushing my head into his hand.

He nodded and leaned close. I rose up to meet him, but he suddenly pulled away and smiled. "Get in."

I blinked, and he was halfway around the hood toward the driver's side. Laughter trailed behind him like he knew what he'd done.

I slipped into the passenger seat and forgot all about his teasing ways. The interior of his Lotus was just as incredible as the body. Black leather with red accents, spotless dash, polished chrome, and sleek… so sleek.

It was small in here, only a two seater. The back window was close behind my head. There was a hard top on this one. A lot of them came with only soft covers, but this was clearly more of a special order car.

I closed my eyes, thinking about how it would be to pull off the piece of roof and let the balmy air brush over my skin.

Beneath my legs, the seat was buttery soft. I was no stranger to luxury, but this wasn't just luxurious. It was sexy.

The driver's seat was all the way back, allowing for Jace's long, lean legs. Instead of looking too big for such a compact car, he just appeared to really own it. The car hugged around him like a lover, like it, too, wanted to be as close to him as it could get.

I didn't pay attention to where we were going. I watched him drive. I watched the way his hand gripped the stick in the center, and I was turned on by his sure and steady movements. The car was responsive, but he seemed to know exactly how to drive it. The performance it gave was beautiful, and it showed me a new appreciation for the way he drove.

"You're staring," he said, not taking his eyes off the road.

"You drive the car the way you do a lover," I said.

"Cars and lovers are a lot alike."

Shivers raced up my spine. "How so?"

"Because you have to be gentle yet in control. You have to be sure but willing to let the it do some of the work." He glanced over at me, his eyes darker than the night sky. "Because the better you treat it, the better you get treated in return."

The words coupled with the sound of his voice reached inside my chest and squeezed. "All this time, I thought you were just an asshole." I smiled.

He winked, turning back to the road. "That's what I *let* you think."

"How many people do you *let think* you're an ass?" I asked, rueful.

He made a rude sound, and I laughed.

That meant everyone.

"We're here," he said a few minutes later.

I glanced up as the Lotus slowed and turned into the raceway where we'd just spent the entire day. "What are we doing here?" I asked.

"Nothing better than a track all to yourself." His crooked smile was nearly my undoing. It was playful, but it did things to me. Things like loosen my lower belly and start an ache in my breasts.

God, everything about him is foreplay to me. Even his car.

"It's closed up," I said, trying to ignore the fact I was horny. I was worse than a guy. Geez.

But when I was sitting so close to someone who literally embodied pleasure, it was hard not to think about sex.

"I talked to someone before I left. He did me a favor." He eased the car through a tunnel, stopping at its closed gate at the end. Without a word, Jace got out, punched in a code, and the gate swung inward.

Flashing a smile that was almost as bright as his headlights, he jogged back to the driver's seat and we drove into the raceway. I turned back to see the gate closing on its own behind us. Must have been on a timer.

"He just let you in here." I scoffed, my stare glued to the empty, wide track.

"I promised him I'd behave."

I laughed. He couldn't even make that sound innocent. What a crock. Jace was far from innocent. "So you paid him," I surmised.

Beneath the fabric jacket, his shoulders shrugged. "Money talks."

Yes, it did.

"Pretty cool, huh?" he said, his voice quieter, almost reverent. His gaze was locked out the windshield. I watched him take it all in, as if he were seeing the place for the first time.

When I didn't answer, he looked over at me. Through the glowing dash and dim lighting, our eyes locked. He continued to drive along the track, but he looked only at me.

My chest felt tight when he stared at me this way. Trying to find the words to express exactly what it was about his eyes or the emotion burning a hole inside my chest was impossible.

I couldn't describe something I'd never felt.

It was like trying to name a color I'd never seen before.

All I really knew was I sincerely hoped whatever this feeling was never went away.

Jace made a small sound, releasing it into the close space around us as the car slowed, ultimately coming to a complete stop.

With the engine purring, one hand dropped off the wheel into his lap as his torso rotated to me. "Wanna drive?"

"You're gonna let me drive?" I stuttered, still trying to exist in a world with so much emotion and at the same time carry on a conversation.

I wasn't sure I liked this. You know, being the one who was a little more interested.

Don't act like you don't know what I mean. How sometimes people say in every couple there is always one that loves the other just a little bit more…

That was me. I wasn't in love, but I definitely was in like. And *totally* in lust. It was very apparent I had it worse than he did. After all, I was the only one struggling to string a sentence together.

He was over there driving a car, looking at me, *and* speaking.

The big, fat jerk.

"You have a total lady boner for my car." He smirked.

"Really?" I scoffed. "A lady boner? Did you learn that in third grade?"

"Probably." He snickered.

Oh my God, he's cute, too.

I am totally going to be the one who loves more.

Oh shit. Did I just think about love?

I grappled for the handle, pulled it swiftly, and ejected myself from the car. The pleasant night air brushed over my burning skin, and I heaved a grateful sigh. The door closed softly behind me, and I leaned against it, listening to the smooth hum of the engine.

"Hey," Jace said from close by.

I glanced over. He was standing beside the hood. The white on his jacket practically made him glow.

"I thought you were coming over for sex," I blurted out.

Way to cut to the chase, Joey!

He laughed. Somehow, the sound relaxed me. "Oh, there's gonna be sex," he drawled, like it was already written in stone.

I kinda liked his confidence.

"And I'm not talking about sexy as hell on the hood of a car sex, either." He went on, moving closer. "I'm talking the kind that takes all night. The kind where even after I have to let go tomorrow to get on a plane, whenever the air around you shifts, you'll still smell me on your skin."

I swallowed so hard I heard it. My tongue jutted out to wet my lips. "Then why are we here?" I asked.

I wasn't the kind of girl to play head games. I didn't like to wonder, and holy hell, was I wondering. He was turning me into a giant tight knot that would never be untied, and if by some chance I was able to untie myself, I would never be the same again.

He moved in, dropped both his hands on the side of the car, caging me between them. "Because, Josie, it won't be enough."

I sucked in a breath for him to say more. The sound of his voice hummed across my skin, making me vibrate. "It won't?" I asked, breathless.

He shook his head, eyes never once leaving mine. "I don't want just sex from you, Josie. I want more. I want your time, your laugh, your dirty, filthy mouth. I want to know you in ways no one else does."

"Well, if that's what you want…" I tried to joke, but my voice literally shook.

"Know what else I want?" he whispered.

I shook my head.

"For you to want the same."

Oh, I wanted it all right.

"Do you want it, Josie?"

My voice didn't shake. Not even a little. "Yes."

"Good. Now get that sexy, round ass of yours in the driver's seat." He stepped back, giving me space to get by.

I held up a finger. "First, we need to get one thing straight."

His impossibly dark brow arched up the side of his forehead. "Demanding."

"Me?" I rolled my eyes. "You're the one who just laid claim to like everything."

He shoved me back against the car, pinning me with his tight body. "Oh no," he growled. "I don't own you, baby. Some things are just too beautiful to be tamed. I'm gonna be a choice, one you make every single day."

"You seem awfully sure of that," I said, dry.

He leaned in to whisper, his lips brushing against my ear and tickling my hair. "I already see it in your eyes."

"Be careful," I warned, turning my head away to stare off to the side. "The untamed are hard to keep up with."

"I'm not worried." He mused. "I'm pretty good with speed."

A rude sound vibrated my neck, and he laughed. Jace stepped back, poking me in the stomach. "Tell me."

"If you ever say lady boner again, I'll shave off one of your eyebrows when you're sleeping."

His smile was awfully large. He must not think I was serious.

I was totally serious.

"And don't tell me what to do," I snapped, pushing him away to sashay my way around to the driver's side.

The sound of his rich chuckle cut off when he closed himself in the passenger side of the Lotus.

I blew out a breath.

Inside, I was a quivering mass of melted feelings. He wanted to be my choice. Words Trent said to me echoed through my head.

We don't get a choice. Love chooses for us.

Love chose for me.

Love chose Jace.

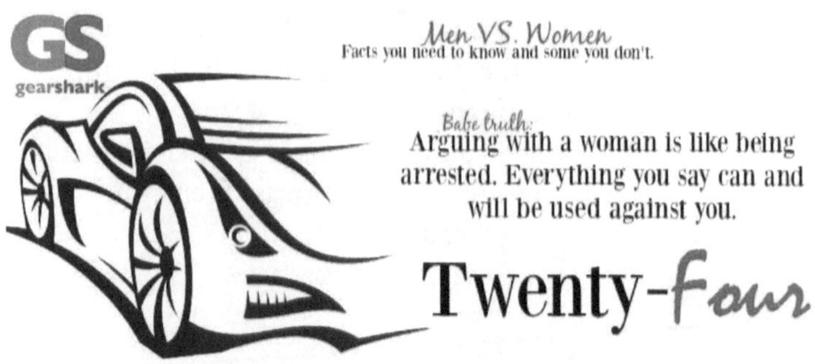

Lorhaven

I was in trouble with this one.

Deep, deep trouble.

She was bossy, stubborn, independent and threatened my eyebrow. Just one of them… I wasn't exaggerating when I called her untamed.

She felt like an earthquake, shaking up everything inside me.

I didn't want ordinary. No woman who was could hold my attention. Josie challenged me in ways I'd never been challenged before.

The way she looked sitting behind the wheel of the Lotus was the shit wet dreams were made of. She could be a pinup with all those curves and, dark, glossy hair.

"Wait," I said, putting my hand over hers when she gripped the stick shift in the center.

"I haven't even hit the gas, and already you changed your mind?" She scowled. "Too bad. No takebacks."

I laughed. "Did you learn that in the third grade?"

"Duh." She scoffed and rolled her moss-colored eyes.

"How about a little night air?" I glanced up at the roof.

The spark of interest in her eyes was all the answer I needed. After a minute, I pulled off the special hardtop over our heads and lifted it carefully down. Cautiously, I placed it on the ground, near the retaining wall of the track.

"Too slow!" she called when I turned back and started to pull away.

"Hey!" I shouted and sprinted forward and jumped in.

Her laughter floated behind. She'd likely tangled in her hair as she sped off and summer air flooded the interior of the Lotus.

She wasn't shy with the gas pedal. In fact, it made me jealous the way she seemed to give it all her attention. My car flew over the track, down the straightaway, and she released a yell up into the air.

Her hands curled around the steering wheel lovingly, like even though she drove like a bat out of hell, her touch was gentle. The respect she had for the car and the road itself impressed me. I felt out of control sitting here in the passenger seat as the car I normally only ever drove barreled through the dark.

Maybe it was the wind or the way she looked driving with sparkling eyes, wild hair, and a big, toothy grin that made me feel so free.

Or maybe it was the loss of control in the moment. The fact that I was pretty much at her whim. I trusted her more than almost anyone. I didn't know how that came to be, but here it was.

I could totally sink into the leather and enjoy the way the night blurred by, how everything was out of focus except for the way she looked.

Being so tightly wound and in control every second of every single day was exhausting. Hardly ever was I the one to sit back and let someone else drive.

Drive my car. Drive my heart.

She downshifted, slowing as we came toward the gravel patch, then spun the wheel and whipped around, only to punch the gas again and tear off in the opposite direction.

I laughed.

"I love this car!" she cried.

"Go for it," I yelled over the engine and the wind.

She glanced over. I caught one second of her questioning eyes before her hair took away my view. I leaned over, pinned back the defiant strands, and said, "Open her up."

That's all she needed to hear. The Lotus shot forward as she pushed the engine to its highest speed. When a curve came, she took it, smooth as butter. Sweet as cream.

Eventually, she slowed, the churning air settled to what felt like a gentle breeze, and one of her hands fell off the wheel and reached for the stick shift.

I didn't think twice about pressing my palm to the back of her hand and slipping my fingers in hers. We rode in comfortable silence. Every so often, she'd look up into the sky where stars painted shapes on a black canvas.

I was surprised when the Lotus rolled to a stop. She turned to me, her eyes sparkling with happiness, her nose pink, and her hair looking like there was a nest of birds living in it.

"Your turn," she said.

Surging forward, I took her mouth. A small sound of surprise floated into mine, and I swallowed it as I ravaged her mouth. In my ear, my pulse pounded, but I didn't stop kissing her. I couldn't. Using my tongue, I stroked her over and over again. Using my lips, I nibbled on her mouth, and using my hands, I tried to show her just how much I coveted her presence.

"Wow," she whispered when I pulled back enough for us to breathe.

I kissed her again.

Her eyes were glassy when I came around to the driver's door and opened it for her to stand. I chuckled, reached for her, and helped her out.

She didn't need my help, but she had it anyway.

Her skin was soft, not like silk, but velvet. Her wrist was delicate. I could easily wrap my forefinger and thumb all the way around.

"I thought I was going to have to pry you out of the driver's seat," I murmured. "I definitely thought you'd want to drive half the night."

One shoulder shrugged. "Maybe I missed the sound of your voice."

My heart skipped. There was beauty in the untamed, especially when something so wild approached you.

Keeping hold of her wrist, I leaned inside my car, hit the button, and shut it off. Since no one was here with us, I left the key fob inside and closed the door gently as I tugged her along with me.

At the retaining wall, I offered her my hands to hoist her up. Abandoning both her flip-flops to the pavement, her bare foot hit my palms. It didn't take much effort to hoist her because she helped. Once she was up over the wall, I took a running leap and hoisted myself up as well.

We climbed over the railings to the seating and climbed the concrete steps between the wide rows to one that was high and overlooked the spacious, still track.

There were lights lit up around the track, sort of like streetlights that stayed on when it was dark, for added security. There were probably cameras, too, but I wasn't worried about those. The only thing those deterred me from was stripping her naked here and now.

I might insist I didn't own Josie, but no one else was allowed to see her naked.

Only me.

For always.

I sat in a seat in the middle of a long row, stretching my legs out in front of me as much as I could. Josie sat beside me, angling her body toward mine, lifting her legs and draping them over my extended legs.

Her feet were still bare, her toenails painted a dark shade. I couldn't tell which because of the dark sky.

"It's peaceful here," she mused, looking up at the star-splattered sky.

"You seem surprised."

"I guess I'm just used to places like this filled with unending chaos."

"You like it?" I turned my head toward her, studying her profile as she studied the sky.

The side of her mouth curved up. "I do."

We lapsed into silence, but it wasn't uncomfortable. Part of me wanted to talk. Just like I told her, I wanted to know her more. I wanted more than just her body.

I wasn't too good at talking. I didn't do it much. Only ever with Arrow, and that seemed easier somehow.

"You drove really great today," Josie told me.

I smiled. "You make a pretty good spotter."

She laughed. "I prefer driving."

"I didn't know you'd be here today."

Her shoulders moved beneath her top. "I don't have a race 'til next weekend. I'll be at all the NRR races I can."

"'Cause you're crossing over," I stated. I knew that was the reason. Still, I couldn't help but want her to say she'd been here for me.

"Yeah." Her voice took on a little different tone with that one word. Kind of guarded.

"I saw you being interviewed right before I hit the track."

She grimaced. "I'm not very good with reporters."

I scoffed, amused. "No?"

Her chin came down; green eyes sought me out. "They asked about you."

That was surprising. "Me?"

"There's a rumor going around I'm crossing over because you and I are involved."

"No shit?" I laughed.

My teeth were still on full display when she gave me a withering look. Apparently, this didn't please her the way it did me.

"When he was done asking about you, he asked about Drew and my father." Her voice was bitter.

Ah. "He didn't ask about your racing."

Josie made a rude sound. "He did when I called him on it."

I laughed again. *That's my girl, giving 'em all hell.*

The thought stopped me in my tracks.

"So, uh…" I started, trying to recover. "What did you say?"

"I copped out."

That surprised me. I forgot all about my private thoughts. "You copped out?"

"I gave some lame, generic answer."

I reached for her hand. "Nothing about you is lame, Josie."

She was silent a long moment. I watched her stare down at our joined hands. There was a storm inside her, one that raged on, constantly trying to drown her. I'd seen it before, and I saw it right now.

"Has anyone asked you about the magazine article?" she asked. "About us?"

Dad did. I shook my head. "No."

"Toward the end of the interview, I said something you should probably know about." The regret in her voice made me kinda excited.

"Oh yeah?" I squeezed her hand.

She rolled her eyes and actually blushed.

"Did you tell them we were dating, Josie? Don't worry. I'll go along with it so I don't embarrass you."

She yanked her hand away and punched me in the stomach.

"Ow!" I howled.

"I didn't tell them we were dating, you idiot."

I bent over my knees like it hurt, but really, I just was laughing. I loved it when she got all feisty.

"I tried to make a joke," she said, not even concerned for my could-be injury. Hell, she wasn't even looking at me.

It made me laugh harder.

"After the disastrous interview, I thought it might help," she muttered. "Wrong."

"What'd you say?" I sat back, reining in the laughter.

"He asked me again to comment on our relationship," she said. "So I said I don't have a comment, but I might if he asks me out."

I felt like I'd just won a marathon. Like a total victor. "He being me."

"Smug is not a good look on you."

I sat back, propping my feet on the chair in front of me. "You want me to ask you out."

"I do not."

I chuckled.

A frustrated sound pierced the space around us, and she shot up to presumably march away. My feet hit the ground, and I caught her arm, pulling her back until she stumbled into my lap.

"Where do you think you're going?" I whispered.

"Leaving."

"Tell me about the interview." I implored. "Why was it disastrous?"

"It's like people don't know how to react to a woman in racing. He tried to goad me. He wanted me to act unprofessional or something."

"It's hard, huh?" I said, nudging her rigid body.

She sighed, and all her weight shifted into me. I leaned back, adjusting my position to make more room in my lap. Her legs draped over the armrest and into her now vacant seat.

"Sometimes it kinda sucks," she whispered.

Her head hit my shoulder. The arm loosely looped around her back tightened, holding her a little closer. My free hand settled over her bare knee, sliding down the top of her thigh. I tucked my fingers between her legs and left them there.

"You have any friends in the pros?" I asked. Since she was so close, I didn't have to speak very loud.

"Just Hopper."

"Your manager?"

"Yeah, technically, he still works for the pro division, but I think he's going to come with me when I crossover."

"Are any of the drivers nice to you, Josie?"

"No." After she realized she spoke out loud, a new tension coiled beneath her skin. I rubbed slow circles over her side. "I can handle it, though."

"I know." She shouldn't *have* to handle it.

"John said the reaction to my announcement wasn't good in my division. It surprised me."

"Who the fuck is John?" I burst out.

Her head lifted off my shoulder. She was so close I could make out all the shades of green in her eyes. "The guy who interviewed me."

Oh. Right. "He's an asshole," I declared.

"Have you ever met him?" she wondered.

Why did I need to meet him? "You agree with me." I pointed out.

"Yeah, well, I talked to him."

"Good enough for me." I shrugged and then pushed her back into my shoulder. "So the asshole said that and you were surprised."

Look at me keeping up with the conversation. I was proud of myself.

"They don't even like me. I would think they'd be glad to see me go."

"They're butt hurt," I told her.

"What?" She started to look up, but I wouldn't let her. I liked her weight against me.

"Maybe they don't like you, but they don't like the fact you're leaving either. It's an insult to them you would leave the top after you made it in. It's like saying they aren't good enough for you."

"John did make out like I was giving up something amazing to go to the NRR."

"You kinda are."

"No," she intoned, absolution in her voice. "And I thought you hated the pros."

"I do. But it's a legitimate division. Only one of its kind. A lot of people still view it as the only division with real drivers."

"That's a bunch of shit."

I smiled over her head.

"I thought I'd get some more acceptance and respect with the crossover."

"But you haven't."

"Not even you think I should drive. Right after you implied my father bought my way in, you said so in *GearShark*."

Well, fuck. "I shouldn't have said that."

She retorted, "Why, because you want to get laid tonight?"

I stiffened beneath her. "No. Because it was an asshole thing to say."

"Yeah, it was."

I could have said sorry, but what was the point? The words were out there. Saying I'm sorry wouldn't make up for it. She might not admit it, but I could tell the words hurt her. I never wanted to hurt her. "You're a good driver."

She laughed, thought I was teasing.

"Seriously." I squeezed her. "I've seen some of your races. And tonight with the Lotus."

Her dark head lifted. I met her eyes so she could see the truth.

"You've watched some of my races?"

It was something I didn't plan on telling her. But I kinda owed her after putting her down in a national magazine. "I watched some tapes, uh, last week."

Her smile was brilliant. Made me wonder why I ever thought twice about admitting it. "You did? Thank you."

"I'll still smoke you, though," I added.

She rolled her eyes. "We'll see."

"Does your dad know how it's been for you in the pros? The reason you want to cross over is because you hate it?"

She ceased breathing for a long moment, like she was stunned I laid it out like that. Stunned I picked up on the fact she didn't like the pros. Josie loved driving; that much was crystal clear.

But the pro division?

It was squashing her. I had a feeling if I'd met her years ago, before she'd signed, I would have met a completely different woman.

Josie was feisty and stubborn by nature. She was also jaded; that came from life.

I was surprised when she didn't deny it. I thought she'd argue and tell me I was wrong.

She didn't.

"Not completely."

"Does anyone know? Hopper?" I pressed.

"No."

I could feel her holding something back. Like it was right there and she wanted to dump it all out, but she didn't.

Even though Josie hadn't said everything, she'd still told me a lot. I didn't think I quite realized how weighed down she was. How tired. I wanted to scoop her up and protect her. But she wasn't that kind.

In a way, it was good because shielding people was also tiresome. "I know what it's like to always be the strong one, too, to bear responsibility and never say too much." She might not want my protection, but some understanding might go a long way.

"Tell me about it." Her voice was soft, and she pushed her face closer into my neck. The soft strands of her hair caressed my skin.

I glanced down, trying not to be so affected by her. By our exchange of words.

Talking felt more intimate somehow, more so than sex. Because baring your body in front of someone was a lot less scary that baring your innermost thoughts.

Her legs were covered in goose bumps. So were her arms.

"Josie, are you cold?" My voice was harsh.

"It's a little chilly just sitting," she said. "No big deal."

I made a noise and pushed her away from my body. She scrambled up. I pushed to my feet, crowding her in the narrow space between the rows. Swiftly, I yanked off the cotton jacket I was wearing.

Already, she was shaking her head.

"Sit down," I ordered, patting my lap again. Her eyes narrowed. "Don't you sass me, woman."

She sat down, resuming the same position she'd been in just seconds ago. I draped the jacket over her side and part of her legs.

Her silent sigh went unheard, but it brushed over my neck when her face pushed close.

"I lied earlier," I said. "When I said no one asked about us. Someone did."

"Who?"

"My father."

"I've always gotten the impression you don't have much of a relationship with him."

"I don't." My voice was clipped, and it was work to unhinge my suddenly tense jaw to explain further. "He never liked my interest in cars or that I street raced. It didn't fit in his business world."

"I'm sure that went over well," she said knowingly.

I smiled to myself. "Pretty much. I did what I wanted anyway. We settled into a tolerable relationship, and he bailed me out of trouble a few times."

"Like criminal trouble?"

"Yeah," I said. "I've done some shit I probably should have done jail time for."

"What kind of shit?" she asked, looking up.

"Illegal betting, fighting…"

"I don't think you can go to jail for fighting." She pointed out.

"When you almost kill some people, you can."

I watched her eyes widen. I measured her reaction to my words. I'd never told anyone that before, that I'd beat someone almost to death. It was a sworn secret between my father and me and only those involved. Everyone was paid to shut the hell up about it. I wasn't even sure how much Arrow knew.

"Did they deserve it?" she asked softly, still staring unflinchingly in my eyes.

"Oh yeah."

She nodded once. "Okay." Then she tucked her head back into my neck.

I wasn't shocked very often, but I was just then. My body went slack, all my energy going to process her reaction. Even the arm holding her fell away.

Such easy acceptance.

No fear.

Not even when I outright admitted to being violent. Granted, it was provoked.

"Jace," she whispered.

Both my arms tucked around her. My head turned enough so I could rest my chin on her head as I gazed out over the empty track. Down below, my car was a bright spot, the white paint standing out in the night like a neon sign.

"A couple years ago, my dad did some things, said some shit that ruined our tolerable relationship."

"Did it have to do with Arrow?"

I paused. "You know he's gay?"

"Is it a secret?"

"Not really," I murmured. But it wasn't something we announced.

"Hopper asked about him, you know," she mused, interest in her tone.

My attention zeroed in. "What the hell for?"

"Maybe he's interested."

Uh, what? "Hopper is gay?"

"Yeah," she answered.

"He's too old," I announced. He could forget it right now, and he could also never look at my brother again.

Josie burst out laughing. "Old!"
I made a sound.
"He's twenty-six."
"Arrow is twenty," I replied, tight.
"Age is just a number…" she mused.
"No," I barked.
She just giggled. "Testy."
"My brother's been through a lot of shit." My voice was hard. "My father only made it worse. He's damaged now. I won't stand around and watch him get hurt again."
"Ahhh," she said, knowingly.
Her tone annoyed me. "What?"
"The people you almost killed… Did that have to do with your brother?"
"Yeah," I said, not wanting to say anymore. It's not really something I liked to think about. In fact, some nights it haunted me in my dreams.
I might have almost killed some guys, but I was no killer. That experience would be something I would never forget.
"Sometimes I wonder if my father had let me go to jail, if I would feel—" My lips slammed shut. I hadn't realized I was speaking out loud.
"Less guilty?" she asked, soft.
I nodded.
"Look, I don't know what happened. I could probably guess, but I won't."
"You wouldn't be right. Someone as light as you could never imagine something so fucked up."
She paused, sat up, and looked me in the eye. It wasn't hard because when she sat straight, our eyes were level.
"I'm not so light."

Oh, Josie. What the fuck have they done to you? I brushed my hand over her hair. "To me you are."

"We walk around a lot of stuff, don't we?" she asked, her mouth turned up slightly.

"Sometimes you don't have to come right out and say everything to understand," I murmured.

"Your father asked about us?" she asked.

I nodded. "He summoned me to his towering offices, and there was our magazine on his desk," I explained. "I didn't even know it was out."

"I don't know how they got it out so quickly," she mused. "I looked up in Target one day, and there it was."

"Did you buy it?" I teased.

She blushed.

It made something inside me feel warm.

"He thought we were dating," I said of my father.

"I think everyone assumes that."

I shrugged. It didn't bother me. In fact, I was glad. Having someone like Josie at my side could never be considered anything but a blessing.

"I think it was the first time he was happy with one of my decisions," I mused.

She laughed. "Then you told him we weren't together."

"I told him I was working on it."

She pulled back, surprise written on her features.

I winked.

"He told me he was proud of me," I admitted quietly. The words felt like a heavy weight. "I don't remember him ever saying that to me before."

Her hand came to rest on my jaw, lightly rubbing over my stubble.

"It made me suspicious, you know?"

She nodded. "Like he wants something."

I nodded. That was exactly it. "He says he wants to make amends and he's sorry for being a shitty father. He claims he checked out when my mom died…"

"Your mom died?"

"When I was six."

She snuggled back into my chest. This time her arm came up to loop around my neck. It was sort of odd to be comforted. No one had ever comforted me before.

It was kinda nice.

So I picked up her hand, kissed the palm, then laid it back around my neck.

"Arrow's mom raised me really. She's a good woman; she was good to me. But it was never the same."

"Can you forgive him?" she asked, cutting right to the heart of things.

I'd asked myself that a hundred times since I saw him.

"For being a shit father to me? Yeah, I guess. But what he did to Arrow… that I can never forgive."

Her arm tightened around me. "Maybe someday you'll tell me about it."

"Someday, I will." I promised. But not right now. Right now I felt like I'd laid out so much I had to keep something in reserve.

Just like maybe someday she'd tell me what kind of hazing she'd gone through.

"What does Arrow say?" she asked.

"I, uh, haven't talked to him about it. I've been avoiding it."

"You protect him," she said simply.

"He fights against it. He wants to stand on his own."

"He's strong."

I agreed. "Way stronger than he looks."

"You love him," she whispered.

I whispered back, "Yeah, I do."

"You're a good man, Jace."

"Sometimes."

"All the time."

"Don't be telling people that. I got a rep to protect."

She kissed the side of my neck. The giggle that escaped her caressed my skin. I patted the side of her ass. "Up," I commanded.

Josie unfolded from my lap, and the jacket slid off her toward the ground. I caught it and stood, wrapping it around her shoulders and tucking it close.

"Let's go." I took her hand and led her down the stands so we could jump back over the wall. "You wanna drive back to the hotel?" I asked.

She smiled. "Not this time."

Slightly perplexed, I grabbed the hard top and installed it back on the Lotus. It was late now, and the air was much colder than when we arrived.

"Thanks for bringing me here," Josie said when I was shut in the driver's side.

I hit the start button and turned to face her. "You want some food?"

Her mouth twisted. "I'm actually kinda starving."

"You like tacos?"

"Are there people who don't?"

"Fuck if I know." I shrugged. "I'll hit a drive-thru on the way to the hotel."

"How long until we get there?" she asked, her voice dipping.

"Baby, I can be there in five if you're that starving," I drawled and put the car in first gear.

"Maybe take the longer route." Her hand reached across the center and brushed across the front of my jeans.

For the first time in my entire life, the car stalled out on me.

"Josie,"

Her fingers found the button and popped it open. Slowly, my zipper came down. My hips slid out farther so she had better access.

"You're supposed to be driving, Jace," she said, turning in the seat so she could lean across. My dick slid out with the help of her hand; the waistband of my boxers were pulled down with the other.

Her hand slid up my shaft. It was growing harder by the second.

The engine fired right back up, and I eased the car forward. "Maybe I'll just take a lap before pulling out on the main road," I rasped, feeling her hand squeezing gently around my head.

"Whatever you say, Jace," she purred.

I loved it when she said my name.

Her mouth slid down over my dick, and I moaned. Beneath my hands, the wheel jerked. God, her mouth was everything. Hot, tight, wet. Her lips wrapped around my shaft with the perfect amount of pressure and worked, slipping up and down.

All at once, she sank even farther, taking all of me. The tip of my head hit the back of her throat, and she moaned. My foot tamped down on the gas with excitement as her mouth released me.

My hand gripped the wheel; my other buried in the back of her head and pushed down so she could take me deep once again. My tires raced over the track while she sucked my dick until I was panting in need.

I was throbbing, desperate for release. I hadn't had sex since the night in the hangar, but I craved her every day. Josie wrapped her lips around the tip of my head and sucked deep. I felt myself jerk inside her, and I groaned. The car swerved, but it didn't matter because there was no one else on the track.

Regretfully, the sudden movement made her release me and look up. "Time to turn around," she said.

I focused ahead, and the gravel section was coming into view.

I grabbed the emergency brake, pulled it, and then drifted around in a wide circle. She laughed, and I pushed her head back down to my center.

Her tongue teased me, licking up the sides, flirting with the head, until finally she plunged back over it.

"Don't stop, Josie." I urged.

She didn't. She sucked me until I almost hurt. Until I slammed on the brakes and brought us to a full-on stop. The second the Lotus was no longer in motion, she took me deep one final time and sucked.

I bucked up in the seat, but she stayed with me, sucking me dry as I shot off a load across her perfect tongue.

I moaned and shouted as I came, white lights bursting behind my eyes until I fell back into the seat, spent.

Josie was still sucking, still lapping up every last bit of me. Before pulling away completely, she gave my cock one last thorough swipe with her tongue, and I shuddered.

I glanced at her face through half-closed eyes when she pulled back, licking her lips.

"Blow and drive," I muttered. "Sex and cars. You just combined my two favorite things."

"I still want tacos," she said. "And I want all night like you promised."

I chuckled and buttoned up my pants.

A fast car, a blow job, and now sex and tacos?

Best night ever.

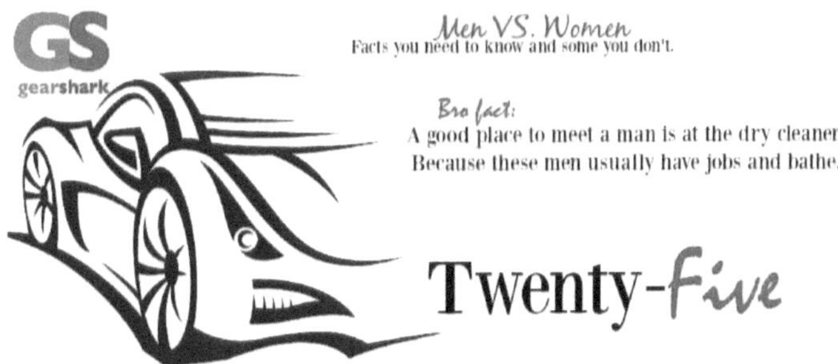

Twenty-Five

Joey

We didn't turn on one light when we walked into my hotel room. It wasn't because I didn't want to see him. On the contrary, I could look at Jace all day and still want to look more.

We didn't speak either. Not one word when we pulled into the hotel parking lot, walked through the lobby, rode up the elevator, and walked down the silent and empty hall. It wasn't because it was awkward or because we had nothing to say. After sitting in the stands in his lap tonight and listening to him and him listening to me I knew conversation would never be a problem.

Have you ever wanted someone so much you couldn't see?

Have you ever felt need so deep the words wouldn't come?

Light and words weren't needed right now. We were past that.

My shoes were the first to go. Jace dropped the bag filled with tacos on the dresser and turned. I didn't even wonder if he would be ready so soon after the car. I saw it in his eyes. I felt it in the air.

The hum of the AC unit by the window was the only sound in the room besides the thundering of my heart.

Jace used nimble fingers to peel his jacket off my shoulders. I abandoned it to the bed. The rest of my clothes came off slowly, excruciatingly slow. Each garment fell to the dark floor without another thought, and the closer I got to being bare, the more anticipation I felt.

My knees rattled beneath my skin. A fine tremor made my fingers clumsy when I reached for his shirt. He must have sensed how far gone I was because he brushed my hands away softly and disrobed right before my heated stare.

Between my legs was soaked. Tingles of pain shot up into my lower belly, and my breasts ached for his hands. Jace's bare skin was like a beacon in the dark. Every line of his body stood out; the strength he emanated seemed to make me feel even weaker.

Powerless wasn't a feeling I reveled in, but *oh*, I reveled in it right now.

Stepping up to him, my palms flattened on his smooth chest and dragged over his shoulders, down his biceps. His hands spasmed around mine, but I kept moving, keeping my touch elusive, letting him feel it, but not lingering any one place long enough for him to be fully satisfied.

I wanted Jace to know how I felt. I longed to make him hurt with need. If I was going to love him, then I would do it better than anyone else ever could.

And yes, I was going to love Jace.

I was already falling, spiraling deep.

He stood beneath my exploration, his body taut. He didn't move but for the rapid rise and fall of his chest.

On impulse, I leaned forward, placing my ear just over his heart. The sound of it beating was so satisfying because of the quickened pace. I closed my eyes briefly, taking in the rhythm, committing it to memory.

Jace's bare arms wrapped around me, and the tips of his fingers found the nape of my neck.

I wasn't yet ready to pull away from him, from the sound beneath my ear, so I dragged my nails gently down his back, enjoying the way his waist dipped in slightly above his ass. Lightly, I drifted farther down, over his cheeks, and flirted with his crack to finally reach the back of his thighs.

Between us, his rod poked me, a constant reminder of all the pleasure yet to come. Slowly, I pulled back, closing my lips around his nipple. Jace sucked in a breath as I sucked and played with the erect bud, nipping at it with my teeth.

After I repeated the process with the other, I trailed hot kisses down his toned abdominals, past his belly button, and to the smooth skin above his dick.

The second my tongue swiped over it, his hands went beneath my armpits and lifted me. He moved around the side of the king-size, and with one great yank, the blankets gave way. Crooking a finger at me, I went to his side and was pressed down into the center of the blankets.

My arm fell out to the side, my fingers reaching for him. Lips unlike any lips I'd ever known lightly caressed those fingertips, moving down over my hand, my wrist, and up my arm. The farther up he kissed, the closer he came, until he was on the bed completely and climbed between my legs.

Jace wrapped his arms beneath me. I arched up to get closer the same time he moved over me, bringing us chest to chest.

His weight pressed me into the bed, and I expelled a satisfied sigh. I liked being skin to skin with him like this, every part of him touching every part of me.

Still wrapped up in his arms, he began to kiss me. First my cheeks, my eyelids, and then the tip of my nose. Emotion swelled up inside me, so much it made me overwhelmed, and I began to wiggle like I wanted to get away.

A little bit of panic intruded on our moment, and I was angry at it, but the feeling was too strong to ignore.

"Josie." My name sounded almost like a command.

Our eyes met.

"It's okay," he told me in a much gentler tone.

I started to shake my head, mortified because this wasn't me. Emotion like this never brought me down, but oh, I was drowning.

I was drowning in Jace.

"It's all right, baby." He assured me.

I wasn't prepared for this. I was prepared for sex, for satisfaction, for mind-bending pleasure. Not for emotion. Not for something deeper than just two people merging their bodies.

This felt like he was trying merge into my soul.

It was scary.

It felt a lot like love.

"Jace, I—"

"I know," he murmured, pushing up on his elbows to look down. His eyes reflected back to me everything I felt.

Before I could say anything else, our lips met. His tongue swept inside my mouth. It felt like he belonged. It felt like home. All the anxiety I felt was soothed away.

Just like that, my body went boneless beneath him.

He felt the give inside me, and he moaned.

We stayed like that for a while, making out, having sex with just our mouths. Eventually, it wasn't enough. His mouth began to explore. Down my neck and over my collarbone he sucked.

My head fell to the side when his mouth closed around my breast while one hand massaged the swollen, needy flesh.

I made a sound of appreciation and spread my legs. He settled between them, the head of his large cock teasing the slick heat in my center.

I moved impatiently, but he pulled back just enough to rob me. Jace worked my body over until my eyes would barely open.

I stroked him when I could and kissed him when his body was near, but slowly, he worked his way downward until his dark head was between my thighs.

Two fingers parted my folds, and satisfaction rumbled out of him. I was almost certain he whispered my name before using his mouth for a whole other purpose.

No one ever explored that part of my anatomy with so much focus and desire. His tongue licked everywhere. His fingers stroked deep and swirled around inside my heat until I was shuddering against the blankets.

But he wouldn't let me come. He seemed content to bring me to the peak, then back off until I was panting to be lifted up again.

I don't know how much time passed. How long we tortured each other in that bed before his body rose over mine in a way that made my stomach flop.

My knees bent, feet flat on the mattress, as my thighs cradled his body between mine with patience the rest of me did not contain.

The fingers on Jace's left hand were still a little slick from my pleasure when he grasped my jaw and stared down into my eyes.

With one hard stroke, he entered me, and I cried out.

His hand fell away, and even though we tried to hold each other's stare, the bliss just took over. My nails dug into his back as he thrust deep. His large, unforgiving size stretched my walls in the best way. Every part of me felt full.

He set the pace, but I kept up, thrusting to meet each of his.

"I want more, Jace." I panted when his mouth closed over my breast and sucked. "Harder."

His mouth left, and his body rose on his hands. He pulled back, almost abandoning my body completely, then surged deep.

My mouth opened, but no sound came out.

He did it again and again.

"Like that?" he whispered.

I nodded. His pace increased until he was pounding into me so hard and fast I would probably have bruises on my inner thighs in the morning.

God, it was so good.

He delivered exactly what I needed, and it felt in that moment my body had been waiting for him my entire life.

"Don't stop." I panted as he plunged into my body.

The veins in his neck stood out, and a sheen of sweat coated my skin. I was so close to the edge, but I didn't want to give in. Not yet.

I couldn't give this up.

It was like he knew. He smiled swiftly the same moment he surged in. I fought against the orgasm and lifted my shoulders off the mattress to fasten my lips on his shoulder.

One of his hands delved into my hair and tugged. My face came back, and his mouth crashed over mine. His tongue fucked my mouth while his dick fucked my body.

And then I was shuddering, coming apart beneath him. He lowered my body to the pillows and rocked in so close our pelvises ground together.

I called out his name, but it sounded like the mewl of a kitten because the peak of my orgasm was so intense it robbed me of almost everything.

Jace's body collapsed onto mine, and with one last shove, I felt him spill deep inside me. His shout was muffled in the pillow above my shoulder, and his entire body quaked with release.

I wrapped my arms and legs around him, keeping his body close to mine.

A short while later, we ate tacos in bed by the light of the moon shining through a partially opened curtain. When that was done, we made love again. I fell asleep in his arms but didn't stay there long.

I came awake with his mouth between my legs, his tongue working my swollen clit. I came right across his tongue this time, and he lapped it up like he'd never tasted anything sweeter.

After that, it was like our bodies gave in despite our hearts' demands. I fell asleep with my hair spilled across his chest and the sound of his heart echoing in my head.

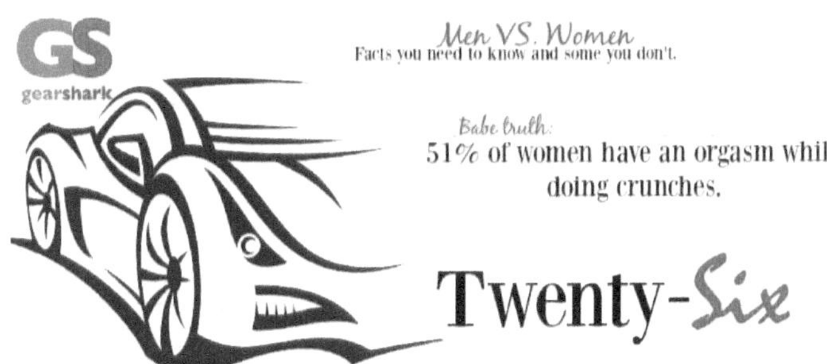

Lorhaven

Passion. She had lots of it.

I was beginning to see Josie did nothing without putting all of herself into it. Even the parts she kept hidden.

I wanted to know her, not just pieces, but entirely. I'd never wanted to know anyone this way. I'd never felt equal parts of wanting to stand beside but also in front of someone before.

I loved my brother. I'd do anything for him.

But this was different… more intense.

Thankfully, the press I had to do today wasn't until noon. Because of the race, we scheduled it later than normal. Race days usually ended in late nights.

Even with it not being until later, I was still tempted to cancel the shit. I wanted to prolong the time I had with her. I wasn't sure when I'd see her again once we left today. We didn't live in the same town; we didn't have the same racing schedule.

It made me feel grouchy and, frankly, pissed off.

As I lay there and considered how irate my manager would be if I told him I wasn't coming, Josie stretched against me like a cat. Her warm, supple body curved into mine, and desire crawled up the base of my spine.

I'd just had her an hour ago. She'd brought me awake by climbing over me and sinking down on my dick. The heat of her core was scorching, but in the best way possible. The way I felt sheathed inside her body with nothing between us was the closest thing to heaven as I'd ever gotten.

Josie wasn't shy with her body, her wants, or her needs. The whole time she rode me, I watched her. The shape of her body was all woman. I loved the way her body curved in and out, the way her hips rotated, and the way her flat stomach would clench when she bore down on me to rub against that perfect spot inside her.

Her tits were full and real. They bounced when I thrust up into her, which I considered an invitation to wrap my hands around them.

And right before she came, her teeth would sink into her lower lip. Like she was bracing herself for the overpowering pleasure about to befall her body.

It didn't matter it had only been an hour. I wanted more. My dick was going to be raw by the time I let her out of this bed, but fucking A, it would be worth it.

I palmed her ass, giving it a pat. She purred and pressed her face into my neck. Without thinking, I turned my face, kissing her forehead. She didn't say anything, but I felt her smile against my neck.

It seemed to me people forgot she was a woman. How anyone ever could was a goddamn mystery to me, but it's what I sensed. Josie wasn't used to someone taking control or showing her tenderness of any kind.

Hell, I wasn't used to giving tenderness. Yet I couldn't help but want to shower her with it, because even the smallest gesture put just a glimmer of awe in her emerald eyes.

What she needed was someone to treat her like an equal, but not forget who she was. Women had needs just like men, but women were a lot more complex.

Frankly, women were pains in the ass.

But not the one in my arms right now. Not the one rubbing her chest against my side while her hand slid down between my legs and cupped my sack.

I kinda liked this one… In fact, I might like her a little more than that.

"I need a shower," she murmured, her lips brushing my chest.

"That an invite?" I asked.

"Yes." She continued to massage my sack while I ran my fingers through her long, soft hair. Neither of us made a move to get out of the bed.

"What time does your plane leave?" I asked after a few minutes

One long sigh expelled from her lips. "Just after breakfast." Her body jolted a little. "I'm supposed to meet Drew and Trent downstairs to eat."

I made a sound. "Tell them you aren't coming."

"They're my ride to the airport."

"I'll drive you over."

"You don't have to." She pulled back a little, and I rolled, pinning her beneath me.

"I know I don't," I growled. "I want to."

"You do?" Her voice was soft.

"I'm not ready to let you go yet," I whispered, then kissed her gently.

"What about Arrow?" she asked around my kiss.

"Can't you see I'm trying to get some?" I quipped and pulled back.

She grinned. Her hair was a tangled mess around her head. Her face was flushed and had a hint of beard burn on her cheeks from my stubble.

"Arrow can ride over with my manager to the interview. I'll meet them there."

"Okay."

"Okay?" I confirmed.

She nodded, and I lowered back down to kiss her, but instead of her lips, I got her cheek because she turned her head. "Hand me my phone."

I groaned and rolled off her.

"Where is it?" I grumped.

She shrugged.

Unbelievable.

Josie pushed up into a sitting position, the blankets tangled around her waist, her chest bare and fully exposed. With a view like that, I wasn't about to complain, so I went about searching for the damn phone.

It was under the bed.

I tossed it to her, and she sent out a text to, I assumed, Drew. A few seconds later, it made a sound, and she laughed at the screen.

"What?"

She typed something else and sent it off before looking up.

"I told them I'd meet them at the airport."

"They know you're with me?" I asked, feeling sort of like staking my claim. It was idiotic. She was texting a gay guy.

"Yes," she said, her voice a little shy. "I told him."

"Him who? Drew?"

She shook her head once. "Trent."

"He gonna come beating on the door to try and kick my ass?"

"Trent wouldn't do that." She defended him.

"If you believe that, you don't know him like I do," I said, thinking back to the time I caught him and Drew in an… intimate position and he slammed me up against the locker. By my throat.

"He's my friend," she announced. That stubborn glint in her eye made an appearance. "Besides, he's the one who told me to—" Her lips slammed shut.

"Told you what?" I pressed, staring at her.

She shook her head.

I dove on her, tackling her into the mattress and tickling her ribs. She squealed. It was a carefree, light sound. So I tickled her some more. She wiggled and twisted, trying to get away, but all she managed was to make my cock hard.

"Tell me," I demanded.

"Okay!" She laughed. "Okay!"

I relented but still kept my body against hers.

From beneath dark, lowered lashes, she gazed up. "I talked to him about you, about stuff."

"Sex?" I pressed.

I really didn't care if she told him we had sex. Hell, she could tell the whole world. I'd own it. I'd be proud.

"More than that," she whispered.

I swallowed. Even so, my voice was raspy. "Feelings?"

She nodded once.

I ran the back of my knuckles across her cheek. "He tell you to stay away from me?"

"No."

That surprised me. There was no love lost between Trent and me. We never had gotten along, and we might never, but I did respect him.

It was sort of nice to know he respected me.

"No?"

"He just wants me to be happy." Her eyes were the vibrant shade of green grass took on after a heavy rainstorm when everything was saturated.

"Are you happy right now, Josie?" I whispered. *Do I make you happy?*

"Happier than I've been in a long time," she admitted, looking away.

My heart swelled. I kissed the place beside her eye, letting my lips linger against her skin for long seconds.

"Come on," I said. "Let's take that shower."

She wore her "shower shoes" in the shower. They were black flip-flops, and it amused the hell out of me. She told me I needed a pair and, when I laughed, resolved to buy me a pair, then insisted I promise to wear them.

I promised. Only because she looked so damn cute with soaking-wet hair and water droplets clinging her eyelashes and trailing over her heart-shaped lips.

Plus, I figured it was a win for me. She'd want to make sure I was keeping said promise, and that meant more co-ed showers with her.

I treated the shower like a prolonged foreplay session. Sure, we got clean, but I made sure I teased the shit out of her while we did it.

The sounds of pleasure she made in the shower stall echoed through the tiny bathroom when I shoved her up against the tiles and sucked her tits until she begged me to stop.

In retaliation, she soaped up her hands and used the slick suds to jack my rod, until the soap was completely rinsed away and my thighs were quivering. Then she dropped to her knees in front of me and sucked my dick into her mouth.

Water rained over her lips and trailed down my cock. She lapped at the water with her tongue, staring up into my eyes.

By the time the water ran cold and we both were wrapped in towels, all I could think about was burying myself inside her body.

In the shower, I noticed she was slightly swollen from all the times I'd gone at her the night before. It held me back until she was combing out her damp hair and the towel fell away and left her standing there completely naked.

"Josie," I groaned.

She smiled, understanding in her eyes.

"Your body's had enough, baby." I forced the words past the desire clogging my throat.

"I'll never have enough of you." She took my hand, leading me out of the bathroom and back toward the bed. I followed along like a puppy who wanted fed.

At the foot of the bed, she released my hand and grabbed the towel tied around my waist. When it was gone, she stroked my still rock-hard length and smiled.

I started to tell her no, but she kissed me swiftly and climbed onto the bed. On all fours.

Her round, luscious ass was in the air facing me. I groaned. Her eyes beckoned me from over her shoulder; the curvaceous ass right before me wiggled.

I grabbed her by the hips, stepped up behind her, and caressed her cheeks. Before sliding inside, I tested her center with two fingers. She was wet.

She was offering herself to me. And she was ready.

I took her from behind. I went in deep, until my hips hit her ass, and then I ground against her. Josie bore down and pressed against my dick. My fingertips dug into her hips. Then I grabbed her ass cheeks and spread them wide.

I pulled out, thrusting back in. Her face fell into a pillow; her muffled groan filled my ears.

"I'm not gonna last," I warned her.

In response, she pulled away, then thrust back down on me.

After that, I started banging into her, holding her ass and hips while I fucked her furiously from behind.

Looking down at her back, flaring hips, and drops of water dotting her skin from our shower made my balls hurt they drew up so far.

"Josie," I ground out. "Goddamn, what you do to me."

"Fuck me harder, Jace," she demanded.

I followed her orders and reached around to her clit. Her sharp intake of breath was all I needed to hear.

Using some of her silky desire, I coated her clit and worked it while I humped her from behind.

"Come with me," I rasped, trying hold myself back. "Right now!"

My body bent forward with my last surge. My chest came up against her back, and both my arms wrapped around her from behind.

Josie rocked onto me as I exploded inside her, and then she was panting and gasping with her own orgasm.

Her body basically collapsed in my arms, so I lowered her onto the mattress before pulling out and collapsing beside her.

It was probably a good thing we had to be places. If we didn't, we'd likely kill each other with sex.

It wouldn't be a bad way to go. Am I right?

I'm totally right.

"I'm gonna walk funny for a week." She moaned.

I knew she was joking, and part of me was pretty fucking pleased with myself I could satisfy her that way, but the other part of me was concerned.

"Did I hurt you?" I asked. She always told me harder, faster, more. And I always obliged.

Maybe I shouldn't have.

She laughed. "No."

"Josie…" I threw my arm over her waist and pulled her into my body. "If I hurt you, you have to tell me."

She turned her face into mine, stroking my cheek with her palm. "You're sweet to me."

I scoffed. "I was just hammering into you like a machine."

"You're sweet to me, Jace," she said again.

"Maybe sometimes," I muttered, looking away. But my concern for her safety, for not hurting her wasn't sweet. It was common decency. It bothered me she didn't seem to make that distinction.

She pulled my face back. "No one's ever been sweet to me before."

Yeah, see? Just what I thought.

"Do you like it?" I whispered, rubbing my fingers against her side.

She nodded. I thought I saw the sheen of tears deep in her gaze.

"I want to see you again." I confided.

"I want to see you, too."

"I don't want you to see anyone but me." Possessiveness rose up within me. Fierce and strong like a gust of wind on the back end of a tornado.

"You say that like I have a ton of offers," she said, sarcastic.

"Do you?" I demanded. I'd beat all their asses. "I already told you I'm not above violence."

She rolled her eyes like I was joking.

I wasn't joking.

"Josie," I warned.

She sighed. "No one's interested in me, Jace. Not like that. I haven't dated anyone in a long time." Her eyes flew to mine, red tinging her cheeks. "Not that I'm saying you want to date me."

"I do."

Her eyes widened like big saucers.

"When the next reporter asks about us, I want to tell them what a lucky asshole I am. I want to stand at your side and be proud to have you there. I want you to be proud to have me there."

"Jace," Josie murmured.

"I don't have a good reputation. I'm not a nice guy. I've already told you I should be in jail. And if someone comes at my brother again… I might end up there."

"Shh," she hushed and laid her hand on my face. "I know who you are, *Jace*."

I couldn't help but feel I was more when she looked at me the way she was right then.

"I come with a lot of baggage." She cautioned.

"No more than the rest of us."

"It will be hard on you being with me. Your career is taking off. I—"

"Are you saying no to me?" I intoned. I wasn't taking no for an answer, especially not when I saw the yes right there in her eyes.

"I—" And there it was, that little bit of hesitation I saw last night. That little bit of whatever she wasn't saying. She sighed. "No. I'm not saying no."

"You want to be with me?" I asked, laying it all out.

"More than anything," she whispered.

I kissed her deeply, then pulled her into my chest, wrapping her up in my arms. Today was a good fucking day.

"Jace?" Her voice was barely audible against my chest. Still, I'd know my name on her lips anywhere.

"Yeah?"

"Just know… whenever you want out, I'll understand. I won't make it hard on you."

Did she think I was some kind of little bitch who ran at the first sign of struggle? "I'm not gonna want out, Josie."

She said something. Even though it wasn't clear, it sure sounded a lot like, "I hope not."

Her face stayed pressed into my chest for long moments as I lay there with her in my arms and wondered.

Suddenly, she lifted her head. "So does this mean I won't pull up to any of your street races and find a rat with her hands all over you?"

My lips twitched. "Why would I want a rat when I have you?"

Her voice turned rueful. "I seriously thought about running her over with my car."

I threw my head back and laughed.

"I'm gonna get ready. You have to feed me and give me caffeine before you take me to the plane."

"Food *and* coffee?" I teased. "You're a lot of work."

She smiled, but it didn't quite meet her eyes. I knew she was thinking about the out she put on the table. The one she promised to make easy when I decided to run.

I wasn't running anywhere.

Again, I wondered why she thought I'd be so eager to get away.

Twenty-Seven

Joey

Wednesday, 10:00 AM

Going to Charlotte this weekend.

I'm gonna need a pit pass.

Read.

Three days. That's how long it'd been seen I'd seen him last. It wasn't like the last time, though. We talked now. Every day.

I never pegged Jace for a guy who called. But he did.

And he texted.

We didn't sit on the phone for hours; our calls were usually only a few minutes. But they were meaningful and all I needed.

Even so, after three days, I started to think about when I would see him again. When Drew called and told me he was coming to Charlotte for my race, I knew that meant Jace's schedule was clear, too.

So I texted him.

He texted back.

It gave me butterflies in my stomach.

I was going to see him again. This time, I'd see even more of him than last weekend, because this time he was coming just for me.

My race was Sunday, but we decided to fly out Friday morning. My car would get there Saturday and would need to be inspected, etc., and I was always there for that. A racer's car was their most valuable and important asset. Making sure mine was in top shape was crucial.

Plus, it would give me the day to get in the frame of mind to race.

Trent and Drew got into town Thursday afternoon. They'd been here so much the last few weeks I was beginning to think it was odd when they weren't. The room they stayed in was now Drew and Trent's room, and even the housekeeper asked when they would be here next.

I loved Drew; he was quite possibly my best friend. But Trent was a close second. He'd become the one I always wanted advice from. The one I thought of first when I needed to talk. He was simple to talk to. He didn't make things convoluted or even analyze them like women tended to do. Trent was straightforward, he was honest, and he had a capacity for understanding that in a lot of ways took me by surprise.

I was standing in my walk-in closet with a suitcase open before me when he barged right in.

"Hope you aren't naked," he said as he stepped in.

He wasn't even covering his eyes.

I rolled my eyes. "What do you want?" I asked fondly.

He dropped onto the rug beside my suitcase. "Drew's in the shower."

"And you aren't with him?" I arched an eyebrow.

His smile was slow. "You have a dirty mind."

"Please," I muttered and turned back to my clothes.

I don't know why it suddenly seemed so hard to pack. I'd traveled to races a thousand times, and it was always the same, jeans and T-shirts. Now I stood here and debated which jeans with which shirt and what color.

I was kinda annoyed with myself.

"I wanted to check in. See how it's going."

"With Jace?" I asked knowingly.

"Pretty much."

I gave up on my perusal of the clothes hanging around and sat on the floor near him.

"He's a lot more than people think," I confided.

Trent tilted his head. "Good or bad?"

"Good."

"You seen him since the race?"

I shook my head. "He'll be in Charlotte this weekend."

"You want him to be?" Trent pressed.

He was totally giving off the overprotective big brother vibe. I kinda liked it.

"Yeah. I do."

"All I needed to hear." He grunted and stood.

I felt my forehead wrinkle. "What?"

"I'll see you in the morning," he said, turning to go.

"Where are you going?" I called after him.

"To take a shower," he answered.

The sound of him leaving my bedroom was distinct. I laughed and got to my feet. "What a weirdo," I told no one.

I sighed. Trying to pick clothes was a pain in the ass. I decided to go back to my usual style of packing and just throw some stuff in there. My hand closed over a dark pair of skinny jeans and sleeveless loose white top. I tossed it in, turned back, and reached for a sundress.

What? It's super-hot in the South during summer. A sundress would be comfortable.

It was made of lightweight cotton in a simple A-line shape that would show off my hourglass shape. It was white with a pattern of tiny flowers all over it. The size and pale coloring of pink and green kept it from looking like grandma's curtains.

Okay, fine. It was girly. The girliest thing I owned.

Nothing wrong with wanting to look nice.

After I added that, I went for a pair of army-green cotton shorts and a fitted black T-shirt with cap sleeves.

Putting something that was more my usual style in there after the dress made me feel a little more like myself.

Now all that was needed was the stuff I would wear to race in and my shower shoes. I spun around to get them and noticed a large figure hovering in the door of my closet.

I shrieked and pressed a hand to my chest.

"Jace!"

"You look pretty cute standing there scowling over your clothes," he mused.

"I do not!" I argued. Suddenly, I felt out of breath and excited. "What are you doing here?"

He pushed out of the doorway and prowled toward me. "I didn't feel like waiting 'til tomorrow night to see you."

He was close enough I had to tilt my head slightly to stare into his rich, dark eyes. "You drove all the way down here to see me a day early?"

A playful smirk tugged his lips. "I could tell you missed me."

"I missed you?" I scoffed.

I felt his hand tug on the knot tied in my shirt, and reality came crashing into the moment of seeing him here, in my room.

Oh my God. I looked like crap!

There I go again with the girl drama…

But seriously! I was dressed in a pair of crop sweatpants and a white T-shirt that was too big, so I'd tied it in a knot on the side of my waist. My hair was wild with curls. I barely even tried to tame it today.

I looked like I was from the eighties.

"How'd you get in here!" I demanded. *And why wasn't I given a warning?*

"I'm assuming it was the housekeeper who let us in. Drew and Trent were in the kitchen eating everything in sight."

"Arrow came, too? Trent and Drew know you're here?" Trent hadn't said a word to me!

He nodded once but scowled; a dark look stole over his features. "Trent wouldn't let me come in here until he was sure you wanted to see me."

I fought a smile and lost. That's why he'd really come in here. "He's sweet."

Jace's eyes narrowed. "He tried to keep me from you."

I rolled my eyes. "You're in here, aren't you?"

"Speaking of…" he growled, grabbing me by the waist and lifting me off my feet. My legs wound around his waist naturally. "Aren't you gonna show me how happy you are I'm here?"

I kissed him—went right in and locked my lips on his. Our tongues stroked together as I wiggled a little closer against him.

"You look fucking hot in sweatpants," he said when I lifted my mouth.

"I look even better without them."

His quick grin was thrilling and rather wolfish. Carrying me, he stepped out of the closet and strode into my bedroom toward my pillow-filled bed and literally tossed me right in the center. I giggled as I sank into the down-filled comforter like I'd fallen into a cloud.

Jace ripped the T-shirt he was wearing off his body and tossed it over his shoulder. The jeans he wore were like always, a little loose and not to committed to hiding his hips. My hands slid through his hair, ruffling the strands as he crawled over me and claimed my mouth.

"Where's Arrow?" I gasped, ripping my mouth free even as my hands explored his bare back.

"With Drew and Trent. They're watching a movie or some shit," he said, nuzzling against the side of my neck.

"The door," I groaned, thinking of the guys' habit of barging in.

"I locked it on my way in," he informed me, even as the knot in my shirt came untied and he went up beneath it to kiss my breast over the cotton bralette I was wearing.

"Oh God, Jace. I missed you." I groaned.

Over my breast, his mouth stilled. I became self-conscious of my words. It was the first time I'd told him that. It was the closest I'd come to really admitting how much he'd come to mean to me.

Slowly, he pulled back from beneath my shirt. His hair was totally mussed when he glanced up.

"Say it again, Josie," he demanded, a deep rasp in his words.

The hungry glint in his eyes made me want to give him more. It made me feel like I'd been withholding things he needed to hear and feel.

I surged up and grabbed his face. The roughness of his jaw was a contrast to the smoothness of his cheeks. I made sure to look directly in his eyes and nowhere else when I spoke.

"I missed you, Jace," I whispered. "So much." His lips pulled up, and I ran my thumb along his lower lip. Even quieter, I said, "No one's ever made me feel like you do."

This time when he kissed me, it was different. Less fierce but more consuming. Less desperate but more secure.

I gave in to him, to the feelings consuming the air around us. I felt more aware of him moving inside me tonight than I ever had before. Everything was amplified, and the slowness with which he made love to me caused a drunk feeling to settle over my limbs and mind.

He was a blanket, heavy and warm; offering shelter and comfort. His body muffled everything else.

I succumbed to it all. To him.

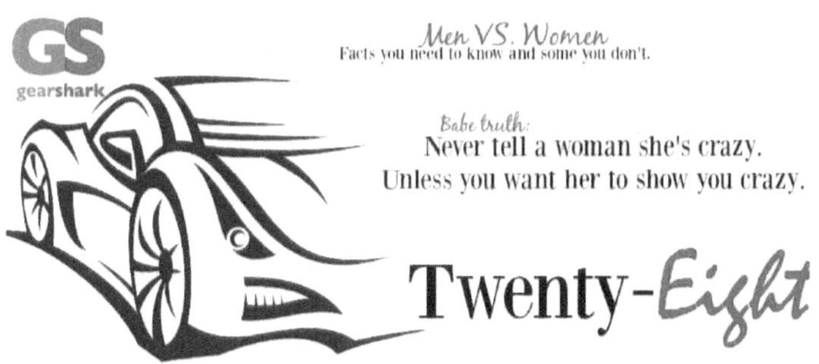

Lorhaven

I handed her my heart last night.

And quite possibly a piece of my soul.

She didn't ask for either, but sometimes the very best things in life are given without request.

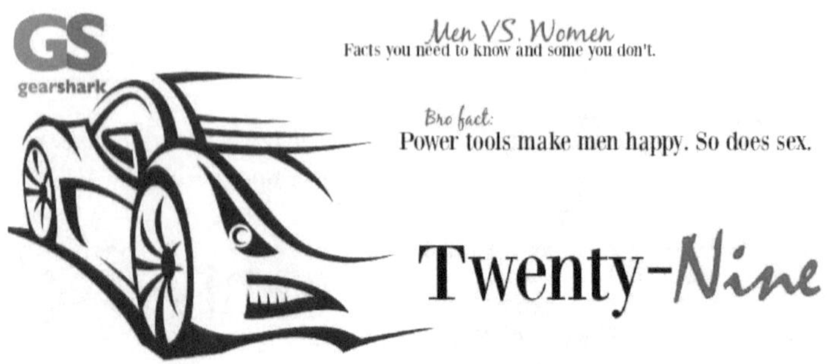

Twenty-Nine

Joey

Friday and Saturday passed in a blur of travel, work, and sex.

Jace and Arrow hopped on our short flight to Charlotte, and surprisingly, everyone got along.

Everyone = Jace + Trent + Drew.

What was even more surprising was the way Jace was with me in front of everyone else. He treated me the exact same way as when we were alone.

Well, except he left my clothes on.

Yeah, we were kinda official (totally official), but there was no easing into it with him. It was all or nothing. He held my hand in public, draped his arm around me on the plane. Kissed me often, no matter who was in the room.

If Drew snickered when it happened, Jace's response was totally tame.

Totally tame = giving Drew the finger. Sometimes both at once.

A girl could get used to that kind of thing.

It frightened me.

I didn't want to get used to something I would miss if it went away.

In the beginning, I thought what Jace and I had was some sort of chemical reaction. A sexual compatibility unlike anything I'd felt before.

It went deeper than that. Much, much deeper.

I never meant to fall for him. Hell, I didn't even mean to like him. But here I was, totally in love, while in the back of my mind, I wondered if it would last.

I wasn't a fan of doubt or clouds hanging over my head. I was straightforward, so I expected everything else to be.

The way I saw it, I had one of two choices:

1.) Walk away.

Or

2.) Tell him.

Walking away wasn't an option. I'd make it three steps before the invisible chain he unknowingly shackled around my heart would tug me back.

So I'd tell him. I'd say out loud what I hadn't before. My secret. Even my dumb past. It could change the way he saw me. That expression in his eyes every time he looked at me could shift. The loss of it would cut deep.

Still, I'd rather hurt than torture myself with doubt every second of every day.

Not 'til after the race, though. Focusing on the track, the win, and my career was my immediate goal. Having Jace in the pit today was like an extra boost of motivation. I wanted to impress him. I wanted to show him I belonged on this track.

I was a damn fine driver. No matter what else happened, of that I was sure.

So far, I was proving it.

Adrenaline was a cocktail in my veins today. I felt like I had an invisible IV of the stuff flowing right into my bloodstream. Despite the rush, my hands were steady on the steering wheel as I guided my car around the track.

I was doing it today. I was proving to everyone I could hack it. Only five laps to go, three cars to pass, and everyone would see me at the top, and then maybe they'd all shut up about a pro going indie. *Maybe they'll all shut up about women drivers.*

My back was sweaty from being strapped in the cab for so long. The vibration of the powerful car beneath me was no less noticeable than it was when I was on lap one. My brain almost hurt from the concentration I put in today, but for some reason, this race seemed more important. Crucial to my career somehow.

Maybe it was because of the interviews lately and the way I sort of bombed them all. Maybe it was because I knew people were watching me more closely than before because I was planning on going indie.

Or maybe it was because I was giving all these dick-toting drivers around me a run for their money.

I grinned as I stared at the bumper of the guy behind me. Yeah, I liked that one.

"Watch it!" my spotter yelled in my ear, and I looked up in time to see a car drafting nearby. I pulled away, doing my best not to swerve out too far and throw my car into a spin. It was a fine line driving at speeds like this.

"What the fuck!" I yelled, straightening out. "He tried to take me out!"

"We're getting down to the final laps, Joey. Tension's building. I feel it."

Why did that sound like a warning and not a pep talk?

"Ease over," he said in my ear. "The car behind you is still really close. He might try and clip you again."

I glanced behind me. He was definitely too close for comfort. Something in my stomach clenched, but I forced the feeling away and turned back around. *Don't look behind you. Only look ahead.*

Through my windshield, I focused on the guy I needed to pass up. I'd know that car anywhere. It was one of my "team members." Notice the quotation marks? Yeah, there's a reason for them. He was a total douche nozzle, and I hated him. What's more? He hated me.

I wanted to place ahead of him more than I wanted to actually win this race.

We'd been trailing each other most of the day. I could almost feel his satisfaction that I'd yet to pass him.

"I'm going for the pass up ahead." I spoke into my mic.

"What? It's too soon." He worried.

I rolled my eyes. "It's not. I need to take him now so I can get even farther ahead on the next lap."

"Yeah, okay, try doing it on the inside."

"He's totally going to pull to the inside," I argued, my hands tightening on the wheel. "That's Cannon's M.O."

"Passing on the outside is too risky."

I ignored him. He knew I could do this. He was just being cautious. This was another example of why it was hard being a racer when I was my father's daughter. Spotters were scared. If they encouraged me to make a move that ended in a fiery crash—or worse, death—the fear of what my father would do to them was intense.

"I'm doing it."

"I'm going to advise against it."

I shoved the mic away from my ear and down my chin. *Fuck him!* His refusal only made me more determined.

The curve came up. I shifted and prepared to move. The driver on my ass swung in because I moved out just a hair. All at once, his speed punched up, his front end came barreling at my rear, and I knew he was aiming to take me out.

I pulled the wheel and guided my car out and over. The driver who'd been trying to clip me was taken off guard by the sudden movement, and his front tire hit the grass. The change in pavement jolted his car and sent it into a spin, farther into the center of the track.

"See ya," I sang, refocusing on the car in front of me.

"They're coming up fast! Boxing you in!" my spotter yelled.

Just as soon as the one car spun out, another replaced him, filling the vacancy I just left. On my right, another car was coming up, and I jerked the wheel, gliding over to push him out, and then hit the accelerator and pushed my car so I was driving parallel with Cannon.

On the outside of the curve, my car had to work harder than his. My fingers ached from gripping the wheel as I pressed down the gas a little bit more.

Pure hostility seemed to slam into the side of my car, and I glanced out my window into Cannon's blue vehicle. His head was turned in my direction. Even though I couldn't see his expression, I knew he was pissed I would try to pass him this way.

"Back off." My spotter warned me.

"What! No way!" I yelled and powered on. I gained on the blue car. He sped up, trying to gain what he lost, but there was no way in hell I was going to let that happen. Up ahead, the curve was starting to straighten. It was now or never.

I gave my car almost everything it had and went for it.

I pulled ahead, barely clear of his car. Movement out of my mirror made my heart jolt when Cannon jerked his wheel toward my back end as if he were trying to shove me off the road.

I cut the wheel sharp, cutting him off completely and taking up in front of him just as the track straightened out.

"Asshole!" I spat and refocused in front of me

I needed to concentrate on taking the lead, maintaining the progress I was making.

Beneath me, the car started pulling a bit, like some bolts needed tightening.

"Fuck!" I muttered and kept going.

"Your car is pulling. You need to come in."

"I can go another lap," I insisted.

"You're risking a whole hell of a lot," he argued.

"I know my car, dammit."

"Next round, come in," he said. I heard his muffled voice yelling orders and demands for the crew to get shit ready. Then it seemed his voice got farther away. I only heard the rumble of his tone, not what he was saying.

Cannon appeared on top of me, drafting hardcore, even worse than the guy who'd just tried to do it to me before.

"Get off my ass!" I yelled.

He pressed in closer, coming up on the inside of my left rear corner. I sped up, my car rattling a bit, but I knew she would hold. Cannon came right along with me.

"What's his position?" I called into the mic, jamming it back against my lips.

No answer.

"His position!" I yelled.

I glanced back nervously. The back of my neck was tingling. Cannon was going to try something. He was going to try and nudge me enough to take me out.

"You're in trouble, Joey. You need to get some space. He's drafting, and it looks bad."

Really? What the fuck was wrong with this guy? He was so getting fired.

"Way to have some confidence," I bitched.

I ignored him, looking ahead to see what my options were. As I drove, a car moved past Cannon and up beside me.

What the fuck?

I looked over, recognizing the driver as someone Cannon was often photographed with. Even through all our gear and the windows, I felt our stares lock.

This was an ambush. He was going to ride my side so I couldn't move over and Cannon would have a better chance of taking me out.

I knew these guys hated me, but what they were doing right now was downright dangerous. Life-threatening.

Sweat dripped off my temple. I felt it trail down the side of my face. I pulled in a shuddering breath and forced my eyes off the driver and back ahead.

I felt a whisper of a touch against my back left side…

"Josie!" Jace's voice flooded my ear, pulling me out of the panic starting to swallow me.

"Jace?" I answered.

"These motherfuckers are trying to take you out," he growled, but his voice was rushed and sort of breathless like he'd been running.

"No shit. Where's my good-for-nothing spotter?"

He made a fierce sound. "I punched him in the face."

Just like that, I felt stronger, more in control. "You got this?" I asked.

"*We* got this."

I hit the gas, asking my car for a little more. The rattling got a little more intense; my car pulled.

"Fight it," he said. "Get through this. Then we'll tighten your shit."

"That bank up ahead," I said, surveying my options in front of me as the driver beside me slid in a little closer.

"You're gonna need that bank," he said, his voice oddly void.

"Jace?"

"Focus, Josie," he commanded.

I wasn't too far behind the two cars in front of me. All the push I was giving the car to get away from Cannon was gaining me a little advantage.

"He's gonna try to take you out. I see the way he's forcing the car into position," Jace said, flat. "Take that bank ahead, go low into it, and then use the way it slopes up."

"Got it."

"You need to keep that car in control, Josie." Jace sounded almost desperate. In a weird way, it made calm wash over me.

When I was a child and woke up from a scary dream, I asked my dad if he was ever scared. He smiled and said, *Never.* When I asked how come, he said, *Because when the person you're with is scared, you have to be strong for them. You have to give them strength.*

I felt the nerves in Jace. I was going to do this. Not just for me, but for him, too. Fuck these guys, my so-called teammates.

One was already out because he tried this.

Now here, two more were trying. They were working together to shut me out.

I was so very tired.

But I couldn't let them win.

The light hit came seconds later. The car to my right drove in, forcing me off the side. I steered into the hit, feeling my back wheels fishtail as I fought to keep control.

The bank came fast, and I took it. The car bounced and jostled, but I held strong, flying through the grass, ripping up the dirt as I sped up the slope of the hill.

The sound of groaning metal behind me was so loud it pierced my ears; all the muscles in my neck went rigid.

"Jace!" I yelled, wanting to know what was happening.

"It doesn't matter," he urged. "Focus, right here. Stay with me."

"Always," I said, forcing out the sounds and staying right there with the car and him.

"Okay, move toward the track there's an opening for you to slide back on."

"Got it," I said, doing what he instructed. My heart rate, which had been so erratic it hurt, started to level out.

"Up ahead, you're going to transition back onto the road. The change in asphalt is going to jar you."

It was jarring, but not as bad as people trying to take you out. I made it back onto the track, taking up position right behind the two leading cars.

Jace whooped with relief. "That was fucking awesome, baby! Goddamn, that was some hella good driving!"

I let out a yell, relieved and happy at the same time. But I only had time for one moment. This race wasn't over. "Where's Cannon?"

"The two cars trying to take you out? They crashed into each other and caused a pile up of metal behind you."

"What!" I glanced back, trying to see.

"Eyes ahead," Jace ordered like he knew. "It's just a pile of metal. Looks like all the drivers are unhurt. The track will be clear when you make it around."

"The cars?" I asked.

"They're done. DNF all of the ones in the pile up."

So Cannon was out. Removed by his own hand. He deserved so much worse. "Karma's a bitch, and so am I," I muttered.

"What the fuck is going on out there, Josie?" Jace said, a little less urgency in his tone. "This entire race has given me fucking heartburn. They've been on your ass this entire time."

"Welcome to my world," I muttered.

There was a pregnant pause. I tuned it out and focused back onto the track, on trying to gain on the cars in front of me.

"Pit is coming up," he said into my ear. "You need to come in."

"Yeah," I muttered darkly. Pit stops. What a fucking waste of time.

"C'mon the crew will have you back out in no time. You'll make up anything you lose."

He was right. I'd already had enough close calls today; I didn't need to take myself out by not maintaining my car.

"I'm coming in." I confirmed.

"Hey, dickheads!" Jace yelled out. "Get ready!"

I laughed. I'm sure the pit crew loved him.

"Hey, Jace?" I said.

"Hey, Josie," he replied.

"Spot me the rest of the race?"

"You know it."

I downshifted as I pulled into the pit. Men swarmed around me, tools out, and chaos reigned. It was like being a popular exhibit in a zoo.

I stayed strapped in, tapping my fingers on the wheel and bobbing my knee nervously. It was hard to come in, hard to sit at a full stop when I needed to be out there racing and my body was still in full throttle.

"You hanging in?" Jace's voice filled my ear.

"They need to hurry up," I bit out.

His warm chuckle washed over me like a gust of warm air on a winter day. "They're moving," he assured me. "Just a couple seconds left."

I made an impatient sound, watching all the people move around.

"If I wasn't up here, I'd be down there at your window," he said, a smile in his voice.

"Wish you were. That would help pass the time." I flirted. Yes. I flirted.

"Few more laps," he said, "Then I'll make up for it."

My heart swelled a little, my lips curving up.

One of the pit crew banged on the hood of my car. My eyes snapped up; people were rushing back.

The man who'd banged on the hood made a gesture with his hand indicating we were done, and I hit the gas.

"There you go," Jace said. "Let's win this thing."

I barely heard him. It wasn't because I was so intent on speeding out of the pit, even though I was. It was because my stare locked on the crew member who told me I could go. There was something about the way he was looking at me, something about the way he seemed less than eager to jump back from the car even as I sped off.

Something sinister.

I forced my eyes away and gunned the engine, rejoining the race.

Hopefully, the speed would dislodge the strange feeling his eyes had left me with.

Thirty

Lorhaven

Disloyalty.

Dishonor.

Fucking turd burglars.

I used to think the pro division was the cream of the crop. The top percentage of drivers. You know why I thought that?

Because that's what the pro division wants everyone to think.

People only know the information they're given.

I've learned a whole hell of a lot in the past few years; most of it turned everything I thought about the world of racing onto its ass.

When you're on the outside looking in, things look a whole lot prettier. Once the door is open, though? You find the cobwebs in the corner, the dust under the beds… the trash that didn't yet make it into the garbage.

This wasn't the first pro race I'd been to. It was the first time I'd sat in the pit. The first time I'd watched on with fucking rocks in my gut and my heart in my throat.

Brutal.

That's what this was today.

Only a few laps in, it became clear Joey was a target. It was like every car on that track worked against her. Driving wasn't a team sport, but today, they all seemed to band together as just that and focus on getting her the hell out of their way.

What the fuck?

Is this what she faced on a daily basis?

I'd rather have my leg hair pulled out one at a time with rusty tweezers than stand here and watch these guys try and run her off the road.

I knew better than anyone driving got heated. It was dangerous. Tension and adrenaline ran high. But this was different. This was vicious.

I paced. Drew and Trent stood by and watched with grim faces. Drew started yelling the first time someone got too close. Josie handled it like a pro and moved on like she didn't even notice. Hopper yelled the second time it happened, and Trent stood there with anger in his eyes and veins bulging in his neck.

About five laps to go, I noticed a car coming up behind her. I looked up at her spotter, and the fucker wasn't even watching. He was supposed to be her eyes. Her ears… a partner.

"What the fuck!" I yelled.

Trent glanced at me. "They're going at her hard today."

"It always like this?" I bit out.

"I haven't been to many of her races, but they've never been this bad before." His voice was grim, restrained with anger.

Hopper paced by, staring straight ahead. I grabbed him, pulled him around.

"What the fuck is going on out there?"

"I don't know," he spat, looking back.

"Those are your guys out there! They're attacking one of your own!"

"I'm working on it!" he yelled back. I shoved him aside, and he put his ringing phone to his ear. "Tell him to back the fuck off, Grimes!" he roared as he swung back around.

My eyes stayed glued to Joey's car as it tore around the track. I wondered if she was okay, how tired she was. How mentally drained she was feeling and how bad these fuckers were messing with her head.

"So help me God, if he doesn't back off, he's going to regret it." Hopper ripped the hat off his head as he yelled into the phone and shoved at the messy dark strands of hair. They were damp with sweat as his eyes were glued to the race.

It wasn't good enough. Him calling the spotter's mates and demanding they behave wasn't enough. I glanced back up at Josie's spotter. He was saying something to her, shaking his head.

The sound of metal crunching on metal stopped my heart. A loud buzzing sound replaced everything going on around me. My hands shook wildly, and I felt unsteady.

"Josie," I ground out, glancing around, desperate to make sure she was okay.

It was like I was suddenly blind. I couldn't find her. All I saw was metal and cars piling on top of one another accompanied by the sound of brakes squealing.

A hand hit the back of my neck, squeezing so hard it brought me back. "There, she's fine, ahead of it all," Trent said, steering my head in her direction.

All the oxygen whooshed out of me in a great heave. Suddenly, I felt like a deflated balloon.

"Thank God," I rasped.

Trent gave my neck a light squeeze and let go.

I sprinted into action. I raced forward and rushed up the ladder taking me to where the spotter was posted up high. The platform wasn't tiny; there was enough room to move around.

There was a hard, annoyed look on his face. "You're in trouble, Joey. You need to get some space. He's drafting, and it looks bad," he said into the mic.

I saw red. How dare he talk to her like that, like he didn't even care!

I made a sound, and he spun. His eyes widened when I stalked forward.

"Give me the headset," I ground out.

His eyes narrowed, and he shook his head.

I laughed. Then I punched him right in the face. He folded like a house of cards. Fucking pussy. His nose was bleeding when I bent and ripped off the headset.

He made a sound, and I shoved his head away. "Shut up," I told him and put it on.

The relief in her voice when I came on was apparent, and it made me feel sick. She shouldn't even be in this position to need relief. She should've had someone in her ear that wasn't an asshole.

Goddamn, I was so, *so* angry. My hands shook with it.

I wanted to ask her if she was okay, if she was upset.

I couldn't.

We had to do this. Races were run by the clock, driven by focused drivers. Right now, she needed guidance and confidence in her ear. Even if I did think this was a giant clusterfuck, I would do right by Josie.

I knew even more fear when another driver started drafting her left back corner and another boxed her in. I felt helpless, completely out of control. I couldn't protect her. She had to protect herself.

But if this guy wrecked her… if she got hurt in any way… I'd be this motherfucker's worst nightmare.

"We got this," I told her, forcing resolve into my voice.

And we did.

She made it out.

The asshole who bumped her end could drive home in his scrap metal with a *did not finish* under his belt. Once they hauled it off the track, that is. I rather enjoyed the sight of him standing on the shoulder, staring at the mangled mess he'd been driving.

The amount of relief I felt when Josie pulled into the pit made my knees weak. I leaned on the railings and stared down at her car. I flirted with her because, even though she seemed okay, I knew she was rattled inside.

Too soon, she was ripping back into the race, and my heart rate was still so high I was pretty sure it counted as cardio for a day.

"Let's win this thing," I said, getting back into the race. She was trusting me with this, with her eyes, her safety.

I wasn't going to be like the bastard who had at some point crawled away and down the ladder.

I wasn't going to be like the limp dicks out on the track, pissed off because she was kicking ass despite what the hell they were doing to her.

How this shit even passed all the pro codes was beyond me.

Fuck that. Fuck them.

She had me now.

Thirty-One

Joey

My limbs were shaking more than normal. The tremble in my fingers was only quieted when I gripped the wheel so hard my knuckles turned white.

I'd been scared out there. I couldn't really allow that thought into my head when I'd been on the track. I couldn't allow myself to realize some of the heart-pumping, skin-quaking emotion I knew as I raced today was because I was being ganged up on.

I was lucky today. Lucky I hadn't ended up in a multiple-car pile-up.

Lucky I hadn't been killed.

But…

I was still alive, and I was smiling.

Second place!

It hadn't mattered what Cannon or any of the other drivers tried out there. They didn't pull it off. But I did.

We did.

Jace and I.

The second my car screeched to a halt, my hands worked ferociously to undo my harness so I could get out.

It seemed to take forever. My limbs felt like Jell-O, and mental exhaustion pulled me down.

Strong, sure hands pushed mine away, deftly removing the restraints. I looked up. Jace was there, the headset around his neck now, his hair standing up like he'd been running his hands through it and his olive skin seeming fairer than usual despite the sun.

He looked like solace.

He smelled like home, and he felt like relief.

I ripped off my headgear, gloves, and sunglasses. Jace had the straps undone, and then I was out of the car. The fresh outdoor air brushed against my cheeks. I launched myself at Jace. He caught me, his arms like vises around my back.

"You tore it up out there!" he exclaimed.

I laughed. "Second place!"

"That was some of the most levelheaded driving I've ever seen, baby. God, I'm proud of you."

He was proud, and it felt almost as good as that win I fought for.

Not many people told me they were proud. Mostly, I just told myself. I thought it was good enough until I heard it from Jace's mouth.

Now, good enough wouldn't be near enough ever again.

"Holy shit!" Drew said from close behind. "Joey, that was awesome."

Jace put me down, and I hugged Drew and then Trent. Hopper was standing there, looking a little worse for the wear. His too-long hair was wild, the hat he'd had on long gone, and the corners of his eyes seemed pinched. But he made up for it with a relieved smile.

"That was impressive," he said and yanked me into a hug.

When I pulled back, I said quietly, "Did you see?"

His full, dark brows drew down. "Oh, I saw. It will be dealt with."

I didn't say anything else because people swarmed us. I stepped back a little, overwhelmed and, honestly, still shaken.

My back came up against a familiar chest, and I melted against him for long seconds before straightening away.

His hand enfolded mine, and I took strength from his touch as the press and everyone crowded in. I answered a few questions, smiled for the cameras, and then Hopper told them all to move back.

"Give the woman time to celebrate! She'll answer questions after the trophies are presented," he called and waved everyone back.

Arrow stepped up beside us and grinned, his blond hair falling over his forehead.

"You owned it out there." He smiled, a little shy.

I bounded forward and hugged him tight. He hesitated a second, but then his arms came around me, and I smiled against his shoulder.

"Thanks," I said, only loud enough for him to hear.

When we pulled apart, I noted Jace watching us, a warm look in his eyes. He stepped up to me, anchoring his arm around my waist.

Beers started being passed around, and a celebratory feeling went through the air. Even though I was excited about the win, my nerves were still strung tight. I hoped the beer in my hand would help me relax, but my throat still felt too constricted to drink it.

"Josie, you doing okay?" Jace leaned in to whisper in my ear.

I glanced up, nodding. "Yeah, it was just intense."

His eyes darkened, lips thinned. "Yeah, too intense."

I felt the guys around me wanting to ask about it, but it was almost like a subject no one wanted to touch. I understood that way more than anyone else could, and I definitely was in no hurry to explain. Hell, I didn't even think I could.

It was getting out of hand… News of my crossover was making it worse.

Nearby, there was some commotion, and I heard some yelling from the press. I craned my neck to see what was going on. Drew, Trent, Arrow, and Jace all did the same.

An odd feeling of foreboding washed over me. It left me overheated, sticky, and churned up inside. My hand gripped the bottle of beer like it was a lifeline… or maybe a weapon.

The crowd parted as three men, all in suits and ties, one with a clipboard and a frown, headed our way through the pit. I swallowed down the vomit rising up in my throat.

This isn't good.

I ripped my eyes away from the men to find Hopper and signal with a mayday look. In seconds, he was there, swiftly at my side. Before he could even ask me what was wrong, he noticed the men. His body stiffened.

Drew wasn't far away, and we locked eyes. He frowned, smacking Trent in the side, who then also noticed. It seemed everyone noticed them in that second. All the noise and celebration died down to be replaced with the kind of eerie silence I'd only heard in movies, up until now.

Jace sensed whatever was about to happen, too, reaching out and trying to pull me into the shelter of his body. I wanted to be there, I craved the shelter, but I couldn't accept it. I needed to face this on my own.

I kinda want him, though.

"Ms. Gamble," the man with the clipboard said, reaching us.

"That's me," I answered.

"The inspection of your car just a few moments ago has provided us with some troubling conclusions."

"Is there something wrong with my car?" I asked, alarmed, looking around for it, even though I knew it wasn't out here. My stomach twisted, and my palms became clammy.

"As a professional driver, we know you've been made aware of the strict policy of making no changes on your car after the inspection the day of the race."

"Of course," I said, confused.

"We inspect the cars again right before the race, then right after," he said.

I made a sound. "I know that. What are you saying?"

"Your car has been worked on since the inspection this morning. Unpermitted modifications have been made."

"What?" I said, my own voice like an echo inside my head. I didn't understand. I didn't make any changes to my car. I wouldn't. Nor could I! I'd been driving it for crying out loud.

The man nodded, referring to his notes like he didn't know exactly what he'd come here to say. Around us, the press was watching, red lights on cameras blinking and everyone waiting with bated breath to see what this official would say.

In other words, the air was scented with scandal, and the media loved a good scandal.

"Your lift plate has been adjusted to allow more oxygen in, which, as you know, results in the ability to go faster."

"That's insane!" Jace bit out.

A wonky, unbalanced feeling came over me. The press started going crazy, yelling out questions, cameras going off. All the noise around us pressed in, becoming almost unbearable.

I glanced at Hopper, unable to form any words. He frowned. "That's impossible," he said.

"It's not," the man said. "I have the inspection report right here."

"Let me see," Hopper insisted and held out his hand.

"As Ms. Gamble's manager, I'm afraid you are also suspect in this, and we are not required to show you any of our reports."

"That's ridiculous!" he fumed.

"We have no choice but to disqualify you from today's race. The professional division of racing does not take lightly to cheating."

And just like that, the bubble I was floating in burst. They were taking away my win. Making out like what I did out there today—the way I survived and pulled through—was nothing.

"Are you kidding!" I gasped. "I have never cheated! I didn't modify my car. If that report"—I jabbed my finger at his clipboard— "shows tampering, then I want to speak with this facilities manager. My car was supposed to be safe here. It was to be under strict lock and key. If someone modified it, then I want to know who it was!"

You already know…

The thought stopped me cold. I gasped and stepped back into Jace. My eyes tore around until I found who I was looking for.

The guy on my pit crew, the one who'd looked at me so strangely during my final pit stop.

It was you…

His eyes widened. Then he looked away. But not before I caught the stench of guilt wafting off him.

"It was my pit crew!" I panted. "They must have messed with my car when I wasn't looking!"

The official gave me a wilting look. "Are you saying the pit crew you hired—your own staff—adjusted your car without your knowledge?" I started to say something, but he cut me off. "Because this division would find it very hard to believe a driver's own pit crew would sabotage their own race."

It was hard to believe, but that had to be it. I wobbled on my feet. Betrayal at every turn. Deceit surrounded me.

All this time. All these years I fought for respect. It all felt like it had been for nothing right now.

Did no one respect me? Did no one think I deserved to be here today?

"I didn't do this." I sounded hollow to my own ears. My stomach lurched, bile rose up in my throat, and my chest became so tight it hurt to breathe.

"You're claiming you didn't know about the changes made to your car?" The official scoffed.

"I'm not claiming anything!" I snapped. "I'm saying it to be true."

"Look, Ms. Gamble, we know who your father is—"

I lurched forward, pushing my face so close he actually stepped back. "Don't you dare bring him into this! This isn't about him. I am my own person, separate from my father."

He acted like he didn't even hear me. "Maybe you thought we would overlook your… changes because of him, because you placed second. Or maybe you just thought he would write a check and make it all go away."

I made an outraged sound and moved forward again.

A strong arm wrapped around my waist and towed me back. My chest heaved as I tried to breathe. I shook so badly I was afraid if it weren't for Jace holding me, I'd fall down.

I glanced around. My ruin was going public. It was probably being broadcast on the news right now. I'd been dogged out there on the track today. Everyone worked as a unit against me. And now this…

They were chipping away at everything I had. My career, my pride, my reputation.

Anger so hot whipped through me it burned. "You actually think I would tamper with my own car, that I need to cheat to win a race?" I yelled.

The official without the clipboard seemed to have an answer ready. "Maybe the renewed media interest in your crossover and subsequently your career has put pressure on you to win so your crossover will be more publicized."

I laughed. It was a strangled and unfortunately helpless sound. I was going to break down right here. Right now.

Everyone would see just how weak I really was.

"Are you fucking kidding me?" a very familiar voice ground out beside me ear. "You peckers aren't actually standing there implying you think she did this. She said she didn't." Jace unwrapped his arm from around my waist and stepped forward, challenging the men. Trent stepped up beside me, and Drew took up position on my other side. Thank God for them…

What if they leave you when they find out how weak you are?

"Why would anyone else want to modify her car?" the man retorted.

"To get me disqualified!" I burst out.

"Surely there is something that can be done." Drew spoke up.

Hopper was shaking his head, a scowl on his face. He knew as well as I did what that answer was going to be.

"It doesn't work that way. She was caught with a modified car. She knows the regulations and the consequences." He looked at me. "You're out. There is no win here for you today. Pack up and go. The division will be in touch with your management as to what this will mean for your future races."

It was my final blow in the epic battle that was today.

Jace pulled me against his side, and I leaned against him for a moment while my head swirled with doom.

My career was over. I drove like mad today. I literally beat the odds—the men trying to tear me down—out there today. I showed everyone I deserved to be on the track.

I won.

I won only to be disqualified after and was accused of cheating.

Even if they let me race again, I would be branded a cheat. I would lose sponsors and credibility. The press was going to eat me alive for this. My father was going to go ballistic.

The man with the clipboard ripped off a piece of paper from the stack and held it out to me. On the top it read: NOTICE OF DISQUALIFICATION.

I stared at it with contempt and shock. Hopper reached out and took it when it became clear I wasn't going to.

I couldn't accept this. I wouldn't.

The men with their suits and judgmental expressions strode away. I gazed after them, anger beginning to build.

Hopper stepped in my line of vision. His features were nothing but a blur in front of my eyes. "I'm going to get to the bottom of this. I won't let this touch your career."

"It already has," I told him. "No matter what, I'm out today. All that out there"—I flung my hand toward the track— "was for nothing."

He nodded, grim. "You're out today."

"Not for nothing!" Jace argued. "There has to be something we can do."

"There is, but not today. They won't change their mind on the win. They won't even bring out the car. They'll confiscate it," Hopper told him.

"Who would do this, Joey?" Drew asked, his voice hard.

I shook my head. I couldn't... My head was spinning.

"Why?" Drew pressed when I didn't reply, his hands balled into fists.

I glanced at Hopper. "They're that pissed?" I rasped.

He paled. He actually staggered back a step. "They wouldn't…"

But they would.

"What?" Jace demanded, his voice wholly suspicious.

I swallowed. "My teammates," I spat. "The other pros I drive with. They're pissed I'm crossing over. They hated me before… but now it's worse."

"I need to make some calls," Hopper said. The paper in his hand crinkled in his fist. "I won't except this. I'll take it to the top of the division if I have to." He pulled out his cell and strode away with angry, quick strides.

The entire crew was standing around looking at me. Some were whispering. My eyes found the man I suspected of making the change to the lift plate. I made sure my stare drilled into his.

He turned and walked away.

"Wait a minute!" I yelled and raced after him. The entire crowd seemed to follow me.

I grabbed him by the arm, and he looked over his shoulder.

"Why?" I asked him, low.

He jerked away from me. "I don't know what you're talking about."

"The hell you don't!" I growled.

"What's going on?" Jace demanded.

"Don't blame me because you got caught cheating," the mechanic said.

I jerked like he slapped me.

His words were like salt in the wound. He just denied what I know he did, and he not only did it in front of the press, but he implied he knew it was me who ordered it.

I watched him disappear into the crowd, leaving me here… with the pieces of my career at my feet.

Paparazzi descended like buzzards on roadkill. They smelled defeat, and they wanted it on camera, captured on film so the entire world could see my ruin, and I would have record of it for the rest of my life.

"Joey G., do you have a comment on being disqualified from today's race?"

"Joey G., why would you cheat?"

"Joey G., do you think your actions will affect Gamble Enterprises?"

They fired at me like bullets out of a machine gun, so many questions with so much force. Each of them hit me; each of them pierced my skin.

The walls were closing in on me. I needed to breathe.

Don't let them see you bleed.

"No comment!" I yelled, stepping away from Jace and straightening. The questions kept coming. The mics were in my face. People stared at me as if I were a criminal.

"Do you think today was your last race?" someone yelled out.

I snapped. Like broke in half.

"No more!" I screamed and threw my arms up in the air. "Pack the fuck up!" I roared.

Everyone stopped and stared. They acted like they were in shock at my outburst. It pissed me off. *I* was in shock. Not them.

It lasted maybe three seconds. Then everyone burst back into a flurry of movement.

"Joey," Drew said, stepping to my side.

I pulled away from him. From everyone. I felt Jace's stare, but I refused to look. I was so angry. So shocked. If I looked at him even once, I'd probably cry.

Crying was the worst thing I could do.

No.

The worst thing I could do was see the look in Jace's eyes. The condemnation.

"I'm gonna go grab my bag," I said to no one in particular and went swiftly toward the giant locker rooms for the drivers and staff.

They were co-ed down here on the track, 'cause you know, up until I started driving, there wasn't any reason for a female bathroom on a male-driven raceway. It would be discrimination to keep me out, so instead of making changes to the buildings, most places added another sign to the door, one of a figure in a dress right beside the male one.

I didn't care. What difference did it make? There were stalls, and it wasn't like I'd never seen a urinal before. Or a penis. I barely ventured past the lockers anyway. Hell, I probably wouldn't even go in there at all if I didn't want a place to lock up my bag and some extra clothes.

I hadn't even used to do that, until of course the tampering started. Until a lock had become necessary.

I should have known this was coming. I should have prepared for it. Although, how did someone prepare for something like this exactly?

I felt like the "preparations" I'd made up until this point had been to harden myself, my heart, and feed the chip on my shoulder until I could use it as a shield.

The thing about shields?

There was always one weakness. Always something that could penetrate to hit its mark.

I'd been busy with my life, with friends who came to town to see me, additional press and travel. With Jace and the way he made me feel.

I dropped my guard. My shield.

I knew better.

This was my punishment.

I went to the sinks, turned on the cold water, and splashed my face. The icy droplets helped rid some of the fog weighing down my thoughts. Feeling sorry for myself wasn't an option. I needed to think, to act.

After I used a crappy paper towel from the dispenser to pat my face dry I pulled the clip out of my hair and let the dark curls spring forward.

I studied myself in the mirror above the sink. I looked deep into the green eyes staring back at me.

Was this really worth it?

It always seemed no matter how hard I tried, it just was never enough.

Despite my best efforts, a tear escaped. With absolute loneliness, I watched it trail down my reddened cheek. Another fell. And another.

I loved driving, the thrill of speed, and spending my days behind a wheel, not at a desk. Was everything that came with it finally starting to break me down?

A sob broke free of my throat, and the dam burst open. Grabbing another paper towel, I buried my face in the scratchy paper and cried.

My body shook like a thunderstorm. I cried out of humiliation, loss, and even defeat.

All these years of being strong, of never letting it break me down… It ended in a win today… Then that win was swiftly stolen away.

I allowed myself to cry longer than I wanted. Actually, my body took over and seemed to pour out so much despair I was frightened. Which, of course, made me cry more.

Eventually, I sniffled, lifted my chin, and stared down at the torn, saturated towel in my palms. Slowly, I looked up. For once, my reflection showed what I was really like on the inside.

Broken. Kicked. Torn down.

The skin around my eyes was swollen and red. The fair skin on my cheeks was splotchy and hot. Dry, cracked skin coated my lips, and the end of my nose was raw from the stupid paper towel.

There was a smudge of dirt on my cheek, likely from the race... and it flooded me with memories of the first night I spent with Jace. Of the way we went at each other and the way he looked in that dirty T-shirt.

I started to cry again.

What if I lost him along with everything else that had already been taken?

I tossed the ruined cloth in my hand away and retrieved a fresh one. After mopping up my tears a second time and wiping my nose, I threw it away and washed my hands.

Enough was enough. Standing in a bathroom and crying wasn't going to change anything. Walking out of here with a face giving away how I really felt was going to be embarrassing enough. If I still wanted to cry later, I could do it in the privacy of my hotel room.

Pity party for one was now cancelled.

At my locker, I entered the code and opened the door. My brown leather hobo bag waited for me in exactly the same position as when I placed it there.

I wasn't quite ready to go back out there with everyone, to face the questions, the conversations... the looks. I stalled for time by unzipping the jumpsuit I was wearing and stepping out. It smelled like sweat and gasoline. The back was damp from how badly the sweat pooled between my shoulder blades. Beneath it, I was dressed in a pair of black skinny jeans and a simple gray loose V-neck T-shirt made of combed cotton.

The brush of cool air against my previously confined skin was like a kiss from Jace. Teasing but refreshing. Soft but exciting.

I had to take off the boots tied on my feet to pull off the suit, so I sat down to quickly do so, but when I went to put them back on, I couldn't. I was so tired… Instead, I reached into my hobo and found a pair of flip-flops. I was stuffing everything in my bag when the door to the locker room opened and slammed shut.

I glanced up, thinking it was Jace, not objecting at all to his presence. I kinda wanted it right now. I just wanted to feel his support. I needed it.

I knew almost instantly, though, it wasn't Jace. My back stiffened as someone stepped around the row of lockers into sight.

All the little nagging thoughts, the suspicions my subconscious held close, rushed to the surface. Along with it came humiliation, defeat… anger.

"If I were you, I'd turn around and get the fuck out," I said, grabbing my bag and slamming the locker door closed with a bang. It made a nice exclamation to my words.

"Joey, Joey, Joey," he intoned, stepping forward. "You look like you've been crying." He made a sad face, and in that moment I knew true hate.

Dean Cannon was an arrogant bastard who thought the world revolved around him. He wasn't a large guy, standing about five seven, with a slim build and a head full of brown hair. He definitely wasn't my cup of tea—or my cup of anything really—but I knew a lot of fans thought he was a heartthrob.

He liked to remind the entire team of that whenever possible.

He had his own line of T-shirts, some with his name on the back. He also had a couple endorsement deals, one of which pretty much made him a household name. Well, for anyone who watched TV and paid attention to commercials.

My father sponsored him, along with a few other big companies, but it was the deal he had with my father that made him part of my "team."

Technically, drivers weren't on teams. But my father sponsored quite a few drivers in the pro division. Our headquarters was at Gamble Speedway. Everyone had apartments there. The garages and mechanics were there. Hopper and a few other managers were there.

We drove together a lot. We occupied a lot of the same training facilities, and we used the same team of people to get us ready for races.

Everyone got along with each other, but no one really got along with me.

I was the outsider. The driver who remained apart even in a crowded room. People recognized it. I downplayed it.

Because really, I didn't care.

Not much, anyway. Okay, fine, sometimes it hurt like hell. Sometimes, I felt like a kid in kindergarten who stood in the back of the class while a popular kid handed out party invitations, waiting for mine, but it never came. Everyone got invited to the party, everyone but me.

Why not me?

When we were at work, I was all business. I ignored the jokes, the looks, and the occasional snide remark. I didn't go out for pizza and beer or watch old racing tapes after hours in the headquarters media space.

I was nice to everyone on staff, but I earned the reputation of being aloof. I knew some people assumed I thought I was better than the other drivers. Some thought I was spoiled by Daddy. I never denied it, but I never confirmed it either.

It didn't matter, though, because I learned sometimes silence had a price. Some people always wanted to believe the worst or revel in the drama, and since I never said anything, they continued to do so.

It bothered me, but in the grand scheme of things, what did it really matter? My job was to drive, to be a professional, and to win races.

Today you didn't win. Today it was all taken from you.

Looking back, and looking at Dean right now, maybe I should have been a little less professional. I'd allowed him and the others to get away with too much.

Hiding behind the stereotype.

"The press is already having a field day with this." Dean guffawed, placing his hands in the pockets of his dirty, sweaty racing coveralls with a smug look on his face.

"That was your intent, wasn't it?" I said knowingly. "To discredit me with the press and take away my win today so I looked worse than you after you tried to take me out and caused a metal pileup on the track."

An angry glint covered the truth in his eyes. "Are you implying I'm the one who fucked with your car?"

"Oh, I'm not implying it."

His hands yanked out of his pockets, his arms pumping when he strode forward. I stayed planted where I was even though my skin crawled with his nearness.

This is the first time I've been alone with him since that night.

"If you know what's good for you, you'll keep your mouth shut," he warned.

I tipped my head to the side and studied him. "You mean like before?"

His eyes flared. "You haven't forgotten about that yet?"

I smirked. "You wish I would, don't you?"

His blue eyes narrowed. It was such a beautiful waste of color on him. His dark soul ruined it.

I stepped forward, challenging him. I refused to show any kind of fear or intimidation toward him. It's what he wanted, and even if my hands did tremble a bit with our confrontation, I was too conditioned to let it show.

I'd become very good and hiding the worst of my weaknesses.

"Is that why you fucked with my car? How'd you do it, Cannon? Did you sneak in yourself after you ate my dust today, then wrecked during your temper tantrum on the track? It wouldn't be the first time you messed with my car."

His face soured. "I didn't modify anything."

"So who did?" I asked. "You pay someone on my pit crew?"

His eyes flashed. "You're a little bitch, you know that?"

So that was it. That look I'd seen on that guy's face. Cannon paid him to modify my car; he paid him to make me look like a cheat.

The worst part? I was sitting in the goddamn car while it happened.

"No, Cannon. You're the bitch. You're such a bitch you tampered with my car because I beat you today. Not only did a girl blow past you out on that track, but I was stealing all the pro spotlight, wasn't I? I was getting all kinds of new attention because of the crossover."

The muscles in his neck corded like he was having trouble containing himself. I guess the truth hurt. "Publicity? No one gives a fuck about you or your career. The only reason you're here is because of your daddy."

"So you keep saying," I retorted, bored. I'd heard him say that so many times I practically heard it in my sleep.

"You couldn't even get a magazine cover on your own. They had to put a guy next to you because no one would have picked it up if it was only about a woman driver."

That stung, probably because part of me believed him.

"If you think I'm going to keep my mouth shut about today you're on crack. There's no way in hell I'll watch my entire career go up in smoke."

"After today, you won't have a career," he growled.

"After today, you won't either." I vowed.

His eyes widened just a fraction. It made me feel like shit. Did he really think so low of me? Did he really think he could push me this far and I wouldn't push back?

Of course he did. You've allowed it before.

"You shouldn't have come in here, Cannon. But you just had to gloat, didn't you? I might have suspected it was you before, but now I know for sure."

"You don't have the proof." He smiled.

"I've got my word. And I have a direct line to the man who signs your biggest check."

All the color drained from his face, and he rushed me. I flew back, my body slamming against the locker doors as I tried to avoid his hands.

Memories rushed me… feelings, thoughts… fear. I made a strangled sound, trying to get away. He shoved me back again. My head bounced off the metal and I shoved out at him, determined to fight.

You know what sucked about being a woman? Being physically weaker than a man.

He body-checked me. Pressed himself up against me and rubbed like he was a cat on a scratching pole. "I know you missed this," he crooned, reaching for my breast.

I spit in his face.

The mean, spiteful look I'd grown used to appeared in his expression. His hand shot out, grabbed me by the throat, and pinned me up against the wall. I grabbed at the hand with both of mine, trying to claw him off.

He only squeezed tighter, lifting me so my feet were off the floor and dangled over the ground. I dug my nails into his arm, and he cursed, but it wasn't enough to make him let go.

I gasped, desperate for air.

"Listen here, you little bitch," he snarled. "You keep your damn mouth shut, go over to that farce of a division for the poor, forgotten indies, and let the real men handle the pros. You don't belong here. You never did, and you never will."

I brought my knee up and rammed it into his balls.

His eyes about popped out, his hand let go of my throat, and I dropped out of the air, down the locker, and hit the floor with a hard slap.

I grabbed my throat, wheezing and gasping for breath. Even though his hand was gone, I still felt like he was squeezing it. I still felt like I couldn't breathe.

Panic tinged the edge of my vision, and I rolled and sat up. I barely made it; gasping for oxygen was all I could manage. Cannon's body folded in on itself. What I could see of his face was beet red.

I knew I needed to get up, so I started to stand, throwing my hands out to brace myself. With a sound of rage, Cannon launched himself at me, tackling me to the floor, and pinned me down.

"Get off me!" I roared, but it sounded like a squeak. He hit me. Pain bloomed across my cheek.

Tears burned my eyes. I was so incredibly frustrated and hurt.

"You just keep trying to show me who's boss, don't you?" He pushed his face down into mine, spittle from his lips spraying me, and I cringed back. "Maybe I should show you who's really the boss, once and for all."

Fear, genuine and piercing, clawed me. On impulse, I ripped one arm from beneath him and drove my thumb into his eye.

He yelled, and I shoved him off, scrambled to my feet. Dean jumped up as I lunged away, grabbed my arm, and yanked. When I spun, I brought along my fist and caught him right in the face.

"Argh!" he yelled, his head snapping back. Blood spurted from his nose. Pain exploded in my hand, but I clung to the feeling. It made me feel alive.

He recovered way faster than I would have liked and struck out.

His fist caught me in the lip. I felt the skin split and the warm trickle of blood. My head buzzed with adrenaline and anger. My hands shook, and inside my chest, my heart pounded. I dabbed at my lip. My fingers came away red.

He laughed like the sight of me bleeding made him happy. Like it proved something.

"Keep your bitch mouth shut or it's going to get way worse for you." Cannon threatened.

I wiped the blood on my leg and faced him. "How exactly is it going to get way worse for me?" I snapped.

He started to scoff, like I was being stupid, so I swung out, hitting him again. Right in the nose a second time. He howled, this time falling back into the lockers, and brought a hand up to cover his nose.

My chest heaved. I felt years of pent-up frustration and refocused anger shift and zero in on him and everything he'd ever done to me.

"What are you gonna do? Stick some more maxi pads to my car? To my locker? To the bathroom stalls? You gonna hang tampons from my rearview mirror and put them in my drinks when I'm not looking?" I advanced on him, heaving. Tears rained from my eyes, but I didn't care anymore. I was wild with anger and misery. I felt ruined, like I'd hit rock bottom.

How did it come to this? How did I end up disqualified from a race, humiliated, and in a literal fist fight with a man?

My eyes drilled right into his, and I took another menacing step forward, he actually shrank back against the lockers even more, still holding his bleeding face.

"You gonna take my car again? Park it across town in the ghetto in an alleyway? Took me an entire day of searching to find it. You know how much that shit cost me? I had to buy all new rims and a stereo system."

"Shut up," he rasped, finally pulling his hand away. Blood coated his palm, his eyes were already shadowed, and his nose was swelling.

I hoped to God it was broken.

"Why?" I cried. "You don't like to hear all the shit I've put up with from you without so much as a whisper of complaint?" I yelled. "Well, too damn bad! You've pushed me too fucking far!"

I couldn't stop now. It tumbled out of me with such force I wondered how the hell I'd kept it in all this time.

"What about the night y'all invited me to a team party? I thought, *Shit! These guys have finally decided I might be worth driving with.* I thought maybe I'd actually see some of the comradery the rest of you showed each other. But I didn't get that, did I, Cannon? I walked in to you holding an inflatable doll with my racing suit on it. Jacobs was fucking it right there in front of you. Did you get off on seeing him get off? Did you take a turn next? You're a sick fuck."

He gasped. "Not another fucking word."

"Oh, and then there was the time you came in the locker room without me knowing and took photos of me in my bra and panties while I changed. You taped them up in the garage. But that wasn't as fun, was it? Because Hopper found them. You still cleaning toilets for that?"

He took a step forward, clearly promising to hit me again. My lip stung where he'd already done so, but I refused to back down.

"But that's not even the worst of it, is it?" I whispered, still pushing him, even seeing he was ready to snap. "Then there was that night…"

He roared and lunged forward. The bloodied hand he'd had against his nose struck me, slapped across my face, and with it, I felt the warm smear of blood. I stumbled, saw my bag nearby, and picked it up, swinging it at him. It hit him in the face, and I took off running.

I wasn't a runner, but I was outweighed, and I'd clearly pushed him too far.

Again, he caught my arm and jerked me back around. My entire body went on defense, ready to fight.

"Let. Go." The deep, menacing snarl echoed through the room.

I looked over my shoulder to where Jace was standing, just inside the row of lockers. All his focus was on Dean, and the look on his face scared me.

This was not Jace… No, this was Lorhaven.

Even more, a Lorhaven not even I had seen before, and I'd seen him pretty pissed off. His feet were planted apart, his hands balled at his sides. The darkness of his eyes looked almost void, like he had nothing inside him that could even try to hold him back from the pure destruction the snarl on his lips promised.

Cannon released me instantly. I stumbled back, out of arm's distance.

"Jace," I panted, "let's go."

He glanced at me, did a double take. "What happened to your face?" His voice was deadly calm.

I swiped at the blood. "I'm fine."

"He. Hit. You."

I nodded.

"She hit me first. Fucking deserved it!" Cannon yelled, like that would save him.

"How many times? You're bruised. Bloody…" His eyes swept down. "Your neck is red. Swollen." He stepped closer to me, peering down. "Purple blotches…" His body went rigid. "Are those fucking fingerprints!" He roared the last word and even I shrank back.

Jace darted down the row of lockers and, in one swift movement, grabbed Dean by the scruff of his neck and rammed his face into the metal lockers.

Cannon made a muffled *umph* sound before crumpling to the ground at Jace's feet.

Jace spun, his fists balled. "Everything you just said was true?" he rasped tightly.

I felt like someone punched me in the stomach. "How much did you hear?" I whispered.

"I heard everything, Josie. Everything." His chest heaved so heavily and so fast I actually worried.

Tears fell once more, and I wiped at them, trying to hide the fact I was dying inside. My God, I felt backed into a corner for so long… and it was hell trying to fight my way out.

"But there's more, isn't there? I heard you say it, but he stopped you. Tell me the rest, Josie. Tell me now."

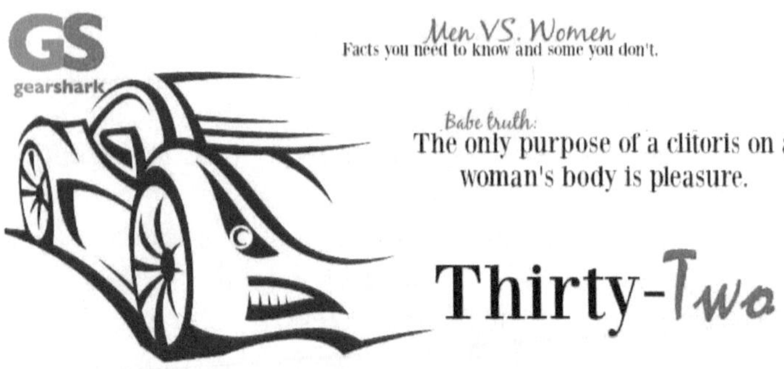

Lorhaven

Déjà-vu: *a feeling of having already experienced the present situation.*

The emotion welling inside me, pooling in my fingertips and clouding out all my judgement, was familiar.

Scarily familiar.

I'd been in this state before. It didn't end well. For anyone.

I pushed into the locker room a short while after Josie did. At first, I let her go, figuring she needed a few to process the shit that just smelled up the entire pit.

I talked to Arrow, Drew, and Trent. We speculated, and I watched Hopper yelling into his phone off in the distance.

The more seconds that passed, the more agitated I became. Fuck giving her some headspace. She was independent, but she wasn't alone anymore.

I looked around this pit crew at all the faces I didn't know. All I saw were people who didn't give a flying fuck. Yes, men. Peckerheads.

No one spoke up for her when she was accused of cheating.

It was absurd.

Her only friends were the ones who came here with her. Normally, none of us came but Hopper. I glanced back to him still speaking heatedly into the phone.

She was totally alone in this.

No wonder she wanted to cross over.

I thought back to her politically correct response to hazing. It made a sick feeling squirm around in my gut, like I suddenly had a bad case of worms. I should have forced it out of her then. I should have seen this.

I walked out of the conversation midsentence. I hadn't been listening anyway. I was with her mentally and wanted to be there physically as well.

When I shoved through the locker room door, I heard an aggressive threat come out of someone's fool mouth.

"Keep your bitch mouth shut, or it's going to get way worse for you."

My back teeth slammed together so hard my jaw vibrated. Who the fuck was this and why did he think it was okay to talk to Josie like that?

Fuck no.

I was about to go around the lockers swinging when Josie started talking. The sound of her voice… I almost didn't recognize it. Raspy and deep. Filled with pain and anguish. It slayed me… It brought me back to that night with Arrow. The night I would never forget.

It got worse.

The more Josie raged, the more horrified I felt.

That's when the déjà-vu rose up inside me, as I stood there and listened to everything she'd been going through. All the shit that peckerhead had done to her.

She said nothing. Not one word to anyone.

She brushed off what in my eyes went beyond hazing. She hid it, covered for these pricks, and they continued to torture her.

Why? Because she was a woman? Because she drove better or her father had money?

All the things I'd thrown at her in the past.

Did that make me the same as the man who was threatening her and who I knew right down in every last cell of my body was the one who messed with her car?

I stood there rooted into place, listening to her strained voice pour out everything as that feeling of wanting to kill grew and grew until my body shook with need.

I was mad at the guys in this division, mad at her father for not seeing, mad at her for not saying a word… and mad at me for being just one of the same when I first met her.

The sounds of a scuffle and the small sound of her distress shattered even the most intense of my rage. I stepped around, my eyes going right to where he restrained her.

He heard the threat in my voice. He saw it in my eyes.

I smelled his fear. I reveled in it. I welcomed it.

Then she looked at me. Blood on her lip. Blood smeared across her cheek; it looked like a hand print. A bloody fucking handprint.

Josie's eyes were puffy, red, and dull. The parts of her that weren't bloody were splotchy, and there was a bruise blooming out over her cheekbone.

And her throat… that explained her raspy voice. He'd choked her, squeezed her, robbed her of air.

There were fingerprints on her neck from the way this man abused her.

He abused her.

Her hair was flat. Her body seemed small somehow. Maybe it was the way her shoulders seemed to slump as if she'd taken all she could bear.

I'd never seen her like this before. Defenseless, turned inside out… broken.

It reminded me of Arrow. Of the kind of people who tortured others just because they could.

I didn't care what she did to him before I walked into this room. It didn't matter at all. He did this to her. I hated him.

When I looked up after the guy she called Cannon was crumpled at my feet, her face was exhausted and closed off.

I understood it; I could see the way she was suffering. But, no.

Before I busted up their little argument, she was about to spill even more. And she was going to tell me. We weren't leaving here until she did.

"Tell me," I demanded again, fighting the urge to yank her into my arms and vow to protect her forever and ever. I'd die if it would wipe the look off her face. I'd take a thousand beatings to never see someone's fingerprints on her skin again. I'd do anything for Josie.

Anything at all.

But I had to know. I had to know exactly what I was dealing with.

Her shoulders slumped even further. That's how I knew just how defeated she felt in that moment. She didn't argue with me, not even once. She opened her bleeding lips and poured it all out.

"One night after a late session of night driving, I used one of the private showers at headquarters." She glanced at me.

It took everything in me to nod encouragingly and not yell for her to hurry up.

"He picked the lock, came into the room, and stole my clothes."

Keep it together, Jace. Don't lose your shit.

"So when I was finished, I had to leave the bathroom in nothing but my towel. I had some extra clothes in my locker down in the garage, so I went down there to get them. He was in the garage waiting…" Her voice trailed off, and she cleared her throat. "I got the usual catcalls, sexist remarks, and harassment. I ignored him and just pulled my bag out of the locker. When I turned around, Cannon was there." She pointed to the douche lying on the floor, moaning like a little bitch.

I kicked him. He curled up in the fetal position, and it gave me a brief feeling of satisfaction.

"He ripped the towel off my body and shoved me against the lockers. He, uh, rubbed against my body and fondled my…" She motioned at her chest. "I tried to fight him off, but one of the other guys was suddenly there, pinning me against the locker so he could feel all he wanted."

"Stop," I demanded, harsh. I couldn't hear this. "Did they rape you?"

"No," she was quick to say. "They didn't. They just wanted to humiliate and degrade me. The whole time he was grabbing me, he was telling me to leave the pros. No one wanted me here. You know, the usual crap."

I took a deep breath. It didn't help.

"I fought him off. Bit the hand that was restraining me, and when he let go, I threw myself at Cannon. He fell back, and I punched him in the face. Broke his nose. Just like I broke it again tonight."

I heaved a sigh and swallowed, trying to get the vivid images out of my head. They were on replay. They might never go away.

"After I hit him, I kicked the other guy in the balls. I left them there, got in my car, and drove off. I was still naked, but it was dark out, and I had the bag with my clothes in it. I just wanted away from them. Of course, I was speeding. I was upset…"

"What happened, Josie?" I groaned, knowing there was more.

"The brakes went out on my Skyline. Later, I saw the line cut clean through. There was a trail of brake fluid leading up to where I finally was able to stop."

Practically raped. Attempted murder. How could she just stand there and calmly tell me this? How was she still fucking standing at all after everything?

Enraged wasn't even an apt description of how I felt. Numb maybe. Hollow. Void. To the point of no return.

That's how I felt.

I already knew I was capable of nearly killing… This time I might go past nearly… This time I might actually succeed.

I forced out the words. "You were hurt?"

She shook her head. "No, just scared. I can handle a car at high speed, so I did. I steered until I came to a steep hill on the other side of town, and I careened up it. The car ran out of speed, started to roll backward. I hit the emergency brake, did a one-eighty in the center of the road, and came to a stop."

"Who'd you call?" I asked, thinking of her naked in the dark in the middle of some road, with a busted car, after some punks sexually harassed her.

"No one," she replied. "I got dressed, called a tow, and took my car two hours away. I had it fixed, came home, and never said a word."

"Josie," I moaned. "Why the hell—"

"She's lying!" Cannon spat from the floor and pushed up to his feet. He had a welt in the center of his forehead from where I shoved his face into the locker. His nose was definitely broken, but it still wasn't enough.

He swayed a little, but his eyes were clear and they still buzzed with anger. "She's making it all up, trying to get out of what she did here today."

I decked him. Right in the side of the head. It felt good to punch him. He went down, and I leaned over, delivering two more swift blows to his face.

"Get off me!" he wailed, blood spouting from his mouth.

I yanked him to his feet, and he swung at me. I laughed, pushing his arm away, and buried my fist in his gut.

He made a sound like he might puke, and I punched him again just because he was a pansy.

"What's the matter?" I roared. "Can't take it when someone you push around pushes back?" I shoved him back, and he fell into the lockers.

I swiped out with one booted foot and knocked his feet out from under him. He fell over with a slap onto the floor.

"Jace!" Josie said, her voice tight.

"You said nothing!" I spat. "You let this little fucker get away with everything he did to you."

I punched him again. He groaned.

Josie grabbed me by the arm, and I swung around, chest heaving, and looked at her. I knew a madman stared back, but she didn't back down. "Let go," I intoned, flexing my fist.

"This is what he wants," she implored. "If you do this, I'm the one who's going to lose."

Her lower lip wobbled.

It was my undoing.

With one final yell, I punched the locker above Cannon, then turned away, unclenching my hands.

"Josie," I whispered.

Her face crumbled. Finally, I swept her up tight against me. I flattened my palm against the back of her head, holding her hard, while my other arm held her strong. She trembled against me, her shoulders shaking.

After a minute, I pulled her back but still held on. I stared at her injuries, the fingerprints, the blood. "Oh, honey. What did he do to you?"

"I'm okay, Jace. C'mon. Let's go."

I made a sound, dropping my hands. Before she could step away, I lifted the hem of my shirt and yanked it up so I could wipe of some of the blood smeared on her face. It only seemed to make the stain worse.

The idiot on the floor laughed. Maybe he was delirious. No one could be that fucking stupid.

"Hit me again," he spat, blood spurting from between his lips. "When I stumble out of here, everyone will feel sorry for me. I bet the media is still swarming outside."

He was right about that. The word of Josie being disqualified spread like wildfire. There was even more press than before.

"You're not getting away with shit," I growled and picked him up by the back of his neck. I moved swiftly, practically dragging him along with me because his feet kept slipping against the floor.

I banged out of the locker room door and stepped into a crowd. People gasped and started talking. I ignored them and dragged his bleeding ass forward.

A camera crew rushed over. A man with a mic glued to his mouth was practically frothing at the mouth. I stopped and pulled the asshole upright, making sure everyone got a good look at his battered face.

"Dean Cannon?" the reporter gasped. "What's happened?" The man turned to the camera. "I'm live with Channel Twelve, and what I have here at the scene at the raceway in Charlotte today is not only a disqualification, but heartthrob driver Dean Cannon appears to have been beaten."

"I have something to say." I interrupted.

Everyone turned to me, including the man with the mic.

"Dean Cannon is a fraud and a liar. He's the one who had Joey G.'s car tampered with. He wanted to get her disqualified."

"Why would he want to do that?" the anchor asked, clearly disbelieving.

"Because he can't stand that a woman drives better. And because it was just one more way to harass her, which he's been doing for years."

I heard Josie gasp from behind, but I made no move to shift so she would be in sight.

"I heard him admit it right after he punched her in the face." I finished. "He also choked her."

A ripple of noise moved through the crowd. Drew and Trent shoved through, appearing nearby, and my brother materialized with them. I knew just by the look on his face what he was thinking. What he was reminded of. I felt bad for it, for everything. But this was something I had to do. She needed this.

I stepped aside and reached a gentle hand out to Josie, pulling her forward in front of the cameras.

"Look at her face," I said tight. Sickness welled inside me. "See the bruise on her face? The blood? The swollen lip. How about the fingerprints on her neck? Dean Cannon followed her into that locker room to taunt and beat her. And it's not the first time."

Dean started struggling. "All lies! He did this to me. I'm suing for assault."

I punched him again. Everyone around gasped and moved closer. Cannon fell unconscious, and I dropped him on the ground in front of everyone.

Silence abounded for long moments.

"Joey G.!" the reporter yelled. "Do you have a comment? Did Dean Cannon really hit you?"

I looked over. Josie was at my side, looking strong and beautiful even with blood on her lip.

"I didn't punch myself in the face," she said. "And yes, I'd like to go on record and make it clear to everyone that I did not modify my car during a pit stop. One of my crew was paid by Cannon to modify the car without my knowledge. I have been continually hazed and harassed by my fellow pro drivers and today, it seems, everything has come to a head. This is why I wanted to cross over. I was trying to get away from the abuse but still stay in the sport I love."

Everyone converged on us like a swarm of ants on a cube of sugar. Josie, shrank into my side. I swept her into my chest, looking at Trent and Drew.

They both wore grim looks and nodded. With one arm tightly wrapped around Josie, I guided her through the path Drew, Trent, and Arrow were clearing with their bodies until we made it out of the group.

Chaos was everywhere, and I felt the weakness in her body. She was so incredibly drained from everything she could barely support herself.

I didn't have my car. We'd flown here. I glanced around at Trent. A set of keys flew at my head. I snatched them out of the air.

"Take the rental. We'll ride back with Hopper," he told me.

Hopper turned up the second his name was said. "Joey, what the hell is going on?" He worried and stepped up to her.

I shoved him back, and I wasn't gentle about it. "You had years to notice," I spat. "Years to see what they were doing to her. You're telling me you never noticed? Or did you just not care?"

Hopper paled.

"Jace, he didn't know." Josie spoke up. Her voice was deep but strong despite how I knew she felt deep down.

"We're leaving," I announced.

She started to say something. I saw the familiar glint in her eye. I pinned her with a steady stare. "You can walk out or I can carry you."

She had no choice.

"I'll see you at the hotel," she said to everyone.

We walked out, side by side. But the second we were out of sight from the crowds and the cameras, she stumbled a bit, leaning toward me.

I lifted her into my arms, cradling her closer than I ever had before, and carried her the rest of the way. Once in the rental, I turned to her.

"Just drive." Her body melted against the seat.

I did what she asked, but the second we stepped into our hotel room, she had some explaining to do.

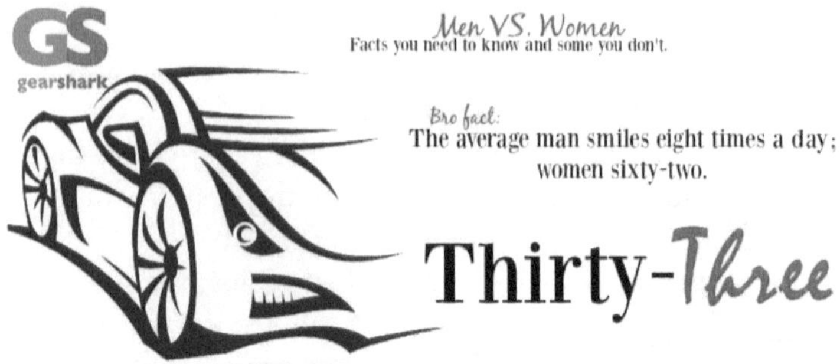

Thirty-Three

Joey

I shut my phone off…

My father called twice in the car ride over to the hotel. I let it go to voicemail.

Just the thought of talking to him made me want to escape to a foreign country and change my name.

I was reeling inside. It was giving me a hardcore case of motion sickness. All these feelings were bouncing around, rebounding off my organs, my skin, my bones… I just wanted it stop.

There wasn't a cohesive thought in my mind; there was too much at once, and it made it hard to process and organize the way I was feeling. Jace didn't push me. He didn't say anything. His palm on the small of my back as we walked through the hotel and down the hall to our room was comforting.

And I needed comfort. My face hurt. My neck hurt. My throat hurt… Hell, everything hurt.

I wondered what he was thinking now that he knew what I was hiding. I wondered if it changed how he thought of me.

He let us in the room, strode past the bathroom, the TV, and the bed.

I went directly into the bathroom. Having Cannon's blood on my face was disturbing. And by the way Jace's eyes would stray to the smears, I knew it bothered him as well.

I washed my face at the sink with cold water. The cut on my lip stung with the face wash, and the bruise on my cheek was tender. The frigid temperature of the water wasn't very welcome, but I figured it might soothe some of the swelling while at the same time clearing some of my mind.

Once I was done, I patted it dry and smoothed on some lip balm on the worst of the chapped spots. The cut on my lip was still bleeding a little, so I pressed the towel against it, hoping it would stop. While I waited, I looked at my neck. Just seeing it made me cringe. I could see now why Jace seemed to snap.

I looked terrible, worse than I'd ever looked in my entire life. Funny, I felt that way, too. My clothes were sticking to me. I felt dirty and sweaty. Placing the towel down, I pulled up the heavy mass of curls. My hair was usually wild, but tonight it just looked bad. I twisted it into a bun at the top of my head and left it there. It wasn't ideal because it made the damage to my neck look worse, but I just wanted the hair out of my face.

Then I pulled off my clothes, even the bra I was wearing, and threw them in the corner without a backward glance. After smoothing on a little fresh deodorant and some eye cream (because my eye bags were seriously on #fleek), I wrapped my body in a towel and stepped out of the bathroom.

Jace glanced at me when I padded out. He didn't say anything when I went to his bag, rummaged around, and pulled out a black T-shirt he liked to wear. I dropped the towel, slid his shirt over my skin, then reached for a fresh pair of boyshorts in my bag.

I wasn't doing this to look better or even to stall for time. I just wanted to feel more human, less like a deflated punching bag and more like myself.

Once I felt a little more comfortable, I leaned against the wall and waited.

I wasn't sure what I was waiting for. For Jace to yell. To laugh. For him to tell me he was done.

"Why didn't you tell me?" he asked, spinning in my direction. I hadn't expected to hear a hint of hurt in his voice.

The pit pass I'd given him still hung around his neck. His T-shirt was red, jeans faded. A pair of sunglasses were forgotten on top of his head.

"I was going to. After the race," I said low. My throat felt raw.

He shook his head; his voice was gruff. "That's not good enough." I watched his graceful movements as he pulled a bottle of water out of the mini fridge, uncapped it, and brought it over to me.

His words made me angry, but the gesture of the water, the way he clearly cared… I couldn't be mad. "What should I have done?" I asked "Thrown myself against your chest the first night we had sex on the hood of my car and poured out all the stuff I kept inside?"

Jace rushed close, his expression a mask of anger. "Don't act like that."

"Like what?" I challenged.

"Like all you are is a goddamn lay to me and all I'm here for is sex."

I glanced away.

"There were lots of times you could have told me, Josie. That night on the track, the night in your room. Last night when we were in bed…"

"I couldn't!" My voice strained under the outburst. I pushed away from the wall. I tried to get away from him, to put some distance between us by moving to the other side of the room.

He seemed to understand the space wasn't just because we were semi arguing. It was because the closeness was too much.

He caught my hand, pulled me around, and didn't let go. "Why couldn't you?"

"Because in the beginning, you made it clear how you felt about me as a driver. You didn't want me in the NRR. You thought I couldn't hack it, and you said women didn't belong in racing."

He started to say something, but I cut him off.

"I know, Jace. I know you apologized. It's forgotten. I'm not holding a grudge. I'm trying to explain." I laughed, a cross between a nervous and frustrated sound.

"Go ahead." He urged, his thumb stroking over the back of my hand.

"Things started to shift between us. The sex was still hot, but there was more, too." I glanced up; he nodded. "I didn't expect it, and it caught me off guard. You caught me off guard. By the time I knew I should tell you, I was already…" I made a sound and started to pull back again.

He tightened his hold and pulled me toward him. "You already what?"

Just go for it. Stop hiding.

"I already fell in love with you."

He sucked in a breath.

I sipped at the water, pretending it was because my voice was hella squeaky and not because I needed a minute.

I'd just told Jace I loved him. I'd never told anyone that before. "I was afraid if I told you, it would change things. It would change the way you look at me, and you would walk away. I wasn't ready to let you go yet."

"Why would you think that?" he asked gently.

I didn't want gentleness. I wasn't used to it. It made me feel even more vulnerable than I already felt.

"You're strong, Jace. Everyone around me is strong. This is a man's world, and sometimes it's all I can do to survive. I've been viewed as the weaker sex since I was born. My father wanted a boy; my mother wanted a lady. I wasn't either. I spent a long time trying to figure out who I was, and it wasn't an easy path. But it made me strong. I got into some trouble when I was a teenager. Did some stuff I shouldn't have."

"What kind of stuff?" He shifted, sat down on the foot of the bed, and pulled me into his lap.

My feet tangled with his against the floor.

"You're listening to me," I said, not meaning to let the thought out of my mind.

"Why wouldn't I listen to you?" he asked, rubbing my back.

My stomach flipped, and I shrugged.

"You listened to me when I told you I beat three men almost to death."

"It was three men?" I asked, curious.

"Yeah. My, uh, father wasn't happy when Arrow told him he was gay. He pretty much made his life hell. Arrow, he's not like me. He's more innocent… softer. So when my father basically unleashed on him, he didn't know how to handle it. He probably never even knew my father was like that."

I nodded, and he continued.

"I wasn't around much, too caught up in my own world and trying to stay out of Dad's. Arrow came looking for me one night. My father kicked him out, and he didn't have anywhere to go. He went onto the wrong turf, someone else's streets. The guys there, they beat him up pretty bad. I'm pretty sure they did some… other stuff he won't talk about."

"Jace," I murmured.

"I found him in the hangar." His voice turned hoarse and haunted. "I went after the guys, beat them almost to death. The only reason I didn't was because a friend pulled me off."

"Kurt?" I asked.

"How'd you know?" He looked up, shadows in his eyes.

"I sensed some history there," I replied, remembering the night of my first street race.

He nodded. "My brother took Kurt's place in my life. He didn't like it too well. But Arrow is my brother. He's family, and my loyalty is to him."

"That's understandable."

"See that?" He looked up at me. The scruff on his jaw pulled up with his half smile. "You listened to me when I told you about how my father bought me out of attempted murder charges. You listened just now when I told you the details. That's what we do, Josie. We listen to each other."

"I thought you would think I was weak," I confided. "You value strength. You like my independence, and you're so strong. I thought if I told you what they did, you'd lose respect for me."

"So it wasn't them you were covering for," he surmised, understanding in his words.

"It was me." I finished. "I was being harassed because they thought I was weak. They thought they could push me until I broke and left the division. Humiliation is a good tool; it makes a person do things they might not. I wouldn't give them the satisfaction. So I never said a word about what they did. Not to anyone, especially not my father. Only the weak tattle. The strong succeed anyway."

"How long did it go on? How long did they do this shit to you?" he asked. The anger in his tone sort of turned me on.

I know. WTF? But he was angry on my behalf. I liked the protective vibe he was totally rocking. It was nearly as hot as the dirty white T-shirt.

"Almost from the beginning," I confessed.

His jaw muscles clenched, jutting out from the sides of his face. Jace stood and put me on my feet.

"Did you think your father would blame you?" he asked, swinging around with fire in his eyes.

"No," I said quickly. My father was a lot of things. He had his faults even in the parental department, but he wouldn't have blamed me for someone else's behavior. "When I was a teenager, I was a hell raiser."

He barked a laugh.

I thought about kicking him for it, but let's face it; this was no surprise.

"I did some stuff, made some decisions that were stupid and reckless. Not really toward anyone else, but to myself.

"My dad found out and put a stop to it. He sent me to therapy and basically put me under house arrest. After a while, I started going stir crazy. I'd always loved driving… you know, with the windows down, wind in my hair, and good music playing. So I asked him for a car, something I could fix up in the garage. He bought one of course, because it gave me something to do at home and he could keep an eye on me."

"That's how you got into racing," Jace surmised.

I nodded. "I started racing at the local speedways, and my father promised to help me get an audition of sorts with some sponsors if I stayed out of trouble. So I did. And I got some sponsors. I think the reason he put down so much money to sponsor me was because it kept me close; it was his way of parenting me. In his own kind of way."

"That actually makes sense." He nodded. "And I gave you shit because he sponsored you."

I made a scoffing sound. "Everyone gives me shit about it. But he's my dad."

"A better one than I have," Jace muttered.

"I wanted to prove I could handle it. To him and maybe to myself. It was always there between us. My dad thought I was going to revert back to my reckless ways. I won't."

"Telling someone you're being harassed doesn't make you weak," he intoned. "You should have told someone."

I shrugged, capped the water, and tossed it down on the bed. "I didn't." I mean, really, what else was left to say?

Rehashing what I did and didn't do and what he thought I needed to do was kind of pointless.

His low chuckle caused a certain kind of full-body awareness to wash over me. I tried not to show it. Instead, I placed my hands on my hips. "What's so funny?"

"Most guys I know bitch about their women running their gums about everything, whining and moaning, wanting to talk about their feelings and decisions until they're blue in the face. Me?" He scoffed. "I find the one woman I have to drag shit out of, and then you look at me like you'd rather jump my stick than finish talking."

Well, so much for me hiding my full-body awareness.

Epic fail.

"First of all…" I held up a finger. "Women wouldn't have to, quote, 'whine and moan' about anything if men wouldn't be such morons and listen the first time they talked." He opened his mouth, and I gave him a death glare and popped up a second finger. "Second of all, you didn't drag anything out of me. I was going to tell you. And I don't want to *jump your stick.*"

By the time I finished, he was full-on grinning, his pearly whites all on display.

"I love you."

The hand I'd been holding up fell out of the air like dead weight. I felt like a crash test dummy slammed into a concrete wall at an impossible speed without a seatbelt.

The breath in my lungs stalled out. The word came out as more of a wheeze. "What?"

He shook his head, his smile still firmly in place. "You're surprised."

Yeah. I guess I was.

The distance between us narrowed considerably when Jace came back across the room to stand in front of me. He twirled one finger around the spiral curl that escaped my bun, tugging it gently.

"I love you, Josie."

A rush of emotion so strong welled up inside me tears pressed against the backs of my eyes. My fingers twisted in his shirt, like I was using him to steady myself.

I whispered, "You're telling me that even after what I just told you?"

"Ah, baby." He abandoned my hair to cup my face. "I think you know me well enough to know by now I don't love too easily. In fact, besides Arrow, you're the only other person I could say it to."

My fingers tightened in the cotton against his abs. "I thought maybe crossing over would make things easier. You know? I could keep driving with maybe a little less harassment. I thought a division with no rules and with Trent and Drew sort of spearheading the message that the NRR was for everyone no matter who you were, especially the underdogs… I'm an underdog, Jace. I thought maybe I would belong there."

"You belong beside me." He spoke soft, his thumb caressing my cheek.

"I don't think you understand," I told him. My chest felt tight. The depth of feeling I knew for him was unmatched. Hell, up until now, I thought it was unattainable. It scared me so fucking bad.

If I lost this, it might crush me. I couldn't accept his words. I couldn't let them pierce my heart until I was sure he knew.

"I'm probably still going to be a target. The guys in my division, they're going to be even worse now because I'm outing them. Cannon…"

"Don't fucking say his name to me," he growled.

"See?" I said, frustrated. "You're already caught up in it. This goes beyond reporters asking us for comments on our relationship. Beyond me thinking it's going to be magically better in the NRR. There's always going to be the guys who don't think a woman belongs. They're always going to look at me, think they can degrade me. Sexual harassment practically comes with my job."

Jace's eyes heated, turning molten, and the anger inside him crackled beneath his skin.

I forged on. "You can't beat up every guy. You can't rush to my defense all the time. You're going to get comments and shit because we're together. Sometimes you're going to have to sit by and see what people do to me."

He released me, moving away, only to turn and pace back.

"People can suck my dick," he spat.

"No they can't." I sniffed. "That's my job."

He laughed, running a hand through his hair. "I've been dealing with assholes and people who want to challenge me for a long time, Josie. If anyone wants to come at me for loving you, then let them. That's nothing."

I opened my mouth, and he cut me off.

"As far as watching men in this profession treat you like shit? Fuck no, I won't. We're gonna get that straight right now. No one, and I mean *no one,* will disrespect you in my presence. And if they do it when I'm not around, they'll hear about it. There's nothing you can do or say to stop me."

"Don't you get it!" I flung my hands out, frustrated. "I've been fighting for years for equality. To be treated the same. If you step in and start fighting my battles and I let you, what does that say about me? It says I need a man to force other men to treat me right. No, Jace. I want respect because I earned it.”

“Some people won’t respect you no matter how much you deserve it,” he deadpanned.

My shoulders slumped a little under it all. He was right. I knew it. But I was right, too.

It was like we were standing at an impasse.

“Then it won’t matter what you do,” I said.

“I can’t make people respect you, Josie, but this shit with the hazing… That stops now.”

“I don’t need a white knight.”

“I’m more of a dark troublemaker with a white Lotus.” He winked.

My lips twitched. I tried desperately not to smile. God, he was so charming. A good guy wrapped up in a bad-boy package. His dark, mysterious eyes weren’t much of a mystery to me anymore. The dark, bottomless way they appeared was just a front. His experiences, the shit that made him jaded, the take-no-prisoners attitude made him Lorhaven.

Deep down beneath it all was Jace.

A man who loved fiercely. A man who was hurt by a father whose humanity got in the way of being a good parent. A man who was haunted by the things Lorhaven did to protect his brother.

“You have a black soul but a heart of gold,” I told him.

“You like gold?” He sidled up to me again, warmth in his gaze.

“I love it.”

“I’m with you,” he said low but no less ferocious. “I do value your independence and your strength, but you don’t have to be strong all the time, not with me. With me, you can have a little softness.”

It's what I want. I want to be strong and soft. I want someone to understand both.

"Do you trust me?" he asked, taking my face in his hands and lifting it.

It was a no-brainer. "Yes."

"Trust I won't do anything that will demean you or shove you behind me. Also, trust I'll step in when I see fit, and it's only because I love you."

I gave in. There was no part of me that could resist even just a small part of him. "I love you, Jace."

"It's me and you now, Josie. Not just you."

"Us," I murmured.

"Us." He agreed.

"And Arrow," I added.

His mouth curved up. "My bro is part of the package, but I don't want you thinking you're any less important. You aren't." He gave me a squeeze.

"I know." I leaned forward, sliding my arms around his waist. I thought about mentioning how I thought Arrow was headed toward becoming an "us," but I had a feeling that wasn't going to be something Jace would be too thrilled about. Seemed like we were already dealing with enough today, so I decided to keep that thought to myself.

"So we good?" he asked against my hair.

"I'm good if you are." The nervous, breathless way I felt was giving way to giddiness. He loved me. He wanted me as I was, and I didn't have to be someone I wasn't.

And for once, it didn't scare me that in order to be accepted as I was, I in turn had to accept him for who he was.

I loved him.

He loves me.

"Just promise me you won't keep this shit from me ever again. When something happens, *anything*, I want to know about it."

Oh, it was hard to relinquish even a little control. "Okay. Same goes for you."

Jace pulled back. My nose wrinkled when I watched him hock a loogie into the palm of his hand. Then he held the same nasty, loogified hand out to me.

"Shake on it," he said.

"Ew!" I squealed and knocked his hand away. "That's disgusting!"

He rolled his eyes and wiped his hand down the front of his shirt. Ew. "Everyone wants to be a dude until they gotta spit-shake on it."

I punched him in the arm (I wasn't about to touch his nasty shirt). "Wanting to take care of myself does not make me a dude."

He laughed. It was more of a cackle than anything.

One thing was for sure: things with Jace would never ever be dull.

I wanted to throw myself at him, but my body was too sore, too battered for the movement. Instead, I stepped up close, and he folded my body into his. The next thing I knew, his hands were tangled in the cotton of his/my shirt, and we were kissing like we hadn't kissed in years.

Eventually, his mouth ripped free and his eyes darkened. "I need to get you some ice for your face and your neck."

"I don't want ice." I fingered the waistband of his jeans. "I want you."

"You look like shit, Josie, and honestly? I'm fucking scared I'll hurt you." He punctuated his honesty by lifted my hand and brushing a kiss across the knuckles that were red and puffy from when I punched Cannon. "This feel broken?" he murmured.

I shook my head.

"That's good." He kissed them again.

"Jace, please," I whispered. Emotion clogged my throat again, a sort of desperate feeling washing over me. Despite knowing he loved me even after he knew the truth, I was still so weepy.

"I can't say no to you, Josie." He brushed a kiss over my mouth. "But none of the 'harder Jace, more Jace' tonight. I won't do it. Slow. Easy. Sweet." As he spoke, he kissed me in between his words. The sound of his voice coupled with the feel of his lips was the ultimate aphrodisiac.

"You know everyone is going to be at our door soon," I half moaned.

Jace thrust his hips into me, still pressing gentle kisses to my face. "They'll wait."

Impatiently, I tugged at his shirt. He lifted up so I could pull it completely away. His body was warm and hard beneath my hands. I wanted to touch him everywhere all at once, and I wanted to feel his skin on mine.

His low chuckle filled the room and vibrated against my cheek. "Easy…"

"Jace," I warned, a desperate note in his name.

His body pushed up, and I reached for his jeans. The second they were unbuttoned and unzipped, he lost them, along with his boxer briefs. I was sitting, and he was on his knees in front of me.

Immediately, I slipped my mouth down over his rigid length. He groaned, his movements stalled out, but then he recovered and pulled at my shirt. I released him only long enough for it to come over my head before I dove back down and sucked deep.

Jace's fingers kneaded my shoulders as I sucked him deep. One hand was wrapped firmly around the base of his rod, and the other reached between his legs and up to cup his ass.

Jace made a deep, throaty sound, grabbed my head, and held it still.

With my lips still wrapped around him, he began to move, taking control of my blow job and pumping his dick in and out of my mouth. He wasn't rough. If anything, he was slow just like he said. It was maddening, nothing but a tease.

The fingers against his ass tightened and pushed him closer, urging him on.

He laughed but didn't increase his pace. Instead, he kept it easy and gentle but somehow still thoroughly fucked my mouth, and I loved every second of it. He was rigid and smooth. The way he felt gliding against my tongue and rubbing over and over against my lips made my own hips start to gyrate toward him.

Suddenly, Jace pulled back, leaving my mouth without any warning.

"I want more," I told him.

He chuckled and pushed me back into the mattress so he could strip off the rest of the boyshorts. When I was as naked as him, I held out my hands, wanting to fill them up again.

He towered over me on his knees, hair fell down into his eyes, his lips were red and puffy, and his cock stood at attention. The corded muscles in his arms stood out like he was trying to hold himself back, but that's not what I wanted.

I wanted him unleashed. The look in his eyes told me he knew it and he relished holding it back.

I sat up abruptly, grabbed his hips, and pulled him toward my mouth. He resisted, but only long enough to collapse beside me and grab my hips.

He guided me so I was above him, and the second I knew his intent, I shifted, both my knees dropping to the mattress on either side of Jace's head. I bent at the waist, my head facing a proudly jutting cock, and grabbed hold. I dragged my tongue over his head, tasted the salty flavor of his pre-release.

He made a sound of appreciation and ran a hand up the inside of my thigh. I shuddered when his fingers parted my folds and his tongue licked my slit.

With him in my mouth, I moaned, my legs shaking.

We continued that way for long minutes, torturing each other with oral pleasure until I lifted my head on a gasp. "Jace," I demanded. "I can't."

"Right across my tongue, Josie," he said, then went back to work with his mouth.

Small sounds began to rumble out of me. I grabbed hold of his cock, slick from my mouth, and pumped him hard as a wave of ecstasy overtook my body.

It was so powerful I collapsed, let go of his length, and went boneless over him, even as the orgasm still rolled.

Jace supported my hips and lower body, holding me up, and continued to work me with his tongue and fingers. I couldn't stop shuddering. Just when I thought I would stop, a new wave would crash over me and I would moan helplessly again.

"Oh my God," I breathed when he lowered me.

Jace grunted, satisfied with the complete ruin of any control I had over my own limbs.

Gently, he rolled so I was beneath him, and in one easy push, he filled me completely. I grabbed onto his biceps and hung on. I tried to work beneath him, but I wasn't much help considering how spent I was from the orgasm that went on and on.

Something told me that was his plan all along, to make it so I couldn't go at him like I usually did. I couldn't even be disappointed because he was protecting me but also satisfying me.

"Jace," I whimpered when he was balls deep.

He lowered, elbows on either side of my head, and kissed me soft and slow. The gentleness ripped a hole in my heart.

Jace made me feel so much, so fast, and all at once. I was overwhelmed in the best way and overcome by someone I never even saw coming.

It's like he'd been there for a while but in my blind spot. The second he pulled up beside me, it was all over. I was all over.

He was it for me.

Between his luxurious kisses and the way he was moving so completely inside me, I told him, "I love you."

His body went taut. I saw the change in his eyes when he pulled back and looked down. I cupped his face as he came apart and filled my center with his release.

When he was done, both his arms slipped around me, holding my body between his chest and the mattress. There was a tenderness to him I don't think anyone would ever believe he possessed. I was glad. I liked having that part of him for myself. Only for me.

He whispered he loved me right beside my ear.

It felt like every road I'd ever driven was to get me right here with him.

My drive wasn't over; neither was his. But from now on, we weren't driving alone.

We had each other.

Thirty-Four

Lorhaven

It wasn't often in life people surprised me. The truth was most people weren't that great. We all had our demons, skeletons rattling deep in the closet.

It was very rare for anyone to remain innocent or untouched by life in general. I didn't know anyone—not one person—who wasn't slightly jaded or damaged.

Because of that, people weren't that hard to read, not if you really paid attention. For me, paying attention was sort of a reflex, a defense mechanism. The faster and clearer you could spot someone's true character, the easier it was to protect yourself or those you cared about.

I'd known Josie had a hard time in the pro division from almost the second we sat down at the *GearShark* interview.

I couldn't have guessed just how hard, though.

The events and truths that unfolded today caught me off guard. I'd always known she was a strong woman, but I don't think I quite realized just how strong she was.

Holy fuck, what they put her through.

Holy fuck, what she endured in silence.

I could have killed Cannon. Maybe I would have if she hadn't been there looking close to falling off her feet.

It was just like back then… back when I found Arrow and went in search of the men who hurt him. Unrestrained anger was a powerful thing. It overruled reason, right and wrong… hell, even value for someone else's life.

After that night years ago when Kurt pulled me off those guys, essentially saving their lives, I walked around with a question deep inside me.

Did murderous rage live deep inside me? Was it a one-time thing or a permanent character flaw that would always make me wonder what would set me off next?

Tonight proved two things:

1.) It wasn't a one-time thing.

And

2.) It wasn't unrestrained.

What lived inside me couldn't be classified as such because both times, I'd been restrained. The dense, angry fog that settled over me had been reached through, reminding me there was more to lose than just some asshole's life.

I understood now.

I loved fiercely.

So fiercely it had the ability to throw me into a tailspin, but it also had the ability to pull me back out.

Love was a catalyst *and* a hindrance for me at the very same time.

No wonder I was so stingy with who I gave it out to. Not everyone was worth the extremes of this emotion.

But Josie was.

All those times I felt she was holding something back, that there was more to her she wanted to say but wasn't ready… It all came out.

I saw all of her tonight.

And I loved her.

There was fragility in strength not many people ever saw, certainly not in Josie's case. But I saw more clearly now than ever.

I was sorry it took everything that happened tonight to bring it all to light. Having her wrapped around me right now, though, listening to her even breathing and feeling the relaxation in her limbs, I secretly thought perhaps it all had been worth it.

Don't get me wrong. The fingerprints on her neck, the damage to her throat and face… I could do without ever seeing that. But now there was nothing between us. We were all in.

I wasn't an *I* anymore. We were an *us*.

It was a strange thought… but I liked it.

I also liked the way she protested when I slid from beneath her as my phone went off continuously.

I'll be real. It made me feel like the fucking man.

The chick just couldn't get enough.

I got up anyway, though. You know how I said today brought everything out in the open? Well, I hadn't meant just for Josie. It stirred up some older, deep wounds for my brother as well.

I'd seen it in his eyes and the paleness of his cheeks back at the track, just before I'd taken Josie out of there. Now that she and I had us worked out, my thoughts turned directly to my brother. I wondered if he was okay, if sitting in his hotel room alone was fucking with his head.

He was the only person that had the ability to get me out of bed with my woman. But I had to make sure he didn't need me.

It wasn't him on the phone, though.

It was Forrester.

However, the call was what led me to the door I stood in front of right now, knocking. My brother cracked open the door a few seconds later, peering out like some little old woman.

"You embarrass me," I told him.

He rolled his eyes, sprang the door open, and gestured for me to come in.

The rich scent of coffee filled the room, and I inhaled with appreciation and a bit of surprise. "You made coffee?"

My brother didn't drink coffee very often.

"There's no beer," he grumped.

I laughed. I kept the hangar stocked at home because little bro here wasn't quite twenty-one and couldn't go buy it on his own.

Yeah, yeah... Don't give me that shit about contributing to a minor. My brother earned the right to drink. He was an adult, and I didn't care what the fuck his driver's license said.

"I need some," I said, going right to the still partially full pot and pouring some into a cheap cup the hotel provided. Once the cup was full, I poured in about four packets of sugar.

I liked my coffee like I liked my women. Dark, hot, and sweet... with just a little bit of bite (hence, no creamer).

When it was mixed together, I leaned against the dresser and stared at him as I took a sip. Arrow was dressed in a pair of blue basketball shorts and no shirt.

The sleeve of tattoos wrapped around his arm were on full display, as was the tattoo of the arrow on his neck.

Yes, an arrow. Because of his name.

He was a thin guy, but over the past year, he'd really filled out. His chest and shoulders had some definition, and his arms were toned. Arrow's skin was paler than mine, but he spent a lot of time in the sun at the airstrip, working on the cars outside, so he always had a tan.

The long, very blond hair on top of his head was swept over to the side like always, the sides and back cut very short. There wasn't an ounce of stubble in sight on his jawline, and sometimes I couldn't help but think he had a baby face because it was so smooth all the time.

He had brown eyes like me, but they were more of a hazel color, with a lot more lightness in their depths. His full mouth was pulled into the eternal pout he always seemed to wear. For a long time, I thought he was just trying to look broody for the ladies…

Then I found out he was gay.

So maybe the guys liked broody, too.

Nope. That was just his lips. Pouty.

"Why aren't you with Joey?" he asked, watching me the same way I watched him.

"She needed a few."

"Is she okay?" That slightly haunted look I recognized earlier at the track floated behind his eyes.

"Yeah, she's good. Well, I wouldn't say good, but she's better than she was."

"What the hell happened?" he asked, sitting down on the side of the bed.

"She's been enduring a lot of abuse, a lot of bullying… She never said anything," I replied, watching him closely.

He swallowed, the Adam's apple in his throat bobbing. "That why you beat up that driver?"

"That bothered you, did it?" I asked, drinking more of the coffee. I could feel the caffeine starting to filter into my bloodstream, and I had to admit it was welcome.

He shrugged.

"It brought up some shit for me, too," I told him. I'd spent a lot of time working on making sure he knew he could talk to me, because with Arrow, bottling up on the inside was a dangerous thing. So I had no problem telling him it brought up the past for me, especially if it made it easier for him to admit the same.

"I wasn't even there… but it still reminded me, you know?" He spoke low, not looking at me.

I drank more of the brew and thought about what he said. Arrow wasn't there when I beat those three men nearly to death. He learned about it later. When I came back with busted-up hands, he knew what I'd done, but I don't think he realized just how far it had gone until our father had to buy me out of a trial and attempted murder charges.

I don't know what Arrow's mind conjured up about that night, but seeing his face today, I knew it was a lot like the picture I likely made standing there holding up a beaten, half-conscious Dean Cannon in my grip.

If only he knew… Those men that night… they looked so much worse than Cannon.

I wasn't going to tell him, though. That was something no one else needed to know but me… and Kurt. And the fucktards who got the beating.

"It's understandable. I didn't mean to bring it all up for you. I walked in… He was hitting her, and she was bloody…" My voice trailed off, and Arrow's face flashed up to mine. An angry glint came into his own eyes.

It was that look that pulled me out of the flashback of seeing Josie like that. It was that look that proved to me just how far my bro had come from back then.

His anger was welcome. It was real, and it would propel him further.

It was when Arrow didn't react at all, when he seemed hollow and unresponsive, that was the most worrisome.

"I kinda lost it." I shrugged, sipping the coffee.

"He deserved it. Men who hit women are scum."

"Word." I agreed.

Arrow snagged his own cup off the nearby dresser and drank some, staring down into the liquid. "I guess me and her have some stuff in common."

"Yeah, and you know… it might help her if you ever want to talk to her about it."

He glanced up.

I nodded. "Might help you, too."

"I'm doing better, Lor," he said without heat.

I nodded. "I know. But I saw the look in your eyes back at the track." *And still see traces of it right now.* "Sometimes the shit comes to the surface, doesn't it?"

"Yeah, sometimes."

"You wanna talk about it?"

He made a sound and stood, pacing away. "No. Thinking about it sucks enough."

"Guys like that, guys like Cannon, they're weak as shit. They're cowards. You're better than them. Stronger."

He swung around, his eyes fastened on mine. There was no hint of anger in his reply. "I know that. You don't have to worry about me, Lor. I'm in a different place now than I was two years ago."

I believed him. Yes, everyone had demons. My brother had more than his fair share. His demons no longer defined him. Arrow no longer fed them. Instead, he fed the parts inside him that didn't threaten to swallow him whole.

I was proud of him for that, and I respected him for it.

I realized then perhaps I'd been wrong before in thinking my brother was the weaker link out of the pair of us. In thinking growing up with my father somehow weakened him where it had strengthened me.

Perhaps my strength was just different than Arrow's because he was tough.

"You know what else you and Josie have in common?" I said.

"What?"

"You're both the strongest people I've ever met."

Surprise widened his eyes.

My lips curved up into a smile. "Even strong people gotta vent sometimes. I'll always be here for you for that."

He nodded, ran a hand through his hair, making it look wild on one side of his head, then spoke. "I want to talk about him."

I guess I should have expected it. I put off talking to my brother about the conversation I had with our father longer than he wanted. It was more than likely the shit that was brought up for him today was more about our father—about the unresolved issues there, than about all the other shit.

"Yeah, I know you do."

"But you don't," he deadpanned.

I set aside the coffee and made a frustrated sound. "It just seems pointless I guess, 'cause it doesn't matter what he says."

"It matters to me."

His words were quiet. Amazing how something spoken so softly could silence everything else.

The words felt like an oversized flour sack was tossed right into my middle. The wind was sort of knocked out of me, leaving behind this momentary hollowness before I sucked in more air to fill it back up again.

I guess I always knew it, that he hadn't been able to write off our father the way I had. It killed me, though, because I wanted to protect my brother, and it seemed no matter what I did, my father would always have an ability to hurt him.

In truth, that was the real reason I put off this conversation for so long. It was an open invitation for my brother to get hurt. Again.

How could I hand that to him? How could I be a party to it?

I didn't really have a choice, because the longer I put this off, the greater chance Arrow would go to other means to find out what the meeting was all about. He might go directly to our father.

I didn't want that.

"He told me he felt regret for the kind of father he's been. He wants a chance to… have a better relationship."

"He seriously said that?" Arrow asked dubiously.

"He said it," I replied curtly.

"But just with you, though, right? Not with me."

The assumption pierced my heart. I might get my asshole nature from my father, but I would never, ever do to one of my kids what he'd done to Arrow.

I rubbed my palm over the back of my neck and went for more of my coffee. "Actually," I said around a mouthful of the stuff. "He meant the both of us."

The small spark of hope that ignited in my brother's eyes left me feeling cold. "Me, too?"

"Yeah, he asked me to talk to you. See if you wanted to, uh, talk to him."

"What'd you tell him?"

"I told him to go fuck himself."

Arrow nodded like he already figured as much. "So you don't think he means it?"

I sighed heavily and finished the coffee. I wanted to say no. I wanted to yell this conversation was stupid as fuck.

I didn't.

My brother deserved better than that.

"I think he meant it when he said it. But with Dad, it's hard to say if he still means it today."

Arrow nodded. "Do you want a relationship with him?"

"Honestly, bro?" I began. "I don't think I'll ever forgive him for all the stuff he's done. I'm not built that way."

I held grudges. For life.

There was no point in pretending otherwise.

A nodded, accepting the truth of my reply. "Is that all he said, that he wants to talk to me?"

"He read the *GearShark* article. We talked about that for a few, but basically, yeah."

"He knew I was going to be on the plane?"

He was fishing, looking for even an inkling of something that might soften all the harsh treatment he'd gotten over the past several years. It hurt me to see it. His vulnerability, the innocence he somehow maintained deep inside him despite everything, cut profoundly.

"Yeah, he knew."

Arrow nodded and fell quiet for a few minutes. He came back around, dropping on the side of the bed.

"Will you think bad of me if I want to see him?"

I made a choked sound and sat down beside him. "I might not always like every choice you make, but I'll never think bad of you, A. I'll always be your brother, and my loyalty will always be with you."

His stare stayed trained down on his feet, and the back of his head bobbed with his nod. "That's good."

I half smiled and gave him a pat on the back (a manly pat). "Take some time and think about it, Arrow. Things might not go the way you want if you see him, but I understand if you gotta do it anyway. When… *if* you decide to see him, I'll go with you."

"Thanks, Lor." He spoke.

"Anytime."

"You heading back over to your room, or you gonna hang?"

"I can hang for a while," I said, kicking back on the mattress. "Josie's probably gonna be a while."

"I'm starving," Arrow complained.

When wasn't he starving? I barked a laugh. "I'll order some pizza and wings. Extra hot like you like 'em."

"What about Joey?" He worried.

I shrugged. "We can take the food over to her when it gets here. Rent a movie."

"She gonna be up for that?"

I scoffed. "Up for lying in bed and watching TV? I think she can handle it."

He grinned like he won the lotto.

It eased me because the smile was genuine, and I knew he was doing all right. It made me silently hope he stayed away from my father, because I was very afraid it would only drag him down.

"What's she doing anyway?" he asked, cutting into my thoughts.

I grunted and glanced at the clock. "Right about now?" I quipped. "Probably answering a whole lot of questions."

Joey

My phone was still off.

I planned to leave it that way until the mess of what happened on the track today blew over… It was unrealistic. This was a big scandal, one that wouldn't just "blow over" quickly.

But I could live in denial for a little while.

The fingerprint-shaped bruises on my neck were pretty much permission granted for a little stay at the denial hotel.

Here's the thing about denial: it's only good if you can avoid whatever it is you're trying to ignore. Some problems come knocking…

Or in my case, ringing.

Jace's phone went off, and his body tensed beneath mine like he might get up to answer. I made a small, husky sound and tightened my body (which was totally covering his) around him so he wouldn't move.

He was a comfort. A true security I hadn't even realized I lived without. If I lost this, it would leave a gaping hole in my life, and I would never be able to go back to not knowing what I missed.

I was sore. Tired. Hurt.

But he made me feel better.

A deep chuckle filled the space above my head. His arm tugged me a little more firmly into him. I sighed, letting my eyes close.

The phone went off again. This time it didn't shut up. Gently, Jace peeled me off him to slide out from beneath my naked form. I protested, but he kept going. "Arrow might need something."

I relented, not upset in the least he would think of his brother. In fact, I loved him more for it. He snatched up the phone, and I perused the strong, lean lines of his body and the strength in his stance.

"What?" he growled into the phone, making my eyes flash up to his scowling face.

Clearly, it wasn't his brother.

He made a grunting sound and then held the phone out to me. "It's for you."

"Who?" I mumbled, pushing up and tugging the sheet with me.

"Forrester."

I pressed the phone to my ear. "Drew?"

"Your phone's off," he stated.

"Yeah, figured the press would be vicious."

He made a sound. "Vultures."

"Is something wrong?" I worried. Clearly, he needed something if he would go to the bother of calling Jace.

"I wanted to give you a heads up. Your father's in town."

"What?" I squeaked. Technically, I tried to exclaim in surprise, but when you're choked out by a man, your voice doesn't always cooperate. I felt Jace's eyes, and I glanced up. He was frowning, then turned away to grab some shorts out of his bag.

"We're on our way to pick him up at the airport. He's coming straight to you."

An anxious feeling turned my belly, and I pressed a hand to it.

"Josie," Jace said, stealing my attention. Concern was dark on his features.

"My dad's in town," I told him. The sound of my voice was rusty and strained, and it made me grimace. I wasn't ready for a talk with him. I still felt shaken and… beaten. I wanted to feel stronger and more together when I faced him for the first time.

Jace made a sound and strode away from the bed. He snatched the ice bucket off the nearby counter, and the sound of the door opening made me crane my neck in time to see him exit without a shirt.

"You might want to put on some clothes before he gets there. We'll be back in about thirty, maybe sooner."

"Drive slow," I implored.

"You doing okay, Joey? We're worried," Drew asked, obvious tension in his voice.

I felt a pang of guilt. I wasn't used to people being worried. Before, shutting off my phone wasn't something that required extra thought.

But now it did.

I had people who cared (more than just my father), people I didn't necessarily want to avoid and make worry more.

"I've been better," I said honestly, "but Jace had been really good to me."

"It's really hard to hate a guy when he's so good to our two best friends," Drew muttered.

Somewhere close by, Trent chuckled.

I smiled. "He's a good person, Drew."

"Yeah, I see that."

"I'm sorry I made you worry. It wasn't fair of me," I whispered.

"Don't apologize. You have a right to a timeout with your person. I wouldn't have called, but I figured you'd want to know who was going to be at your door."

"Thank you." The sound of the door latching had me craning my neck again to watch Jace stride back into the room.

"We'll talk soon, okay? You need anything, just call."

My eyes filled with tears, much to my own admonishment. I'd hoped I was done crying today. "I really appreciate you both," I told him, near whispering.

"We know," Drew quipped, and I smiled. The split section of my lip pulled, and I grimaced.

After I punched the END CALL button on the screen, I dropped the cell in the sheets and looked up.

Jace was standing there with a towel wrapped in ice. "I don't know where to put it first," he admitted, eyes roaming my neck, face, and lip.

I held out my hand, and he surrendered it. I pressed it to my lip.

"My dad flew in."

Jace nodded. "You ready for that?"

"No," I admitted. Now that I'd had just a little practice not having to put on a steel front at all times, it was easier to say when I felt vulnerable.

He pushed a loose strand of hair away from my cheek. "Want me to stay while you talk to him?"

I shook my head. "No, but thanks."

"I will if you want me to."

I lowered the ice from my lip and smiled. "I know."

After that, I grudgingly put on some clothes that weren't Jace's shirt and pulled my hair up once again because half of it had fallen out.

Jace went to Arrow's room to give me some time alone with my father, but I admit the second I was alone, I wanted to call him back. I didn't, though. This was a conversation that was solely between my father and me.

Not quite thirty minutes after Drew called, there was a solid knock on the door.

Standing on the inside, I felt my father's presence even through the thick wooden layers. Ron Gamble was an imposing man, but he was my dad.

With one deep exhale, I pulled it open. He stood there looking a little less pulled together than I think I'd ever seen him. His suit was the usual tailored, expensive kind, but it was rumpled, like he'd been wearing it too long and was ready for a good dry cleaning. The silk black tie at his neck was askew and slightly loose. His gray hair was untidy, as if he'd been either running his hands through it or leaning against the seat in the plane.

Beyond that, it was the look in his eyes. The slightly harried, stressed look that overcame his usual steady, cool-as-a-cucumber expression.

"Dad," I rasped. I swear my voice was worse now than earlier. It was like all the swelling and soreness had finally set in.

His eyes dropped to my throat. It was on full display thanks to the bun on my head, but either way, I figured it wouldn't look good, so I chose to stay comfortable.

"I want an explanation, Josephine," he responded, gruff. Slightly shocked he used my full name, I stepped back so he could stride inside. The lights were on to brighten up the room, and I'd pulled the covers up on the bed to hopefully hide the fact I'd been in it with Jace not so long ago.

"You didn't have to fly here," I told him.

He gave me a wilting look. "I saw the news coverage. Did you really think I would see my daughter on national TV, looking like a domestic dispute victim, and not come?"

I winced. So I looked that bad. Wonderful.

"Not to mention all the assault and hazing accusations and the fact that Lorhaven is all over the news with a bleeding, half-conscious driver of mine in his grip."

"Dad…"

"You didn't answer your phone, Josephine," he went on, stern.

"I didn't want to deal with the press."

"Or me." My father was never one to mince words. I wasn't about to try and talk around his bluntness.

Instead of denying his words, I merely shrugged.

"Have I been that poor of a father?" he asked, a hint of weariness in his tone. It actually matched the way he appeared.

"What?" That caught me off guard. Shock rippled through me.

"Have I been so difficult to live with that you would rather put up with abuse than come to me?"

"You're not difficult to live with," I rebutted, a little bit of shame burning inside me. I never meant to imply he was a bad father; that's not what any of this was about.

"Why did you say nothing?" He pressed.

"Because I wanted to show you I was stronger than anything they did."

"What did they do, Josephine? I want names, and I want details." Oh boy. He had that cool, calculating look in his eyes. The kind he always wore when he closed huge deals or was determined to get exactly what he wanted.

"Why? It won't change anything." I insisted.

"You can tell me now, or I'll find out by other means," he intoned.

I sank on the edge of the bed. I wanted Jace. I wasn't exactly happy about it, but it didn't change the fact I wanted some of the shelter I always felt with him.

I told my father. I spilled it all out. Even about the night I was harassed while naked and my brake line was cut.

He listened without a word. He moved to the window as I spoke and stared at the curtain marring the view of the night. I wondered if he even noticed he only stared at fabric, that the view was closed off. It seemed to me he was lost in the pictures my words conjured up… lost in vivid images the details conjured.

I tried to speak matter-of-factly. To just lay out the bare bones of the naked truth… but emotion clogged my throat as I, too, relived not only what happened tonight at the hands of Cannon, but during all the nights past.

When I was done talking, I fell silent and moved to get a fresh water to try and soothe my raw throat.

"Have you been to the doctor?" he asked, still staring at the mundane hotel curtain.

"I don't need a doctor."

"There could be damage to your vocal chords." His voice was strained, as if he, too, had been choked.

"I'm fine."

"You're not!" he yelled.

The sudden, powerful outburst made me jump. My father was a powerful man, but he never yelled. He never had to. He always got exactly what he wanted without ever raising his voice.

Yet he was yelling now.

Some of the water from the bottle spilled over the top and trickled down my hand. I wiped it away and looked up. He was facing me now, watching me with sharp, angry eyes.

His voice quieted as he took in all my injuries once more. "Cannon did all this to you?"

I nodded.

"He'll never race again." My father didn't make empty statements. Four words and Dean Cannon's fate was permanently sealed.

"He paid someone on the pit crew today to alter my car. That win today should have been mine. He took it from me."

"This is the real reason you wanted to cross over so badly," he stated.

I nodded.

My father's eyes went flat. "You should have come to me."

"And say what?" I burst out. "Oh, Dad, the guys at the club are being so mean to me. They don't like girls. They don't want me around." I mocked. "What would you have done?" I pressed, jumping back to my feet. "You would have thought I was being weak just like everyone else."

He lifted his chin to stare at me, sliding both hands in the pockets of his trousers. I saw the challenge in the set of his jaw, the stubbornness settling on his shoulders.

"I'm Joey for a reason, dad." I began, feeling some defiance in me crumble. Maybe his defiance was stronger than mine.

Maybe I just didn't have any left tonight.

"You never wanted a girl. I was a disappointment to you from the day I was born. I tried so hard to be what you wanted. I will never be a man, but I thought maybe if I grew into a strong enough woman, you might respect me just as much."

His chin dropped some as I spoke, but now that I was talking, I wasn't about to stop.

"Me trying to be what you wanted made me everything Mom didn't want. She was too weak for you, and she never did give you that son. She wasn't interested in me when she moved to Paris. She never asked me to go with her, did you know that? Not once. It was like it never even occurred to her to take her only child."

"Your mother is a selfish woman," he said, some regret in his voice.

"But I always had a place with you. You made that clear, even when she didn't. It was like no matter how disappointed you might be in me, you still made room in your life. Even as a teenager, even when I was determined to push you away."

"I have never been disappointed in you."

"Except for the fact I'm the wrong gender."

He measured me, pulled his hands free of the pockets, and stepped closer. "I wanted a boy. I've never hidden it. I was hoping for more than one child, but that wasn't in the cards for me. Neither was a son. That doesn't mean I'm disappointed in what I do have. I regret you feel you've never measured up in my eyes. I regret I never told you different."

"You don't lie," I said, as if that explained exactly why he never told me any of those things.

"Then you will believe me when I say I *am* proud of you. More proud than I think you will ever realize. It was a fool thing to openly admit to wanting a son so much, because the truth is you are not and could never be a disappointment to me. In fact, looking at you right now, I am more convinced than ever not even a son could measure up to the person you are."

I swayed a little on my feet. His words were like piercing arrows that hit their mark in the deepest part of me, the most tender flesh.

"I wanted an heir, and that's exactly what I got. You're my daughter, and I love you."

Well, fuck.

I was going to cry. And not the sniffle, sniffle kind of cry either. The kind of ugly cry people needed to look away from. The kind that left your face swollen for a full day after you were dry.

I expected a lecture, a stern talking to, and yes, concern… but I didn't expect to hear he loved me. That he was proud of me.

I sniffled, sat on the end of the bed, and looked down, trying to gain some composure.

How long had I wanted to hear what he just said? How deep did my feelings of not being good enough go?

Deep.

So deep I was pretty sure they were the roots from which the rest of my character grew from.

I never realized how wholly those words would heal something inside me.

"Maybe if I'd told you this sooner, things wouldn't have gone as far as they have. Maybe you wouldn't be sitting there battered."

"This isn't your fault, Dad," I said as he came to sit beside me on the bed. Despite his weary appearance, he still smelled like fresh aftershave, the kind he'd worn as long as I could remember. Old Spice.

"Not entirely. Cannon and a few other members of the club are going to have a rude awakening in the next few days. This behavior stops here and now."

"What are you going to do?" I asked. Looking up, my stomach clenched from the steel I heard in his words.

"Do what I should have done a long time ago. Clean house."

"What does that say about me, then?" I asked. "That I had to have my father step in and fight my battles."

"This isn't just your battle, Joey. It's mine, too. We're a family, and we fight together. I shouldn't have let you believe coming to me was somehow a black mark against your character. You endured abuse too long, and it stops right now."

A tear slipped over my cheek, followed by another and another. My father put his arm around me, and I leaned into his side. I felt his lips on the top of my head, and it caused tenderness to awaken within me.

A girl would always have a soft spot for her daddy… no matter how old she was.

"I love you, Dad," I whispered.

"I love you, my daughter," he echoed. "Now…" His voice was brisk as he tightened his arm around me. "No more of this silence bullshit. You don't ever have to prove to me how strong you are. I know. I see it on a daily basis. If someone is harassing you or just treating my daughter poorly, then I want to hear about it."

I laughed. It was a watery sound. "Yes, sir."

"Good. Now get your things. We're going home. My personal doctor is waiting to look you over. And we'll be meeting with my lawyers as well."

"Lawyers!" I gasped, wincing because it hurt my throat.

"Oh, that criminal Cannon is going away for a long time. And you don't really think I'm going to let that disqualification stick, do you?"

"I still want to cross over," I stated, pulling back to look at him.

"I figured. You have my complete blessing, but Joey Gamble doesn't drive out of the pro division with a disqualification under her tires."

Dad always seemed to make everything seem a little less terrible, you know? Jace was my rock, my security… but not even he was as strong of a force as my father.

I leaned my head back on his shoulder. He nudged me. "Come on, then."

"I'm not ready to leave yet. I'd rather wait until morning."

"You need to see a doctor."

I sat back. "I will tomorrow."

My father's shrewd gaze landed on Jace's duffle bag. "This have to do with the owner of that bag?"

I nodded.

"The staff at the house says he was with you the night before you flew here."

Of course they did. The staff was a bunch of big tattlers. "I'm an adult." I reminded him.

"You'll always be my little girl."

I melted a little at his response.

"So you and Lorhaven… I guess that explains why he bloodied up Cannon so good."

"I caused some of that damage, too," I protested, indignant.

He chuckled. "Of that I have no doubt." He stood from the bed. "All right, I'll have the doctor at the house tomorrow, late morning."

"At the house?" I wondered.

He nodded. "Less press that way."

I agreed and walked with him toward the door.

"So when am I going to get to meet this Lorhaven?"

"Soon." I promised.

"Looking forward to it. I'm sure he must be something to have caught my daughter's eye."

I smiled. "He's something." I agreed.

Before opening the door, he glanced at me. "There's something else I need to ask you about, Joey."

I nodded.

"Did Hopper know about this? Did he sit idly by why you were hazed?"

I was shaking my head before he was even done asking. "They never did it when Hopper was around. I honestly don't think he knew how bad it was."

"But he knew something was happening…" he surmised, a displeased note in his voice.

"He saw the pictures they, uh, taped up in the garage. He came down on them. Hard. They stopped for a while. I think Hopper just assumed they never started again."

"I see," he murmured. What it is he saw I wasn't quite sure.

"Please don't take it out on Hopper, Dad. You know he has his own personal demons to battle. Battling mine isn't his responsibility."

"It is as a manager," he replied, tight.

"If I had spoken up, Jay would have come to you," I said, absolute surety in my words. Jay Hopper was a lot of things. A tortured soul. A recluse. A private man. My friend.

He was *not* an abuse enabler.

I could never believe he would stand by and allow men to abuse me.

"You let me worry about Hopper," he said, leaning in to kiss my forehead.

I wasn't sure what that meant, and it made my stomach clench.

He must have read it on my face, because when he pulled back, he sighed heavily. "You know I have a fondness for Hopper. Don't worry."

I nodded, tears coming back into my eyes. My father frowned, and I tried with all the will in me to snuff out my emotional display.

"You're sure you won't come with me now?"

I shook my head. "No, Jace is right next door. He's coming back."

"Drew and Trent are just down the hall," he said, as if that made him feel better.

"I know." I smiled.

"I love you, Josephine."

"I love you, too, Dad."

When he was out in the hall, I called out to him. He turned. "Thanks for coming."

"You're my daughter. And a damn good one at that."

I watched him until the elevator closed and he was completely gone. A shuddering breath left my chest. I was still stiff and sore from everything that happened tonight, but I felt lighter. Less bleak.

My father was proud of me. Of the woman I was.

I had Jace, free and clear, no secrets or pride between us.

Today had been a shitty, shitty day…

But maybe not as shitty as I originally thought.

Lorhaven

I'd never been a nervous guy.

I wasn't about to start that shit now.

It didn't matter that Ron Gamble was a powerful man. He wasn't the first the one I'd ever dealt with. It didn't matter I was standing in the center of his office, which looked more like a study off the set of a movie. I'd been in offices with equal prestige.

He was my girlfriend's father.

Correction, my one-and-only's father.

I'd never had a talk with the girlfriend's father before.

Correction, yes, I had.

When I was sixteen and horny as hell. Those conversations went in one ear and out the other. I didn't listen to that shit.

This was different. Josie was different, and Gamble was her father. I wanted his respect.

Okay. Fine. I was nervous.

Fuck if I'd show it, though.

Josie wasn't even here. She was at the track with Drew and Trent, likely having the time of her life speeding around in my damn Lotus.

Maybe that's why my guts were churning. I gave the woman the keys to my car.

It was going to get me some serious bedroom action later, though. *wags eyebrows*

The sound of a throat clearing had me spinning around. Gamble stood near his desk, looking at me, his eyebrow raised.

"Did you say something?" I asked.

"You got a hearing problem?" he asked, gruff.

"I gave Josie the keys to my Lotus," I deadpanned.

Gamble threw back his head and laughed. "Have some scotch, son. You're gonna need it." He went over to the bar where glasses sat along with a dark bottle of liquid and poured two glasses. I accepted it when he handed it over.

"You call my daughter Josie," he said, staring at me over the rim of the glass. He had quite the stare on him. I'd like to see him and my father in the same room. This guy was probably a match for him.

Well, his reputation preceded him, but I'd never met him until now. Even after a couple months of dating Josie and being with her every chance we got.

"Unlike you, I'm pretty happy she's a girl," I quipped.

His eyes narrowed. I took a sip of the scotch and appreciated the way it burned my throat. I might not be my father, but I definitely had some of his, uh, gumption.

"I've never made a secret I wanted a son. But I love my daughter very much. She's the only child I have."

"I know that. She loves you," I told him.

"Then you must know I'll do anything for her."

I lowered the glass from my mouth. "This the part where you try and run me off?"

"I had someone look into your background."

"Ah, found out all about the skeletons in my closet, did ya? Should have asked. I would have given you the information personally."

"I actually believe that," he mused.

"I'm not a liar," I said.

"Illegal betting, gambling, and attempted murder are nothing to be proud of."

"I'm not proud of it."

"I've met your father. We actually do some business together," Gamble said, dismissing my criminal past. For now, anyway.

"I don't like him," I said, taking another sip of the scotch. It was some good shit.

"Me either."

I smiled.

Gamble scrutinized me from behind a shrewd stare. I bet he read people better than most people read books. "You're nothing like him, though, are you?"

"No. And I never will be." I confirmed.

"You beat up Dean Cannon, outed him to the press."

"He hit your daughter in the face," I growled. "He deserved worse than that."

He pushed away from the bar, carried his glass over behind his desk, and set it down on a stack of papers. He was still dressed for work even though he was at home and it was after hours. His suit was clearly tailored, and his red tie looked freshly tied. I was willing to bet he wore red just because he was meeting me and wanted to have a touch of the color of blood on him.

Like that would intimidate me.

"I agree with you. That's why I told him if he pressed assault charges against you, he'd find out exactly how much worse I thought he deserved."

I stared at him in shock. "That's why he didn't press charges? Because you threatened him?"

Gamble held up a finger. "I didn't threaten. I merely informed."

I laughed. "Right. Well, thanks for saving me the trouble of a lawsuit. And thanks for the hurt you put on him and a few others that were involved in Josie's hazing."

All of them were out of his club. Cannon was totally blackballed from racing and actually serving time for cutting her brake line. Stupid shithead didn't know him sneaking in and cutting her line was on surveillance cameras. The little scene of harassment they pulled on her when she was fresh out of the shower and in the garage for clothes was all caught on camera, too.

When I saw Cannon in court, he looked worse than a baboon's asshole. Something told me Gamble had some connections on the inside, and Cannon's stay in lock-up while awaiting trial was anything but peaceful.

"A lot of men with the same amount of power I have do business differently. I don't lie and cheat in my dealings. My deals are all honest."

I didn't say anything, just stared at him.

"But I'm not a fool, and I wasn't born yesterday. This world is cutthroat, and when you have money and power, everyone always wants a piece."

"That about sums it up." I agreed.

"This wasn't the first time scum has messed with my daughter. This is the first time it went on so long without my interference. She's older now, has her own life. Even so, it probably won't be the last time she's a target for what she does and who she is."

Just the words made my blood boil. I slammed the glass down on the other side of his desk and leaned over it to look at him intently. "I won't allow it."

Gamble's mouth curved up on one side. "I know. I certainly hope you don't get caught up in illegal dealings in the future, but I will admit, your checkered past seems more like a plus than a negative."

I laughed. "Well, that's a first."

"When you have a daughter someday, you'll understand."

The vision of Josie and all her wild hair with a small pink bundle in her arms swam before my eyes and pierced my chest. Possessiveness wrapped around me and that image like the heaviest blanket I'd ever felt.

"I'll do anything to protect her," I told him. "I'm in love with your daughter, and love isn't something I give out freely."

Gamble nodded, pulled out his desk chair, and sat down. "Good. Glad we got that out of the way."

I blinked. That was it? I passed father inspection? And I did it by being the dick I always was.

"You seem surprised," Gamble mused.

I sat down, snatched my drink off the edge of the desk, and took a swallow. "I am."

He made a scoffing sound. "My daughter is happier than I've ever seen her. Keep her that way and you won't have a problem from me."

"Fair enough," I said.

"Now, about your brother,"

I stiffened, my body tense. "What about Arrow?"

"I hear he can drive."

"Who told you that?" I asked, suspicious.

"Drew, Trent, my daughter," he listed.

"He can drive," I allowed.

"I'm down a whole lot of drivers since the shakeup in the pro division."

I felt the bottom fall out of my stomach. "Are you saying you want my brother to drive for you in the pros?"

"It's crossed my mind."

Everything inside me went flat. "No."

Gamble's eyebrows rose. "No?"

"My brother is gay."

His eyebrows rose with the news, but then he said, "So is Drew Forrester."

"Drew Forrester drives for the much more liberal NRR. The pro division is stodgy and old school, a fact you well know, especially after what happened to Josie."

"I can understand your concern." He agreed. "I think the pros are changing. My daughter was the catalyst in that. Your brother could be coming in at the right time."

"My brother isn't your guinea pig," I refuted tightly.

"Maybe think about it. Ask him if he would like a tryout. Hopper is anxious to get him on the track."

Hopper. I bared my teeth. "You sure it's his driving Hopper's interested in?"

Gamble pursed his lips. "Your fierceness extends to your brother."

"My brother has been through a lot. He and Josie are at the top of the short list of people I care about." I paused, then sat forward. "And frankly, I'm fucking shocked Hopper is still on payroll. You actually believe he didn't know about all the shit Josie was being put through?"

"I've spoken to Hopper. At length. I will admit, I think he was in the wrong, but I don't think he knew everything Josie was going through. He'd come down on Cannon in the past for his actions. I think Hopper was foolish and thought he'd dealt with it."

I snorted. "What a crock."

"Hopper will not be managing my daughter in the NRR. He's staying with the pros, much to his displeasure. I'm sure that will make you happy."

"That he's away from Josie? Yes. But the fact you want to stick him and my brother together? No."

"Noted."

I stood up. I was done here. "I'm going back to the track. Gonna make sure my car is still in one piece."

Gamble pushed out of his chair.

I held out my hand over the desk. "Thank you for taking the time to meet with me."

"I respect a man who takes time to get a father's blessing."

"I didn't ask for your blessing," I said as he shook my hand.

"Not in so many words, but that's why you're here, isn't it? You want to make sure I approve because you plan to marry my daughter."

"I plan to marry her," I said with no hesitation. "But not right now. I don't even have a ring." I mean, shit, I'd never even really thought about it 'til now. Sure, it was a given I would marry her. Someday. We were too busy right now dating, driving, and getting to know each other better. We hadn't even moved in together yet. But that was about to change. This driving back and forth to see each other was shit. I wasn't doing it. I wanted her in my bed every single night.

As if he read my mind, he said, "All in due time." He released my hand. "This house is plenty big if you two want to live here."

"I'm not living off my girlfriend's father."

A satisfied glint came into his eyes. "I was hoping you'd say that."

Ah, a test. Lucky me, I passed.

I headed for the door. His voice rang out behind me. "After you save your car from my daughter's clutches, dinner will be on the table. Drew and Trent will be here, too. Bring your brother."

I glanced over my shoulder. "Okay. We'll be here." He nodded.

"But this doesn't mean Arrow will drive for you."

"Understood."

I liked the guy. Respected him. I definitely understood where Josie got her stubborn mule head from. I could see how it might be hard to grow up with such a father. Hell, in a lot of ways, I had, too.

I liked his no apology way of living. He didn't back down from who he was. He didn't try and change. It was what it was.

Although, he did apologize once. To Josie. For not seeing what she went through sooner and for making her feel like she had to hide any struggle she faced. They had a long talk about her past, how he wasn't holding it against her now or expecting her to revert back to her hell-raising ways. In short, she finally got the approval she'd always wanted from him and his respect. After talking with him today, I knew she'd had that a long time ago, she'd just never realized it. It took him telling her flat out to make her finally see.

Shocked the shit out of Josie. She still had a shell-shocked look on her face when I met her after their talk. But really, that's what made me respect Gamble more. He gave her something that day no one else could give her, something she truly needed.

It pushed them closer, made her a little less bitter she wasn't born a boy.

Note: I'd never tell her I thought she was bitter about that. She'd kick me in my sack.

They were even in the process of creating a foundation for people who felt alone, bullied, or just plain needed someone to talk to. It had become a pet project for the duo. It gave Gamble a chance to see his daughter in a new light and her a chance to do something that made her feel empowered.

God, she was amazing. Like hella good.

I loved her more every day.

But if she messed up my Lotus, I might have to amend that statement and just love her the same today and even more tomorrow…

Yeah.

Watching her with her father made me wonder about my own. If maybe I should give him a chance. I just didn't think I could.

But Arrow… I saw it in his eyes when he didn't think I was looking.

I told him about my talk with our father. I told him he wanted a relationship and he might feel bad about everything that went down.

I honestly thought my brother would shoot it down just like I did.

Apparently, my little brother had been holding on to hope dear old Dad would come around. It made me sick. How Arrow could have the capacity to forgive him even just a fraction blew my mind.

It also made him a better man than I might ever be.

He was sitting in Josie's Skyline, his ass in the driver's seat, when I walked up. When I got out of the car, I'd been the one driving. Guess he decided he needed a turn.

I opened the passenger door and leaned in. "What the fuck are you doing?"

He tossed the blond hair out of his eyes. "I'm driving."

"You need a haircut," I bitched.

"Yeah, yeah, I know," he muttered.

I got into the passenger seat and motioned for him to drive.

"How was meeting the pops?" he asked.

I grunted. "Fine. We're going back for dinner after we rescue my Lotus."

"I'm starving," he said.

I rolled my eyes. He was always starving. 'Course, I was, too, so…

"Hey, A," I said.

He glanced over at me as we drove out of the gates on Gamble's property. "Yeah?"

"You like, Josie, right?"

He laughed. "You know I do, bro. She's way too good for you."

I smacked him in the back of the head. "Asshole."

"For real, though, she's cool. She's the only one who doesn't treat me like a kid."

"I don't treat you like a kid," I argued.

He gave me a withering look.

I grunted.

"She's good for you," he said after a minute. "You're happy."

Was that a little bit of envy I heard in his tone?

"She's family now," he said, nodding once like that was that.

It was that. She was family.

I debated for two seconds, then let out a curse. Arrow gave me a sidelong look out of the side of his eye before staring back at the road.

"Gamble wants to see you drive. He's looking for new pro drivers for his team," I told him.

The wheel jerked beneath his hands. "Are you fucking for real?"

"Unfortunately, I am."

"You don't think I'm good enough," he said, flat.

"Fuck no!" I protested. "I know you are. But look at all the shit Josie just went through."

"I'm not a kid, Lor," he argued angrily. "If I want to try out, I will."

"I know that," I said, calm. "That's why I told you about the offer."

"I'm not the same kid I was two years ago. I want a life, one of my own."

"Tired of being my sidekick, are you?" I asked.

He laughed. "Maybe." Then he said, "But seriously, you're building a life with Josie. I'm glad about it. But I need to build a life of my own."

"Yeah," I said. I knew he did. It was hard to give up control, though.

A few minutes later, we pulled into the lot at Gamble Speedway. Arrow parked, and the sounds of the cars' engines inside the track carried out to the Skyline.

"Lorhaven," he said as I was moving to get out. I stopped, turned back in the seat, and looked at him. "I don't think I ever thanked you for all the shit you've done for me the last couple years. In a lot of ways, you literally saved my life."

"Arrow…" I began. My chest got tight really fast.

He shook his head, and his Adam's apple worked when he swallowed. "Thank you. You're a good brother. The best. My loyalty will always be with you, and I'll never do anything you're dead set against. For a long time, you were my brother, but more recently, you've been more like a dad."

Not a father… but a *dad*. This kid, who wasn't really a kid, got to me. He got me right in the damn feels.

"I want to start making my own way, but I won't do it unless you give me your blessing."

It was a day of blessings apparently.

I looked into his eyes. They were brown, not as dark as mine, and they were sincerer than I think I could ever look.

"Take the tryout, A," I said. "And if you decide the pros aren't right for you, you know we'll get you a spot in the NRR."

"Seriously?" Once again, he seemed shocked.

I grinned. "Of course. Gamble is interested. That's not gonna change. Especially after he sees you haul ass."

My brother grinned. Excitement sparked his eyes.

It made me kinda happy.

"Thanks, Lor!" he said and bounded out of the driver's seat.

We met at the front of the car. "Hey," I said. "I'm proud of you."

He launched himself at me, folding his arms around my waist. I closed mine around him, hugging him tight.

"C'mon," I said after a minute. "We need to go save my car."

He laughed. We were almost through the entrance when he said, "So you think Hopper will be at the audition?"

"What's it matter?" I barked.

He shrugged. "Guess it doesn't."

No dating. I ain't ready for that shit.

Especially not when the guy sniffing around my brother was a douche who, despite what he said, had to know Josie was being fucking harassed. If Arrow was going to get involved with someone, it wouldn't be a guy without a spine.

I'd kill him first.

A few minutes later, we were standing alongside the track, and my Lotus was nothing but a white streak on the other side of the track.

When it finally made it around to where we were, she glided to a stop not far from where we stood.

The engine shut off, and she bounded out of the driver's seat. Her hair was wild, her jeans tight, and the green in her eyes resembled that of a sparkling emerald.

When she jumped, I caught her.

"I love that car," she announced.

I laughed.

She tossed the key fob at my brother. "Here, why don't you take it for a turn? Cool the engine down a bit."

Arrow caught the fob and looked at me with wide eyes. I'd never let him drive it before.

I nodded. "Go on."

He was gone in a flash, leaving Josie and me alone. At least until Drew and Trent made it the rest of the way around the track.

"How'd it go with my dad?" she asked, running her hands through my hair.

"He thinks we should move in together," I announced.

She laughed. "I'm sure he didn't say that."

I shrugged. "I'm saying it."

Her eyes settled on mine, realizing I was being serious.

"Really?" she whispered.

I nodded. "I want your ass in my bed every night."

She tilted her head to the side. The wind blew and ruffled her curls. "Just my ass?"

"Your heart, too." I kissed her softly and pulled back. "Yes?"

She nodded once. "Yes."

I was one lucky bastard.

Joey

To **EmilyM@gearsharkmag.com**

Subject **The real story**

Dear Emily,

I know you already did a feature on me for an issue of GS. But I didn't really give you the real story. Instead, I gave you a version of me everyone expected. Attached is what I should have said, what I really wanted to say. I hope you take the time to read it.

Regards,
Josephine Gamble
joeyg@gmail.com

To **joeyg@gmail.com**

Subject **RE: The real story**

Dear Joey,
I knew there was more to your story. Thank you for trusting it with me. You're an inspiration to women everywhere. I want to print this. It will be a full page spread, with an image we took of you at the previous shoot. Solo. It's time you shine on your own. You earned it. Sign the attached consent for us to go to print and return it to me. Drafted copy of the article is attached.

P.S. That ride Lorhaven said he'd give me never happened that day. He was too busy staring off in the direction you drove off in to even remember I was there.

Regards,
Emily Metcalf
GEARSHARK Magazine

You might remember the history-breaking issue we printed just a couple months ago, featuring our first ever cover with two models. That feature received a lot of attention, and our staff here at GearShark was flooded with questions about Lorhaven and Joey G., both separately and together.

It seemed everyone saw what the pair didn't on the day of the shoot. The sparks between them. Since then, this duo has ignited into a full-on inferno both in their personal lives and on the track.

With every fire, there is always destruction. In this case, most of it came down on Joey G. After our feature, several things happened: the press became curious about this pair and their behind-the-scenes relationship, Joey G. was disqualified from a pro race due to illegal modification of her car, and allegations came to light of the abhorrent hazing she endured throughout most of her career.

And of course, no one will soon forget the sight of bad boy driver Lorhaven dragging a bloodied used-to-be heartthrob, Dean Cannon, out of the locker room to call him out in front of the press.

But we aren't here to talk about Lorhaven today (not much anyway). Joey G. reached out to me after all of the above unfolded because she wanted to tell me what she really wanted to say the first time I interviewed her.

This feature isn't my usual format. It's not an ask-and-answer interview. It's a letter of sorts, from the previously ignored (and dare I say suppressed?) driver to our readers here at GearShark and, beyond that, to all the true fans of racing.

When I opened this email and read what she had to say, I knew instantly this was a story I wanted to bring to you. As you'll read below, Joey G. doesn't think she has much "#swag," as we proclaimed. I'm going to have to disagree. And you will, too, once you read what she has to say.

In fact, you might even make a case that Joey Gamble might be the very definition of the word.

* * *

I don't have as much #swag as GearShark would like you to believe. Sure, it was a snazzy headline. And it made me and Jace (that's Lorhaven to you) look pretty cool, but to me, #swag is being confident.

Up until recently, I couldn't really say I was all that confident in myself. Oh, I talked a big game, and I drove one, too. Sometimes people use strength as a means to cover up the lack of confidence they feel. I didn't want anyone to know how bad some days were for me in the world of racing.

Be professional. Be positive. Never let them see you sweat. Those were my mantras.

As a female in racing, I had to be tougher than most. I could never let my guard down. You know why? The truth is I was an outcast. In a lot of ways, I will always be. In my first interview here with *GearShark,* I was awkward, rude, and on the defensive. I was pretty much like that all the time, and a lot of times, I still am today. Truth is the sport of racing is predominantly a man's world. Testosterone flies around here. Men are competitive, they're aggressive, and they all want to be the best.

Estrogen doesn't mix with that, and neither does having feelings.

I was pigeon-holed from day one. I've been discriminated against, looked down on, and sometimes flat-out ignored. No one wanted to interview me. No one wanted to print my scores. And when I won? It was almost an embarrassment to everyone.

People brushed me off, said my father, who is Ron Gamble, bought my way into the pro circuit. They said the races I won, he bought, too. I couldn't possibly have earned my trophies or the right to drive… because I'm a woman.

I refused to bend. I refused to be shoved off onto the shoulder. I kept driving, I kept working, and I pretended none of it bothered me.

The truth was I was being hazed. Heavily. By racers who were what we would call "on my own team." Tampons in my drinks. Maxi pads taped just about everywhere. Pictures of me in my underwear found their way onto the walls of the garage. I was verbally harassed, challenged, and left out of everything behind the scenes. The only time I was treated fairly (note: in this case fairly = treated with silence and scalding looks) was when my manager and other staff members were around.

One night, the brake line was cut in my car. I could have died.

I said nothing.

I was embarrassed. I was humiliated. I was too proud to come forward.

I realize now I was part of the problem. I enabled them. Nothing I did was my fault. I didn't ask for any of it, and I never retaliated. But I never spoke up.

Here I was, this "badass" female driver, breaking down walls, trying to gain equality for women in the world of racing, and fighting against stereotyping. But I wasn't really.

I realized later I was hiding behind the stereotype.

I should have been fighting against them, making everyone aware of what women face in male-dominated fields. I didn't want to be seen as weak. Or as someone who couldn't handle what was thrown at me. So I kept quiet.

Let me tell you what something like hazing does to a person. It degrades them. It makes them feel vulnerable and alone. I looked over my shoulder every single day, and sometimes I didn't want to go to work. But I didn't quit. It's what they wanted. They wanted me gone. They didn't want to race beside a female. And when I won?

The harassment was worse.

This is one of the reasons I decided to cross over. I wanted away from the situation I knew wasn't going to change, but I didn't want to give up my passion.

Drew Forrester is a close friend of mine, and so is his manager, Trent Mask. Could you really blame a girl for wanting to go to work and see people who accepted her? Who she called friends?

I love the NRR. The whole revolution. This division is for the underdog—that's what I felt like in the pro division. I hoped the NRR would be more accepting of a female driver, and honestly, who doesn't want to race without rules?

My crossover was seen as a betrayal in the pro world. The men who tormented me for years were even angrier I would turn my back on a sanctioned division for one they view as less. That's right. A lot of the pro drivers see the NRR as fake. They were embarrassed I would leave a legit world and go to the NRR. Again, they thought my actions reflected on them, as if I were saying they weren't good enough.

Let me make it clear: I don't think they're good enough. As men. Not as drivers. I have deep respect for the pro racing division. Maybe if I had been more readily accepted there, I wouldn't want to cross over, but that's not how it is, and I feel in my heart I belong in the NRR.

Suffice it to say, it was that "embarrassment" that led to my car being modified during a pit stop at my final pro race. Upon a mandatory inspection after I placed second, the change was discovered, and I was made to look like a cheater. I was also disqualified on the spot.

<For details on that, go to www.gearsharkmag.com/joeygdisqualilfied)>

It has since been publicized that ex-driver Dean Cannon was behind the modification. I've also gone on record that it was Dean Cannon who spearheaded the hazing I experienced.

Besides him being removed from the pro driving division, legal action is being pursued at this time, and I am advised by my lawyer not to say anything further. My father, Ron Gamble, has pulled his sponsorship from all those involved in the hazing, and so have many other sponsors.

This letter isn't about Dean Cannon. It isn't about any of the other men who participated in humiliating me. This letter is about me wanting to make it known to all the girls out there—hell, to anyone who's ever felt like *less*—that you don't have to take it. You don't have to suffer in silence because you think that's what makes you strong.

I'm speaking out to say what they did was wrong. It hurt me. But it didn't ruin me.

If you're going through anything remotely similar to what I've experienced or you're just struggling with demons you can't seem to control, know you aren't alone. There is strength in numbers. Even just two.

Jace Lorhaven helped me see this. He helped me realize strength comes in a lot of forms.

If you don't have a Jace in your life, then you can call the new hotline Gamble Enterprises has started. It's my passion project outside of racing. Someone will answer, someone will be there, and you don't have to feel alone.

<*Hotline information:* ***Strength in Numbers Foundation: 1-800-CALLONME***>

As for me? I'll be starting up with the NRR in the new season, and you're going to see me as you haven't before. That's a promise.

And for all the "would you like to comment on the rumors of your and Lorhaven's relationship" questions… Yes, I would like to comment.

He asked me out. I had a great time. He kisses really good.

And I'm in love with him. We're in a relationship. And no, I'm not worried about driving against him this coming season. The best driver will win, and it won't matter which one of us it is.

Drive fast,

Joey G.

* * *

See? Joey G. has #swag. We at GearShark *want to thank her for speaking out and for the founding of* STRENGTH IN NUMBERS. *With everything going on in her world, I feel pretty confident ending this article by saying this will definitely not be the last time you see her in the pages of* GearShark.

Lorhaven

Sunday, 7:31 PM

I read the article.

I'm sitting right beside you, Jace.

You like my texts.

They're okay. 😋

You told the
world you love me.

Forever, Jace.

Forever, Josie.

Come over here
and kiss me.

Read.

Thirty-Nine

Joey

You know what I learned through everything? Sometimes in order to shine on your own, you need the support of someone else.

In my case, that someone was Jace.

And sometimes, real strength is being able to admit you can't do everything alone.

I drove into the world of racing with stars in my eyes. I left the pro division with a chip on my shoulder.

I would drive into the NRR with the same chip and no more stars. I traded the stars out for friends. And for love.

Nothing in life is ever easy. Not even matters of the heart. You have to accept someone for who they are—not just the pieces and parts you like, but even the parts you don't.

And if you're lucky, that someone you do it for will give you the same.

And if you're *really* lucky, he'll also rock your body on a nightly basis.

Where do I see myself in five years?

Who the hell knows?

But one thing is for sure… Jace will be at my side.

And we'll both still be driving way too fast.

The Finish Line.

GearShark Magazine presents
Arrow Ambrose

Nothing but a...

#Blur

Our next issue hits newsstands soon!

Author's *Note*

I'm writing this note cross-eyed. And my butt is numb. No really. Cross-eyed and a numb booty is not a good look on anyone. But I've been tied to a chair forever! Yes, forever, staring at the screen and trying to work out the ending of this book.

I feel like this was the book that never ends… I have a feeling I've said that before. Whatever. Sometimes they all feel like that. Ha! Maybe it was because my personal life kept getting in the way. It's not always easy to write with two kids, a husband, and some animals. During the process of this book, my family had to say good-bye to our fourteen-year-old retriever. It was a hard time, and the house is very quiet without her. We're also in the process of trying to train an outdoor/indoor cat to be only indoor. It's surprising how much he acts like a one-year old. If that cat is awake, he is into something. No, seriously. I'm exhausted. LOL. I also released another book during the writing of this one, a *Take It Off* novel, *Taxi*. It's a romantic suspense, so different than this series, but still fun to write.

Personal update aside, I really was nervous going into this book because I really wasn't sure where to start other than the fact they weren't too fond of each other. And let's be real, following up Trent and Drew is an almost insurmountable task.

Once I got into their "voices," it went a lot faster, and I have to say, I really like the chemistry between Josie and Jace. It was different from how I thought it would be. I kinda always thought they would be hot, so that was no surprise, but the other parts they drew out of one another, the softer, sweeter sides, I found really amazing.

I always like when a story unfolds and the characters seem to develop on their own and when they push toward each other instead of away. I feel like that is what happened with these two. They started off far apart, and by the end, they were sitting on the couch, texting each other from inches away. Not really something I ever thought Lorhaven would do, but I'm glad he did.

I also LOVED getting back with Trent and Drew. I missed them so much. The first day I wrote them, I was so happy all day. I love those boys. LOL. I also really love their friendship with Josie (and the grudging one they have with Lorhaven).

I have to say I wasn't sure where this book would end or how. I'm still a bit surprised by the way it did. Not because it was like a super surprise or twisty end. It wasn't even overly dramatic (which I hope the readers aren't upset by; I know we all love our drama!). I just like where they ended up. I hope you all like it, too. Some books go out with a bang… and others seem to drift slowly to a stop like a racecar trying to cool its engine. Plus, I feel like this book had a message behind it about bullying, feeling alone, and understanding strength doesn't mean suffering in silence. Hopefully, my writing got those things across. I know I tried to impart that.

I truly hope you enjoyed this read and you thought it was a great addition to the *GearShark* series. Next up (as you probably just saw) is the final installment of the GS series with issue four, which is Arrow's book. I admit I have no idea where that book is going to go. I guess we will all find out together.

As always, thank you for reading and please consider leaving a review. Oh, and if you want to stay in the know on all the 4-1-1 in my world, sign up for my newsletter, the link is on the next page in my bio!

I genuinely appreciate the time you spend reading my books and hope they continue to give you entertainment.

Until next book…

XOXO,

Cambria

Cambria Hebert is an award winning, bestselling novelist of more than twenty books. She went to college for a bachelor's degree, couldn't pick a major, and ended up with a degree in cosmetology. So rest assured her characters will always have good hair.

Besides writing, Cambria loves a caramel latte, staying up late, sleeping in, and watching movies. She considers math human torture and has an irrational fear of chickens (yes, chickens). You can often find her running on the treadmill (she'd rather be eating a donut), painting her toenails (because she bites her fingernails), or walking her chorkie (the real boss of the house).

Cambria has written within the young adult and new adult genres, penning many paranormal and contemporary titles. Her favorite genre to read and write is romantic suspense. A few of her most recognized titles are: *The Hashtag Series, GearShark Series, Text, Torch,* and *Tattoo.*

Cambria Hebert owns and operates Cambria Hebert Books, LLC.

You can find out more about Cambria and her titles by visiting and following her here:

Website: http://www.cambriahebert.com.
Email: cambriahebert@rocketmail.com
Facebook: http://smarturl.co/CambriaHebertFanpage
Twitter: http://twitter.com/cambriahebert
Pinterest: http://pinterest.com/cambriahebert/pins/
Instagram: @cambriahebert
Sign up for her Newsletter: http://eepurl.com/bUL5_5

9 781938 857928